Who is reading *Shattered*?

"*Shattered* creates a vivid, intense world of intriguing and complex characters, plot, and story. From the first foreboding words to the last resounding blast, the reader is treated to a thrill ride in a hot fast car that careens along, hitting lots of bumps and making many a sharp, tire-screeching turn along a twisty road. Don't forget to breathe! And for sure, fasten your seat belts! Pay close attention to the scenery too, because during the cruise-control portions, this tale unfolds with dream-like glimpses caught out of the corner of your eye. *Shattered* grabs you and takes you in all the way, deep inside. It bounces you around, then releases you, spent and breathless. This thing is cool, it's hot, it's sexy, savvy, riveting, and reality-expanding—with plenty of suspense and stunning turns. You're in for a treat. Go there if you dare!" ***Victoria Olson,*** *Transformational Health and Wellness Practitioner, NYC*

"Spellbinding! Kevin Hogan's vast knowledge of influence and persuasion and what makes people tick, makes this book captivating. I literally couldn't put it down and neither will you!" ***Katherin Scott,*** *www.makingloveworк4u.com*

"Wonderful story...a must read." ***Dr. Jonathan Twomey***

"A fairy-tale life tragically changed in a split second. Deep faith and trust in humanity restores one's body and soul." ***Dr. Michael J. King***

"A first novel from the master of communication, Dr. Kevin Hogan. Kevin has outdone himself and shocked the rest of us with this masterpiece. Destined to be a blockbuster and number one bestseller, this is a must read. Kevin has shown himself in this, his first work of fiction, to be a wizard at story telling. I recommend you buy this book today and guarantee you will become so engrossed in the plot, you will struggle to put it down." ***Peter Tamosaitis,*** *Former Operations Director LWR, London UK*

"I am a book addict and this is my favorite kind of fix – compelling characters in a quandary, written in a way that makes me care." ***Sunny Carlson,*** *Costa Rica www.sunnyincostarica.com*

"The title of this book says it all. *Shattered* is an incredible roller coaster ride of enormous challenge, perseverance, and triumph."
O.J. Rinehart, *Interstate Companies President and CEO*

"*Shattered* is a gripping, unpredictable story of real life disaster that leaves Megan to rebuild her once perfect life. As someone who works with disabled people daily, I found this an interesting recovery story with numerous twists. This is a must-read for anyone who has dealt with disability issues personally, or peripherally." ***Gary Domstrand,*** *CEO, Allied Technologies: Low Vision Store*

Warning!

The following endorsements contain spoilers.

"A drunk driver shatters the life of beautiful Megan. She barely survives, but even when awakening from a coma, she is unable to grieve for her lost husband as she cannot speak or cry. Recovering, she learns she may never flirt or have sex again. Then when terror strikes, she questions whether she lives in the world she once knew. *Shattered*, based on a true life story, speeds you down a traumatic path struck with disappointment, despair, courage and strength. Riveted to the book it will lead you to wonder what can be done to prevent these needless injuries and deaths." ***Pamela S. Erickson****, Publisher, Campaign for a Healthy Alcohol Marketplace*

"Compelling read! A sobering account of how fragile and unpredictable life can be and how one can adapt and triumph when confronted with extreme adversity." ***William H. Rosenberg***

"This novel *Shattered* is a first rate psychological thriller that portrays the anguish of dealing with intrusive tinnitus. I could not put it down."
Scott Mitchell*, Board Member, American Tinnitus Association*

"*Shattered* is the story of a woman who had it all, lost it all in an instant, and slowly healed through the unceasing help and love of a steadfast friend and one truly remarkable therapist. What a journey! Having lived through disabling sudden onset tinnitus, I very much sympathized with Meagan's plight, and rejoiced with her as she regained dominion of her mind after an extremely traumatic experience, and resulting tinnitus. I even found myself wondering at times if she had been the victim of some kind of creepy technological trans-human experiment! *Shattered* takes you from the mundane through a labyrinth of psychological, sexual, and auditory intrigue. The troubled and sometimes terrifying world of tinnitus sufferers is brilliantly addressed in this novel." ***Renée deWolf-Gibbons***

shattered

shattered

Kevin Hogan • Cheryl Boldon

This book is a work of fiction. Some of what happens in *Shattered* is based on the true life experiences of Janet Snyder. All other characters you meet in the book are constructs of the imaginations of the authors. Any similarities between characters in the book and people in real life are purely coincidental. Most of the places mentioned in the book are real.

SHATTERED

Published by Network 3000 Publishing Corp.
3432 Denmark Ave. #108
Eagan, Minnesota 55123 USA

www.network3000publishing.com

ISBN-10: 1-934266-23-X
ISBN-13: 978-1934266-23-6

Printed in the United States of America

Chapter One

Day One

Today… would be his last.

Gunshot!

Megan jerked at the sound, and tried to make herself as small as she could in the passenger seat of the rare, six-year-old red mini-Mercedes. David owned two of these and had given one to Megan just last year.

Geezuz, David, come on!

He opened the driver's side door, slid in and clicked the seat belt in one motion.

"You OK down there?"

"Didn't you hear that gunshot?"

"Probably a few blocks away." He was reassuring her, but he was also playing with her a bit. He hated the fact that one of his stores was right in the heart of one of the most impoverished sections of Minneapolis. Over the decades profits at a drug store didn't always correlate to the lower income customer. But the safety of the store and the employees was something that had concerned David since he took the store over from his family almost a decade ago.

"I don't want to get killed." She was still scrunched down as low as she could get.

He looked in his rearview mirror. From this vantage point in the parking lot he had a clear view to the store, and there was no one entering or exiting Dresden Drugs. His family's drugstores had been a constant in the Minnesota/Wisconsin landscape for forty-seven years, but times were changing. The family-owned drug stores could rarely compete with the big chains any longer. He owned four stores, and they were all in trouble

"Can we go, David?"

"We're going to wait a couple minutes, make sure everything is OK with the store, and then we'll head out."

"David, the people who work here are *inside* a building. They are *fine*. We are outside in a car. We're *not* fine." She was remarkably composed and clear thinking for someone compressing herself into a ball on the seat of a bright red Mercedes in the poorest part of town.

Megan had no idea that David had a Glock in the glove compartment. He wasn't much of a gun guy, but he was savvy enough to be able to legally carry and conceal in the city. His pistol wouldn't stop bullets, but it could act as a strong deterrent to problems in certain situations. Fortunately, he'd never had to remove it from the glove compartment, except to clean it.

Wisely, Megan hated guns, and she hated gunfire.

Megan considered the stress that David had been under lately. He'd become aware that he was going to lose the store. But he had three other drug stores in town, and frankly, Megan would be happy when the city took this one down. Megan knew David was angry because it had been in his family for half a century, and it had made him and his family before him rich.

I'd be so glad if I never had to come here again. Eventually someone is going to get killed here and it will probably be David. I wish the city would just give him a million dollars for the place and be done with it.

Half of Megan's wish would come true. She would never return to that store.

Still sitting scrunched down in the seat, Megan regarded the third finger on her delicate and soft left hand. It boasted a four-carat round diamond ring that was worth right around $100,000. She didn't know the exact value of the ring – David never told her such things. She wondered if she were ever held up by a robber, whether the man would take her ring from her. Usually it was the only ring she ever wore, and it wasn't something anyone would likely overlook.

Today she wore her large gold hoop earrings, which accented her face rather nicely. She was dressed to kill – not to *be* killed.

They sat in the car. David gave it a good ten minutes, and when he was convinced that the store and his employees were going to be fine, he turned the key. He loved to listen to the engine purr. He loved the feel of it. And he loved that Megan loved the car.

He looked over at her, wondered how she was able walk in her four-inch heels, and how she could keep shoes like that so clean. He gave his cowering beauty an adoring smile.

"C'mon. Sit up, honey. All is quiet on the Lake Street front."

She hesitated, but obeyed.

He took his foot off the brake as he put the car in reverse, only to nearly hit a twenty-six-year-old blonde racing for the car from the store.

He had to laugh.

"Are you laughing at me, David? It's not funny, you know. Someone is shooting out there, and I just don't want to be shot before we go to the fundraiser."

Then he really laughed.

"What? David, you are always making fun of me."

"I'm not making fun of you, Megan. You make me laugh and that just makes me love you more."

Ashley ran around to the driver's side door. Ashley, whom David thought a very pretty and talented girl, managed the Lake Street store. She looked at bit like a voluptuous version of Nicole Kidman, with that same long reddish-blonde hair and fair skin.

Ashley knocked on the window five times, as if he couldn't see her staring in by the time she'd rapped once. Megan was sure that Ashley must have been terrified by the gunfire, too.

But it wasn't the gunfire that had Ashley worked up.

David pressed a button to roll the window down. Ashley leaned forward into the car, giving David a director's view.

Megan straightened up completely and looked at her best friend and space invader, Ashley Drexel.

Megan often thought about how close Drexel and Dresden were in spelling, how close she and Ashley were as friends, and how close Ashley could get her chest to David without him batting an eyelash. Megan rolled her eyes. *Ashley, button your blouse.*

She surveyed her own body, which was almost equally exposed and as poorly protected from the elements as Ashley's. Megan's fashionable and somewhat sheer dress was now a bit worse for the wear.

At least I don't go shoving myself in her husband's face.

Ashley's husband was Robert, one hundred percent United States Marine Corps, and one of Megan's only true male friends. Megan didn't know that she wouldn't be seeing Robert for quite some time.

Ashley was about to explode as the window rolled all the way down. David was clueless as to what she was in such a huff about.

She has a list in her hand? Megan thought. *We have to be somewhere else! Like, now! Work is over!*

"You didn't even say goodbye. You guys just took off! We still have stuff to finish!" Ashley looked down at her list. "Now look, David, don't go pissing off the City at the fundraiser tonight. We need this store and we need to keep the other stores as well. So both of you behave yourselves. Next, David. David, you've got to keep your donation in line with reality tonight..."

And the words kept streaming from her mouth like the Colorado River rapids that flow from the Rocky Mountains.

Who the hell does Ashley think she is, talking to David like this? He would never take this from anyone else. I would never even consider talking to him like this. He just sits there and seems to drink it all in. I swear to heaven, if they aren't sleeping with each other they should be. But what am I supposed to do? Put a camera in the ceiling in the store and watch them 24/7? Listen to her roll.

Megan wasn't jealous, typically. Only of Ashley. David and Ashley's relationship was quite unusual. For one thing, Ashley spent far more time with David than Megan did. And he trusted her completely with his life and business. And she drove him nuts.

"...the guy who can help you the most is Anderson. Scott Anderson. He's our only friend left in Planning. If we don't get him to try and block the rezoning, we're out of here. Maybe ninety days. They're talking about giving us $200,000 for the store. And you know it's worth a million, David. And if they get one of the stores, they're going to take all four. You know that too. So talk to him and win him over."

David still hadn't said a damn thing. He simply moved his eyes around like he was watching a sporting event.

Megan straightened her dress a bit and hoped it would look perfect when they arrived at the fundraiser...if they could ever get out of the parking lot. Megan would say absolutely nothing. Any words she uttered would give birth to a thousand more words from Ashley, and she just wanted the Colorado River to be tame enough for Megan and David to hop on a raft and navigate downstream to the fundraiser that they were obviously going to be late for. Being fashionably late was fine for a party, but not so fine for a fundraiser for a little boy whose parents had died.

And I am hostess for the evening. Come on, David!

"...and the Hiawatha Store is out of Percocet. When I called up there today because we were running low they were *out*. Now *that* is ridiculous. She needs to know that she can't be *out* of anything."

She thinks she runs Hiawatha too? Megan wondered.

Then David made the mistake. He spoke. "Why don't you take care of that, Ashley?"

He should know better than to speak, and certainly never to ask a question.

"I sure will and I will give that girl a piece of my mind. She is not watching out for us. We have enough problems without screwing up any of the easy stuff, like ordering."

David would talk to his manager at Hiawatha tomorrow and tell her to just blow off what was about to come her way... and to make damn sure that she did have Percocet in stock.

David trusted Ashley not only with his store, but in many ways, with his entire future. Ashley didn't know it but if anything were ever to happen to him, she would take over and run his business. He had granted Ashley his Power of Attorney for all kinds of unlikely life and death scenarios. It definitely was an unusual relationship. But he knew she was fiercely dedicated to him, and he respected and relied on that.

"Now you guys are going to be *late* for the fundraiser. I can't believe you haven't left already! Go, go, go – and keep that checkbook in check. We don't know what our financial situation will be like tomorrow. Literally and truly, David! Now go!"

She removed herself from the open window. David pressed his foot lightly on the gas and slowly crept out of the parking lot and onto the street.

He saw the pawn shops and "checks cashed" stores across the street and immediately considered, for the eight hundredth time, whether he should ever let Megan venture into this part of town.

But the fact was, she had been to the drug store fifty times before, and there had never been a problem.

"Do you seriously think it's OK for Ashley to talk to you that way?"

"And what am I going to do to change the way she talks to me?"

"David, I'm not going to tell you what to do..."

"You aren't going to tell me what to do because you just watched someone else tell me what to do and you realized how that might wear on a person?"

He smiled.

"What? David, my point is – she goes on and on and on like she controls your life and – "

"And who picked her because she was great for this job five years ago?"

"Me, but – "

"And what did I say when I hired her?"

"That it might not be a great idea to have my best friend working for you."

"Because?"

"Because I'm the jealous type and because she's the controlling type."

"And?"

"Because she has always liked you and – Oh, you are a pain in the ass, David Dresden. Do they have wedding chapels for...for...for... work wives? Can you get married at City Hall in front of the justice of the peace so you can at least get a box of peace of mind when you get divorced?"

He laughed again. Megan had always made him laugh. She didn't say much, but most of what she said was funny and very cute. He took it all in stride.

"Megan – is Ashley really your best friend?"

That shut Megan up. Traffic was now at a standstill. The side streets were cordoned off.

Something weird was going on. They wouldn't shut down access to the side streets if it was just an accident.

They must have slept together. They had to have. You can't work with someone for five years that closely and not have. And look how she talks to him. My God. I bet his own mother didn't speak to him that way. And I got her the job. I was in her wedding. She was in mine. I know everything about her. Everything! She knows...well...almost everything about me. I don't know...whatever...I mean, think about me! Would I flirt with Robert? NO WAY...never in a million years...well...OK...yes...but not like Ashley. We'd just talk and stuff.

The fact was, Megan acted differently around Ashley's husband Robert than she did around David. Around Robert she was flirtatious, spoke about little else other than sex, and David couldn't have cared less.

David might have been concerned about his wife's faithfulness, had she not insisted on having sex like a daily vitamin, and he was happy to be that vitamin.

It never once dawned on him that Megan might have slept with Robert. He never thought to think it. Megan had often joked about David and Ashley being together, but the fact was that David barely had time to tie his shoes in the morning. He had no time... and even less inclination to have an affair. Truth be told, he was married to one of the most beautiful and sweetest girls he'd ever seen.

She turned her iPod up to a volume where even David could hear it, and she closed her eyes.

CRACK! The sound of another gunshot rang out.

Another one? What the hell? David looked around wildly. He knew it came from the general direction he was heading in, but there was nothing he could do about it. Megan hadn't heard it, apparently. He drove on.

She set her left hand lovingly on his right thigh. She wanted him to know she was with him.

David didn't talk much when he drove. He was an introspective driver and not the more social animal that Megan could be. The touch and the gunshot so close in time to each other triggered some kind of somatic memory, taking him back to their trip to Africa a few years ago. It was his second trip there. That trip he took with Megan probably qualified as the most fulfilling two weeks of his entire life.

We've got to get back to Africa. This time next year. She helped so many people. Ahmed...the man. She was his age and his life expectancy was no more than my age. He was so appreciative. Megan helped his family personally. She gave them enough money to get ID, passports and papers along with enough money to bribe the family's way on to a boat to Yemen where their family would be safer than they would even have been here. Who would have guessed Yemen was safer than anywhere in the world?

She gets upset about a gunshot and she should… but when she was in Africa she didn't think about the dangers there for a second. She wasn't thinking about herself, at all. That one afternoon in Somalia, it seemed like every second she was stopping to feed a baby, help a little girl, comfort a mother, and talk with the few men who were miraculously alive. One spoke English, another had taught English and these kinds of men had value in negotiations with U.N. groups that would bring food. A few were spiritual leaders that could calm the locals when necessary.

We were lucky. Aid workers have been kidnapped and butchered there. There was never a real way to know whether you might live or die.

If everyone went to Africa the wars would all stop. But no one goes. The wars will continue. No one could watch that much suffering and not demand the U.N., the U.S., the U. SOMEONE go in and clear out the warlords and install a stable government.

The next day she asked why the people of the community were digging such big holes in the ground. "What's that you're working on, sir?" It was going to be a mass grave to be filled with the dead from the day before. Starvation was the most common cause of death. Those who were stoned added to the daily toll as did mass shootings of men and women who were often beaten and raped then taken aside and gunned down. Then there might be a week or two or three of "peace" when the militants would leave one part of Somalia and go to another.

Megan desperately tried to get everyone to eat. So many couldn't eat. She didn't know that when you were nearly dead from starvation, keeping food down was nearly impossible. You could see the panic in her eyes. "I want you to live." It was her will and her will could be strong when she had power, but in Africa, like all people, she had no super powers.

She held that little girl. She was not really prepared. I probably should have given her warning of what it was going to be like. And it was bad. They were all so malnourished. Fifteen-year-olds who looked like they were seven. How had the teenagers even lived that long? They were fortunate to be alive. Or were they? Maybe the dead were better off. It's one of those things where you hope the good guys will come in and save the day, and we could... and Megan cried daily for "us" to save them...and Western society, we easily could do just that. The Western countries could actually make Africa stable for almost nothing. It wouldn't require much more than a hundred billion a year and the continent could eat, sleep, drink safe water in relative peace. She wanted to know why we weren't doing something. She got mad at me like I had something to do with it. 100 billion. It's a lot of money. It's 3% of the U.S. annual expenditures. A tax no one with a heart would deny.

That one little girl died right in her arms and Megan had to give her back to her mother. Dead.

The mother simply teared up, but she didn't cry. The mother had AIDS. Her three other children probably did too. But the little girl was her fourth that had died in two years. Death was the release from pain. It was also the release from hope. When your children die one right after the other, there is no hope. You simply see it all. There is no comparison in the U.S. to what Megan saw in Africa. Thank God for that. It's like she always says, "Americans have no idea how lucky they are."

She always speaks about Americans as if she isn't an American.

That trip in a lot of ways was really everything to her. It didn't simply change her perspective *on life. It changed her life.*

Three years ago she was the nicest self-absorbed girl I ever met. But two weeks in Africa shifted who she was. It changed her.

They're probably all dead today. We alleviated a symptom. We gave people a week of life… maybe two. We gave them the illusion of some kind of safety for a week but the thing was that the warlords would be back. Next time they would kill random aid workers. Next time they'd steal most... but never all... of the food. I wonder if I should have told her all of that. She wants to go back so badly. She tried to collect names of people and wanted to remember them so she'd be able to see them again someday. And it's possible that a few of those people will probably survive 'til our next trip. But mostly I don't think so.

I swear to God that she was more passionate about feeding people and giving them shots than she was the week before when we were lounging on the beach in Mauritius. I never figured that. Mauritius was the most amazing tropical paradise in the world. Not a fear to be felt. Pure heaven. And she could only talk about the starvation, the bloodshed, the tears. She even asked about the diamonds. She learned a lot on that trip.

So which is the real world?

The world where she wants to heal people at the possible cost of her own life?

Or is the real world the world where she walks into the room, everyone turns, looks at her and can't stop looking because no one looks that drop-dead gorgeous in real life. She takes your breath away.

How does she sort it out in her mind? I guess it doesn't matter. How do I sort it out in MY mind. I work all day over here… they die all day over there.

There is no comparison.

"What's on the agenda tonight, Megan?"

David knew full well they were en route to a fundraiser, of course. They had agreed on a donation of $25,000 to the young boy whose parents had been killed in a car crash two weeks ago.

"I'll be at the front of the room and seeing if I can swing some nice checks for that little boy."

Twenty-five thousand had been the maximum allowable Dresden check for pretty much all fundraisers for several years now. Her gift giving had gotten out of control a few years ago when she persuaded David to write a check for $250,000 to Children's Hospital Cancer Ward. That one check was about a quarter of David's pretax income for any given year. That pretty much meant that David had worked seventy-hour weeks all year... for free. Every penny he earned that year went to charities or taxes.

He remembered the call from the hospital while he was working the Lake Street store.

She said she needed $250,000. There was no way we could do that along with everything else we had committed to that year. But we gave it and I worked it off. I'm glad we did and if nothing else it got the conversation going about limits and limitations. We aren't Buffett. We aren't Gates. She thinks we are, but she doesn't understand money.

That little boy Jeffrey at Children's really captured her heart. I wonder if he's still alive. I swear, she must've been there twice a week visiting him and his mom. Then it all tapered off when he started getting sicker... when his immune system got so compromised that she wasn't allowed to visit anymore.

He looked at her again and flashed back to their first meeting, at another fundraiser, while she was finishing her degree at the University of St. Thomas.

He had simply walked up to her, asked her out, said "Great," and walked away. Then returned to ask her name... and phone number. He had never been so nervous in his life. Even though he was twenty-nine by then, David hadn't had a lot of practice in asking girls out. Megan, it turned out, had just celebrated her twenty-first birthday.

Megan unconsciously continued to adjust her dress and turned up the Red Hot Chili Peppers. David almost said something about his memories of their first meeting, when he realized she was comfortable in her own world of music. He was glad she had it. She closed her eyes and didn't let the traffic jam get to her. What would be the point of interrupting?

He took his eyes off the road and looked over at her.

Megan was not put together like a runway model. At a petite 5' 4", she could never have modeled for anyone. That noted, almost no one could compare to her in striking beauty. With chestnut eyes and long flowing black hair, her classic beauty and full lips would captivate anyone at first sight, he thought.

The girl simply never uttered anything except what was on her mind. She thinks, she says. That was Megan. She generally didn't think long enough to censor herself, but that made her one of the most entertaining people in the world to be around. She was so much like a little kid, more real than profound.

She was simply a straight shooter who made people laugh. People loved to be around Megan.

David laughed out loud.

Had anyone else said it, it would have sounded so cliché. She's standing there at the front of the room at the March of Dimes fundraiser that night and who knows what possessed her. I couldn't believe it when she called out to the Vikings football team head coach and sassed him. "Dennis, is that your checkbook you're pulling out or are you just happy to see me?" And the whole place died laughing. We raised a fortune that night for The March.

Traffic picked up and he was moving again... finally.

He looked over at her again. Still off in Sergeant Pepper Land.

She's a princess.

Ashley can be a pain in my ass, but she gets the business. If I made her the general manager of all the stores, I'd get more time off. Well, maybe I'd get a whole day off, anyway. Or would everyone quit because she'd drive 'em all nuts? Or would she have things running so efficiently that the customers wouldn't recognize the stores? Life has been so damn stressful lately. And Ashley was right. The city would screw us.

They are going to shut down the Lake Street store now and they're going to shut the other three down as soon as they can come up with a rationale. That's the price for not kissing politicians' butts. I hate it. These people do nothing all day but figure out how to rezone places to make Group A happy and punish Group B. Well. I'm in group C and we are going to take some major hits for speaking up in the elections and not supporting any of them.

He looked over at her. Her hand still on his thigh. She was off in dreamland. That made him happy.

He put his hand on hers as they came to the stop light at the Calhoun Beach Club. She opened her eyes, looked up at him, and smiled. She leaned over to him and gave him a kiss on the cheek.

He hadn't gotten farther than the center of the intersection when things came to a standstill again. He didn't care...

"Don't worry so much, David. God will watch out for us." She put her ear buds back in and closed her eyes.

His world was good.

One kiss meant everything.

I am the luckiest man in the world.

With a life-shattering BANG that came out of nowhere, everything went into a tailspin.

A fifteen-year-old Chevy had crashed into the driver's side of their car. Police would later estimate the car had been doing in excess of ninety miles an hour and propelled the Mercedes thirty feet before the two stopped moving.

It was a drug bust in progress, and the felons didn't want to get caught. Two shots had been fired by police but to no avail. Instead of two dead drug dealers being the headline in tomorrow's paper, for the Dresden family, it was about to be much worse.

The driver and his passenger, both high and drunk, had weaved in and out of traffic, making use of sidewalks, and otherwise terrorizing the local citizens. When they rammed into the Mercedes they were killed instantly.

The Mercedes didn't even look like a car anymore. A crowd of people stood and stared, their jaws hanging open, people pointing, kids running. There was silence after the Chevy and Mercedes came to a stop. No one had ever seen anything like it. Two minutes later emergency vehicles arrived. It wasn't quiet anymore and it didn't matter.

David's heart stopped pumping at 6:06 p.m. on September nineteenth. That was Day 1.

Chapter Two

September 20, 2:40 AM

Day 2

Six people in blue scrubs and surgical gloves walked past Ashley into the operating room. The first team would soon exit the room. It had been eight hours. She wondered when it would be over.

The first person out was one of the surgeons.

"Ashley Drexel?"

"Yes." She stood.

"I understand that as Mrs. Dresden's legal guardian, at least at this point, you need to know this." Ashley said nothing. Her heart seemed to stop. Her mouth went dry.

"Mrs. Dresden is in critical condition. We've been operating for seven hours, but the process has only begun. I don't want to give you any false hope by telling you that I think there is a significant chance she will live. We will do our best. I will be back in the afternoon to continue working on her. For now, the second team is taking over, and they are excellent. However, I don't think that they can possibly finish doing all of the work that needs to be done before I return at two o'clock."

The doctor, obviously exhausted and emotionally drained, sighed.

"Mrs. Dresden has suffered incredible injuries. She has a brain injury. She has three basal skull fractures..." The doctor stopped before he'd started, practically. To tick off all that was wrong with Megan would require an hour, and a textbook. He decided to take a different tack. "There is every likelihood that she will be permanently paralyzed if and when she comes out of this. From the neck down, every bone we have worked on or seen has been shattered, crushed or broken. Mrs. Drexel, your friend is in a situation that might require you to make some very difficult decisions. Please be prepared for that possibility..."

"What else?"

"Her legs have been completely crushed. I don't know if we can do anything with them. We will of course make every effort and use every ounce of our skills and every bit of surgical technology available. Mrs. Dresden's eyes, ears and hearing apparatus have suffered significant damage.."

"If there is one piece of hope for you, it is that she has no internal injuries to her major organs that we have come across at this point. But beyond keeping her heart beating, I don't know that it's going to make any difference…"

"My team will be back at two in the afternoon to relieve the shift that is coming on now. I expect surgery to take about thirty-six hours in total. The surgeons will continue until all of the work is done. When I've finished working on your friend I will speak with you again. Go home and rest. There is nothing you can do here now. Nothing can or will change for the better in the next twelve hours. Please get some rest. You are in for a long wait. Good night, Mrs. Drexel."

"Good night, Doctor…" She didn't catch his name. She whispered the words. She sank down and could do nothing but cry.

David was dead. Aside from her husband and daughter, she had loved David more than anyone.

And Megan, my best friend. She's going to die too.

Chapter Three

December 22

Day 95

Three Floors Up From the Operating Room

She lay there… staring at the ceiling. She would have loved to beep a nurse, but the beeper was about three inches from her fingers. The clip attaching the gadget to her wrist had somehow come loose. She could thumb the ancient device if it had been in her hand, but it wasn't. The pain was great, the painkillers were greater, and her thinking muddled, at best.

I wonder if Jeffrey Stein is still alive. That was three months ago at Children's. I can't remember. I hope so. I hope he gets out of his hospital room and does something with his family. I hope they don't just let him lay there and die. He's such a wonderful boy. I wonder if they had the fundraiser. I wonder if they raised the money for him. I wonder if Ashley wrote the check for me and David. I wonder... but I might never know.

I went to the bathroom on the bed twice today. It's gross. I'm gross. I can't eat or drink by myself. I can't talk. I can't communicate with anyone.

Why did I have to wake up? At least when I was in the coma I was not here.

This is existence. I don't want to be here anymore. Existence is not life. Life is how life used to be. You wake up excited about your day. Or maybe you wake up sad. But you don't wake up inside of yourself unable to do... or say... anything. The only way they know I'm alive is when I go to the bathroom. That's it.

I want to cry but my eyes won't tear. I need to cry. No one knows what happens inside of you when you hurt and you can't cry. People always look down on others when they cry. It's wrong. I can't cry and it makes me want to die; everything makes me want to die.

God, did you know I might never have an orgasm again? Did you know that I probably will never be kissed or held by another person who wants to love me and not pity me? How would you feel if YOU couldn't have an orgasm, God? No one thinks stuff like that but I know you do or you wouldn't have made us this way. I was paying attention in college. I know EVERY animal can have an orgasm. I think it was every animal. But you get the point. YOU can have an orgasm whenever you want and what does everyone say? "Well, he's God, of course he can." But you can stop people from experiencing pleasure, just like you stopped me. Are you proud of yourself? Does that make you feel powerful? Like you are in control?

I can't believe you would do that. Not to me. Not to anyone.

The doctors said something about what happened to my tear ducts. I guess it makes no difference what it is. There are no tears. No one will ever see me cry. They will never know when I hurt. No one will ever know when I need love. No one will ever know anything about me.

If I opened my eyes now I would just be more depressed. I don't want to see this room. I don't want to see the wall. At least in here sometimes I can get away. I can't be out there so why open my eyes to look. There is nothing to see.

The doctors were right about one thing. It hurts when I have to cry. And I really do need to cry right now. Any normal person would just cry.

Maybe it's good that I can't cry, because there's no one here to wipe away my tears. So the part of crying that has to do with someone helping you is gone. But you still need to cry because it hurts.

God, does time go slow. It's been three months they say. But I have no way to check that. None. It could be three years. Or three decades.

I'd never know. Well, I guess that isn't entirely true. Ashley still looks the same. So I guess it really has just been three months.

They always bullshit me and tell me I'll get better.

Really?

Like what?

You WILL be able to go to the bathroom someday without having a nurse's aide wipe you twice each day!

You WILL be able to turn from your left side to face up in bed.

You WILL be able to talk... someday!

I love that.

Some day.

Some day when? Someday, never.

Why me, God? God, are you listening? I always try so hard to be a good person. I fight for people's lives. I help children and their families. Why did you let this happen to me, God?

Do you know what it's like to be trapped inside of your own body? Do you have any idea? It's going to push me over the edge, God. It would push anyone over. If you could just let me talk or walk or write or move my hands or anything. I would do anything to be able to talk.

If this is one of those lessons where you're supposed to learn something, I don't know what to make of it. I don't know what I'm supposed to learn. I guess you're tired of hearing me ask you questions.

Do you want me to talk about David? Do you want me to talk about the other men I slept with? Really? What do you want me to say? What do you need to hear?

Do you need to hear, "I'm sorry, God"?

You hear me right now and you know that isn't true. So do you want me to say it anyway so I can open my eyes and go to the bathroom "someday"?

Think about it, God. You made me who I am. You made me pretty. You made me a sexual person. I had nothing to do with that.

Even my mom had nothing to do with that.

That was one hundred percent on you, God. Do YOU accept responsibility? Really? What about all those kids we fed in Africa? I held children, as they died. We were too late. The mass graves were everywhere.

So why, God? Because they were mostly Muslim? I mean Muslims aren't a Jew's best friend but the fact is, God, they are people too. They starve. They die. How do I know you aren't Muslim or whatever?

Why did you make life so complicated? Why not just say, "No guys, THIS is the way it really is, so throw your books away. The answers are in HERE."

Those people really believed they offended you. They have no idea what they have done and they die.

Why?

And I'm supposed to say I'm sorry because I had sex with someone? My God, God, when you got mad you flooded the WHOLE WORLD! Geezuz. I wouldn't flood the whole world! You were going to kill innocent people and needed to have Abraham intercede on behalf of an entire city. You let Job's family DIE to TEST JOB?

I was paying attention, God. I love you. You gave me life. You gave me my mom and dad. But you really have a temper issue. Are you mad at me because I'm telling you that?

It really isn't because I slept with someone else. It's because I called you out. You might be perfect, but you are perfectly temperamental.

If you know everything from the beginning, then why make evil men that you know you are going to wipe out? It's like watching a football game on video that you heard the score of the game on the radio on the way home, but you're HOPING SOMEONE CHANGES REAL LIFE. It doesn't happen, God.

But God, for all YOUR faults, I love you. I was glad you made me. I appreciated that. But you only loved me when I was doing everything by your rules. Then when I thought for myself you killed David.

What did DAVID ever do?

You didn't like him because he was Christian? So you just took him from me? Why? Because you wanted to mess with me? Because you didn't want to give him a life? Do you know how many people he helped in this world, God? A lot more than me. That man was honest. He was a GOOD MAN. He didn't deserve to die. I swear to God, God, you should not have killed him.

David never did anything wrong. The man is almost as perfect as you are. I can't think of any time I was ever really mad at him...not really. Sure, I yelled that time from the hospital, but big deal. I was emotional that week. You made me that way.

Is this all your fault, God?

No. It was that stupid drunk driver.

But God, was any of it David's fault?

None of it was.

You don't need to make me better. No one will ever make me better. I can't get better, can I? Have you watched the video? How does it end, anyway? Just TELL ME NOW. I'm really angry with you, God. Yes, I love you. No, I'm not sorry. You are a person, too. You gave women their cycles. I have my period. I get upset. I don't flood the world. I don't ram cars into innocent people's lives. I would STOP THE CAR and get help for the stupid drunk.

But it's your world, God. You make the decisions. Obviously, I don't. You are the only one who comes out without being hurt. How are you feeling right now? Are you proud that you put me here? Do you feel like a man?

Did you feel like a man killing David, a man who really was after your heart, except that he was NICE.

If you want me to die, God, just let me die now and give everything I own to Ashley. She has done everything for me. But you didn't do anything when David died, did you? Or did you kill him?

He believed your son Jesus was real. He really TRIED to be like him. He never talked about it, he just DID it every day. And his reward? Well, it's in Christian heaven, right, God? Because his reward was his wife who's a brain in a body, and himself dead. Think about it, God. Yes, I love you. But do you love me? I don't believe it. I think YOU have some explaining to do. I'm open to the discussion. TALK TO ME.

She couldn't speak. She had learned to communicate with her left eye. Move to the right and left: No. Move up and down: Yes. If she wanted to point, she could guide her eye in that direction. It wasn't really deep communication. It was simply all she had.

She couldn't eat solid food because her jaw was still wired shut, though there was a small hole in between the wires for a straw.

Three knocks on the door woke her up from a light sleep. She was so uncomfortable. There were tubes for everything. The bed was cold. The sheets felt like napkins, papery and rough. Being unable to move. Trapped alive inside her body, she wanted to get out. She had to get out. She couldn't stay like this for much longer.

It had been two months since she woke up. It had been over one month since they told her that David had been killed. Ashley told her that day when her world was over. Ashley shouted in her ear so hard it made her shudder, except no one could see what she felt. Only she knew, because no one ever asked.

Yes, Ashley, I know he's dead. You didn't need to shout or even tell me. It was fucking obvious, wasn't it?

She was now sleeping a fairly normal cycle. When she was awake, her only real connection with the world was through her sight. She could hear a little, and everything was muffled. The hearing aid wasn't set properly, but she couldn't let anyone know. It needed to pull a lot more sound in for her to hear anything more than a few feet away.

She could recognize her name pretty clearly, but most of the rest of what she heard was a mumble. Her left ear couldn't take a hearing aid yet because it needed another surgery. The bones in that ear had been significantly damaged. The surgery was scheduled for after the first of the year.

To a great extent, her legs had been crushed. Metal braces were taken off yesterday, and that appeared to make sleeping a little more tolerable, and being awake a little less devastating.

She prayed. She knew there was a reason for all of this. She just didn't know what it could be.

"Megan? Hi, sweetie." It was Ashley, a middle-aged woman with her. Megan couldn't tell for sure. She could barely make her out with her left eye. Her right eye was patched. Ashley had said something about not being able to get it open.

Megan wondered daily just what she must look like. No one had handed her a mirror yet. For all intents and purposes, she might as well have been crushed in a trash compactor.

Megan had mixed feelings about her lack of visitors. Ashley was by daily. Robert came when he could. The room itself was pleasant enough. It had nice light blue walls with a big TV at the end of the bed. This was not standard hospital issue but the work of Robert when he was on leave. Having the large private room was nice, but of the 168 hours in each week, she slept half of them and was useless the other half.

Everyone called her the "Miracle Lady." *What miracle? This is a miracle? Not yet,* she hoped.

Ashley had her typical energy level up even higher than usual, and Megan needed that today. The boost picked her up a bit inside.

Ashley immediately noticed the beeper was not in Megan's hand. She grabbed it and pushed it and held it down.

"Megan, honey, how long has that call button been out of your hand?"

Megan moved her eye from left to right. She didn't know.

"I want you to meet Grace. Grace is going to be your personal aide. She's going to be here with you during most of the day. She'll make sure you're taken care of."

"Hi, Megan. Nice to meet you."

Megan moved her eye up and down. She couldn't move her head. It was still in a brace. Megan had no idea if she'd be able to move her head once the brace was removed.

"I called around and finally found someone who came highly recommended. I'm still going to be here every day, but Grace will be here to help you with the daily necessities of life. Where is that stupid nurse?"

In she walked.

"You called?"

"Megan's call button was not in her hand. It was supposed to be taped right there. If anything happens she has no way to let you know, aside from that button."

"Sorry. Is there anything else?"

"No, there is nothing else."

The nurse left.

What a bitch, the nurse thought.

What a bitch, Ashley thought.

Megan was starting to doze off again.

"Megan, I want you to try and talk to me today."

Who are you kidding, Ashley? Megan rolled her eye as best she could. Her jaw was wired shut. She could only partially control her tongue. She couldn't move the right side of her lips but she did have a bit of control of the left side.

Megan knew what she wanted to say. She wanted to say she was *ready to go home.* She couldn't stand this horrible hospital anymore. Suicide had crossed her mind about a month ago, when she realized that it would be impossible to carry it out. She couldn't swallow pills, lift a knife, slit her wrist. Nothing. She couldn't even entertain the idea for long enough to formulate a plan.

Even when she was awake she was tired. Tired, and in severe pain. The painkillers took the pain level down but made the world seem unreal.

"Megan, I think you can say, 'ugh.' Like 'ugh.'"

Megan was thankful to have Ashley there. Thank God she was there. She would have gone crazy without Ashley. Sometimes it even seemed that Ashley could read her mind. But not that day.

Why would I want to say 'ugh'?

She closed her eye. She thought about the word 'ugh.' She thought about an old Scrabble dictionary her Mom had. If she was ever going to say any of those words, she had to start somewhere. It seemed like a monumental task to say 'ugh.' She would never get to the dictionary. It was impossible.

"Megan. Open your eye, honey, and look at me. *Ugh.* OK?"

Ashley was no nurse. Her bedside manner went from managerial to authoritarian to paternal to maternal to dumb blonde. She could be abrasive. She could be sweet. But she was always determined.

Megan thought that a cough had that *ugh* sound… sort of. She thought she would try to cough. She opened her eye. She moved her eye up and down.

"Uh."

It was soft but it was there.

"Good job, Megan!"

Maternal was not fun. There was no part in Megan that liked being treated like a child. Or was she actually a child? Maybe Ashley was serious. Maybe she was excited, and maybe this was really good. She just didn't know.

"Uh!"

She took every ounce of energy she had in her lungs and exhaled again.

"Uh."

Not as loud, but it was there again.

"Uh."

Better.

She closed her eye. She thought about making the "guh" sound. How could that happen? She could try and gag herself to get that "guh," but there was no other way she could do it.

Megan breathed in until it hurt and with all of her life energy she tightened her throat and let out "guh."

"Wow! This is great."

She closed her eye. *Who are you kidding, Ashley?* She opened her eye and moved it from left to right.

"No, honey, it IS! You are gaining control of the muscles in your chest and in your throat."

Megan closed her eye. It was like taking one step up the Rocky Mountains and then celebrating. It was a joke.

Months ago the doctor had told Ashley that Megan would never be able to cry again. It simply wouldn't be possible. Something happened to her tear ducts in the accident and the subsequent reconstruction of her face. She understood a lot, but not this part. She knew that if Megan could cry, Megan would have cried right now.

The most powerful nonverbal expression of compassion, sadness, and love was something Megan would never again be physically capable of doing.

Three raps on the door.

Ashley turned around. Megan opened her eye. Grace stood at attention.

Robert walked in with Lauren, their daughter.

Lauren was seven and she was scared. She had known Megan since she was a baby. Her parents had told her that Megan looked different than she used to. That was a *big* understatement.

Megan saw Robert enter, but not Lauren. Lauren wasn't tall enough to enter her field of vision.

Robert. Good-looking Marine. Strong. Focused. But even his strong presence weakened as he walked in and saw Megan. It was a lot to take. Megan was once a beautiful brunette, good-looking enough to have been on TV. But not now. Robert was able to hide most of his discomfort. He came over and sat in a chair that was near the head of the bed. He sat close to Megan without being so close as to overwhelm her.

"Hello, Megan. Last week when I was here, I noticed the flowers were getting a bit shabby, so I asked the girl in the gift shop to bring up some more."

And in walked the girl with a cart of flowers. There were a lot of flowers. Ten bouquets. Plants, both flowering and green. Everything.

"An early Christmas present, Megan. You need something to give this room a little – " he almost said "life," and caught it right before it hit his tongue, " – pizzazz." He was very sensitive to her position. A mind inside of a body that didn't work. He'd seen such a thing often enough in Iraq. It wasn't pretty. He'd never seen anyone live through it.

He distributed the flowers all over the room. Within five minutes there were flowers and plants everywhere.

Megan wanted to cry. It was so beautiful. She just adored Robert. She and Ashley both had such great husbands, of course. And then she stopped thinking and closed her eye again.

He was gone. *God, how could he be gone?* It wasn't possible.

"Megan honey?" Ashley didn't know where Megan's attention had gone. "You OK?"

Megan opened her eye and moved it up and down.

Robert wondered for the millionth time in three months just what kind of life Megan could have. Whether she'd even live had been a big question for the first month. Now she was alive, and internal organs were functioning well.

Megan used to joke a lot with Robert about sex. She flirted a lot with him and he flirted with her too. David would just roll his eyes at them. So would Ashley. For some reason, neither of them was ever concerned.

But now, there would be no more jokes about sex. His mind went there and had to come back. He knew that she had to think about it, still. She used to talk about sex with him like no one else. They had a good friendship and they both could talk with each other about things that they couldn't discuss with their own spouses.

He felt her pain. He'd been hit by fire in the war, but he'd never seen anyone who looked this rough. Not even after being shot. Not after anything.

"Can I put the cart on this side of the bed and leave the rest of the flowers next to you?"

She moved her eye up and down.

"Got it." And he did.

He wanted to cry. He didn't want to cry. He was on a mission. He had told Ashley he was going to try to do the impossible today.

"Can I get you some water, Megan?"

What was he thinking? She moved her eye up and down.

She was well aware that she was the biggest freak in the freak show.

Megan could in no way suck water from a straw. Impossible. Couldn't grasp a straw in her lips. Tried it last week. The right side of her mouth simply wouldn't move at all.

Robert held a straw that bent near the end, and a styrofoam cup of water. He came over to the side of the bed with the flowers. He pushed the button for her bed to go to what would have been a sitting position, if it had been anyone else in the bed. This was her Stephen-Hawkingin-a-wheelchair position. He didn't ask her if it would be OK. He had gotten permission from the doctor and Megan trusted him. He knew she would be in pain when she tried it. She closed her eye then opened it again.

"Did that hurt much?"

Yes, but it didn't matter, she thought. She lied and moved her eye from left to right.

"Now Megan, here's the deal. Are you able to breathe through your nose?"

She had to check that. Then she moved her eye up and down.

"Great. When I tell you 'when,' I want you to exhale most of the air from your lungs then suck on this straw and bring the water up into your mouth. I cut the bottom of the straw so the water doesn't have as far to go."

"Now I know what you're thinking. You're thinking, how do you know which pipe it's going to go down? I think it's pretty clear that we don't have a clue. It's at least 50/50 it goes down the right pipe. If not, you'll cough, it'll be uncomfortable, and you might get scared. But it's not like you're going to," he paused, "die, or anything."

Megan thought it would be a lot worse than uncomfortable, but she trusted Robert and Ashley and she was going to do this. Ashley, who was used to running a household, Megan's life, and a million dollar store, was even a bit nervous. She wondered about her husband's wisdom. But she didn't second-guess him out loud. She said nothing.

He placed the straw between Megan's lips on the left side of her face. He pushed the straw past the metal grid that made up her wiring system to keep her mouth and jaw from moving. There were three little holes that the straw could fit through. One was on the left. He gently slid the straw through the hole. The water would fall on Megan's tongue and she would feel the wetness. It was probably going to be cold. God, he hoped it would go down the right tube.

She could move her lips a little. Very little… but a little. And she did.

"OK, now exhale most of the air out of your lungs. Not all the air. Most of it. Then suck that water into the straw and into your mouth. Got it?"

Her eye moved up and down.

She looked down at the water. God, it looked good. It had been three months since she had a sip of anything. She sucked up as hard as she could. The water raised into the top part of the straw, onto her tongue. She wasn't choking.

"OK, a little more, keep going, don't worry about the overflow, just keep going."

The water hit her tongue. She couldn't remember something more pleasant. It was heavenly. Robert pulled the straw out of her mouth. Half the water went down the right tube, the other half dribbled out. He would have jumped for joy and scared the living hell out of everyone if he wasn't trying to restrain himself. Instead, he acted like it turned out as he had expected it would all along.

"So, what do you think? Good stuff?"

Up and down.

God, I love you, Robert.

"That's good, because it won't be long before I'm bringing you a chocolate shake."

A chocolate shake. Oh, that sounded incredible. She closed her eye. She couldn't remember what it tasted like, but she knew it would be good.

He knew there was no way she'd get much down but he'd bring it, she'd sip it, and it would work.

Megan felt like she was crying. There were no tears, of course, because the accident had made it physically impossible for her to cry. She had no sad expression on her face. But still, she thought, this is how it felt when she cried. Her chest heaved a bit. She made some sounds.

"Are you OK?" Robert was immediately concerned.

She opened her eye. She moved it up and down.

For the first time in a month she felt hope.

She would give Robert anything to hug her right now, but he didn't get her mental message. Instead, he gave her a kiss on her forehead. She craved more closeness than a held hand or a kiss on the head. But it would have to do.

Chapter Four

September 19

Day 366

One year ago today… David died.

He never felt a thing. It was instant.

Today would be a painful day. The emotional pain would likely outweigh the physical pain, which was still enormous. The choice between taking heavy doses of painkillers and having complete clarity was always difficult. There was no good answer.

Megan lay in the same hospital room that she'd been living in since before she woke up. It was actually decorated now, and felt a bit more homey, if that's really possible in the hospital. At least there were no more tubes hooked up to her. All the braces had been removed, from head to foot. The metal holding her face together – her jaw, her mouth, everything that had been crushed – was either gone or no longer visible. She had metal plates in her head but she'd never see them, or scans of them. She often wondered if she could ever get on a plane again. She'd set off all those metal detectors 'til they were flashing like a Christmas tree. Scars remained, everywhere. Some were starting to change in color closer to that of her skin. Some were still ugly graphic reminders of everything that had happened to her.

The general insurance rule is that as soon as a patient can receive no beneficial health care advantage from being in the hospital, they have to be transferred to a long-term care facility such as a nursing home, or they have to go home. Megan was now at that point.

The cost of Megan's stay had already far exceeded the maximum lifetime output on her insurance policy. In just one year Blue Cross Blue Shield had maxed out the two million dollars lifetime benefit of payments. Ashley would never have insurance again. She had incurred bills that averaged $7,000 a day for the last year at the hospital. Two-thirds of that money was spent in the first three months of her hospitalization. In addition, their car insurance had covered a large amount of medical payments, as the drunk driver was uninsured. That insurance money lasted all of two months. One hundred percent of all future medical costs would now be out of pocket.

As soon as Megan was out of the hospital, Ashley had calculated she was going to be spending about $4,000 each week on medication, physical therapy, reconstructive surgeries, psychiatrists, and visits to seven different doctors. Another $1,000 per week was budgeted for Megan's caregiver, including salary, food and insurance.

Ashley would be writing checks for Megan's care in excess of a quarter of a million dollars per year for the rest of Megan's life. To say this was a crisis understated the facts. The money was there for this year and next year and the next ten years, but Megan was only twenty-eight years old. Paying her medical bills would leave her destitute before she turned forty. This of course assumed nothing else went wrong.

Facial reconstruction on the right side of Megan's head resulted in the placement of a small pebble-sized ball in her eyelid. Set up with a spring, it enabled her to close and open her eyelid. It wasn't attractive, but it was an ingenious surgeon who had come up with such an idea. Both ears had been operated on and with hearing aids she could hear fairly well. As for most people with a hearing deficit, the hearing aids sometimes caused a hollow or echo-like sound, but it was indeed *sound*, a huge improvement over the first few months that she'd heard almost nothing but garbled noises when people spoke.

From head to toe she had been patched and repaired. Still, not everything worked. Not only were her legs unable to support the weight of her body, but she couldn't put any weight on them at all. She could move both of her arms in a deliberate fashion. Slowly. She could squeeze with her hands though she had not yet tried to write with pen and paper or hold a cup of water. That would be stretching it a bit.

The black and blue marks, the swollen and puffy body – at least all of that had subsided.

She still couldn't sit up without help, though she could now stay in a sitting position without falling sideways or backward. She was helpless in a traditional wheelchair because she couldn't self-propel. There was no guarantee she ever would have that kind of strength.

She had not been off the hospital grounds in the entire year of her stay. She had only recently been stable enough to handle being outside at all.

She could turn her neck to the left and right but it was an arduous process.

She could finally communicate, albeit slowly and with great difficulty. Not all her speech came out clearly. Anything that required moving her lips simply didn't sound right.

Several cranial nerves had been severely damaged. There was no movement on the right side of Megan's face, except for her right eye. She could move that and it had finally started working in tandem with the left eye.

Physical therapy, speech therapy, bathroom therapy… some were better than others and she was tired of all of it. Complaining would have been pointless.

Megan certainly didn't understand the ramifications of having the insurance money run out.

Ashley had to get Megan back home as soon as possible.

Who am I?

In her dreams, Megan was carefree, and dressed like she felt. She never wore blue jeans. She wore dresses, and wild ones at that. Tight. Short. She was a celebrity. She had purses and coats of every color imaginable. She liked to dress like a Paris fashion model. Sometimes she pulled it off. She wasn't as tall but she was just as beautiful and magnetic in every way.

Was…

Grace had lasted until this week when she finally announced that she had to quit. The combination of being aide, therapist, bathroom assistant, cook, gopher and nurse had simply been too much. Grace had never worked so hard in her life. She'd been well paid but she couldn't do it anymore; it was time to take a vacation and go work anywhere else.

Megan was a great girl but Grace was exhausted. Megan was going to be a 24/7/365 job for the next caregiver, too, and whatever she'd be paid, it couldn't be enough. The work was too much for any one or even two people to do. Whoever had the job was completely tied to Megan. It was almost like being a slave.

Grace had helped Megan a great deal and had grown to really like her, but to preserve her own sanity and whatever was left of her sense of balance, she had to quit. She'd helped Ashley a lot in that first year, but finally sent Ashley her resignation.

The doctors agreed that Megan would probably never walk again, but continued to be amazed at what she was able to do. She could speak with great effort. She could move her upper body a bit and she was gaining some control of her arms. They were divided as to whether or not her hands would ever be able to do anything useful again.

She was alive.

That very existence was a curse not nine months ago. Today it was… sufferable. Megan was ashamed of the moments she'd thought of taking her own life. She wasn't religious in the sense of being an observant Jew, but she was very spiritual, which extended to a passing interest in *The Course in Miracles*, an interest that would later rekindle. She respected the people of her religion and really, all religions. She believed in God. She thought God was good. She trusted in God, or she had.

Now, though, she didn't understand anything. She would repeat in her mind, "There is a reason for this. There is a reason for everything." Trying to figure it out was maddening. What purpose could there be for a mind in a box. A mind in pain and tired from painkillers.

Still, she believed. She prayed a hundred times daily. There wasn't much else to do. She could utter words now, and she was understandable. Helping Megan learn to talk again was Ashley's great task. She would stay for hours working on getting the first sentences out. Ashley was tenacious – she took pride in her stubborn nature. Working for David had taught her to be unyielding in the acquisition of her goals. And now her goal was to get Megan to walk, talk, eat with her own two hands, and be able to use the bathroom. She knew the score. So did Megan. But Ashley had known it on Day One when the score was even worse.

Ashley would never give up on her BFF. Now she was Megan's trustee, as well, since David had had the foresight to name her for that possibility years before. How could he have been that smart? No one in their thirties thought about stuff like that. But he did. That's why he was who he was. He'd always thought of everything and he had taught Ashley to think that way.

Ashley did almost everything David used to, plus had her own family where she was a mom and a wife, and now trustee and caretaker for Megan. She was the most loyal human being anyone could ever meet.

This year had been exhausting.

When she was reminded on that first day that it was she who had the power to pull the plug or not, there was no hesitation. She wouldn't let her friend die. This was personal. David had said a hundred times, "If anything ever happens to me, you take care of her." She took it seriously but she'd never envisioned this. They were in their twenties, not their seventies. Nothing was going to happen, and she assured him of that once a week. This worry was his only weakness. He was invincible in every other aspect of life.

David had paid Ashley well to be his right arm. She had no title, yet she was the boss. She did the books. She did everything David didn't do, and when he was gone she did everything he did as well. Life couldn't be more complicated. But she never complained.

Megan had her own burdens, and she also would never complain about anything, except to God. Megan had no energy, and so the weight of the world was on Ashley's shoulders. They talked about their problems but not as much as people who only had one-tenth of their problems complained. What was the point? Their problems were so big that they only had one choice: take another step up the mountain.

Ashley walked in the hospital door with half a bag of groceries. Groceries were a strange sight in a hospital room unless you were a semi-permanent resident as Megan was. She didn't knock. Didn't say hello. She carried them across the room where she had a minibar-sized refrigerator put in about six months ago. At that time the food and drink were for the visitors, the caretakers, and herself. Like David, Ashley thought of everything. She looked over at Megan and put the groceries away, bread and fruit on top of the fridge. She wished Megan could eat those kinds of foods. It would be a while, still.

When she was finished, she straightened up. She looked at her employer, her friend, David's wife. She was determined. Everyone told her that she didn't have to be *so* dedicated, but she did. Hadn't David been this dedicated to Ashley? David gave Ashley his knowledge, his wisdom, his drive. They were confidantes about everything except Megan. They talked about Megan but rarely said anything that was in any way more than newsy. He never complained about her. She never bitched about her.

Megan was the free spirit, and Ashley had become the driver. If not for Ashley, Megan would not be where she was in the healing process at this time. She would have made no progress. Ashley viewed it as a process. One step, then another. It was like business. There was no doubt. This was simply going to work and it was her will alone that was willing it to work, and everyone knew it. With all the will of her twenty-eight years, Ashley was willing Megan to have a life again, by the sheer strength of her determination.

"Megan. Megan? Megan, can you wake up for a bit, sweetie? I need to talk to you about some stuff."

Her left eye opened, then her right.

"Hahhhhi Ashhhhleeeey." The two words took about eight seconds to get out. She could say any letter that didn't require the lips to be involved. "P" sounded like "b" and "b" didn't sound all that understandable. But she could talk.

"How are you doing today, honey?"

"Good." Again, slowly, but it was clear.

"Listen, I have news. We're going home."

Megan couldn't smile. Her facial muscles wouldn't permit it. But the relief coming from her was palpable.

"Oh, good. Thank you Ashley." It took work to get her tongue up to her teeth to make the "th" sound, but she could do it. Megan hated the way she sounded but she was glad that she could finally get "out of her body" in at least this one way.

"December 21 is moving day. Robert and a friend are coming to bring you home. I'll be here. We've bought a van that will hold the wheelchair. It's pretty neat. I got a good deal on it. And today the doctors are going to be visiting you. You'll probably be poked and prodded a lot. They want to make sure that you are good to go."

Megan squeezed the button on the bed control, bringing herself to an almost sitting position. Thank God for these kinds of beds. As uncomfortable as they are, at least they can move a body that won't move much on its own.

"Ya know, I think we'll bring a hairstylist in on Tuesday and get your hair done. It's long enough now for you to get back to your style."

The idea of getting her hair cut and shaped triggered all kinds of emotions. Megan felt angry. She felt sad. She was thrilled. She felt humiliated. She felt happy. All at once.

She closed her eyes and thought about what she used to look like. She had never been self-critical. She knew she was beautiful. She knew she was all but flawless. That was no longer the case. It was hard for her to look at herself in the mirror. She couldn't wince, but if she could she would have. The thought was hard to swallow.

How wonderful it would be to be beautiful again. That was one dream that didn't seem possible for Ashley to make come true.

It had been one entire year since she'd had sex. She missed David and she missed him in bed. She had thought about it hundreds of times in the past year. Before this, she had probably not gone a day without pleasure for nine years… then there were 366 of them. It was something she ached for. She didn't even know if she could feel the feelings again. What would it be like? Would she ever know? Who would ever make love to her? How? It was impossible.

She raised her hand slowly to her hair and touched it. It was at her shoulders. At least it was covering her head. After the accident there was no hair at all. Surgery had taken care of that. At least she had hair. But that was a far cry from ever being touched or caressed by someone again.

Who has sex with someone who can barely move? Who makes love to someone who can't give pleasure? It was again time to face reality. Life was going to be very different.

Reality. Sometimes she faced it. Sometimes she lived in a different world. The world where she was beautiful. When she had everything she wanted to live in the moment. Now that she was disfigured, she wanted nothing of the moment.

She opened her eyes.

"Grace had to quit. She'll stay until you move home. I told her I completely understood. I hired a new caretaker today as well. I've had a bunch of interviews with her. I went with her to one previous employer's office, too, and I'm good with her. Her name is Mary. She's middle-aged and she has a decent resume. I checked her out and she'll move in when you go home. She'll have the room down the hall from yours at home and take over Grace's job."

Megan could nod… slowly… and she did.

What kind of a person can do 24/7/365? The homeless?

Home. She was going home. Did home look the same, or was it disfigured as well?

"I can't ...ait to go ...ome."

"We can't wait to have you home."

"Tuhday…"

"Yes, honey, it's the day David died." Ashley was way ahead of her and knew she'd have to stop doing that if she ever wanted Megan to speak clearly again.

"He is with ne," Megan said, with her *m* turned into an *n*, "you know."

"I know he is. You can feel him here."

"I can heel him."

Chapter Five

December 19

Day 457

The moon cast its light through the open windows in the bedroom. David looked up at Megan and saw the mirror behind her. Her back was straight and her dark hair was blown just a bit by a breeze that came in.

She straddled him, leaning just far enough away from him that he couldn't touch her breasts. She wanted him to admire her first.

It wasn't hard to do.

He looked at her face. Her dark brown eyes had a mischievous look in them. Her lips were full and her mouth was open. Her complexion clear, perfect. She touched herself for a moment and then she moved forward.

She was warm and she rubbed his chest with her hands.

He didn't touch her. He just looked.

The perfect body.

She inched up, sat up and then came down on top of him. He felt good. She felt full of him. She closed her eyes.

He didn't.

She bent forward and placed her hands on his shoulders. They felt strong but that was nothing compared to the feeling inside.

She grabbed each of his hands and brought them to her chest. He gently touched her. Held her breasts in his hands. Soft. Full.

She felt electric inside. Her head tilted back.

She started to move faster. He didn't take his hands from her breasts. She wanted to do it all. And she did.

She moaned.

His forehead tightened and the expression on his face changed in intensity.

She took her hands from his shoulders then held them again.

She began to move in shorter faster movements, gripping his shoulders tightly, almost painfully, as her fingernails dug into his skin.

The bed began to make that unmistakable shaking sound that only a bed moving under the weight of passionate lovers can make.

She opened her eyes briefly, looked into his, and then came in spasms that seemed to last forever.

She moaned again… mentioned a deity… and he pulled her close to him, kissing her forehead gently and running his fingers through her hair.

It was quick. It was her choice. Sometimes she could be in bed for an hour. Sometimes she wanted it fast. Today she needed it *now*.

***

"Megan, Megan, Megan. Wake up. You in there?"

Her eyes opened.

"You were having some kind of dream or something. Mumbling in your sleep."

It was Mary, the new caregiver, looking down at her. There was concern in her gray eyes, and she fiddled nervously with a strand of her salt and pepper hair.

It was only her second night on the job and she didn't want anything to happen to her patient and boss.

"Are you OK?"

Megan looked up at the woman who looked older than the fifty that Ashley had surmised. Maybe sixty was closer to the truth. Her hair was both black and gray. Mary was spending Megan's last night in the hospital with her.

"I OK." Megan uttered.

At least Mary hadn't awakened her two minutes earlier. Why couldn't she always live in the world where everything was fun and filled with pleasure?

"I OK," she said again.

"Can I get you anything?"

She wanted a glass of water. "Otter?"

Mary moved away from the bed, relieved that Megan was OK. She poured Megan a glass of water and got a straw.

She put the water and straw down on the table by the bedside and clicked the bed button to sit Megan up. Then she put the straw in the glass and brought the glass to Megan's mouth.

Megan opened her mouth a little and grabbed the straw with the left side of her lips. She drew in the water. Cool. Fresh. It felt good

When she had taken in most of the water and had enough, she loosened her lips. Mary almost intuitively gently took the straw from her lips.

"…ank you."

"You're welcome, Megan."

"Sleet."

"You want to go back to sleep?"

She nodded.

"OK." *Thank goodness.* Mary had no idea what they would do there at 3:14 in the morning if there was another choice.

She fluffed Megan's pillow.

"Do you need help putting your head back against the pillow?"

Megan slowly shook her head. She moved her head back and successfully negotiated the few inches to the pillow without incident.

Mary clicked the bed back to a horizontal position.

"Good night, Megan."

"Night."

Mary walked away, leaving the door to the hospital corridor wide open. She went straight back to her bed and plopped down.

God, how Megan wished she could do that.

She closed her eyes wishing she could move back into her dream, knowing that it would be gone. It wasn't long before the sleeping medication took effect. Her last night in the hospital would be restful. Tomorrow she would go home.

Chapter Six

December 20

Day 458

Mary was relieved by Ashley early and was sent straight to the Mansion to prepare for the homecoming.

Mary straightened up her own bedroom first. Megan's home of many years was now going to be Mary's new home for a long time to come. Megan has quite the place. *I wonder if they'll sell now that her husband is dead?*

That girl is half my age, has a million times what I have. It is WRONG. There is something WRONG with our country to let this kind of thing happen. The rich get richer and the poor get poorer. Cute girl marries rich man. It's how it always is.

Nice enough room… nicer than anything I've ever had in my life and it's one little room in this mansion. Who deserves this? These people must worship money to have this kind of a house.

At least they are paying me $800 a week. I'll have SOMETHING finally. But they have MILLIONS of dollars. It is not fair. They have NOTHING to worry about. Nothing. They can just sit on their butts and money comes straight to them.

How can one person deserve this much money? How can you build this kind of a house and shove it in the face of all the poor people around here? People who scrape and save pennies to buy food. To make rent. And she owns a fourteen-bed, twelve-bath, miniature hotel complete with a wood paneled library, wine cellar and an entryway as big as a fucking basketball court. It's sick. How many people could they feed with all of this money? You could put fifty people, a hundred people in this house and it wouldn't be crowded.

No one deserves this much. No one ever gave me anything like this. No one ever gave me anything.

It's bullshit, is what it is.

She brought clothes down to the laundry room, which really was a room. It was enormous in size.

This is so much nicer than the nursing home.

She had been taking care of old people, forty hours a week. *Cheapskate rich owners of the nursing home pay you $350 a week and expect you to LIVE on that.*

At least these people have the decency to pay me a pittance.

Megan probably deserved being in the crash. You can't live like this and not have God get you in the end.

These people steal from the poor. They take advantage of us. They pay us dirt while they stash their millions and live on their yachts.

They've never had to work for a thing in their life. She was throwing the clothes in the washing machine now. *I've worked for everything. I've scratched and clawed just to survive.*

I never had a man help me make it. I did it myself. Now she doesn't have one either. Wonder if he went to heaven? Rich man through the eye of a needle… I doubt it. Bible says the poor shall inherit the earth. We should get SOMETHING for all this.

She turned around and stood with her back against the dryer, looking out of the laundry room into a hallway of the mansion.

Everything happens for a reason. You live a certain way and God will punish you, it's as simple as that. I don't know what she did but it must have been bad. You don't end up looking like that without doing something mighty bad. There are no coincidences in life. She is being punished big time for whatever she did wrong.

Probably cheated on the husband. Maybe they got their money illegally, selling drugs. You don't get a place like this, working for a living.

You're gonna have to screw SOMEONE to get this kind of house. You either screw the owner or your screw the poor people.

She looked around and started walking around the house. Now instead of thinking in terms of "you" she was thinking in terms of "I."

What a gorgeous house. Most of the time it looks like NO ONE is here. I'm going to be driving that Mercedes to the store. I'm going to be using these bathrooms. I'm going to be sleeping on these sheets. I'm going to be living the life of a rich woman. I'm the only one who can walk here. I'm the only one who can get around this place. This is basically gonna be MY place. There's a housekeeper that comes once a week to clean this place.

Think about it. Who is the rich bitch now? The rich cripple laying in the bed upstairs? No. I'm living here now. I've got the run of the place. Hell, I endear myself to these people, who knows what they will do for me.

Ya know what, Mary? You are gonna be living in this place the rest of your life. Your ship has come in. You play your cards right and you will be living in this house for the rest of your natural life.

No one… no one is going to screw this up or I'll screw them up. My ship has come in for sure.

Chapter Seven

December 20 - Late

Day 458

They had brought Megan home in the van with the wheelchair and gotten her back into her own room in her own house. Megan felt relief.

It took two trips; there had been a great deal more in the private hospital room than anyone imagined.

Now she was home. For more than a year she had been institutionalized in hell. Now her life was about to change.

The first moments inside, she thought about David. He'd be somewhere in the house, probably his study. Only he died over a year ago. The last time he was here was the last time she was here.

She wanted to cry but she wasn't able. She wept instead. A loud strange guttural sound that Mary had never heard come from a human being.

Mary continued working, not knowing if she should console Megan, let her weep, or walk away.

The bed Megan would spend most of her hours in was like a hospital bed. It moved up and down but it still almost felt like a real bed. Probably because it was at home. What was here was everything she owned and everything she loved.

She shifted in consciousness between *the world that was* and *the world that is*, wondering what the world would become.

By ten o'clock it was time for Ashley, Robert, and Lauren to head home. They had gotten Megan settled in, with Mary's help.

Mary was about to retire to her own bedroom as she closed the door on the family. Then a stroke of genius hit her.

She moved quickly upstairs and went into Megan's room.

Megan was awake, watching the end of a TV show.

"Megan, I've been thinking. It's a lot of work to get you from the bed to the bathroom and the shower. If you were in the room that I'm in at the end of the hall, and we put the bed near the door, you'd be ten feet from the bathroom. Right now, it's about forty feet. If an emergency ever happened I don't know what we would do. How would you feel about moving to the room that's closer to a bathroom and shower?"

Megan loved her room but she could see that it might be a good idea to be closer to the bathroom. Maybe it was hard on Mary to push her to the bathroom from here. Probably be easier if she was closer. She was thankful to have such a nice lady who would be here to keep her safe and help her do everything, every day.

"Talk to Ashley. She says it's OK, it's OK." Megan was slow but she surprised herself in that she was able to speak that so clearly. Then she realized what she said didn't have any of the hard letters. There wasn't a *p* or a *b*. There was no *w* or *v*. There was no *f* or *m*. No hard *y*. But still, she had done well.

"Good idea, Megan."

That Ashley is going to always be a problem. Ashley seems to have an answer for everything.. She's probably a rich bitch too. Either that or some leech that sucks up to Megan, which would make her rich anyway.

"That's right, Megan. I'll talk with Ashley about it and we won't do anything without her OK."

She looked around at what she thought might just be her room. Maybe she'd give it to herself for Christmas.

"Megan. Can I get you something to drink? Protein drink sound good?"

Megan nodded her head. It sounded very good.

Megan thought to herself that Ashley had set up this bed perfectly. She could see the TV, change the channel by touching the special remote, move the bed up and down and buzz for Mary. Thank God for Ashley.

She closed her eyes and thanked God.

Chapter Eight

December 23

Day 461

Ashley sat in her office in Megan's house. Although Megan hadn't been in there in over a year, Ashley was there almost daily.

Having Megan home from the hospital took one of life's major challenges off the board. Now there were only about 121 left. At least she could avoid the daily drive to the hospital, which ate up a lot of time. Now she could get back and forth from the drugstore fairly quickly and avoid almost all traffic. A big plus.

Most importantly, it allowed her to check on Megan whenever she was here and still get work done.

Pictures of her and Robert on the walls… and Lauren. Calendars. Notes. Lots of filing cabinets. New computer on the desk.

She was on the phone.

"You know, we really want to do something special for the staff at the hospital, now that Megan is home…"

Mary was walking past the office. She stopped as she got to the other side of the doorway when she overheard Ashley talking about a surprise for the hospital staff who had helped Megan. Mary wasn't thrilled that Ashley was now likely to be here a lot more often than Mary had anticipated.

I am going to get that girl to talk. For real. No more of this laborious crap. We are going to get her to really talk. No more speech therapists necessary. I am now the official speech therapist. I will get her to talk if it takes the rest of my life. How hard can being a speech therapist be? You need to get the person to talk. They move their tongue, their lips, breathe. Then have her repeat a sound or a word. Can't be that hard.

I mean, she can already say a lot of words and communicate in a very slow and deliberate way but I am going to get Megan to talk…like a real person. This IS brilliant.

And I think I should grease her wheels too.

Ashley hung up the phone.

Mary turned around and walked into the office.

"Afternoon, Ashley."

"Hi, Mary." She looked up from the desk. "How are you doing today?"

"I'm doing well. Listen, Ashley, I want to do something really special for Megan for Christmas." Megan was Jewish and she was a Jew who loved Christmas. She loved the spirit of the holiday and had celebrated it her entire life. Mary, now well aware of this fact, was going to use it to endear herself to Megan.

"Ashley, I'm thinking that maybe we invite her aunt, your family, the twins, a few friends, for maybe an hour or two. I know it's short notice, but what if we got a tree and put it right there in her bedroom. Put all kinds of decorations on it. Do the whole room. I think…"

"That is a *great* idea." Ashley was ecstatic. She had been so busy with the store, the other properties and Megan's health, that she hadn't thought much about Christmas at *this* house.

"If I gave you a list, would you be willing to call everyone? Have them be here, say, for Christmas Day at one o'clock, maybe?"

"'Course I would. I think it would be great. If you like I can run to the store and pick up some special decorations and gifts for everybody too."

Ashley didn't have a true Southern accent but there were times where you could just tell she had spent a lot of time in of Alabama or Mississippi.

"Boy, where did you come up with all this energy? You're on. Check in on Megan, then come back down in about a half hour. I'll bring up a Christmas gift list and a guest list for you to call. You can use the phone in the annex off the bedroom, while you keep an eye on Megan. How are you going to get to the store?"

"I do drive, you know," Mary smiled. She was going driving!

"Insurance?" Ashley asked.

"Of course." Mary lied. She hadn't had a license or insurance in a decade.

Ashley opened the top right desk drawer. There were key rings on top of key rings. She grabbed a ring with three keys on it.

"Here ya go. These are for the red Mercedes convertible in the garage. You can take that one after you make your calls and I get the lists made up. Thank you *so much*, Mary, you are a saint!"

"Thanks, Ashley. I'm going to go see how Megan is doing."

She slowly turned holding her anticipation and excitement in. *What is it going to be like to drive a Mercedes? A Mercedes convertible!*

She walked up the staircase and turned left down the hall to Megan's room.

Megan was finishing her soap opera. Mary just stood in the doorway until the Ivory Soap commercial came on.

"Megan?"

Megan's head slowly turned to the right, and eventually she made eye contact with Mary.

"I have something wonderful to tell you!" Her enthusiasm was real, if not a little misplaced.

"I'm going to invite some of your friends and family to come over on Christmas. Have a little get-together here in celebration of Christmas and you coming home."

Megan nodded.

"Oh that's nice." She got all three words out with feeling, without too much difficulty, though very slowly.

That reminded Mary.

"And Megan, I want to start helping you speak more clearly and quickly. You'll feel a lot better if you can talk at a normal pace. Don't you think?"

Megan nodded again. "That's right." Again, a sentence with no *p, b, w, f, m, v,* or *y*. Slow, but not terribly difficult.

"Ashley asked me to go run some errands, get some Christmassy things and so forth. So if it's OK with you, I'm going to head out shortly and get everything she asked me to. I told her I'd call your friends and family first, make the invitations for Christmas and then take off. But I'm worried about you. Will you be OK while I'm gone, as long as Ashley's here?"

She nodded again.

"Uh course."

"See now Megan, if we work together every day we can turn 'uh' into 'of' in no time. Are you game to start tonight?"

"Uh course." Megan nodded her head.

"Don't worry about it. I have no problem understanding you. I don't think anyone does. We just want you to be able to express yourself faster so you won't be so frustrated."

Wasn't that the truth, Megan thought. She nodded, sparing the work of getting the words out. She had no idea that Mary could help her speak better but it would take too many words to find out how. Was she a speech therapist and a voice therapist too? Ashley had really hired the right person. She would make sure that Mary had a special Christmas.

Mary was already in the annex off the bedroom on the phone. First call was to Megan's Aunt Rebekkah.

"Hi, Mrs. Neumann, this is Mary, Megan's personal aide at the house. Ashley and I are putting together a special Christmas afternoon for Megan. Would you be able to come over about one on Christmas? That would be wonderful. Yes. Of course you can... she'll love it, I'm sure. Great, see you at 1:00 on Christmas. Thanks! Bye-bye."

Mary took a walk through the house and decided that Christmas would take place in a great room on the main level.

Must be a thousand square feet.

She had lived in apartments as big as this bedroom. She figured that twenty guests could fit in here easily, even if there was a Christmas tree and decorations.

Mary's excitement continued as she plowed through the few numbers she had on her emergency number list. She'd get the rest from Ashley shortly. She emerged a few minutes later.

"Megan, this is going to be a wonderful Christmas." Mary smiled a truly happy smile at Megan.

Where the happiness was emanating from was another question altogether. She wondered what Megan's favorite things to drink were. What would she get for the friends and the family? She'd be doing the cooking so she wanted it to be great, but didn't want to have to kill herself.

She asked Megan everything and Megan had what seemed like good answers throughout.

Ashley popped into the room. Megan looked up at Ashley, and the sheet of paper in her left hand.

"Did Mary tell you that we're going to have a special Christmas get-together here?"

"She did."

"Isn't that wonderful? I am so excited. Mary, here's a list of the rest of the people you can call to invite to the party, and a quick list of special Christmas gifts. You can stop off at Target and get most of them on the way back."

Mary glanced down. She quickly considered whether she would work off Ashley's list or what Megan had told her. She thought about it and realized she would do both.

"I need to stop at the library too, if that's OK."

"No problem. I'll hang out with Megan until you get back."

"OK, I'll be back in a couple of hours. I'll make the rest of the calls when I'm out."

"Sure, just be careful."

"Will do. See you in a few hours, Megan." She waited until Megan's eyes met hers. Then she smiled at Megan and waved and left.

There was a spring in her step as she walked down the stairs to grab her warm coat, through one of the kitchens, back out into the garage. There were seven Mercedes, all told. She didn't begin to understand what two people would need with seven Mercedes. Gotta spend it on something!

She opened the door to the red Mercedes and slid in. She started the car and it purred. The car was like a new car but it had 40,000 miles on it. No dirt, no scuff marks, no nothing. It was mint inside and out.

The garage door was open, probably from when Ashley had come in this morning. She backed out of the winding driveway onto the road. And off she went. There were no highways nearby to really see what the car was like at top speed, but it didn't matter. She had a Mercedes, a pocketful of prepaid credit cards and a shopping list with instructions to go shopping, get Christmas gifts and yes – she was getting paid to shop. Her world was turning upside down.

Who knew they made prepaid credit cards. There must be $10,000 here!

There was not one car on the street nicer than her Mercedes. She drove with her head held high.

Lots of people looked as she drove by. The sight of a red Mercedes is a bit unusual anywhere on the planet, and definitely in Minneapolis.

The drive to Target was all too short. She parked near the back of the parking lot. She didn't want anyone scraping up against her car. One nick and Ashley would notice. No one was going to screw this up for her.

She walked away from the car, turned to look at it and admired how it stood out. It was actually… beautiful.

Her note from Ashley said to get something for Megan from her, meaning from Ashley, on Megan's credit card. That didn't really make sense… or maybe it did.

I'll do whatever I can to give Megan a memorable Christmas. And everyone who comes will have a Christmas that they will enjoy.

How did Ashley put together this list in such a short amount of time? She would need two shopping carts to get everything. Ashley had suggested lots of iPods. So many, in fact, that Mary bought the store out. Then she grabbed as many point-and-shoot cameras as she could find. All the electronics stuff was expensive as hell, but it didn't take up as much space as she had imagined it might. She might need to make two trips in and out. Gifts for everyone, including Ashley. Everything that wasn't for Megan was to be from Megan, except for the gift from Mary.

Nowhere on the shopping list did Mary see cosmetics.

That's where she started looking. Ashley hadn't thought Megan would need it or want it. *If I were Megan I would want perfume, make-up, eyeliner, lipstick, the works; and I'm going to get it for her. There isn't anything she will like or appreciate more than that.*

Makeup was an excellent notion. Megan knew how she looked. Some makeup and perfume would help her feel like a woman again. *There was a mangled car crash victim now at home, but maybe I can make that image of herself change over time.* Mary was thinking of everything!

She went through the store and began picking up everything on the list. Ashley hadn't written down anything for Lauren, Ashley's daughter. Well, that wouldn't do. Megan would buy them both something very special. In fact, something memorable... even if it was Target.

Mary didn't even consider a budget. She bought the best of everything. She guessed that Ashley would have suggested going to the Galleria had it not been so close to Christmas, but time was short.

She made sure she picked up plenty of decorations for the Christmas tree she imagined she'd have to get tonight or tomorrow. Where would she put it? Certainly not on top of the Mercedes. She'd get to that later.

Lots of decorations and ornaments, wrapping paper, everything. Nothing would be left out.

By the time she got to the counter her carts were overflowing. Mary had never seen such a thing. She swiped the prepaid cards and they all went through. Oddly, she wasn't asked to show her license. How strange… but what a relief.

The total came to $6,294.33. The checkout girl stacked bags on top of bags on top of bags. They had to get yet another cart as somehow the organizing of all the gifts had made the stacks bigger. She wheeled the carts out of the store, one at a time, and slowly she maneuvered back and forth to the Mercedes at the rear of the lot. Fortunately the manager offered to pull a cart for her. She didn't want anyone grabbing her goods.

She hadn't considered whether everything would fit in the trunk, and indeed, it did not. No matter: it did fit in the trunk, the back seat and the front passenger seat combined.

She scooted the last cart away from the car and decided to go back to the house, empty the shopping bags and check in. She had been gone quite a while and didn't want to do anything to upset Ashley. She turned grabbed her cell from her purse and called Ashley.

"Ashley? It's Mary. I finished here at Target and I filled the car completely so I need to come back to the house before finishing up the errands. Can I get you anything while I'm out?"

Fortunately, Ashley declined. There wouldn't have been room for even one more Christmas card.

She put the key in the ignition, turned it, and listened to the car purr. She looked at her list and found the next phone number to call.

"Hi Kendall, this is Mary, Megan's personal aide. Yes that's right. Listen, we're having a special party for Megan on Christmas Day, at one o'clock at her home. Yes, she just got out of the hospital and she wants you to come. Would you and your husband be able to make it? I know Megan will be thrilled if you could. Yes, only about a couple of hours. Gifts aren't necessary but just so you know, I believe there will be something under the tree for you! Thanks Kendall, see you day after tomorrow."

She looked up and got her bearings. Talking and driving is something she hadn't done much… ever… and it was a bit difficult. Looks easy, but how do people talk on these phones and drive at the same time? She punched up the next number and let it ring.

"Hi Krissy, this is Mary, Megan's personal aide. Yes. Listen, we're having a special Christmas party for Megan at her home on Christmas Day at one o'clock. Yes, she just got out of the hospital. Would you guys be able to make it over? Lovely! We'll be expecting you, yes, Megan has bought gifts for everyone so if you like, that would be wonderful. Maybe a blouse? Colorful, yes, exactly! OK, great, thanks so much and see you on Christmas."

Again she put the phone down and oriented herself to simply driving.

This was too short of a trip.

I wonder if all these other people have money too, or if they're normal people.

A police officer was coming up on the car. She immediately looked at the speedometer. She was doing the speed limit. She didn't even touch the brake pedal. *If I get pulled over, I'm dead.*

Her heart raced but she kept driving and didn't call anyone else. The cop turned right before Lake Calhoun. *Thank God. What a mess that would have been.* She'd have to make sure she got a driver's license right away.

Her heart didn't slow down and arriving back at the Dresden house didn't help things, for some reason. She parked the car carefully, got out and went around back, opened the trunk and lifted out two bags. She carried them to the door, and turned a handle with one hand woven through the grip on the bag.

"Hi, Ashley, I'm home."

"Do you need help?" The voice came from what seemed like a hundred feet away.

"No, that's OK, I've got it."

She went back outside and got two more bags. She certainly *had* bought a lot. As she lifted the packages out of the trunk, there was Ashley, and Mary startled. She felt guilty but didn't know why. Ashley looked at her as if something strange was going on or maybe she just thought that.

"Here, let me have those. Looks like you found everything. Excellent!"

"It's going to be a lot of fun. I hope you don't mind, I came up with a few extra ideas for Megan, and a little something for you. So no snooping."

Ashley smiled.

"Absolutely not." They walked in together, put the bags down on the center island and went back out, each grabbing two more bags, Ashley from the trunk and Mary from the back seat.

"Wow, these are heavy!"

"Don't peek! I think that one has something for you in it."

"You didn't have to do that!" she said, wearing another big smile. Ashley loved Christmas.

"Yes, I did. You've really made me feel at home here and I appreciate it." *Is that enough grease or do I need more? No, no more. She'll think I've been drinking.*

"You get a hold of everyone?"

"Yep, I did. Everyone is coming." She pulled out some of the long tubes of Christmas wrap. She would take them to Megan's room if Megan wanted to be part of the wrapping… the "watching" part. If not, she'd do all the wrapping in the front dining room. "I'll just slip my coat off and then I'm going to see if Megan wants to help wrap. If she does, I'll bring some of this up there."

"Good idea. I bet she'll want to."

Mary strode through the house to the stairs, walked fairly quickly up, and Megan was watching yet another soap opera. Mary didn't want to startle her. She knocked three times. "Megan? Megan? Megan?"

Megan turned. "Hello."

"I just got back with the Christmas shopping for you for your friends and family. Do you want me to bring the presents up here and wrap them in here, or should I do it downstairs?"

"…ring the …resents uh here…I ont to see hut you got."

"Wonderful. I'll be back in a minute."

I'll tell Megan what everything is, who it's for, all that kind of stuff. Should make her feel good. Maybe Megan didn't deserve all of this happening to her. She seems to care about her family and friends.

She trekked back downstairs to get some of the gifts that weren't for Megan and bring them up with some wrapping paper, oversized tags (she'd just figured out why Ashley wanted them), scissors, tape and bows.

She can't help wrap, but maybe she can tell me what to write on the tags. Ashley, you are one smart girl. You think of everything.

"Megan," Mary was walking in the door when she realized she had carried too much. She was close to dropping everything. She moved quickly to the bed and gently placed a few things on the bed and then the rest on the floor so there wouldn't be the appearance of an earthquake. "I think I was carrying too much at once!"

Megan nodded. You never knew what Megan was thinking or feeling because there was no expression; her facial muscles just weren't able.

"You need a truck." Megan uttered each word slowly.

Mary looked at her and laughed. She was fine.

"You have to tell me what to put on each of the cards because I don't know very many of these people."

"OK." Megan nodded again.

Mary rolled out one of the scrolls of wrapping paper and placed the first gift on the paper. She looked up at Megan.

"Ashley gave me a list of who gets everything. This American Girl doll is for Lauren. What should I write on the card?"

"Uhnerican Doll at Target?"

"Well, now, Ashley popped it in one of the bags when I was coming up."

"Ha ha."

Mary didn't get the joke but she smiled and laughed. She had no idea how Megan could have known she didn't get the doll at Target. Maybe the girl was psychic or something.

"Right. Ashley must have picked this up today somewhere... I guess."

Mary was fairly adept at Christmas present wrapping. She moved fairly quickly and elegantly. Megan was certainly impressed. With all of the iPods, cell phones and other gadgetry, Mary had wrapped a pile of red and green packages adorned with bows and neat folds at the corners. It was a sight worthy of Norman Rockwell.

"Very nice." Final piece of tape, and Mary sat on the bed next to Megan and wrote the last message on the card. "Megan, I think you should sign each card."

"Can't sign."

"Sure you can. Doesn't have to be legible. Please. It would mean so much to everyone."

"OK."

Mary held the card after strategically placing the pen in Megan's hand. She held the card with two hands, hoping Megan could move her arm or hand enough to make an "M."

The signing was arduous and time-consuming but there were a million reasons to do it this way. In the end the first "M" looked like the first time a kindergartner made a letter. Megan must have been devastated by what she was unable to do.

"See, I told you that you could do it. I had a boyfriend once who didn't write that legibly." She slid the card into the envelope and taped it to the package.

"Ha ha." Megan didn't laugh but she said the sounds. Mary wondered if Megan would ever be able to laugh. She laughed herself, a bit nervously.

OK. Let's see who's next...

***

She pulled into the greenhouse, or garden center, or whatever they called these places. Ashley had insisted on a ten-foot-tall real tree. She said Megan loved the smell of a pine tree and it would make her happy. The tree would need to be delivered almost immediately.

She picked out a tree that was not so big as to be impossible to get in the house and decorate without help, but big enough to be full. It was indeed all of ten feet tall. Mary told them she'd need the stump sawed off and a tree stand to go with it. She wrote down the address, gave the cashier the credit card, watched it go through again and asked how long it would take to get the tree delivered to the house.

"About a half hour, I would think."

"OK, it's really important it's delivered soon."

The girl looked at her kind of strangely and simply nodded as Mary walked out the door and returned to her Mercedes.

Arriving back at the house, she walked in without making any announcement of her presence. She could hear Ashley on the phone talking to someone, and Ashley was upset. *Mad* upset. Something about selling the house, and the drugstore. Whatever was happening, it certainly didn't sound good.

She walked over to Ashley's office and poked her head in. Ashley put her left index finger in the air. She knew that meant, "Stay put. Wait." That's what Mary did. Ashley finished yelling at whoever it was and hung up with a loud *"Good-bye!"*

She put her head in her hands. Breathed in, then out, then looked up at Mary. Mary had plenty of time to think of all the wrong things to say, and she could find nothing that was right to say. So she said nothing.

Ashley looked back up at Mary.

"Any luck finding a nice tree?"

"Yes. The nursery is going to deliver it in a half hour. They'll bring a stand."

"Thanks. She's doing really well. She really appreciates you going the extra mile. It means a lot to her you know."

"I'm glad I can help. You folks are taking good care of me and I appreciate that too."

Whatever internal struggles Mary was having with the grandiosity of the mansion and Ashley were nonexistent on the eve of Christmas Eve.

"I'm going to check on Megan and see if I can bring her anything. Ashley?"

"Hmm?" She was distracted by the phone call, to be sure.

"Do you think Megan could have a little wine if I could find some in the house? I saw some books about wine in the library. Seems like she has more than a passing interest."

"There's a wine cellar down there." She pointed. "I can't see any reason why Megan wouldn't be able to have a sip or two. Could do her good."

"Thanks. I'll find out. It would be nice to have a toast on Christmas. Wine or Champagne. Something, you know?"

"Great idea."

"If it's OK with you, I'd like to sneak a peek downstairs after I spend some time with Megan. Is that OK with you?"

"Of course. I'll catch up with you in a bit. Mary, I've got to finish dealing with this problem I'm working on."

"Thanks."

Chapter Nine

Christmas Day

Day 463

The great room was filled with a beautifully adorned tree, Christmas decorations, and a second hospital bed for Megan and presents underneath and around the tree. Almost two dozen people had gathered. Bing Crosby and Rosemary Clooney provided background music for the crowd.

Mary found it odd that a girl not even thirty years old enjoyed the music of someone who died forty-five years ago.

A table of food was laid out against one wall. Everyone had a plate in their hands and most were working on sandwiches, hors d'oeuvres, or holiday desserts. People were split into cliques of three, four, or five, including a small group of three kids, one of whom was Ashley's daughter Lauren.

Ashley asked Megan if she wanted to wear a hat into the living room. She was preparing the wheelchair and was looking at Megan, all dolled up for the party. It wouldn't be right to say she looked "nice" or "pretty," but she was dressed festively in a red blouse and a long red and green skirt that only Megan could wear.

Megan's hair was not her signature flowing black hair but it was below her shoulders, and that made her feel good. It actually looked nice. But her head was not symmetrical and her face didn't look good. A hat would help hide some of that.

"Yes, thank you, Ashley."

Ashley brought out a loud hat that would match Megan's outfit.

Megan looked better than she had in over a year. Though she was nowhere near being independent, she was getting a bit stronger after months of intensive physical therapy. She had recently beaten her inability to chew food. At fifteen months, she was finally at square two.

"You're talking a little better every day, you know?"

"Thanks. Mary is helting a lot." *Helting* wasn't *helping* but it was progress. The words were coming slowly.

"OK, you are ready. Are YOU ready?"

"Yes. Let's go."

Ashley turned the wheelchair toward the door and they were on their way to the living room. Now it was Ashley who was a bit nervous for some reason. Some of the people in the room, mostly the kids, hadn't seen Megan since the accident, and she was not easy to look at.

As they approached the living room, Ashley called out, "Hey everybody!" Everyone who hadn't been looking was now. Most of the faces appeared happy and excited to see the two of them. A few guests, especially Lauren's two friends, had some anguish on their faces. It was evident that there had been conversations with parents before the party. Those who were uncomfortable were very polite.

The twins were Megan's cousins, and ten years older than Megan. Very pretty women in their late thirties, wearing matching outfits. *Odd to everyone anywhere at this age except this family,* Mary thought.

They rushed to give Megan a big hug. "How are you, honey?" one of them asked.

"Getting good." Megan refused to stumble over the b's in the word better.

"Last we heard you weren't able to speak at all. You must be feeling much better."

"Yes. Thank 'ou. How are you two?" The words were slow and there were breaths being held as the words came out, but they were all there.

"The flight in was delayed but it was fine. I was so excited that Mary called! We couldn't wait to see you. You know, she must be a big help around here."

Mary was over in the corner keeping things in order. It wasn't her job, but her job had been taken by Ashley for the afternoon. Her ears perked up and liked what they were hearing.

"So glad you are here." Megan looked the second twin right in the eye, wishing she could make her face smile because she was so happy to see the two women.

"It's great to see you! We were so worried for so long. How is your therapy coming?"

"Let ne show you. Ashley? heel oder to the hostital ded." She did. She pulled up right by the bed, the back of the chair nearest the pillow. This hospital bed looked like it was made for a princess, with a beautiful bedspread and pillows to match. Elegant.

"'Otch."

Everyone watched, as they had been told to do. All anyone could hear was Bing Crosby. Otherwise, there was silence.

Megan pushed herself up out of the chair. It took time. It was an uncomfortable moment for everyone. She did not stand straight or support her own weight, but leaned up against the bed and rolled onto it. She lay there looking at everyone.

"Ashley, you can helt ne now!"

Everyone applauded. Even Ashley was stunned. Ashley straightened Megan up, laid her head against the pillow and gave her the controller.

"Megan, you didn't tell me you could do that!"

"I didn't know." Slow, deliberate, but the words were all there. Everyone laughed.

The tension was lightening up. Megan grabbed the control of the bed and pushed the button so the bed would help her sit straight up. The new bed worked like a charm.

"This is a great Christnas dresent. Thank you, Ashley."

There was a tear in Ashley's eye. Megan had gotten from the wheelchair to the bed and Ashley simply couldn't believe it.

Physical therapy had paid off. And nothing was going to change. Therapy was still going to be every day. Seven days a week. One hour in the bedroom. The therapist had purchased a weird looking device that looked like a swing that a baby would sit in and not be able to fall out of. It was set up on parallel bars and every day Megan would stand in the swing and move her body forward. Take a step, in a manner of speaking. She was able to move her legs. She was getting motion in her arms though she couldn't grip well. The therapy was helping, finally. But they were only at square three. She still couldn't support half her weight. She couldn't easily grasp or use her hands for anything other than rudimentary things. But she had come a long way from being trapped completely inside of her body. She was beginning to speak, albeit slowly. There was progress. Each day.

Ashley thought it must be just like a baby growing up. That it would be a decade before Megan could walk without a walker or canes, if ever.

Square three.

***

Megan was still in bed in the vast living room as she, Ashley and Mary saw the last guests out. It was coming up on six o'clock, and their guests had stayed longer than intended. Megan was very thankful. She needed to see people she loved and she needed to see that people still loved her.

Ashley walked back in the room. Some new-age solstice music played in the background.

"You were a *hit!* I couldn't believe you actually got from the wheelchair to the bed." She walked around in front of the bed and put her hands on her hips. "Have you done that before?"

"No. I didn't know I could do it." The words came very slowly.

"I can't wait to tell Dr. Norton. He'll be amazed." Ashley changed gears. "Wasn't it nice that everyone was able to make it?"

"It is great." Very slowly. She couldn't move her lips to say "was" because of the "w" so she simply changed the tense of the word. She was becoming skilled at knowing what was coming next and rephrasing things so she could actually communicate in real time.

"Listen, honey, the other day your aunt called and for whatever reason, she told me that she wanted to be the final say-so on your therapy, the house, the stores, the investments, your, well everything. What do you want me to do?"

"No 'ay. Ashley!"

Megan was not happy about that at all. Ashley had taken care of her and Megan didn't want Aunt Rebekkah involved in anything. She loved her aunt, but Rebekkah knew nothing about the drugstores, nothing about the investments, nothing about anything. Megan wouldn't have even wanted *herself* in charge of all of it. And Aunt Rebekkah would have no idea what to do.

Mary listened from the hall and was as quiet as a mouse. *This* was interesting, she thought.

Megan wondered, and said, "You think it is about dollars?" She couldn't pronounce the "m" in money.

"I can't believe that would be the case," Ashley responded immediately, but actually, she wondered herself.

Ashley was naïve about very little, but she was about this "money." Money can do funny things to people. "She said she was thinking of going to court to get an order." Ashley sat in a chair where she could still see and talk to Megan comfortably.

Megan slowly shook her head. It was nice to see her move her head. Megan was disgusted. She didn't need this from her aunt, and Ashley didn't have the time to deal with anything else other than what was already on her plate.

"Answer is no chance. You take care uh it all."

Mary thought Ashley was pretty slick. She really got Megan's support on that. She was starting to understand how these two thought. Ashley wanted control of everything Megan had, and Megan was going to let her do just that. Two could play at that game. But part of that game was knowing today is Christmas, and that meant she would come back to this later. For the moment, Mary simply filed the conversation in the "critical" folder in her mind. She turned the corner into the room.

"Well, that really was a wonderful party." They both looked up at Mary.

"Nary, tank you." Megan was sincerely appreciative of Mary. She was very happy Ashley had found her. "You got a great holiday."

Mary beamed.

"You're welcome, Megan." Not missing a beat, she said, "Well, I'm going to clean up and get things put away. You going to watch *CSI* tonight?"

"Yes. Good idea. *CSI*."

"Sounds good."

Ashley's mind wandered to Robert and Lauren. It was Christmas, they had left an hour ago and she should be getting home to cook supper there. Was this really a holiday? Did she ever stop working? Had she ever not worked?

"OK, listen, I told Robert that I'd be back shortly after he got home. I think we're good for the night." She stood and went over to Megan and kissed her on the cheek. "You really captivated everyone today, Megan."

"Tanks, Ashley. Couldn't done it 'out you."

"Merry Christmas, Megan. I'll see you tomorrow after I finish at the store."

And no, there were no days off. There were no hours off. It was one continuous sweep second movement from second to second, minute to minute, hour to hour, day to day. Week to week. Month to month.

"Merry Christmas, Mary." They exchanged an awkward hug and Ashley headed for the door, stopping to get her purse and coat on the way out. "Goodnight, you guys." She caught the door behind her.

"Megan?" Megan moved her head slowly toward Mary. She'd be so happy when she would be able to move like everyone else again.

"Would you like to stay out here tonight? I'm not sure it does us any good to bring you all the way back into the bedroom, especially when you have this beautiful new bed with all these neatsy features. Lot closer to the bathroom over here."

It was, too. Maybe fifteen feet away instead of forty in the bedroom.

"OK." *Why not try it. Might be nice.*

Mary went about her work as Megan slid her arm forward to grasp the remote. Magically, the big TV in the living room turned on. Megan clicked the channels until it landed on the news. She decided to watch.

Mary began to wonder how else she could become the lady of the house.

The phone rang. No one else was there to answer it, but who cared. It would be someone wanting money or something and she wanted a break from all that. Mary decided she wouldn't give in to the nonstop ring. Then she heard the upstairs phone ring. Probably Ashley. She'd call her back later. Not to worry.

It's Christmas and I'll be damned if I'm going to be some kind of secretary for the house.

Chapter Ten

Three Years Before Day 1

It was a hot and sunny summer day. Megan lay beside her majestic pool. She reached into the small bag that contained her lotion and as she turned over to lie on her stomach, she rubbed lotion wherever she could reach.

As expected, her self-care drew the attention of the gardener who was still trimming shrubs around the far side of the pool. Why would he work quickly, now? Now he was watching Megan do nothing but lie there in the sun.

She didn't know whether she wanted to have sex with him or not. He was only modestly attractive but he was here and no one else was. Her little boom box was pumping the music from her favorite station.

No one would be around today until 3:30 when the cook and housekeeper would arrive. Until then her palace was empty. Just her... and the gardener.

I wonder what his name is.

It didn't really matter. She would never ask. She would never say a word.

Why do men sit back and look without doing something? They never say anything when we're alone.

The four-carat diamond on her third finger, left hand, could have something to do with it. Who would want to mess with the guy that bought her that? Only the foolhardy. The gardener had no idea how much that ring cost. Had he known, he would have gotten his mind off of the girl and back to the trimming.

She stood, arched her back and moved to the side of the pool where she would step slowly into the pool. The water felt cool. She knew the water temperature was kept at eighty year-round, but it always felt chilly when she went in.

She watched herself step down into the pool. Once she was deep enough to where the water hugged her just below her chest, she stood still and simply stared up at the gardener. She removed her top and let it float on the water. Her eyes didn't leave him for one second. Then she took what was left of her two-piece off and let it float the other way. She wasn't going to be wearing either piece for awhile.

She stared. She glared. She didn't smile. She said nothing.

He looked at her. He looked at his work. He looked at the door to the house. He was considering the possibility.

She simply stared at him. She moved her hands over the surface of the water so water would splash enough to draw attention and not make a scene… well, at least a different kind of scene.

He put his tools down.

There was a ring on his third finger, left hand, too. She never saw it. Her eyes were riveted to his. Magnetic. She kept moving her arms and hands, making half circles with them.

She took one step back in the pool. That was his cue. He didn't know why he knew. He just knew.

He saw the movement and unconsciously took one step toward the pool. There was now nothing in the world other than this woman. It no longer crossed his mind what would happen if David were to come home.

The sweat being produced now came more from the intensity of the moment than any labors in the garden. She took another step back and he moved another step toward the pool.

The fish was on the hook.

She stepped toward him, one step.

He faced her and took another step toward the pool. She continued the hypnotic semi-circular movements of her arms. He couldn't really see her eyes. The sunglasses didn't permit it. She had no expression on her face.

She nodded three times.

He walked to the steps descending into the pool.

A brief thought passed through his mind. *This is a bad idea. If he comes home, he will kill me.*

He slipped off his sandals, pulled his t-shirt over his head and removed his jeans as he walked into the pool. She faced him and moved back into deeper water. She had snagged her fish. That hadn't taken long. Two minutes, perhaps?

He was hypnotized.

He should have winced a bit when the water swallowed him up to his waist, but there was no involuntary response.

She smiled just a bit.

He walked toward her.

She stopped moving her hands and arms in semicircles.

She raised her arms straight in the air, bent them at the elbows, brought them behind her neck. She showed him what he wanted to see.

With five steps he made his way to her. He stopped about five feet away.

She still hadn't let her eyes leave his face. His eyes broke with her eyes and moved to her body. Riveted. She took two steps forward, put her right hand on the back of his head.

He was about a foot taller than she was. She stood on her toes and brought his lips to hers and she closed her eyes.

Their bodies met, and danced under the water.

She wrapped her legs around him, and they became as one. For two people who had never been together before, it felt natural and familiar.

Finishing together, she placed her hand on his cheek. She smiled. She stopped looking at him. She walked away from him after she snatched her bathing suit's two pieces, deftly slipping them on while moving, as if she had done this many times before. By the time she was at the top of the steps he was still standing, paralyzed.

Her eyes went to the tiny box of music. She walked over to the baby boom box, bent over and picked it up with one hand while she grabbed her bag with the other. She had been in the sun for nearly a half hour and didn't want to risk a sunburn. The tan was all she wanted.

He turned around and tracked her movements as she walked into the house. He was naked and alone in the pool. He had never experienced anything like that in his life. He was left wondering just what he had done.

She had a towel waiting for her inside the door. She would dry off, then make her way upstairs for a shower. She had an early evening fundraiser in town. She would be running a bit late.

***

It had been a difficult morning at the office for David. He'd brought Ashley into the main office today and promoted her to vice president in charge of operations. Ashley was stunned.

"Ashley, I can't think of anyone who I trust more with my business. You are the new vice president. In effect, you will run the management, administration and buying for all four stores. It's an enormous responsibility, and I know you can handle it."

He was on his cell calling Megan. He tried the house, he tried her cell. He rang the phone that rang in her office, his office and in the pool house. None of the phones were answered. He tried her cell again. Everyone answered their cell phone.

"Strange, she has to be home… today is the fundraiser, and the gardener doesn't have keys."

"Try the upstairs phone in your bedroom, David."

He let it ring a few more times. "Good idea."

It rang for a good minute.

"Huh. I wonder if she's OK?"

She looked at him, doe-eyed. She wasn't worried about Megan at this moment. Megan was young and healthy. But what the hell was Ashley doing as the vice president of a small but still multimillion dollar business? She blinked.

"Thank you, David."

Her promotion took her from being assistant manager earning $54,000 a year to vice president with a salary of $110,000 annually, and potential for significant bonuses for hitting targets. She didn't know what all he had just done – but she knew it was big.

"Take Robert to dinner tonight. He'll be a happy man, I imagine."

Happy wasn't the word. Lauren in her final year of preschool might never see her mother again, with this kind of a workload, but with this kind of money she could hire a nanny. And then some.

"Tonight, Megan and I are going to the Pediatric Aids Charity Fundraiser down in Bloomington. Means a lot to her. Ever since she went to that hospital when we visited Africa, this cause has meant everything to her. She wants to make a big impression on the audience and the community through the media. They asked me to present a check to the foundation, but I deferred to Megan."

"Sounds exciting." Ashley was still in shock. Just where do you begin when you are the vice president?

"I've got to take off now if I want to get my portfolio in line at home and still have time to get to the event. The media is going to broadcast part of the event live on the news today. So, I'm going to surprise Megan, stop and get a sparkling bottle of bubbly and so on."

"You know she'll love that."

"Listen, Ashley. You have done great work here and I appreciate it. The outline of your job description is in this folder. Don't let the thickness of it worry you, there's a lot of repetitious stuff in here. But do read it before you call it a day. And listen, it'll take me about a half hour to get home. Would you try Megan in about fifteen minutes and let her know I'm on my way? I'm a little worried that she isn't answering any of the phones."

"Of course."

He grabbed his coat. Ashley often wondered why he wore a coat and tie on a day that was 97 degrees and humid, but never said a word.

"Have a good afternoon, Ashley. And congratulations."

"David. Thanks. I hope you know what you're doing!"

"I do." And he was off. He knew.

His Mercedes was the last car in the parking lot. He inserted the key and turned. He knew the seat would be hot – that was the only drawback of leather. He opened the door and the heat just poured out of the car.

He slid in, ignored the noisy gadget demanding a seat belt, and turned the key.

Get her favorite bottle of wine, maybe spend a half hour in the pool? Should be nice.

Stopping at a liquor store was not his favorite thing, but it was convenient, just a few blocks from the house and they'd take care of him quickly. He was back in the car in no time and was moving toward his goal. A nice interlude with his wife, then back to work before heading to Bloomington. He had it all planned.

He pulled into the oversized garage. *Is that what a building that houses eight cars is called? A garage?* He hit the remote and the garage door quietly closed behind him.

Grabbed his coat, the wine and some papers from the back of the car.

Turning the key he slid into the house. He'd pour the wine into her favorite crystal glasses. He almost found himself tiptoeing into the kitchen. She always wanted him to be more spontaneous and unpredictable and he was rather liking it. He'd done something like this less than a handful of times in their short marriage. He opened the cabinet.

He heard her baby boom box. She must be out swimming. The boom box. It was Megan's only real break from elegance. She was after all only twenty-four, and this was part of her childhood.

He had a tough time opening the wine. He rarely drank and never served. How did she open a bottle so easily every single day? Finally he withdrew the cork.

He hoped that Megan didn't hear him.

He slowly poured the red into the glasses.

That done, he took his comb out of his back pocket and ran it through his hair. He was hot to be sure, but it was cool inside and that was helping already.

He looked at the door out back to the pool. A bath towel hung from the hook in the foyer leading outside. She would be in one of her bikinis and that was a good thing. He started to grow with anticipation. He slid a hand around each glass and headed out to the pool. He took about fifteen steps to get to the outside door and as he pushed the handle down with his elbow, the door opened and nudged his arm. Somehow he didn't spill the wine.

"Ouch!" He jumped.

She jumped higher. She came out of the trance she had been in for the last half hour.

"Oh my God! You scared me." She pushed him back in the house. "What are you doing home, honey?"

The gardener, watching all of this, jumped out of the pool. He grabbed his shorts and pants off the side of the pool deck and raced behind some of the shrubbery. *Dammit!* He knew he was dead. What the hell had he been thinking. *Jesus.*

"Megan, I think I heard something outside." He peered over her head and saw nothing but water moving in the swimming pool.

"Of course you did, honey. I hopped out of the pool as soon as the gardener finished in the front. I didn't feel all that comfortable with him working back there, so I came in."

Still looking over her shoulder. "I don't see him. Are you sure?"

"Positive." She carried herself as if she were immune to the danger at hand.

She pushed him back with the tip of her finger, happy he had both hands full. She saw the wine, considered the situation, and figured out what he had in mind.

Finally he gets it. It's too bad his timing is off a bit today.

"I have chlorine in my hair and I smell like a swimming pool. Let me get a quick shower and then we can spend some time together. How's that sound?" She moved forward with her body until his hands parted and her wet body came up against his. She kissed him on the lips and walked forward as he walked backward. Their lips locked and he was ready.

She rubbed her breasts against his chest. She refused to take one of the glasses.

"Now, let's go."

"You go up, I'll be up in a second."

She hesitated but only missed one beat. She walked toward the hall leading to a set of stairs that would take her upstairs when she turned around. She set her baby boom box down.

"You have one second and after that today's special might not be available." She showed him her breasts, moved just a little so he would understand at every level of his being.

"Quantities are not limited, but I might get bored waiting, Mr. Dresden."

She dripped the remaining pool water all the way to the stairs and up she went on the spiral staircase.

The gardener had gotten his pants on and raced back over to his equipment on the other side of the pool. There was no way out so he had better get it together and fast. He couldn't believe no one was coming outside. He threw his shirt on and started clipping, his heart pounding. He was drenched. His clothes were drenched. He might as well be dead in the water.

David looked out the window. The first thing he noticed was that the gardener's hair was dripping wet.

He opened the door and stepped out. "Ricardo!"

His heart pounded through his chest. He could barely look at the man in the eye. "Si, Señor?"

"What the hell are you doing? You're going to die of heat exhaustion. Take a ten-minute break and if you need to, get a swim. Don't die for my shrubbery, for heaven's sake."

His mouth went dry. God had spared his life and he would never make this mistake again.

"Muchas gracias, Señor. It is very hot today. Thank you, sir."

Crazy Mexican. Good kid. Works hard. We'll keep him.

He turned and saw the wine glasses. Time was short. He picked up the glasses and bopped up the stairs. The shower had stopped and Megan stood facing him in the Roman bathroom like a goddess. Naked.

Most women would be uncomfortable. But not Megan. She owned the world.

"You have seconds left, Mr. Dresden." She turned and smiled. "Did you get me my favorite?"

She held out her hand and took a glass.

***

Two hours later, David pulled his blue Mercedes up to the hotel valet, who opened the door for Megan. It was still light out, though the sun had inched down behind the hotel on the west side so they were in the shadows.

The Radisson Hotel in Bloomington was by no means the nicest hotel in town, but this was for charity. The Pediatric Aids Society of Minnesota was something David and Megan had supported for the last four years.

As always, David was dressed impeccably for the public. Young. Healthy. Perfectly tailored suit. Megan, on the other hand, was dressed in her typical outlandish fashion – like a twenty-four-year-old Parisian fashion model. Today it was a tight green dress with a plunging backline, and a stunning green hat. The dress hugged her neck in front to create a stunning contrast to her white pearl necklace and emerald earrings. She had seen the hat on a beautiful girl in a fashion show in Paris on their last trip to Western Europe and she had to have it.

She loved the looks and the attention. It wasn't ego, as many thought. It was just a desire and the fulfillment of that desire to be unique, one of a kind, to feel and be special and free. And to be courted by every human being who saw her.

Her right hand was laced through David's left and they walked at a modest pace down the long hallway to the ballroom. Every eye from the bellman to the registration clerk turned and followed her. Sexy? Yes. But it was more than that. It was a boldness and her statement of independence and individuality that drew everyone's gaze.

They walked the entire length of the hall, nodding at their subjects without comment until they got to the door to the ballroom. There were probably four hundred chairs and four tables at the front near the podium. Everything was as perfectly decorated as if Megan had supervised it herself.

"Welcome, Mrs. Dresden. Mr. Dresden. I will take you to your seat at the head of the room."

All the seats were filled and only two remained where the master of ceremonies now smiled. The host seated them at their two chairs next to the podium.

Megan smiled and thanked him.

The President of the Pediatric Aids Society was gratified by their presence. He stood and brought the room to attention. He spoke for about four minutes, at which time he began his introduction of Megan and David Dresden.

Megan reached into her purse and made sure the check was in the envelope. *Thank God for Ashley.*

"...in the last thirty months the Dresdens have personally donated over $150,000 to the Society and their gifts have given the gift of life to hundreds, if not thousands, of children across the globe."

She looked out and saw television cameras from Channels 4, 5 and 11. Only Fox wasn't there. Not surprising.

"Ladies and gentlemen, Megan Dresden."

A rousing standing ovation brought a radiant smile to Megan's face. A dozen cameras flashed.

"I have a question for you. Do you think this dress is a little too much? David was telling me that he thought I was overdoing it today?"

Everyone laughed and a hundred people shouted, "No!"

She looked at her husband and grinned. "See, I told you honey. They think it's conservative."

More laughter. She was twenty-four, and she owned every ballroom and every pool in the world.

"Ladies and gentleman, I can't tell you how we will eventually cure AIDS. I can only tell you that when David and I were in the Horn of Africa two years ago we visited several villages. We helped medical personnel give shots to children ranging from infancy to sixteen years old. Many of these children had AIDS. In fact about a third of them did. They live in squalor. They face the most difficult life imaginable. We were more than touched by the dignity of these beautiful children in the face of all their suffering. We gave immunizations for two consecutive weeks. We helped distribute medication and condoms. We know we only made a dent, and maybe not even that much."

A tear came to her eye. If there had been any doubt about the genuine affection she felt for the children they had helped in Africa, it was dismissed.

"David and I are very fortunate people. We had only planned to visit one village and then move along. The gravity of the situation caused us to change our plans and stay two weeks. We canceled our vacation and did what we could to help in any way we could.

"Ladies and gentleman, today I want to offer you a challenge. I want you to provide medication for a child. You all know what it costs as it's in the program you received when you arrived.

"Just because these children don't live in the house next door to yours, just because they have different colored skin and most not a stitch to wear, they are wonderful people crying out to live a life that has meaning.

"I don't know if anything can make those dreams come true for them. I don't know if the experimental medications will extend their lives but the doctors assure me that they almost certainly will.

"I don't know anything except that we are all incredibly fortunate to live in the healthiest state of the greatest nation on this planet."

She pulled the check out of her envelope. She looked at the dollar figure and she cried. She wished she would have written it for a bigger amount.

"Today, David and I would like to present the Pediatric Aids Foundation with this check for… one hundred thousand dollars. Will you please give generously today? God will bless you and the Foundation in your efforts to save the lives of these wonderful children.

"Thank you."

A standing ovation erupted as she sat down. She dabbed a tear from each eye. She thought back to the children they had helped, the families they had flown in food for, the fighting that was going on not ten kilometers outside the city. It was all coming back. This was what she had wanted to do all her life. Be a representative of good works. She felt in some small way that she had achieved that, and she truly appreciated their appreciation.

David looked at her and when she sat down he put his arm around her. She looked into his eyes. He smiled and nodded. The master of ceremonies acknowledged the incredible generosity of the largest non-corporate donation ever made by an individual to the organization. He knew that he had to make the rest of the audience feel Megan's mission so they also would make a difference tonight.

He looked down at the saint in the loud green backless dress, a beautiful young woman who was obviously not a simple woman.

Chapter Eleven

April 19

Day 576

It had been almost four months since Megan surprised everyone at Christmas. Megan, Mary and Ashley were now all into a new daily routine.

Megan lay in bed watching *The Price is Right*. It was OK with her that Mary now used her room and that she used Mary's. Why not? It was a long way to the bathroom in the master suite. Who would have ever thought that would have been a problem?

One of the beautiful models was framing a brand new car. It was a Ford. Nothing compared to a Mercedes… but The Beauty, she was beautiful. She had the same color hair as Megan, and a striking figure.

That's me. That's what I looked like two years ago. Why would God let this happen to me? Is there some kind of purpose that I'm supposed to fulfill? It doesn't make sense. My legs used to look like her legs. My smile was as pretty as hers. Am I really lucky to be alive like they all tell me? Really? Lucky for what? So I can sit and watch The Price is Right *for the rest of my life? I can't take a step without falling. It's been seventeen months.*

Same thing every day. Get up and go to the hospital. Get up and go to the physical therapist. Fall down, they pull me up with a stupid pulley. Like a five-month-old baby. Except the baby will walk on her own in a year. I won't. I probably will never walk. Can't support my own weight for more than a second or two.

That blonde is cute too. But I'm prettier. I was prettier. They can do more surgery and work on my face. I want to be able to walk like that girl. On heels. I can do it. I've got to do it. I will go crazy if I have to sit in this bed for the rest of my life.

She removed the blankets with her hand. It took a few minutes but she was gaining a mobility in her hands and her arms that she didn't have at Christmas.

I want to be able to walk on my own. I want to be able to go to the bathroom on my own and not on that stupid commode. I want to go TO the bathroom. I want to be able to put my own makeup on. I'm getting stronger. I know I can do it.

She lowered the bed to a horizontal position. Once it was there, she rolled toward the side of the bed and maneuvered her legs off the side of the bed. Her head and back on the bed. Her legs off the bed.

She couldn't easily lift herself to a sitting position. She kept falling back down. She got her head and upper back off the bed but her lower back wasn't cooperating as her stomach muscles weren't yet strong enough.

She allowed her legs to drop toward the floor. They dangled uselessly, but she was determined to make this happen.

This turned out to be a mistake as her body didn't quite work the way she thought it would. There was no way she would be able to stand. She now realized that only a Chinese acrobat could actually stand from this position.

She twisted onto her stomach and decided to push off the bed facing it.

Without having hips to help her, this was a much more arduous task than she thought. She heard the TV host telling the audience to get their pets spayed or neutered.

I might as well be spayed or neutered. Dammit. I want to walk. I am GOING to walk.

Her feet were now touching the floor, or at least her toes were touching the floor. Her toes were extended, as she couldn't flex them flat.

Now, with a hefty grunt, she used her shoulder and elbow strength to push herself up, her entire body weight balanced above the tips of her toes, while she pushed backward until the soles of her feet finally connected with the floor.

No wonder babies have such a hard time doing this.

The moment of truth.

With all of her will she pushed down on the bed. Tensed her legs. She found the muscles in her back to help her come toward a vertical position. Her body was clear of the bed and only her hands remained supporting her weight.

Yes!

She pulled with her back muscles and in seconds her hands were off the bed. She was now bent over the bed. Her hands were between her and the bed, and a feeling of elation came over her.

Her right leg couldn't hold her weight and it collapsed under her. She fell over to the right, her head like a domino slamming onto the floor, her right arm providing no brace for the fall.

The carpet provided some padding but the fall caused enormous pain. Unfortunately it didn't knock her unconscious. At that point she would have welcomed the oblivion.

She lay there in a fetal position feeling the pain, wanting to shout out for Mary but refusing to. It was all part of wanting, of needing, to do this on her own.

Oh God…now what? Do I yell for help?

She wasn't going anywhere. The pain in her head was severe. She waited until she could think through the pain.

It was fairly easy to roll onto her stomach and now she was face to the carpet. No blood. She had to pull her right arm out from under her body and that took some finagling. She needed to get her face off the carpet. She brought her hands up by her shoulders and was surprised that she had more strength than she thought.

She was going to do a pushup, the kind she'd done in elementary school. She readied her knees to take the weight of her lifting her body. She pushed herself a couple of inches off the floor but that was all. Her upper back wasn't strong enough to help her.

I'll crawl to the damn bathroom.

She curled her toes and bent her feet so she could "push off" them. She didn't know how that was going to work.

She couldn't bring her hands too much more forward or they'd provide no leverage at all. So she simply willed herself forward. Her hands, butt, knees and feet pulled or pushed her forward. Three inches.

She turned her head and lay her right cheek on the carpet.

How can I be tired? I haven't even moved. I can do this. God, what if there was a fire right now? How would I get out? I'd yell and Mary would come get me out of here.

She pushed with her hands, pulled up with her neck and back, pushed with her legs and the bottoms of her feet and plunged forward.

Four inches.

What if a spider or some gross bug decides he wants to come say hello to my face? Ugh.

She rested again for a few minutes and immediately did the plunge forward. Maybe three or four inches this time.

OK. I'm going about one foot every ten minutes. It's about fifteen feet to the bathroom. I should be there in….150 minutes. That's like two hours.

She dropped her face back into the carpet.

Two hours is a long time to get to the bathroom. What if I had to GO to the bathroom? This is INSANE. DAMMIT.

She plunged again. Four inches. The anger helped. The after-effect of the burst was exhaustion.

What does she do all day? I'm paying her $45,000 a year to do what? To sit in my bed and watch TV? To go grocery shopping? What DOES she do? She has no idea I'm laying on the floor here. Why didn't she hear my head slam against the floor? Didn't they hear that downtown? Could it have been louder? No, Mary, please don't worry it was ONLY MY HEAD SPLITTING IN TWO on the floor. Please don't trouble yourself.

She plunged again. Three inches this time.

"Dannit. -hy not talk to nyself… decause the dords cone out too slowly…ugh. It's easier to not try and talk. Dannit."

How far have I come? One foot? Two feet? This is ridiculous. What the hell am I doing here kissing the floor? I can live without walking, can't I? Can I have sex if I can't walk? Will ANYONE ever want to be with me again, even touch me? Even look at me?

Her facial appearance had dramatically improved in the last seventeen months. The left side of her face showed no actual damage from the accident. But the right side was still crunched in. She remembered the expressions on some of the kids at the party. She didn't look good.

She plunged again. Five inches?

I'm going to walk again and I'm going to talk clearly like a normal person and not some handicapped wheelchair person for the rest of my life. There is NO WAY I will kiss the ground forever. I want to kiss a MAN. A MAN.

What kind of a man is going to want to kiss ME? No one. I'll have to find a nice man. A nice man. That by definition means he's ugly. By definition, I'm ugly…by definition…I better be nice.

She plunged again. Three inches.

So the question is, do I want to kiss an ugly guy? Here's another question then. Does an ugly guy want to kiss me? How gross does a guy have to be to think, "Oh, I want to kiss her but I don't know if she'll be happy or not"?

And then there's this: Do I want to kiss a guy who would be stupid enough to kiss me?

Stupid or blind. What's up with that? Why do people kiss anyway? Why not just rub thumbs or ears together?

What do wheelchair people do anyway for sex? If you can't have sex and you can't even do it for yourself, do you simply go insane? I have GOT TO be able to walk and get this stupid body to work. Mary, do you hear that? I'm actually feeling really horny for the first time in a year.

This is good. Feeling horny and I'm not dreaming. This would be a terrible dream. So this is really good news.

But what do I do with the news? Mary comes in. So would I ask her?

Mary, would you… and then what do you say? I know it's not in your job description but…

I'm sorry, I know I look like I came from Phantom of the Opera, *but would you be nice enough to give me an orgasm? Oh yes…absolutely. I'd be happy to do that. I won't feel WEIRD at all about that, Ms. Dresden.*

Excuse me, if I gave you $50 would you…No, not for $50. If I gave you $500 would you…For $500 a lot of people will say yes. How much would that be for a hundred orgasms in a year? That would be...oh, where is Ashley when there is math to be done? That would be 500, 5,000, $50,000. Wow. That is a lot for a hundred orgasms. But it would be so worth it if he was hot. Or if she was hot. Who cares? I just don't want to pay $500 to someone who isn't attractive. I've got to talk with Ashley about this. She can make it happen. If we pay in advance we can probably get a good price.

Is that legal? What would they do? Throw me in prison?

Hiring someone to be a hooker...but isn't everyone a hooker in one way or another?

She lunged again, almost six inches this time.

Wow, that was pretty good.

Is there a service in the Yellow Pages for normal people stuck in bodies that don't work but are dying to have sex? What would that be under? Charitable organizations or illegal prostitution?

What if there was a charity within prostitution rings? They're people, too.

They just get paid to have fun. Why not? Then when they come across someone who is really needy, they look at the requests and say, "Oh, we should help Megan Dresden out. She's a really good cause."

People donate clothes, cars, tons of money, their time volunteering, why not orgasmic relief? The Orgasmic Relief Society. Helping people who can't help themselves. Would I have donated?

Hell, yes, I would have made a contribution!

"MEGAN! Are you all right? Where is Mary? Oh, my God!"

Ashley had come over to have lunch with Megan and she was early.

"I'n tine Ashley."

"What are you doing there and where is MARY?"

As if on cue, Mary appeared at the top of the stairs.

"What's the matter? Oh my GOD! Megan, how did you get there? Are you all right?"

"Yes, I'n tine. I'n tine."

"You have a HUGE mark on your head. How did THAT happen? How did this happen? Was anyone here?" Ashley was loud and clearly she was anxious.

"Don't worry. Nothing happened. I'm tine. I just wanted to go to the dathroon… dy nyself."

"Are you nuts, honey, you can't go to the bathroom by yourself." Ashley motioned to Mary to help her pick Megan up and get her back into bed.

"I has to go to ze dathroon!"

"You can use the commode, for God's sake." Ashley didn't know how to feel.

"I crawled all the hay oder dere."

"Honey, you crawled two feet. What are you thinking?"

"Ashley. Ashley. I has to try. I can't de here the rest of ny lite. I'll go insane."

"Honey, you aren't going to be here for the rest of your life but … how did you get out of bed?"

"It's a long story."

Mary had gone and come back into the room with an ice bag. She held it up to Megan's head. Mary was not only shocked, but of course she was scared she would be fired.

"Megan, you have to call me when you need *anything*. I am so worried about you." What was Mary going to say to get out of this? She hadn't been in the room to check on Megan for over an hour.

"I'n tine. I just anted to alk."

"Megan, if you want to walk, you let me help you." Mary was firm and sounded resolute.

"OK."

She was too exhausted to talk about her escape and how she had crawled just two feet. It was more than two feet, wasn't it?

She created an entire nonprofit organization for orgasmic relief... it had to be at least three feet!

Maybe not.

Chapter Twelve

October 29

Day 2230

Six years.

It had been six years.

When David died, the City decided to postpone the destruction of the Dresden Chicago/Lake Store.

Ashley seized the opportunity with various legal maneuvers, the effects of which she knew would be temporary, but that would give her time. She had underestimated herself. She bought them six whole years.

But now it was over.

And it was bad. Not only was the City going after the Chicago/Lake Store, they were going to close the other three stores as well. Yes, the City would write a check, but it would be perhaps one million dollars in total, instead of their actual worth, which would have been as high as eight times that figure.

When David Dresden died, no one in the city administration wanted to appear cold and uncaring to the community by stealing the sole income source of Dresden's disabled wife. But cities don't forget, and Dresden had been a thorn in the side of city politicians and administration for years. Now, six years later, they would take all four stores through rezoning projects that would be rubber-stamped within days.

Ashley had no way to tell Megan the facts, except to tell her the facts.

"The reality of it is that the City has succeeded in forcing us out of the Chicago/Lake store and that means that we're going to get taken again on the valuation and what they are going to pay us. It's not us, it's them. We can appeal again, but we're appealing to the guys they take out for drinks every night.

"It's a joke. The law says they have to give you fair value for your property but the City is who determines whether they can take your property or not, whether they *will* take your property or not, and how much you will get for your property. If you don't like it, then you can appeal to someone in the office next door… at the City. But listen, Megan, it's not just Chicago/Lake. It's all the stores. They're finally pushing us out completely."

Ashley sat across from Megan, who was in her wheelchair at the big dining room table. The view overlooking the backyard was soothing even on this most stressful of days. The fact was, the "yard" was more like a perfectly manicured park.

"I don't want to move, Ashley. We have to stay." Megan spoke at about half the speed of anyone else. Almost all the letters and words were clear now, at least most of the time.

She slowly reached for her cup of tea and brought it up to her lips, and she gently sipped it. Megan clearly felt disturbed. In her estimation, her life had been nothing for six years and now it was going to get worse. They would have to sell the beloved marital home that David had bought for her.

"Expenses have caught up with us. We have enormous property taxes, Mary's salary, speech therapy, physical therapy, doctors, dozens of costs that didn't exist before the accident. We've been losing ground for the last couple of years and as the City has taken the stores from us things have gotten worse at a faster pace."

Ashley didn't want to get too stubborn about the issue because there really was no choice. By autumn there was going to begin a wholesale selling-off of most of David's Mercedes. Most of the art and an awful lot of other "stuff" was going to be sold. The cost of treatments, therapies, and surgeries alone was $250,000 annually. That didn't include the house payment, the car payments, the gardener… so many expenses.

There was still net worth. Assets. If Ashley took a second mortgage on the house, their monthly payments would begin to chew up that diminishing net worth. "Once we sell the house we move into a condo in Edina and there will be a few million dollars left after selling off the rest of the Mercedes. Then we're fine. But right now, we're feeding the alligator, and it's getting big fast."

Megan was shaking her head. Edina was a beautiful city, home to many mansions. She wouldn't be living in one of them, though. She'd be moving to an upscale condo, but a condo, nonetheless. Edina boasted one of the top ten zip codes in Minnesota for wealth. But Megan didn't want to leave her home.

Her life had been shattered already, and she didn't know if she could take any more.

"What if we just sold most of the Mercedes? That would give us hundreds of thousands of dollars."

She just doesn't get money. Ashley wouldn't say it, though.

"We're going to sell the Mercedes, but we won't raise much because we still owe on them. The net on them will be about zero."

"But there are a bunch of them. They're worth $40,000 to $100,000 each, Ashley!"

"I understand that, but we owe the bank the money that we borrowed to buy them. David didn't pay for them in cash. We *have* to sell all but your red Mercedes just to break even on those monthly payments. You never get for cars what you think you should. And there aren't a lot of people out there buying Mercedes in this economy."

"Oh. How much are we making at the stores every month?"

"After all expenses? Perhaps $10,000 per month per store but remember, in just a couple months, they become the property of the City of Minneapolis, because they are putting us out of business. So the answer is that in a couple of months, it will officially amount to nothing."

"What about David's investments?"

"There's still money left but the market has been going down and we've lost a lot. The investments aren't bringing in money anymore. We've spent about two million dollars since you've been out of the hospital."

Megan put her teacup down and slowly folded her hands into her lap. She looked at her hands. At least they worked pretty well nowadays. She could lift, grasp and do most things that most people could do with their hands.

"Is there any way we can keep the house?"

Ashley shook her head.

"I'm sorry, honey. The insurance company from the other driver only paid so much and now the bills are all ours. Once we sell the house we'll be able to pull out the equity and put that away. We should be able to invest that and you should be able to live off it for the rest of your life. But even though it seems like a lot of money, when you look at our expenses, you'll run out of money before you turn forty. As long as I was able to fight the City, we had income to keep the house. Now we simply don't have it. The City has shredded us. They aren't just taking one store, they're working on all four."

"Ashley, why did they hate David so much?"

"Mostly politics. David was a pretty conservative guy. The people who work at the City get pay increases when they can bring in more revenues, taxes from people like David who build businesses. The government by nature is made up of liberals. Heavily tax the businesses and the people earning the most money. Distribute first to the government, then to everyone else. David aggressively campaigned for pro-business candidates and small government candidates. Think of it this way. All those people at the City? David was basically saying, 'You aren't going to be working there anymore if our guy gets elected because he is cutting government.'

"You think it isn't personal, but it is. David knew that two of his properties were in prime locations for malls, like the Calhoun store was. Now the City gets your property and will begin to get twenty times the money in taxes every year, starting next year after they build the mall. That pays the City employees their paychecks and that's the way the world works."

Now it was Megan shaking her head.

"But Ashley, this is all wrong. They can't put people out of business who have worked their whole lives and have employed hundreds of people. Look at all those families who won't have incomes."

"Megan, you will drive yourself nuts if you start to think about all of this. David was a good guy who worked long hours, had great employees, loyal customers and the people at the City over time simply grew to not like him. It was politics. He would put up signs for the people that City employees didn't want voted into office. Council people, senators, representatives. People who proposed to cut taxes and cut government are the kind of people who obviously the city or the county or the state government or the federal government can't have in office, because cutting expenses means taking out the people who don't do anything and having them go look for work elsewhere."

"You're right, Ashley. I don't understand it at all."

She looked away from Ashley. If she had been capable of crying, capable of tears, they would have been there.

"When do we have to move?"

"Right after the holidays. I've already put a down payment on a nice condo in Edina. It's at 4190 Stinson. It's really a beautiful place, easy to navigate for the wheelchair and as you start walking more. It's not small, but it's more convenient than the house."

"It makes me nervous moving somewhere, when I can't get around all that well."

"I know, Megan. Hey, listen. Do you realize it has been six years since you've been shopping? Think about that. Six years and the only places you've gone are to doctor's offices and therapists."

"That's a long time."

"So I was thinking, maybe tomorrow we go to The Galleria and go shopping. Buy some jewelry, some clothes, just treat you to a fun afternoon out."

Megan looked down. This wasn't the first time that leaving the house for non-medical issues came up. For a long time, Megan hadn't wanted to go out in public where strangers would see her face.

But now, Megan's face, while not attractive, was not the frightening visage it had been six years ago.

"Maybe we could buy you a Halloween mask, Ashley. I don't need one."

"You know what, Megan, your face is not anything like it used to be. The puffiness, the discoloration, it really is all gone. The surgeons have done such a good job on your entire body, including your face. Once your lips get some more motion and your left facial nerve lets you have some movement, you're going to be a pretty girl again."

"But not now."

"You know what, while we're out we *should* get a mask. You need to give out candy to the trick-or-treaters this year. Mary has been doing it for the last few years, but you should do it this year. You can stand in your walker by the door or use your wheelchair, or both. What do you say? Let's go shopping."

Inside Megan was trying to sort her way out through the crushing ambivalence. She didn't want anyone to see her. But it was true that she hadn't seen much of anything in six years. She did need to get out. It was time. She could move in her walker or Ashley could push her in the chair like she did when they had to go to the hospitals.

"Let's go to The Galleria after lunch, Ashley. I'm up for it if you are."

Chapter Thirteen

October 30

Day 2231

"Couldn't be better."

Mary was on her cell with Jake in Las Vegas. She and Jake had been close since high school.

"I've got so much money stashed away it's unbelievable. They pay me $900 a week. All my living expenses are paid and I drive a Mercedes. Megan feels sorry for me because I can't leave. I'm indispensable to her. It's OK, really. I live in a bedroom as big as the house we had in Scottsdale. No kidding. Yes. It's her room but she still can't be in there… too far to get to the bathroom. Exactly… only in a wheelchair. Yes. No one can hear me. That is by far the worst part. Morning visits to the bathroom… or not. It's getting better though… hasn't been too bad the last year or two. The first couple years were terrible… every day another mess or two or three. Worse than being in a nursing home.

"No, I haven't taken a day off in years but it doesn't matter. Even though I have a lot to do, where could I go that would pay me this much? She has no understanding of money. Sure, I need a vacation and it'll happen soon. No, she can't, she's at the other end of the hall. About forty feet from here and I'm on my cell. Yes, a master bath with a whirlpool. A few times a week. Wonderful. I eat the best food on the planet. I have no expenses and about $100,000 socked away in that account that I emailed you about. No. There's nothing to spend it on. Everything I could want is free."

She paused, looking out of the door to what was once Megan's room… now her room, down the hall to what was the guest room… now Megan's room.

"Well, see, that's the thing. There might be even more money coming. She has to sell the place. I guess most of her money is wrapped up in the house. As soon as she sells there is money here… lots of money. Hmmm? Maybe four million! No, I'm not kidding. She loves me. Yes. Never. I do too much around here. Someone has to be here and I am the one. No. No one else. Just me. Job security is not an issue. It never will be."

She looked outside the room again. Not a peep.

"No, of course I can't just grab a million bucks and run... but I can do some other things that might not be all that different from that. Well, that's what I'm thinking. If I can get her to be steady with her walker…exactly… if she can move even a little better she'll be able to travel fairly easily. Hard to say… she's getting better slowly… it is a miracle. I never dreamed in all my life I'd be here. Of course I'll take care of you. Not until after we move… right after the first of the year, but I can't get out of here without her or they would replace me. You only see a golden goose once in your life and I'm not going to kill it.

"That's the problem…she'll be here a lot more often pretty soon because the government is shutting down all their stores. Started with one in a bad part of town. Then somehow it became all four of them... Don't know. They're screwing the girl but there's nothing I can do about it. I'd like to go shoot the people in the City. They have no idea how they've screwed up my original plan.

"I think I heard her call. Yeah I gotta go. No, there's nothing I can do about Ashley except get Megan away from her. Once you are traveling then it's a new world with new possibilities. That's coming soon, Ashley be damned."

She turned off the phone. She was surprised her heart wasn't pounding harder. When you have $100,000 in the bank you just don't worry much about anything.

With her plan, she would soon be a millionaire. She had all the time in the world.

"Megan, did you call?"

"Hi, Mary. The remote won't work for the TV."

Mary looked down at the remote and saw that there was a crumb blocking the sensor. Flicking it off with her finger, she almost told Megan how stupid she was, then thought better of it.

"See if that works." She handed it back to Megan who tested it.

"Thank you."

"Listen Megan, do you want me to get anything special for Halloween tomorrow?"

Megan had been thinking about this since discussing it with Ashley the day before.

"Get me a mask and a costume. I want to hand out candy at the door."

"You want to look like someone from *Twilight*, *True Blood* or Kim Kardashian?"

"I'll never look like Kim Kardashian again."

"Megan, that's ridiculous. You get better looking every day. You know, I think you guys are the same age or close. Maybe you're a few years older. One thing is for sure, you both have the same type of body."

"When I can walk I'm going to get this body back in shape."

"You will, honey. You will. Hey, have you figured out how the door is going to work?"

"If the weather is nice I can sit in the wheelchair most of the time and stand up the rest of the time, if you help me."

"Of course I will, dear. Should we get you to the bathroom before I head out to do some last-minute shopping, then?"

"Yes. Thanks. Mary, you are so wonderful."

Chapter Fourteen

Halloween

Day 2232

Mary had the gardener hard at work on what would be his last day for the Dresdens, after eight years. Megan never told her about the gardener. She never told anyone. He was good-looking then and good-looking today. What she didn't know was what he thought about her. Was he repulsed by looking at her? She didn't know because he rarely made eye contact with her.

He put carved pumpkins along the long walk leading to the Dresden house. Leaves were everywhere on the ground as the trees had all long since peaked. The afternoon was spent making the place look spooky, which was really not that easy to do because of the estate's gracious beauty. He did a good job, though. He always did.

This year the theme was very vampire. All kinds of special props and decorations.

Mary had set up a fountain of candy and gifts to hand out to the youngsters who would be coming by within the hour. Megan would have no trouble reaching the fountain, whether standing or sitting in her wheelchair.

Megan was both excited and nervous about the evening.

Part of her didn't want to wear either of the masks that Mary had bought her. She had considered the vampire teeth and cloak, or being one of the Fantastic Four, but she didn't know which character. In the end she decided to see how the kids would react to her real face, and she decided to dress and look just as she did every day.

The day before Halloween was really the first time she'd left her home and gone out in public in six years, except for her many trips to the various hospitals she had to visit. She had gone to The Galleria where there happened to be no children. It was a mall designed for people with money to burn, and on an afternoon weekday that was a demographic made up mostly of wealthy women.

Megan was no longer dramatically facially disfigured. She had regained some motion in the right side of her face. Surgery had straightened out her features for the most part and though it was obvious she wasn't without accident, she was not an image from a horror movie by any means. More stigmatizing was the wheelchair. Having people look at you, and look down on you, as you were pushed around by someone your own age was humiliating. You could try and keep a stiff upper lip, but it was a very uncomfortable experience at best.

Instead of dressing in costume, Megan found the most normal-looking of all her clothes. The vast majority of her wardrobe was made up of wild Parisian outfits, specially designed fashions from New York's finest shops, and gifts from people who were equally audacious as Megan, sent to her from various parts of the world.

Essentially, everything in her closet was unique.

Megan hadn't been in her room in months, and now she stood in the closet with her walker for a couple of hours As she stood looking at dresses, finding outfit after outfit that was right or wrong by whatever criteria she was using, she moved her walker just an inch at a time. She browsed the various racks of clothing that reminded Mary of a dry cleaner's. Hundreds and hundreds of outfits. No two the same. Not even close to the same. A rainbow of primary and secondary colors with only a rare outfit that was black or brown.

That's what she would choose for today. A black pantsuit made sense for Halloween. A standard American boring black pantsuit, and a white blouse with a conservative scarf.

Megan pulled a little walkie-talkie out of her pocket and brought it up to her mouth.

"Mary."

"Yes, Megan," The voice came over loud and clear.

"Would you come up and help me with my clothes?"

"Of course, dear. I'll be there in a moment."

And within seconds Mary was in the bedroom closet with Megan.

"What have you decided, Megan?"

She pointed to the outfit and Mary nodded with approval, although she was shocked, too. This was the last outfit she would have expected Megan to have picked.

"Looks beautiful. Very conservative and the color is right for Halloween. OK, I'll get the chair and we'll get you over to my bed and get you changed."

Megan hated needing help with changing, but after six years it was almost second nature. Soon she would be able to dress herself. She could already get in and out of pants and loose fitting shirts. Everything else required more flexibility than she had.

Mary had a four-foot-square space for Megan to stand while she handed out the various treats to the trick-or-treaters. Mary didn't know how long Megan would be able to stand after having been on her feet for almost two hours in the closet, but she knew that this was working out well – particularly if she was going to be able to implement her plan anytime in the near future.

Most trick-or-treaters waited for you to bring the candy to them. Megan left the door open and each of the kids came in to her. It was about 40 degrees and Mary had raised the heat in the house to compensate for the chilly air coming inside. There was simply no way that Megan could open and close the door, and the kids were coming in droves. Kids were smart. Trick or treat in this area and you could hit the jackpot. The drawback was that the homes were very far apart. Nevertheless, the kids played the candy lottery here.

There were lots of cheery "Trick or treat!" demands from the kids. No one seemed scared. No one seemed to care how Megan looked. None of the kids made any uncomfortable comments. She was just a thirty-something-year-old woman dressed up in a business suit handing out candy, and of course, that was what was truly important to the kids. She was ordinary to them, it seemed, and for the first time in her life, Megan loved the idea of being ordinary.

About an hour and a half into giving away the goods she needed to sit down. She dreaded sitting in the wheelchair, but did so with Mary's assistance. The kids did stop and look and some were even uncomfortable when they saw Megan in the wheelchair, but that didn't make her feel as bad as she would've felt if they'd reacted to her face. Megan guessed that the chair was what made her the object of pity.

The last trick-or-treater that Megan would serve left at about nine o'clock. Tomorrow was school and the kids would be on their way home, their bags stuffed with treasure.

Mary closed the door and wheeled Megan to the kitchen so she could get herself something out of the refrigerator. Mary intentionally made herself scarce so Megan could get the feeling of being "independent." Both of them knew that was a ruse but it was important for Megan to at least experience doing some things on her own. And she could get herself a bottled water. Opening it was something else altogether. Sometimes she could and other times she needed help.

For Megan, the night had been a success. She was improving all the time and she felt for the first time that it wouldn't be long before life began to normalize and be more ordinary.

That's what she thought. She couldn't have been more wrong.

Chapter Fifteen

May 28

Day 2441

Three-bedroom, two-bathroom condo. Hardly a home. It was a condo and Megan disliked multifamily dwellings. Everything about the condo was "nice." It was all "very nice." It was the kind of place she'd like to go visit someone, and then at the end of an evening go home.

Megan didn't like being in her new "home," at 4190. It was certainly pretty for a condo, but it wasn't home. After four weeks of living there, she had regressed into depression. She thought about her life: David, her home, her cars, her face, her body. Everything she once knew was gone or changed.

Moving had been a terrible idea. But Mary had supported Ashley and Ashley was appreciative that Mary had been so helpful in every aspect of the big move.

Mary had asked Megan if she wanted to watch a movie. She did. Tonight Megan picked the Alfred Hitchcock psycho-thriller, *Marnie*.

Ashley had gone home two hours earlier.

It didn't matter whether you were thirty or sixty. *Marnie* was one scary movie.

They had popcorn and wine. Another of Megan's idiosyncrasies. They dimmed the lights and allowed themselves to be absorbed into the movie.

Tap Tap Tap

Marnie, played by Tippi Hedren portraying a troubled young woman, walks toward the train station. Her heels click off each step. She has just robbed her employer of $9,000 in cash. Straight from the safe. The detectives learn that she was a beautiful woman who had been given a job for that very reason. Hitchcock wasn't politically correct; it was a concept that didn't exist in those days, anyway.

Marnie goes home to her mother's house, and at the sight of some red flowers, her psychological state changes from cold and calculating to bitter, anxious and tense.

The color red is a psychological trigger for Marnie. So is seeing and hearing a thunderstorm. Eventually the reactions that Hitchcock wrote for Marnie would be known in the psychological community as post-traumatic disorder, something similar to panic disorder.

No such designations existed in the early 1960s, but the problems themselves did.

Marnie had sent her mother money so she wouldn't have to babysit the next door neighbor's six-year-old girl any more. Marnie doesn't like the little girl, at all.

Marnie's mother brushes the girl's hair.

"I never had time to take care of Marnie's hair when she was a kid," Mommy Dearest tells the little girl, as Marnie watches with jealous eyes.

Megan had watched this particular film numerous times in the last six years. Thank God for DVD players and TiVo. It was one of her favorite movies. In six years there were a lot of movies that have become favorites. Hitchcock was such a master – all of those viewings, and she was still engrossed tonight.

Tap Tap Tap

The blinds tap against the window.

Marnie is asleep in bed. Having been slapped by her mother, she was told to go to her room and she obeyed. It was as if her mother was disciplining a little girl, age six.

Marnie is having a nightmare.

"Marnie, Marnie, Marnie – wake up!" Mother tells her to get up. It's time for supper.

Tap Tap Tap

Mother's shoes clicking down the stairs.

"I'm having the same old dream, whenever there is tapping," she tells her mother.

Sean Connery plays Marnie's boss, future husband and lay psychologist, and gives Marnie comfort when a thunderstorm hits. Comfort and a kiss.

Tap Tap Tap

Marnie cries in her sleep as Sean Connery knocks on the door before entering her room. She's dreaming about her Mother wanting Marnie to get up and get out of a room. Marnie doesn't want to go because she's afraid of what's going to happen to her mother in the room, but she can't remember what that might be.

Near the end of the movie Connery prods Marnie to relive the memory of what happened that caused her panic, her post-traumatic stress – and she does.

Later, Marnie's mother tells Connery and Marnie that it was a sign from God when Marnie lost her memory and couldn't remember what happened that night when Marnie was just five years old.

A sign from God.

No one could have guessed the impact of the movie on Megan.

Chapter Sixteen

May 29

Day 2442

"...and she hates the new place." Ashley complained to her friend Freddie over a glass of red wine. "She looks around and sneers at the walls, the floors, the ceilings. It's like she wants to fly out of bed, just bolt. And the place is beautiful."

"It's not home, and there's no 'feeling' of David there. That's what my friend is missing."

"That, and sex."

"She speaks of this often?"

"All the time. It's not a one-track mind like you men have, but it is definitely a very deep and profound track. I really never gave her sex life any thought until the last few years. She's become obsessed with hiring a gigolo."

"Really? I wouldn't have guessed that of Megan. But it's more than understandable."

Freddie looked at Ashley with both compassion and irritation. The lighting in one of the Twin Cities' finest restaurants, Ciao Bella, was always low, always romantic, even for two longtime friends. A soothing setting, for someone who definitely needed soothing.

"Ashley, I want to change the subject if I may. It's been seven years. That's a big piece of your life. Your family misses you. Your friends miss you – "

"Freddie, no. I don't care if it takes twenty years, I'm going to get her back to normal. It's not as if my family doesn't see me. I get home by eight or nine most nights. And Robert is OK with it all, really."

Freddie smiled. He had heard this many times before. Lauren was now a teenager and at the age when fathers didn't want their daughters to date. But they already had.

Since Megan was a little girl, she was a night owl. She would go to bed at one or two in the morning, and often it was three or four. She was back on her old schedule now. Ashley would stay at Megan's as late as she could every night, but eventually she'd have to get home to her family. It tore her up inside, every day, and that was her baseline for what seemed like… forever.

Ashley had so many things to be grateful to David and Megan for. David and Megan had given Ashley and Robert a celebrity-worthy wedding in their home. David had hired Ashley when she needed a deserved break in life and she could never thank him enough for the faith and trust he placed in her, and for the responsibility. David had all but entrusted his businesses to Ashley and indeed put her in charge of executing his will upon his death.

For Ashley to let Megan fly into the wind now would simply not be possible. Ashley knew that Megan's progress was largely dependent on Ashley's attention and commitment to getting her well. Ashley felt more than an obligation to nurse Megan back to some semblance of good health. Nothing better could have come of the tragedy that Megan had suffered than to have Ashley in the driver's seat from that moment forward.

"Ashley, you told me that emotionally and mentally, she's getting worse! Yes, she's very slowly improving physically. It is a miracle and so on and so forth, but my God, Ashley, what about Robert? What about Lauren? Don't they need a miracle too? Don't they at least need more of you?"

Born and raised in northern Italy, Freddie didn't move to the States until he was fifteen. He still sported a thick Italian accent, which was one of the things Ashley adored about him. It was so sexy. He was young and good-looking, single and… disabled. Freddie only had one arm, the result of a car accident. The left sleeve of his suit coat was professionally tailored to solicit as little distraction as possible. His right hand and arm were fine. Having been through a horrific accident himself, he knew what hell was like.

Megan and Ashley had both helped him ten years ago after the accident. He and Megan had met in college, and they were very close. Ashley and Freddie had come into each other's lives through his friendship with Megan.

His rehab time was laborious but eventually he was able to obtain his law degree, and he became one of Minneapolis's more successful young attorneys.

Freddie knew that there was nothing he could say to get Ashley to cut back her hours from taking care of the business, Megan, and everything else in the world except herself. He could, however, put his dear friend to the task. He had been the best man at Ashley's wedding in Megan's house, what seemed a lifetime ago. His best friends on the planet were Ashley and Megan. And today it was his duty to encourage Ashley to invest in her family as she had Megan.

Ashley's defiance retreated as she took a more conciliatory tack with Freddie.

"Freddie, sometimes she's fine and focused on therapy, and other times she's distant and I feel like she's not even in the same room. She might mumble to herself one minute and be sharp as a tack the next second. She makes progress physically, fights for it with all of her will, and then it's like she checks out for a few minutes, and then comes back."

"Like how?"

"Yesterday, I gave Mary a day off and I took Megan in to Dr. Parduhn for a simple checkup – if there ever is a simple checkup with Megan. We're in the waiting room and she asks why we're there."

"So?"

"We had already discussed it twice on the way over."

"Ashley, that doesn't mean anything. You and I both forget things all the time."

"She didn't know after I had told her twice in the car, Freddie. We had the same conversation twice. It's like her brain is constantly being knocked offline."

"The stress could be getting to her. Have you taken her to talk with a psych? God knows it would be perfectly reasonable and expected for her to develop some kind of mental or emotional problems after everything she's been through."

"She doesn't like seeing anyone with that in their job description. For seven years she has totally argued against seeing any psychiatrists or psychologists. In her mind, she was in a car accident and she is fine. She'll tell you that nothing works except her mind. Well. That used to be the story, and now she *is* getting mobility. You saw that at the holidays."

"Huh!"

"*Huh!* is right, Freddie. If I leave her to Mary only, she'll be OK, but she'll just barely be OK. Mary isn't always playing with a full deck either, you know. Or maybe she's playing with a trick deck. Maybe both. I can't put my finger on it."

"Home help. Well…"

"Sure, she's not the most skilled person to walk the planet. But it's not that. She's different. She's like a woman with a mission, and I can never figure her out. Sometimes I wish I hadn't hired her. Megan has grown very close to her. I get into arguments with them about what Megan can do and where she can go."

"What do they propose?"

"They want to go on a trip, to Las Vegas or Europe or something."

"Those are two pretty different options. But why not? Megan can be in a wheelchair. It's humbling, but I survived a couple of flights over the years doing that. I still do."

"I know, but I don't entirely trust Mary. She'll leave Megan and go off playing and spending her money, or something."

"That's crazy. Why do you think so?"

"It's a feeling."

"Women's intuition?"

"Freddie!" Ashley acted offended, but their friendship was too strong to give or take offense.

"I mean, what is the evidence that she's going to take Megan to Vegas, dump her in front of the Bellagio and take off to go see a show? Let's see, Megan watches the waters dance to Sinatra all night while Mary, a middle aged woman, parties all night? Come on."

He paused, letting the picture sink in. Problem was, Ashley *could* envision that picture. That's what made her nervous.

"Wouldn't that just make Megan upset with her? Surely you can't think that Mary would do anything that would jeopardize her job. Look what you're paying her. It's ridiculous. You pay her double what anyone else makes doing the same thing."

"I know. I know. Logically, yes. But Mary is too cunning."

"How do you know she's is cunning? What has she done?" The attorney in Freddie had come out to play devil's advocate again.

They both sipped on their emptying wine glasses. Ashley looked at her watch.

"You've been here eleven minutes. Would you please breathe, for God's sake."

"I'm fine, Freddie. She *is* cunning. She's up to something. I don't know what it is but I can feel it."

"OK, you can feel it. That'll stand up in court. 'Your Honor, she *felt* it.'"

"Shut up, Freddie."

"Well, come on, Ashley. What could she possibly be doing?"

"Planning to steal Megan's money."

"You have all the bank accounts sealed up like Fort Knox."

"But not the credit cards."

"How much is there?"

"A lot. Maybe a couple hundred thousand in credit lines between them all."

"Huh. But nevertheless, Ashley, the fact is that you'd get the online statements if anything weird happened. You pay all the bills."

"But they could be out of the country before I ever got a statement."

"Online you see all pending charges the day of the transaction. But that's not the point. What is so wrong with a trip, even overseas? Megan could use getting back to paradise in Mexico or Vegas if she wanted. What's so wrong with that?"

"She – "

Freddie hit hard. "She would be vulnerable and out of your control."

Ashley blinked a tear back. She looked down at the bread on her plate.

"I can't let anything else happen to her."

"But as crazy and impossible as traveling is for someone so disabled," and he looked at the absence of his own arm and leg, "disabled people deserve to travel, too."

"She's different than you, Freddie. She's a mess. She has no real strength. You have two good legs. She has neither."

"She seems to be much better."

"Yes. She's a miracle, but it would take her an hour to get from a hotel bed to a bathroom without a wheelchair."

"And with a wheelchair?"

"Fifteen minutes. But she'd never use it. She is going to walk. I can't get her in a wheelchair unless we go shopping and that's rare."

Freddie stroked his chin. "So let me see if I have this straight. Megan is getting forgetful, and she has bouts of temper after having been virtually immobilized for seven years. Mary is cooking up some dastardly plot to steal Megan's credit card money, or at least use it on a trip, where Mary would leave Megan vulnerable to the elements or whatever."

"You can be a jerk."

"I think you need to just sit back and let go. I mean, say it was all on target. Say Mary was plotting to take over Megan's estate. *You* are the final answer to everything Megan owns. Nothing gets spent or paid without your OK. No changes to the estate, the trust, nothing. It *all* comes back to you. If Mary has some kind of a plan, she is going to have to sell you, and I don't see that happening."

The sigh was like a balloon letting all of its air out. Ashley had been whipped in thirteen minutes. She never lost, but that's why she loved Freddie. Freddie would see every angle about something she didn't.

"What if she tried to hurt Megan?"

"Ashley, if you're that concerned, fire her and hire someone else. You're going to drive yourself nuts."

"Megan would never go for it. She loves Mary. Mary this, Mary that. Mary does everything!"

"And she does do a lot, yes?"

"Yes."

"And so far, we have what appears to be a close friendship between Megan and Mary and a rivalry between you and Mary. And you still hold all the cards. Ashley, Mary isn't in the will. There is nothing for her if anything bad happens to Megan. You might be right, but whatever is hitting your intuition buttons hasn't got it all figured out yet."

The waitress was dressed like a waiter. Formal restaurants. She put the halibut and asparagus in front of Freddie, and the salmon in front of Ashley.

"Can I get you two anything else?"

Freddie looked up, pasted a smile on his face as the waitress moved her eyes from his absent arm to his face.

"No, thank you. Everything is wonderful."

"Let me know if I can bring you anything else." She put her smile on and walked away.

Freddie was intent on getting Ashley to see that her seven years of work were well spent.

"Ashley, *you* have given Megan *life*. No one else. *Your* will. *Your* fortitude. *Your* desire. *Your* determination. Whether it's today or in ten more years from now, you are going to have to let go one day. And you know what? Megan will hurt. She will be sad. She will have bad days. She will be the victim of life again, as we all are at times."

Ashley opened her mouth to speak. Freddie lifted his index finger from the wine glass. It was one of the few gestures that could silence her.

"Megan is weak but she is as strong as she is, because of you. If David is up there looking down you can know that he is proud of you. And Robert, through his frustration, is proud of you as well. Think about adding someone to 4190, to help Mary help Megan and give you some rest. It has been seven years. You need a day off. Mary needs time off too. Now then, that's settled. Eat."

They did.

"Someone part-time is going to cost a chunk of money."

"Ashley, come on, Megan is not impoverished."

"No but two million bucks doesn't get you what it used to. There is no more that's going to come in. I've got to make that money last fifty years. That's a long time. Another accident or taking steps backward in therapy, or anything that costs a couple of million would wipe her out."

"Money is the least of her problems. I love my dear friend, more than you know. But today is about *your* family. It's about *you*. Are *you* happy? Are *you* getting anything from life? Are you living your dreams?"

"Freddie, look, I promise I will spend more time with Robert and Lauren. I'll put an ad in the paper and hire someone to come in a few hours a day to help out at 4190."

"Excellent. Ashley, I wish I could help more."

"Freddie, don't even go there."

Freddie thought it was amazing how good Ashley looked for someone who'd gone through the stress and trauma she'd experienced these last seven years. She had added a few pounds but nothing that took away from her girl-next-door look. Robert was a fortunate man indeed.

Freddie wished he could help Megan more. But he could do nothing other than be her friend and attorney. And that had been mighty important. But he was still nagged by the feeling of humiliation that comes with being disabled. They could say "physically challenged" or whatever euphemism they wanted, but it only made "them" feel better. He was handicapped. He didn't consider himself disabled… and he was clear there was a big difference between the two.

"You will put the ad in the paper tomorrow, yes?"

"Yes. And Freddie?"
"Hmm?"
"Thanks, Freddie."

Chapter Seventeen

May 29 – Late

Day 2442

The woman moaned with what might have been pleasure. Or if it wasn't pleasure, she faked it well. The bed moved so much it made the walls seem to vibrate.

He was an older man, more than six feet tall. In his mid-fifties, and probably wealthy. Wavy brown hair, clean-shaven, with the looks of someone who was successful… and stressed. He looked like a typical businessman.

She was in her late twenties. Long blonde hair with piercing blue eyes, when they were open. They weren't right now. She moaned and seemed like she was in another world.

She gyrated and groaned almost as if to a script, while a compressor-like sound mixed with hissing, and the chirps of crickets almost covered her screams. It was like having sex at a construction site… except the bedroom was lavish.

Her name could have been Kylie. She was a pro. Five hundred dollars for a hand job, a thousand for oral, fifteen hundred for penetration. For Minneapolis, those were good numbers, and her "manager" was the man who sat watching television in the living room. He would give her half at the end of the night. It was the only way he could afford to live in this beautiful condo. Otherwise at sixty he would have retired to a small apartment.

His wife of multiple decades was in the other bedroom sleeping away, oblivious to what was happening. She simply didn't care.

Meanwhile, the woman decided she was going to get him to finish. She didn't particularly like this one. Sometimes you like them and sometimes you don't. An annoyance in a profession that had its definite ups and downs.

It was time.

She opened her eyes and looked at him. His eyes had been riveted to her chest. Now they locked with hers. She pulled his head down against her chest, cupped both of her arms around his head and squeezed tight.

There was one more thrust and he was finished, just like that. Had she not had a martini with him, it would have been seven minutes flat. She was nice to him. She let him think he was a stud. He'd be back. And a neat $750 for putting up with that. Could do worse.

Every now and then the guy was good or attractive and she actually got into it. Not tonight, though, or most nights.

He had paid her manager on the way in, so there was no need for him to pay on the way out. He went into the bathroom, straightened himself up, combed his hair and asked her if she was available next Friday night.

She said he should check her schedule with her manager. He said he would.

He slapped her on the leg, she smiled for him, and he walked out of the room, saying goodnight to the man waiting outside the door.

He just nodded.

She hopped out of bed. She would have another customer in less than an hour. She liked the next one. Good guy. Attractive, and money to burn. He was a tipper... a doubler, actually, which was particularly rare and particularly appreciated. And, like a magician, she would make his fifteen hundred double in value. It would end up being a profitable night and only two customers.

She hopped in the shower and cleaned up.

Minutes later she strode out of the bedroom and told her manager to turn the compressor up. It was hidden away in a utility room behind the bedroom, where no one would ever see it. She didn't know if the next customer would want the full treatment or not, but she wanted to have the massive vibrator powered up and ready.

He got up, moved to the utility room, and hit some switches to kick the compressor as high as it would go. He came out, and smiled as he looked at her naked body, which was less than half-covered by a skimpy white towel.

She smiled at him and blew him a kiss.

She returned to the bedroom and found some clothes.

She took the old sheets off the bed and got out some new ones. Each man was special, of course, so each got special treatment. They were special not to her, but to themselves. This was part of customer service.

The bedroom was as big as a hotel suite. Coffee table, desk, beautiful bathroom, colorful drapes, contemporary art and accents. You disappeared into her world.

No one would ever know. They were on the top floor and owned this condo as well as the one next door. It was unlikely that the people on the other side of the hall would ever hear anything. The woman who lived directly below was apparently some kind of an invalid. Plus which, she used hearing aids, and no one wore hearing aids to bed.

It was the perfect set-up.

They had four girls and two other bedrooms. His wife didn't care. She wasn't an active participant. Everything happened after she went to bed at about ten, and business was concluded by four in the morning.

He had finally found the perfect place to run his "upscale" business.

***

Megan awoke to the sound of the compressor and the feeling of the bed upstairs shaking the wall. She had the vague remembrance of an elaborate dream. She was nearly jiggled out of her own bed. It sounded like the air compressors that are used to fill tires at the gas station, except much louder. The sound had both qualities of the high-powered air hose: the sound of the motor rattling and the high-pitched sound of the air being injected into the tire.

She lay there and listened for another hour, and then it stopped. She looked at the clock. It was three a.m. She'd been told that no one had moved in upstairs yet.

Why would they lie about that?

After the noise stopped she called for Mary. Mary was on the other side of the condo in her own room.

Mary heard her and looked at the clock: three a.m. What in God's name did Megan want at this hour of the night? She usually didn't have to go to the bathroom 'til morning.

"What's up, honey?"

"Did you hear that racket upstairs?"

"What racket, Megan? There's no one there. Yesterday the manager said that the Harris family won't be moving in for a few more days.."

"Well they're there now!! They were having sex up there. Twice. About an hour apart. And there was the sound of this really loud compressor. It nearly shook me out of my bed."

"You were having a dream, Megan. Listen, it's quiet."

"No, I'm telling you it was loud. *Really* loud."

Mary sighed. "OK Megan, we'll take care of it in the morning. Can I get you anything?"

"No, but if you hear anything though, would you go up and tell them to keep it quiet?"

"Of course, honey."

She turned around and flipped the light switch off. "Good night Megan."

"Good night, Mary… thanks."

"No problem."

Crazy girl. What is she thinking? Oh, well. Whatever. I'm going back to sleep.

Megan slept the rest of the night and woke up around nine, to the sound of hammering and sawing.

What is this condo going to be like? What has Ashley gotten me into here?

Mary walked into Megan's room. "Oh, good. You were able to sleep through the racket. I'm glad. They woke me up at seven when they started. The new tenants will probably move in over the weekend."

"They're already up there, Mary. They were having sex last night and they had a bunch of weird mechanical things going, like a compressor."

"I didn't hear anything like that, but they sure did get to me at the crack of dawn. Come on, let's get you up and on your way to the bathroom."

Megan slowly edged her way to the side of the bed. She wanted to do this herself. And she did. It would take twenty minutes to get from there to the bathroom and twenty minutes to get back. These were mind-numbing minutes for Mary, who seemed to be able to tolerate anything. She always reminded herself that she was getting paid a lot of money to make sure Megan could get balanced in front of her walker, and safely escorted to the bathroom. The only bad part was the nursing-home-like work that would typically take place in the bathroom. She had never quite gotten used to taking care of adults who had no ability to take care of themselves, when it came to the bathroom.

Today was going to be a difficult day. It was getting *very* loud overhead.

"My God, have they got to be that loud?" Mary was noticeably upset.

"All day, all night. Maybe they'll stop soon." Megan wasn't optimistic. "I want to call Ashley when we're all done."

"OK, Megan." Mary looked at her watch. That would be in well over an hour from now. One thing was for sure, there was an awful lot of racket going on up there for an expensive place like this.

What are they doing?

Chapter Eighteen

May 30

Day 2443

Ashley got there at around one. *It's not the house, but it is pretty. She'll get used to it. I hope.* She used the remote to lock the car and turned to head into the condo. There were two construction vans parked across the street. One plumbing, one electric.

People are moving in Sunday and they're just getting to this now? What idiot planned that?

She shrugged it off. She learned long ago that she was of a rare breed of good planner and good doer. She figured out the problem, came up with a solution and typically executed it flawlessly. That was Ashley, in a nutshell.

"Hello?" It was *noisy.*

"We're in here," Mary yelled from the other side of the condo.

Megan was sitting up in bed having lunch. She was slow but the food was getting on the fork and being transferred to her mouth, however slowly. It was happening. It made Ashley feel good.

"Hi, guys. Hey, guess who I had dinner with yesterday?"

"Who?" They both chimed in, Mary a little quicker.

"Freddie."

Mary couldn't have cared less.

"How is he, Ashley?" Megan was sincerely interested. They were best of friends even if they hadn't seen much of each other the last few months.

"He's great. He's a junior partner in the law firm now, and he's making a pile of money. He looked so adorable in this suit he had on. He says to say hello and he wants to hear from you soon!"

"Oh, we have to call him today. Can we do that, Mary? I really want to say hello to him."

"Of course we can. Ashley, do you have his number?"

"How long did you say this racket has been going on?"

"Since last night when I went to bed. They were having sex up there and then this morning they're doing something else."

"Started at seven. Been driving me nuts ever since," Mary corrected Megan. Had anyone been making noise up there, she would have heard it. She hadn't slept well since moving in with Megan years ago. She couldn't. She needed to be aware of everything Megan might whisper or yell.

"I'll go up and see how long this is going to continue." Ashley dropped her stuff in her small office, really a third bedroom that she converted to her new in-condo office. She ran into one of the plumbing guys on the way out, carrying a bathroom fixture.

"You guys are making a lot of racket for my friend who lives here. How long before you're done?"

"We'll be out of here tomorrow. Don't work Sunday. I've got to replace the stool, hook up a different shower for these guys, and then my work is done. Probably dinnertime tomorrow if I take my time."

"Then you're done for good?"

"Done for good."

"What about the electrical truck?"

"Don't know what they're doing, but I know they'll be out of here tonight. They don't work weekends at all. Hey – "

"Yeah?"

"This fixture is getting heavy."

Ashley had been oblivious. "Sorry." She opened the door for him and he went in.

Returning to Megan's condo, she felt relieved. *Today and tomorrow and it will be over.*

***

You could tell when it was five o'clock. As she peered through the window, Ashley watched the electrician put the keys in the van's ignition, and the plumbers were closing the door to the back of their van too.

Whatever the electrician had worked on almost certainly was completed. Tomorrow the plumber would be back. Well, the worst was almost certainly over. Blessed silence.

Megan was using her walker to make her way out of the bedroom, with Mary standing next to her. Apparently Megan was going to come all the way to the dining room with no assistance other than from Mary spotting her.

Ashley looked at them as she headed back to her office.

"You'll sleep better tonight, honey. They're gone, and not a minute too soon."

"They are so loud upstairs," Megan said in her strongest voice.

"I know, but it's over for the day. Then just the plumber tomorrow."

"They're still making all that racket upstairs."

"I just saw them leave. You have to remember it takes you time to move from room to room. That electrician is on his way to where ever service people have beers and brats on Memorial Day Weekend. But the plumbers will probably wake you up again in the morning."

"Why do they have to be so loud?"

Ashley ducked into her cramped spare-bedroom office, choosing to let Mary deal with this one. Ashley had been working on trying to acquire some real estate for Megan. The stock market had gone south and though she didn't expose a substantial part of Megan's money to the markets, what was there had been cut down in the last couple of years. She knew that it was the markets and not her, but she still felt responsible for the loss. She'd done such a great job in the past, or at least the market went up like a rocket ship. Now? Sputter, plunk, ugh. Terrible.

She had looked at some commercial properties in and around the Twin Cities in the last year. She wasn't going to jump instantly on any of the proposals she had been offered. She would either get a decent property, or no property. It took more time than she ever dreamed to do the legwork. But she was learning and it would happen very soon.

If I can take a million and put it in real estate, that is where people are going to be making money with the markets going like this. Buy today for a million, sell in five years for two million? Maybe one point five? Maybe I'm dreaming? Well, we need to get a property or two first, then we'll see. Strip center would be nice but most of them are kind of dumpy and rundown. If Megan's going to own something, it's got to be beautiful, even if it is small.

God, I wish she were happier with this place. It's a nice place, for goodness sake. Who wouldn't love it? Rent's ten percent of what the monthly payment was on Lake Calhoun. Ten percent. Someday Megan will have money to travel and entertain again, whether it's with Miss Snippy or someone else. But she'll have it.

There was a huge thud upstairs. Ashley almost jumped from her chair. She raced out into the hall. Megan was there looking up, and Mary was equally as curious.

It was quiet again and as Megan's eyes came back to Ashley's, she said, "I told you. They're making more noise than they were all day!"

Ashley thought it strange but not unheard of. One of the men probably left something heavy on top of a sink and it simply fell. Of course things don't just drop. But, of course there had to be a logical explanation, She didn't need to know what it was, herself, and she didn't have time for banging on doors of vacant condos.

Back to work.

"You'd think she'd have the courtesy to go check it out, don't you think, Megan?" Mary prodded her.

"I wish she would. It's so noisy. They never turned off the compressor either."

Mary had no idea what Megan was talking about. She had made her point that Ashley didn't care, and that was all Mary cared about.

As time had passed, over the years Mary had developed a very close relationship with Megan. She knew that as long as she took care of Megan, Megan would always take care of her. She had said as much numerous times. Taking care of Megan was a pain but Mary believed Megan was worth a few million and eventually some of it would be Mary's. It would all be worth it, and she had time. She was middle-aged and had had nothing for her entire life until she met Megan. Now she had bank accounts stashed away, with real money in them.

It took no money to live with Megan and she got paid well. Megan paid all of her expenses, so she was getting rich! She saved almost all of it. She didn't know how much she had, but it had to be at least $150,000. It seemed like a dream come true, but she knew that wouldn't support her for long in real life. Five years? She figured she'd live 'til she was ninety. She wanted a million. She was going to get it, and maybe get it all.

Chapter Nineteen

Monday Morning

Daybreak arrived with the sounds of people calling for their favorite deity, and the loud sound of a compressor.

Megan had a quivery feeling throughout her body that wouldn't go away.

She looked up at the ceiling and called, "Mary, when are they going to stop that?"

"Stop what, honey?" Mary came to see what was up.

"All that sex up there. It's a prostitution ring. I know it. They're having sex all day and night."

Mary looked up and heard nothing. She had no idea what to say, but one thing she had learned was that there was no reason to argue with the woman who was making her rich. So what if Megan was hearing things. Or maybe there was something going on there, but they were taking a break or something.

"Would you like me to check on it?"

"Oh, would you? They are driving me crazy. If you could just knock on the door and ask them to stop."

"OK, Megan, I'll do that right now."

Mary left, wondering what would happen when she knocked on the door upstairs. "Hi, I'm here to stop your prostitution ring because my patient Megan is being driven nuts by the sound of your having sex all day up here."

She opened the door to the hallway and found the steps, which were closer than the elevator at the other end of the hall.

Sounds quiet to me.

She got to the front door of the condo above. There was some sawdust on the floor. Someone hadn't cleaned up all that well. She listened at the door for what seemed like an eternity. Nothing.

She put on her most intense face and knocked on the door. Silence. She rang the doorbell. She knocked again. She rang the doorbell again. She repeated this over and over for about five minutes, after which she was convinced that either no one was home or that no one was going to answer her. She reached out to turn the knob, not knowing what she would do if it opened.

It didn't open.

She turned and quickly went back down the stairway, into 4190 and back to Megan's room.

"Did you tell them to stop?"

"I went up there but there didn't seem to be anything strange going on. I knocked on the door and no one answered. I rang the doorbell and no answered. I'll go back later on, OK?"

"Thanks, Mary."

The racket stopped. Maybe those were the only two days they were going to have that kind of wild sex up there, Megan thought. She hoped so. Lack of sleep was starting to get to her. It was so hard to work on therapy when you were not awake and alert. Doing therapy while sleep-deprived was almost impossible.

Megan's biggest problem in walking, with or without the walker, was that she had little feeling in her legs. So she had to look at her legs, her knees, and her feet, and move her body with great intention and thought. It looked easy enough when watching someone else, but when you can't feel a thing, well…

Who would understand?

Many times she thought she had good footing, only to collapse. Without watching, it simply wasn't possible to be certain that your muscles were doing what they were supposed to be doing.

Today she would go to the physical therapist for four hours. She would walk almost 200 steps and it would take most of those four hours to do that.

Each step was taken methodically.

It began by being stable in the first place. Then she would "lift" her walker about an inch and move it forward, perhaps the length of a hand. This was when she would fall if she was going to fall.

Then she would move her left foot forward, generally scraping it across the floor those few inches to where it would rest, if she were fortunate. Then she would intentionally shift her body weight and move forward with her other foot, again, hoping it would rest safely behind her walker.

She would breathe, never taking her eyes off of her feet and her knees.

Then she would begin again.

She would do that for four hours today. Hunched over when standing, Megan's eyes wouldn't leave the floor for the five hours it took to walk painfully slowly from the car to the office, do her session and walk back. Unable to straighten up, she would never see her physical therapist after the session started, at least, she wouldn't see her face.

Megan had grown accustomed to the necessity of this brutal regime. It was either do it, or never walk again.

She had canes which she had sometimes successfully used for a few steps, but she well aware that she wasn't ready for the relative instability of canes.

Falling, tripping, collapsing… all were part of her daily life. If she wanted to walk she would crawl, fall, trip, collapse. She would continue to take steps that were shorter than her shoe for the next decade, if necessary.

She would never give up.

Unfortunately she now had to deal with these noisy neighbors, too. If they were just walking around, she wouldn't consider that a problem. But they weren't. They were having sex. She hadn't had sex for years. For – ever, it seemed.

More than most things, she missed sex. Everything about it. And it seemed not to be in the cards for her for a long, long, long time.

That was why these last couple of nights were so frustrating. These people were having fun, really living life. And she was crawling and falling, with no one to even talk to for most of the day.

She couldn't complain. She was lucky to be alive. They told her that all the time. Everyone still talked about how lucky she was. She rarely felt sorry for herself but the neighbors upstairs were rubbing her nose in the ground and it was hurting, badly.

After Megan returned from therapy, Ashley came into Megan's room. Megan was watching television. Ashley didn't care. She was gleeful.

"Megan!"

"Hi, Ashley," Her eyes turned away from the TV as she used the remote to lower the volume. "How are you?"

"Honey, you aren't going to believe this! I went up to Edina today and there is a wonderful strip center there that you just bought!"

"Really?"

"Yes! It is lovely. Let's see. It has two restaurants, one's Chinese and one's a steakhouse. There is a Pottery Barn, a Barnes and Noble, and there a few other stores too. We picked it up at a really good price because the owners are getting divorced and the wife wants a cash settlement."

"Oh, that is wonderful, Ashley. Will this mean we'll be able to move back to the other house?"

Ashley's elation was quickly punctured, but she continued to smile.

"No, honey, that is not going to happen. But this gives us the insurance on your future that we need. Would you like to go with me when I sign the paperwork on Friday?"

"Do you really want me there?"

Ashley knew Megan didn't want to be seen by anyone, ever. But this would be a big success, even if Megan didn't see the importance of it today. It *was* big. The mall had been successful for a decade, it was in as good shape as you could ask for, and it had steady tenants with great payment histories. Mostly corporate tenants and franchises. She had gotten a bargain. She knew it. *They* knew it.

"OK. I'll go."

"Oh good, we'll sign the papers at one of the restaurants then. That way you can see what you own. How was your day, Megan?"

"I didn't sleep well."

"Again? I'm sorry to hear that. I tell you what, I'll call a doctor and ask for a script of some Ambien or something."

"That would be good." She was simply down in the dumps and there was nothing that was going to lift her up.

"Honey, what's wrong?"

"I just couldn't sleep. There was too much racket going on last night."

Ashley looked puzzled.

"Are you OK now?"

"Just tired, that's all."

"OK, well, listen… where is Mary?"

"Didn't you see her when you came in?"

"No. You don't know where she is?"

"Maybe she's taking a shower or a nap."

That woman. I don't pay her to take midday showers or naps. What if Megan needs help? What if she fell and couldn't yell for help or get attention by hitting her canes softly against the wall. That Mary is so thoughtless. She may not be working here much longer.

"I'm going to track her down and have her put Friday on her calendar as well. Meanwhile, do you need anything?"

"That Ambien sounds good."

"All right. I'll get that for you right away."

She raced out of the room. She was pissed. *Where the hell was that woman? If Megan were laying dying… Damn it. Damn it.* Ashley stopped at the entrance of Mary's room.

There she is. Sleeping. Damn it.

"Mary! How is Megan supposed to get you to help her if you're sleeping in the middle of the day with the TV on full blast?"

"Huh?" Her eyes flickered open. "Megan needs something?"

"No. Yes. She needs a script for Ambien. She isn't getting enough sleep."

"How am I supposed to get her Ambien?"

"Forget it. I'll do it."

"So Megan doesn't need anything then?"

"She needs to be taken care of. Please, Mary. Please."

She hated to raise her voice above its already loud quality. But this was ridiculous. Megan was on the other side of the condo and had no way to get Mary's attention if she really needed it. This was just ridiculous.

"I'm going to get Megan some sleeping meds. I'll be back in an hour. *Please* go see how she's doing."

Mary's look would have frozen water in the desert. She had never liked Ashley. Nothing was wrong with Megan and there was no reason to be such a bitch. But that was Ashley, she thought to herself… that's Ashley.

Chapter Twenty

Monday Night

Mary opened the Ambien and shook one out of the container. She gave it to Megan and then gave her a small glass of water to swallow it down with.

"I sure hope you sleep better tonight, Megan."

"Me too. Maybe they won't be having sex up there tonight."

"I'm sure they won't." Mary had no idea why she said that. It was a knee-jerk response. She didn't imagine that anyone was having sex "up there." She wished she were having some – anywhere. She was almost sixty, but she wasn't almost dead.

"Would you like me to turn out the light for you? I know it's early. It's, what, just about midnight?"

"Yes, please turn it off. I really want to sleep."

Mary clicked the light and returned to her room, hit the remote and turned on the TV. Not a lot of new stuff on at midnight. She flicked it off and hit the light switch. She was going to sleep as well.

In minutes she was snoring away.

***

Megan looked at the clock. It was 12:06 and they had started again upstairs. She was screaming at him, or having an orgasm, or something. Whatever it was, she was definitely having sex. Maybe it would be over soon.

She lay there looking at the ceiling. She felt the walls shake. She felt her body shake. She felt dizzy and like she was falling.

"Oh my God… what's happening?"

She screamed but no one heard.

***

At about a quarter after five, Mary woke up.

She was groggy. The TV was still on. She hadn't turned it off? She didn't look for the remote. She walked to the TV and pushed the power button off.

Her head itched and she scratched it as she walked to Megan's room.

Might as well check on her.

She peeked in the door and saw Megan lying on the floor. She looked like she was dead.

What the hell?

She shook Megan. Her body was warm. Thank God.

Megan took a minute to wake up.

"Megan, Megan, are you OK? How did you get on the floor? Megan!"

Megan opened her eyes and saw Mary. There was relief in her eyes. "They shook me out of bed."

"Who did, honey?"

Mary helped Megan sit up. She would maneuver her back into bed as quickly as possible. Whatever happened, she didn't want Megan to think that she had dropped the ball, fallen asleep on the job… whatever.

"Mary, they were having sex and it was so loud that they started shaking the walls and then I got dizzy and they shook me out of bed. I think I hit my head."

Mary looked but saw no marks. "Can I turn a light on?"

"Sure."

She got up and flipped a switch. Megan squinted and looked at Mary. Mary ran her fingers through Megan's hair. No. There was no bruising or anything like it. She ran her hands over Megan's head looking for a bump. Nothing.

"I think you're going to be OK. How do you feel?"

"I am so tired. They kept me up until almost four o'clock, and then it went crazy."

"An hour ago? OK. Well it's quiet now."

Megan looked up and at the walls. Mary was right. Quiet. Mary pulled Megan up and set her up against the bed where Megan took over her own movement, and set her head back on the pillow.

"I'm so tired, Mary." She began weeping. There were no tears. Just loud weeping.

"It's time to get some sleep, dear. That Ambien didn't help?"

"It made me sleepy but they were too loud. Nothing could have made me sleep."

"You poor dear."

"Can you stay with me for a minute?"

"Of course. And I'm going to give you another Ambien. That'll help you fall asleep. We're not going anywhere in the morning."

Thankfully the sun wasn't up yet. Megan would never be able to get to sleep once it started getting light.

Mary picked up the cup from the night stand and went to fill it with water. She came back, opened the Ambien container and grabbed the second one of the night. She handed it to Megan. Megan placed it on her tongue, then sat up for the water. Sitting up wasn't half as hard as walking. From the waist up she could feel things – she had normal sensation.

"Will you tell Ashley to get them to stop it?"

"We'll go see her tomorrow after therapy. How's that sound?"

"Oh, good. That will help.

***

Ashley had a big 16 x 18 office in her home, but she wasn't as busy there as she had been in the past. She used to bring home work from Dresden's. Of course, the office was still tastefully decorated. Everything in its place. Everywhere you look it said "organization." She was neat, clean and organized.

She was concerned about Megan but assumed Mary had been exaggerating Megan's crying and fears.

Once they arrived in the driveway, Ashley knew it would be an hour before Megan actually made it to her office. Maybe more. Each step was tedious. Slow. Methodical. Honestly, it was painfully slow. Mary somehow survived the tedium. Every time Ashley asked Megan if Mary might want additional help and more time off, Megan balked. So did Mary. Ashley never understood why. It made no sense. Of course, being with Megan certainly wasn't a bad thing. Megan was great. But being with any human step by step, inch by inch, minute by minute, is far more than an act of love.

She shook her head at the thought and went back to her computer.

Buying the building was going to happen. She was excited about the prospects. She had told Megan it was already a done deal, but the fact was, it wasn't quite wrapped up yet.

Robert had felt some of the tension of recent years lessen when Ashley moved back to the house for most of her work hours. Ashley was there more for him, for Lauren, for the family in general. And for herself.

For so long Robert had played second fiddle to Megan. He loved Megan. Everyone did. And she was his best female friend to be sure. But for several years the strain of Ashley gone what seemed like 24/7 was more than he wanted to deal with. He was a great father, but he was a lousy mother. Most men were lousy mothers, he guessed. Lauren as a teenager really needed her mom and now, finally, she had that. The pressure at home had eased up a great deal.

When Megan moved to 4190, sanity took hold in the Drexel household. Robert was thankful that Megan had found a place she could be safe in, a place where she could continue her healing process. Somewhere that was nearby. A good move. Thank God.

The world was starting to become normal, for the first time in almost a decade.

Ashley looked up from her computer. Robert would be home in a couple of hours. Lauren would precede him, but only by minutes.

Megan inched into Ashley's office. It would still be fifteen minutes before Megan would be in a chair. Lift, replace the walker a few inches forward, step, steady, confirm stability, lift, replace. And Megan almost never looked up. Usually when she did, she fell. It was as predictable as night following day. When she walked, all concentration was on the ground, on her walker and her lower body.

"Hi, Megan."

"Hello, Ashley." Head focused down. "How are you doing, Ashley?"

"I'm good. Working on your new property. It's really something. If everything goes as I'm planning, you'll own it in a couple of months. We'll have an office in there long before that."

"What stores will be there?"

Ashley had been over this ground with her already. Perhaps Megan was forgetful or just making conversation. "Everything. Byerly's, Chinese Panda, Rocky's Sports Bar, Barnes and Noble, Pier One, Office Max, Pottery Barn. I mean, everything. About a dozen stores. All but one has been there for at least a few years. The last store is a greeting card store. Competes with Hallmark, I guess. Mom and Pop deal. Might make it. I doubt it."

"Why are they selling it to us?"

"Divorce sale. Honey, we already had this conversation, remember? They're splitting everything and need to sell it all to cut it up even-steven."

"That's too bad they have to get divorced. People shouldn't do that."

"I know, honey, but that's the way the world works."

Megan was now less than five feet from the chair she would occupy in Ashley's office.

"What's it going to mean to us once we own it?"

"We'll have a small positive cash flow every month even if the greeting card place goes under and that spot is vacant. You're looking at about 10K without the card place, maybe 13K with it."

"That's a big difference."

"It is. They aren't done yet, just fighting to survive."

"I hope they make it. It's so hard to be in business."

"We'll do everything we can to help them succeed, honey. You know that."

"I do."

"How was therapy today?"

"Same as always. Nice good-looking guy worked with us for an hour today. He was relieved by a young gal, in her early twenties."

"New people?"

"The guy was, yes."

"And you noticed he was good-looking?"

"My eyes aren't *always* on the ground you know."

"I know."

Megan got to the chair. Now came the next piece of work. Mary had remained silent through it all. There was no "Hello Mary," for Mary didn't have a welcoming look. There was no "Hello Ashley," either.

But something was different. Mary wasn't her grumpy old self today. She didn't exhibit anything that could be confused with happiness or joy; she was simply not grumpy. It was a rare occasion.

Mary helped Megan down. Ashley kept typing, always wanting to get up and help but knowing that Megan never wanted more than one person helping if she could have her way.

She was finally seated. Now she could look up.

"Oh, I like your hair. It looks very nice."

"Thanks, Megan, you're looking pretty spiffy yourself. I like your necklace."

Megan laughed. Her self-evaluation was worse than reality, but reality wasn't all that good and she knew it.

Then Megan changed the conversation.

"Ashley, you have to tell them to leave me alone. Every night from about eleven 'til five in the morning they are having sex, taking showers, scraping their feet across the floor. There are two or three men each night going in and out of there and sometimes two at a time. They must have some huge sex toys up there because they are shaking the building. Last night they shook me right out of bed."

Ashley was dumbfounded. Part of her wanted to laugh. Huge sex toys? Part of her wanted to scream in anger at these people – how dare they not let this poor woman sleep!

Ashley could be tactful when she thought about it, and right now she was thinking about it.

"Mary?"

"The racket is keeping Megan awake and it's scaring her. Last night they made so much noise and caused such a ruckus that Megan fell out of bed. You need to put a stop to it, Ashley. This new condo you found us is a nightmare. If you can call the manager and have them stop, we'd sure appreciate it."

"You heard the noise too?"

"Ashley, I work my butt off all day and sleep like a rock the few hours I sleep. It just so happens that I have heard some of the noise, though most of it is up over Megan's room. You need to put a stop to it or get Megan a nicer place to live."

Ashley's eyes rolled. Then before she said what she was thinking, she went back to Megan.

"Tell me what's been happening."

"I think it's a prostitution ring. They have a few girls and there are a few guys up there every night. Usually they turn the compressor on about eleven or midnight. And it runs the vibrator until morning when they all go home."

"A prostitution ring? You're putting me on? How do you come to that conclusion?"

How can you have an entire "ring" in a condo?

"It's the same hours every night and it's in the middle of the night when it happens. There is screaming. I know what sounds there are when people have sex. And they're having a LOT of sex, Ashley. Last night, the compressor was so loud, the girl was screaming at the top of her lungs, the bed upstairs shook *my* bed and shook me *out of it,* Ashley."

"OK, Megan, be calm. I'm going to call the police and the building manager. We will have this taken care of tonight. There won't be anyone having sex in there tonight."

"Are you sure? This is getting crazy. I'm getting no sleep. I'm going crazy. I need sleep."

"Megan. Megan. Megan. Look. It's over. There won't be anything happening tonight. I promise."

Chapter Twenty One

Tuesday Noon

Mary decided that it was time to reduce stress for the day. She drove the Mercedes down to Lake Calhoun and found a handicap parking space as close to a sidewalk as she could. Megan was going to be wheelchair-bound whether she liked it or not.

"No please, Mary, let's not use a wheelchair. Not on such a nice day. Let's take a walk."

Mary looked over at Megan.

"Once we're over there," she waved a finger at some benches, "you can be out of the wheelchair all you want. But it would take hours to get over there, and we don't have hours."

Megan was quieted. She hated the goddamned contraption! It brought so much attention to her and it brought her own attention to her inability to control her life, or any aspect of it. She said nothing more. Mary was going to get her way today no matter how much Megan complained.

Bound to a wheelchair and feeling very unattractive. Not just plain, but almost a curse to look at. She tried to think of something good. It would be nice to be outside by the lake. She loved the lake, though it made her think of her home not far from there… or whom ever it belonged to now. She didn't know and she didn't want to know. Her roots, David, her home, her possessions, her ability to move in a way that was even close to normal, her physical appearance, her dignity... had all been stripped away from her.

She didn't feel sorry for herself often. Nor did she feel God had it in for her. In fact, she could often be heard mumbling, "There is a reason for everything."

Part of her believed it.

But why the tenants upstairs? Why do they have to have a prostitution ring in her building? She couldn't understand anything about it, except that Ashley would take care of it. That was comforting.

It was relief to be away from the sound of the giant vibrator, the compressor, the sex. Sometimes she was upset with the noise. Sometimes she was upset that she wasn't having sex. The women upstairs were having sex several times each night.

Granted, she didn't have sex several times each night when David was alive, but she had more sex than there were days in the year. She always felt bad for people who didn't have a decent sex life. How could you survive without it? She used to wonder. Now she yearned for the feelings, the closeness, the tenderness, the intensity, the savageness – all the aspects, whether loving or brutal. She would pay an enormous sum to have sex today. But the opportunity wouldn't surface. Not for a long time.

"Come on, Megan, scoot your butt into the chair."

Mary had yanked the wheelchair out of the trunk of the Mercedes. It would be so simple to push Megan over to the benches where Mary could just sit and relax beside her.

Megan plopped into the chair and Mary flipped out the foot rests. When Mary's cell phone rang, she answered it at light speed. Someone to talk to other than Megan. Thank God, there was one person she could talk to.

"Hello? Yes. Oh, Megan, it's my cousin Jake in Vegas."

"Tell Jake I say hello."

"Here? It's seventy or seventy-five degrees, not humid.... One hundred? Already. Yes, I know, dry heat. Well, I don't know, Megan and I are at the lake. Yes, Calhoun. No, we had to sell the house. Because the medical costs and other expenses began to be bigger than the money in the bank. No, she's fine. Plenty. Sure.

"I suppose we could talk about that. I'd like to see you." Then she spoke to Megan. "Megan, Jake wants to have us come to Las Vegas. He wants us to get a hotel room at the Cosmopolitan or maybe the MGM and stay for a few days."

"Oh, I don't know…" Megan thought of the looks she would get in Vegas. She knew the Cosmopolitan was one of the nicest hotels in Las Vegas… the world, even. Everyone would stare at her there. She would be so out of place. She didn't like to gamble. But she would love to see something other than 4190. In fact, she'd love to see anything other than 4190.

"Jake says that the MGM Grand has some nice big suites that are about half the size of our condo, if not a bit bigger. Easy access."

"Oh. Well, that sounds good." And it did. A big space was different from a hotel room. If she could get around, it could be a nice change of pace.

Mary listened to her cousin talk and then she said to Megan, "Well, what do you think? Should we go for it, girl? Could be fun, don't you think?"

"OK, but we'll have to talk with Ashley."

They arrived at the benches. Mary pulled the wheelchair up next to a bench and turned it facing the lake. She stood behind Megan and continued to talk on the phone.

"She'll talk to Ashley about it. Huh? Oh. Hang on."

Mary walked to the front of the wheelchair and set the brake. She stooped and looked Megan in the eye. She reached over Megan's left arm and grabbed another cell phone out of the bag on the back of the chair. It was packed tight with Kleenex, emergency bathroom changing supplies, and some snacks.

"I'm going to take a short walk. Jake wants to talk with me about some personal stuff, honey. You can watch me over there." She pointed with her phone, indicating that she'd be on the path heading east.

Megan's heart palpitated, but what could she say.

"Don't be long, OK?"

"Don't worry honey, you just give me a ring on your cell phone if you need me. I'll be back in a few minutes."

She put a cell phone in Megan's hand and flipped it on. Then she turned and walked away.

Megan watched Mary move quickly. It seemed quick to Megan, anyway.

A turtle would seem quick.

I hope I don't have to go to the bathroom. She won't be long. She loves me. Maybe the walk will do her good. She deserves to take a little walk and get around, after all. She works so hard.

Darn.

She looked at the cell phone. She wasn't good with a cell phone. She hadn't been able to push the buttons without fumbling, but she knew if she had to, she could in an emergency... or she could, if the cell phone had power. This one had none! It had gone dead in the few minutes since Mary had turned it on. Megan pushed the power button. The little hourglass came on the screen, then disappeared with a flash as the phone went dead again. Just enough juice to start the phone and then die.

That's OK. I don't need the phone anyway. Mary won't be long. She just wants to have some private time to talk with her cousin. If she doesn't deserve it, no one does. She has to do so much every day. I'm glad we're here.

As people walked by in shorts and t-shirts, bikinis and on roller skates, Megan's heart broke. Some would look at her, then quickly avert their eyes. They knew it was rude to stare. Or was it? Didn't everyone stare at a beach?

As she looked around she noticed many attractive men and women, and even more who were fat.

My goodness, how can they do that to themselves? Oh, now, he's good-looking, my age, I wonder if he cares if I stare? Probably not. He'd never know because he's not going to look over here twice. One look and poof. He'll turn around so fast you'd think he was in a race. Yup. And back it goes. See, I knew it.

I used to have a bikini just like that. She looks as good in hers as I did in mine. I wonder if I'll ever be able to wear one again… or even a bathing suit. Scars… everything… probably but what about my eye? It makes me look so goofy… scary… I can't cry, without that stupid metal thing in my eyelid, I wouldn't even be able to close my eye. Makes me look hideous. Maybe we could go to Las Vegas at Halloween when everyone is all dressed up scary and I'd fit right in. They'd think, "Oh, what a great costume that is!" I'd win first prize. Another good-looking guy. Darker hair. But still nice. No muscle men. I guess there really never were here at Lake Calhoun… and I'm not so sure you need a muscle man. Do you want one? I mean, what are they thinking?

"Hi, what do you do for a living?"

"I'm a body builder."

"And how's that business nowadays?"

"You don't do it for income, you do it for competition, for the love of the sport."

"So how do you live?"

"Not well."

Then why the heck would you be a body builder? Wouldn't you want to be a mechanic and a body builder or a doctor and a body builder? Are you that small that you have to sit in a gym with a bunch of guys all day to make the rest of you big? Or are you big and you want to make the rest of you match up? But why all day in a gym? Where are the women? When do you have sex? Or do you have sex? When do body builders who spend all day in a gym have time for sex? And who are they going to have sex with anyway?

What do you talk about? I mean, if you're good in bed, you don't have to talk to me, honey, but my God, what is the point? The gardener was trim and had nice shoulders but who the hell cares! It's the sex, baby. Let's take a poll. Women… yes: ladies… what do you think? Do bodybuilders look sexy or gross? About a third of the women raise their hands and say sexy and about two-third think it's gross. I wonder if some of them are lying. Like, do all of them who think it's sexy really think it's sexy, or is it just that the way these monkeys look is ten times better than their fat-butt husbands… and what about those who say it's gross. Is it really gross or is it being healthy and people are so unhealthy that we get annoyed at people who focus on getting the most out of their bodies?

Oh well… I guess at this point, I don't care. I'd have sex with a monster. Anything.

"How long has it been since you had sex, Kylie?"

"Seems like forever. Maybe a month."

"Oh, you should see Megan. She hasn't had sex in like seven years?"

"Oh my God, even Rachel had sex this decade…"

Yeah, yeah… on the bell curve, I'm waaaay over there. No sex. No kissing… kissing. OK, sure, there have been kisses. Freddie kisses me on the cheek. Ashley and Mary both kiss me on the head sometimes. But those are all pity kisses. I mean like a kiss where someone looks at you and says, "I want to kiss her."

Where are all those guys?

They are all here, but who wants to kiss someone in a wheelchair?

Right. Almost no one.

Who wants to kiss someone in a wheelchair whose eyelid needs to have a metal ball in it to help it blink and whose face is like what you see when you look in a funhouse mirror at a carnival.

That would be… no one.

No one.

What if someone came over and kissed me but he had a strong magnet in his pocket and my eyelid wouldn't open or the ball crashed through my eyelid and got caught by the magnet?

Kissing would likely come after seeing, and no one wants to look at me.

You know, it's interesting. My body… except for my face… still looks pretty good. I lost all that weight after the accident, now it's back. There's no tone but I'm slender. And my legs… well, they still are pretty beat up but you have to get closer to actually see the scars.

And my face… well, that's a different story. I mean there are people that are worse off than me… just not many. No one says, "Oh Megan, think about all the headless people out there and how much better off you are."

The fact is that I've got Ashley and Aunt Rebekkah and Freddie and Mary and all that is pretty nice so, it's true that I am better off than others. But does that mean I want others to be less well-off so I can feel better?

Now that is sick thinking. I'll never say that to anyone in my life.

"Oh, just think Ashley, there are a million starving kids in Africa who have nothing, and they die of AIDS every day, so be thankful you are only a cripple."

Screw that. Never again. That's a sick, sick, sick attitude.

Oh, what a cute little girl. Hey! She's looking at me. Staring. So curious. She's not even disgusted. Uh, oh. Mom looks up. Yup, there goes the little girl's head, pointing away as Mom tells her how tragic I am and how she needs to not stare. It isn't polite.

HELL, LADY, just tell the kid, "Honey, you should ignore all people in wheelchairs. In fact, NEVER look at them." Just tell the world, "Oh, my God, they are all disgusting and revolting. Never look at a person in a wheelchair and when you make eye contact… if you do, by accident, BOOM! Look away instantly. Or if you are stuck, nod and move on. NEVER engage in conversation. NEVER say hello, because what are you going to talk about? Poor things, they are nothing but tragic figures."

What is it about someone that makes them not want to talk to people who get hurt? I never was like that. You go to the hospital and you talk to the kids with cancer and AIDS. It makes them feel good and it makes you feel good. But most people aren't like that, are they? They are uncomfortable around handicapped people. That's why they changed the name from handicapped to disabled to physically challenged. Now they don't have to feel guilty when they don't look at us. Screw that. Call me handicapped and talk to me. It's OK. I AM handicapped. I can't even go to the bathroom myself. Which by the way, if Mary doesn't get back soon…

Politicians. Dumb politicians. Good job, guys. Brilliant. I am handicapped. But I'm not disabled. I'm… OK, I'm mostly disabled. I can go to the bathroom, just not get there without help. I can walk with the walker, but I can't actually go anywhere. I can't get on a bus or a train or a plane or anywhere without help, a lot of help. Darling Mary. My God, she is a saint. To put up with me all day. Why does she do it?

Hey, he's got some muscles. He looks good. Not like that implant look with grease all over. Just nice. Heck, they all look nice today. Even the ones that used to make me go "yuk" inside look good. What's that saying?

Everyone is a ten when you are a one.

See now, there is a nice couple, with smiles. Real smiles. No fears. No worries. Course in Miracles says that love is the opposite of fear, so they must be not fearing anything. If there is a reason for everything, then does it matter if I fear or love? I mean if I'm going to be this ugly beat-up woman who can barely walk and can't do much else, that is because I did something. There is a reason, a cause, right? A cause for the fact that I am sitting here in a wheelchair and a thousand other people are out getting a suntan, jogging, rollerblading, and having fun. I don't remember not ever loving anyone. I always loved everyone. I still do. So does my loving do anything? If everything happens for a reason and I'm the result of some reason, then what does that mean?

Does it serve God and the Christ Consciousness for me to be here, an invalid in a wheelchair? I mean, It's not like I feel sorry for myself. I don't. Well. Maybe a little. But, whatever... the point is... the question is... How am I serving God's great purpose and grand design by sitting here in a wheelchair and causing people to look away and feel uncomfortable? I don't get it.

People are afraid. What are they afraid of? That couple isn't afraid of love. Everyone else looks away too. Just like they did. They had those happy faces and then they saw me, and now they have those sad pitiful faces. I might be full of love but I'm sending people away. People aren't being drawn to me like light. The response I feel from everyone is fear. Of course fear is an illusion. At least that is what The Course says. The Bible says to fear God but The Course says that fear is an illusion. Maybe the words mean different things. One of those "context" things.

I do believe that God put me on this earth for a purpose. There had to be a reason that David died. A reason he died and another reason that I lived.

What's my purpose?

To sit in a wheelchair and be the object of pity?

That's a lousy purpose, God. I can do better than that.

Or is the purpose so I learn the lesson of what…pride?

Too much?

Only when you aren't crippled up?

Maybe David is in a better place now. Right? I mean, I was the one who had the fling. He didn't. I mean, I thought he and Ashley did, and maybe they did. No, I don't think so. Not David. Not Ashley. So if I sinned, then why didn't I die, and why didn't he live?

Or… is this hell? It really is sort of, right? And David went to heaven so he is in a better place and the reason that I'm in the wheelchair is because I wasn't faithful to David, and so I've been punished to hell. But I thought Christians thought hell was like burning forever. Would that be any worse than being stuck without talking or moving for ages? I guess it would. Burning can get really hot. But how much worse would it be?

So the reason I'm here is that I was unfaithful. David was taken away from me to punish me and… the purpose of me being unfaithful in God's plan was… ugh. I just don't know. It's like I'm spinning in a circle.

I love people. I always helped people. But I liked to have sex. That's not a crime. Or maybe it is in Minnesota. I wonder if it is in Las Vegas.

That city is run on sex right? Sin City? What happens in Vegas stays in Vegas right? What the hell happens in Vegas and can I do it too?

They seem to be a little more liberal there and we are really liberal here. Of course we are conservative-liberal here and they are liberal-liberal there. I wonder if that makes sense to anyone else besides me.

I wonder where Mary is.

She is nowhere. It must be dinner-time. Maybe I haven't really been here that long.

If I had the walker, I'd be able to make it back to the car on my own. But there's no way I can get the wheelchair there.

And she does deserve a break. Maybe there is a big family problem. Wow, I don't think I know anything about her family. Now that doesn't show love, does it? But she must hate me. She has to deal with me all day and she has no life of her own.

Could I ever help someone to the toilet? Wash them when they don't get there on time? Be there every second of the day? I could now, but could I have then? Maybe that was the purpose of the accident, to teach me humility. I've sure learned that. But then, what was the purpose of the accident for David? To teach him what?

I want to cry. But I can't because I'd just wail and everyone who's left here would come up and wonder what to do with me.

"I know it looks like I'm losing my mind, but I'm actually crying, you just don't see tears because there aren't any because the tears don't come out any more, so all you get is this weird wailing sound. Make sense, ma'am?"

Maybe the cell phone has sat long enough to charge enough to call her.

I wonder if it works that way. I think it does with a car, right? You leave it sit and sometimes ...how does that work... the juice goes back in the battery and you have enough to start it? I wish I knew. I am so dumb about some things.

Give it a shot.

Light... good. Hourglass. Good. Hourglass turns. Good. Poof. Power is off. No good.

OK. So, Mary needs to come back here to get me. It would take me about four hours to walk back to the car, though I could ask someone to push me there and I'd be there in two minutes. But I don't even know if there is an extra set of keys in the bag. Probably not. Why would there be? "Megan going driving today?" Ha. Ha. Not likely. No. There are no keys.

At least I don't have to go to the bathroom. At least not yet. Thank God for that miracle.

What if I get mugged?

Who mugs an ugly girl sitting in a wheelchair? Gonna steal all her money? Yeah those wheelchair people they carry tons of money with 'em. OK. So I'm not gonna get mugged. I wonder if muggers will look at a handicapped person? Or do they walk by and look down at the ground and thank God that it isn't them? Or do they just think, "No cash in those pockets." Muggers have moms. I bet they don't want to be muggers. I mean, when you're growing up and the teacher asks you, "And Johnny, what do you want to be when you grow up?"

"Oh, Miss Teacher, I'm going to skip out of going to college so I can go straight to being a mugger or maybe even a murderer if I'm good enough."

Or are people, even children, really mean enough that they will answer Miss Teacher and say, "Miss Teacher, I want to be a mugger or a murderer because I hate people and I want to get them back for all the bad things that have happened to me and my family."

Some people ARE mean. Look how mean the people at the City were to me and David and Ashley and all the people that worked for us. They didn't care if they put us out of business and hundreds of people out of work. Didn't care in the least. We were good for the neighborhood. Good for the community. Helped poor people get jobs with us. Helped sick people a lot of times for free. The people in the City should have been nice because we were, but that isn't how life is, is it?

Some people are just mean.

That is true. There are a lot of mean people. I wish it weren't true but there are so many people who are just mean. And there is no reason to be mean. Don't people realize that even though our skin color is different, that we're all the same inside?

I think that things are going to start changing. A new age? Maybe people will start being more tolerant of others. Be nicer. They'll talk to the girl in the wheelchair, for God's sake.

Mary... where are you, Mary? It is really time to get going.

It's getting cool out. The bikini tops are even getting covered by tank tops and t-shirts. The muscle-y guys are even putting on their shirts. Not the fat guys though. They are always last to get dressed. That extra person around them keeps 'em warm, I bet.

Didn't Dear Abby say that fat women shouldn't wear bikinis, that they should have appreciation for other people's feelings as well? I wonder if she's right. Isn't she like a hundred years old? Or did she die? She doesn't have a bikini, of course she wouldn't because she IS always thinking of what other people think. I mean I could put on an old bikini...if Ashley kept any of them. But what would happen? It's an exercise in futility and like a practical joke. From neck to waist I'm fine...basically...just a few reminders of scars. But below the waist it's scary...and my legs...

not what they used to be. I wonder if they will ever take their original shape. Or whether all those scars from where the braces were will go away, or if I'm stuck for the rest of my life.

See I am better off than some people. What about Siamese twins? How the heck do they make it? My God, THEY have problems.

"Hi, meet my sister Mercedes. Oh, and I'm Madison."

The guy doesn't know who he's going to have sex with. Ugh. Now that is disgusting. But why is it disgusting? I haven't had sex for years. So that must mean that I'm disgusting. What's the difference? Me? Siamese Twins? All the same.

So maybe it's not disgusting for them to have sex. Oh…it is…damn… I wish I could get over the prejudice I feel about other people. Damn. And I even get it.

"Excuse me," Megan spoke to a couple walking on the sidewalk in front of her. "Could you tell me what time it is?"

"7:14."

"Thanks."

"No problem."

At least he didn't look freaked out.

OK, well, we have a problem. We've been here almost two hours. I've been here almost two hours. Do normal people say "we" when they talk to themselves inside of their head? My God, when you have such a hard time communicating…sure…everyone must do this. I'm not THAT nuts. Who wouldn't be crazy after what I've been through. Crazy or dead.

So let's just calmly figure this thing out.

I have no way to contact Mary. What if she got hurt? What if SHE got mugged? Oh my God, that would be very bad. She could be raped and I couldn't do anything to help her. Oh my God. I hope she is OK.

I can either wait here…or I can…yell for help to get me to the car where I can't get in or do anything…or I can ask someone to borrow a cell phone and try and call her…wait. I don't know her phone number! OHHHHH. I don't know her phone number. How could I call her? She thought I knew her phone number. Why would I know her number? She's always here. If she ever leaves me, Ashley's there, and Ashley knows her number. I never have to call her.

Well, I know Ashley's number. She's at home. Probably...so if worse comes to worse...what a stupid saying...worse already is worse or it would be better. If dogs come to dogs...if apples come to apples...if sex comes to sex.

God, do I think a lot about sex. I think I actually think more about sex with each passing year that I don't have sex. Shouldn't I think more about crab and lobster? I haven't had them in my entire life! Being a Jew should make you want all that stuff right?

So really there is nothing to be worried about. God will take care of it. Just like he takes care of me. And David. God, he does such a bad job at his job...or does he have a purpose for all of this? And the answer is yes, he does, but I'm just a human and I really have no place questioning God or how he does his thing. If more people respected God the world would be a better place. Maybe that is part of this purpose thing... I don't know.

So I'll give Mary a few more minutes. Then... then... I will have to do something.

I do have to go the bathroom though... but I still don't want to rush. I'm fine. There are plenty of people around. I could always move the wheelchair onto the sidewalk and ...well... no, that does seem unlikely... we'll just have to hope she gets back here soon.

David was such a good man. He took care of me. Wouldn't let me stress about anything. What would he have done if he had seen me like this? He would have gone insane. He wouldn't have known how to help. What to do. He would have done his best but he never had a great bedside manner. But he was always thinking into the future. If something could possibly go wrong he had it figured out so far in advance. Ashley's just like him...well, she gabs more than David ever did...but aside from that, they're a lot alike.

I sure do miss him...I miss him so much. My life revolved around him...his life revolved around me and his businesses. Both. I guess sometimes I wanted more of his time but I wasn't going to go whining about it. I was happy. He was happy. We were happy. What more could you ask for?

Then, poof. His life was snuffed out in a second. It is so tragic. He was so young. His parents must have been so proud of him...and then when he died...they must have wept and wept and wept. How could you not? It's your child. They loved him so much. I don't imagine anyone wants to bury their children. Don't most people think that they want to go before their kids? I know I would if I had kids. Ashley certainly wants Lauren to outlive her. It's not natural for children to die before their parents.

God, I wish I had kids...but I'm glad I don't. I guess that doesn't make sense, but there is no one here to know but me. How could I have taken care of kids? I was always running around. Charity work, swinging by one of David's stores, taking care of the house, being a Mrs.

Would I have been a good mom?

Honestly? No. I would have stunk. I would have wanted my baby to cuddle for an hour, and then I'd want to go dancing or go to an event or a function. I would have hired a nanny, wouldn't I? Yes. I would have. So, no. I'm glad I didn't have kids. But it would have been nice. Christmas time...especially for a Jew who follows The Course. Guess I never made sense in my religious beliefs, whatever they are. I mean I love God. I believe God is within me. I just don't know what good that is to anyone else.

I'm sitting here at Lake Calhoun. It must be sixty degrees out, people are starting to go home... and if Mary doesn't get back soon, I'm going to be here all alone. Now that wouldn't be good.

This is not a crisis but it is not good.

I think that before everyone is gone I better take care of this.

Next person that walks by I'll ask if they have a cell phone. Thank God for cell phones. How did we live without them?

"Excuse me sir, could I ask you a question?"

"Sure."

Thank God he stopped. "My... the person who takes care of me... I think something happened to her and I'm wondering if you would be nice enough to call my friend to come and get me."

It was an awkward request, but he was sympathetic. His girlfriend said nothing and avoided eye contact. He pulled his cell phone from its little case on his belt.

"What's the number? Or do you want to call?"

"My fingers don't work as well as yours. If you would dial 612-555-4951 and ask for Ashley that would be great. "

"Hello, is this Ashley?"

The voice on the other end was loud. "Yes, it is. Who's calling?"

"There's someone here who wants to talk to you." He handed the cell phone to Megan. She gently took it from his hand.

"Hi, Ashley."

"Megan, are you all right?"

"Yes, I'm fine. I have to go to the bathroom and I'm at Lake Calhoun and this nice..."

"You're where?" You could hear the screech through the phone and halfway to St. Paul. She was freaked out.

"Ashley, I'm at Lake Calhoun and I have to go to the bathroom. Can you come and get me?"

"Megan, where's Mary?"

"I don't know."

Megan looked up at the man who had the strangest look on his face.

"You don't know? Oh my God. OK. Where are you?"

"I'm at Lake Calhoun. In the park. I'm fine. I just have to go to the bathroom and I need help now. Can you come and get me?"

"Yes. Oh my God. Exactly where are you?"

"North side in the park. Can't miss me. I'm the one everyone is walking past... I'm in the wheelchair."

"OK, I'll be there as fast as I can."

"Thanks, honey. I'm sorry."

"Don't worry about it. I'll be there shortly."

Ashley hung up and Megan gave the phone back to the man who stood there politely.

"Can I take you over to the restroom?"

Megan smiled at his kindness.

"Sir, you have done enough. If I had you take me to the bathroom, you would never get home today. I move pretty slowly. Please, both of you go, have a nice evening. I'm fine and my friend will be here in a couple of minutes."

"OK, well, have a good night then." The woman gave a weak wave of her hand and they said nothing until they were far enough away from Megan that she couldn't make out the words. She couldn't make out most words spoken at a distance of more than twenty feet. Her hearing was just not good. Even with the hearing aids.

Ashley is going to want to fire Mary and we can't have that happen. Mary must have gotten involved in a conversation with her cousin. Must have had some serious family problems. Poor Mary. I do wish she would have told me she wasn't going to come back.

I wonder where she did go… she didn't have to wander out of eyeshot to talk with her cousin. She knows I can't hear much. She could have gone to the building over there and I would never have heard a word of her conversation. How odd.

I DO have to go to the bathroom. Darn it. I will hold it. No way will I do that here in the middle of the park. No way.

Maybe she quit. Maybe she just got sick of me. What am I going to tell Ashley? I don't want Mary to get in trouble. She's been such a good friend for so long. I don't want Ashley to fire her.

Maybe I could say that I told her to go walk around the lake. No, that wouldn't work… she'd have been back by now.

Oh, I don't know what to say. I'm sure Mary has a very good reason for disappearing. Maybe Penn and Teller made her disappear.

Megan laughed, drawing the attention of a couple passing by.

She straightened up and stopped her chuckling, lest people think she was nuts as well as paralyzed.

She would just tell the truth and hope the best came out of both Ashley and Mary, if she ever showed up. What if Ashley didn't show up? What if she had an accident coming over?

Who would I call then? I think I would start getting scared at that point. No one else has the keys to 4190, even if I could get a ride.

Oh my… and I hope the hookers are quiet tonight. I wonder if Ashley really did get a chance to talk with them today. Oh, I hope so. I want this to be a restful night. Things have been so hard this last week.

***

A blonde woman came running at full speed toward Megan. It was Ashley.

"Megan. Are you all right? Where is Mary? What happened? Are you OK?"

"She went to talk to her cousin on the cell phone about some private matters and she didn't come back."

"WHAT!"

"Well, her cousin from Las Vegas called. They invited us to come down there and visit. Everything was fine, then I guess they had to talk about some family business and she walked away for some privacy. Really. It's OK."

"It's OK? It's *not* OK. She is going to get fired when and if we ever see her again."

Megan began to weep, in the only way she could.

"No please, don't fire her. She's my friend."

"But Megan…"

"No. No… please… don't… she didn't mean to do anything wrong. I know she didn't. She's a good person."

"OK, listen we're going to get you into my car. We'll get someone to come get your car and bring it back to the condo. I'll take you home. You said you had to go to the bathroom?"

Megan nodded, still crying, though no tears coursed down her face.

"OK…OK…let's go."

Ashley was as mad as a human could get. But she wasn't mad at Megan. She was mad at Mary. What the hell was she thinking, leaving Megan in the middle of the park… alone? Stupid woman!

I will give that woman a piece of my mind when I see her. I cannot believe she left Megan. Stupid damn woman. GOD I can't believe this.

Ashley nudged Megan into the passenger seat and then folded up the wheelchair, placing it carefully into the oversized trunk of the car.

***

When they pulled into the driveway it was about eight o'clock. No sign of Mary whatsoever. Where the hell was she? They both wondered, with a different set of emotions attached.

Ashley moved quickly out of the car, opened the wheelchair and pulled Megan from the car. They moved rapidly toward the entrance and Ashley opened the door. All was quiet. That made Ashley feel a *little* better.

Finally they got to Megan's room. Ashley hustled Megan to the bathroom. Once her business was done, she put Megan into bed.

Ashley was dumbfounded. She felt silenced by the whole thing. Megan didn't know what to think either.

"Thank you for coming to get me."

"Well, honey, of course. I just can't believe this happened and I can't believe Mary hasn't gotten back here or called or anything. What can she be thinking?"

"Well, she said she had some family business to take care of on the phone. It was private and I saw her head around the right side of the lake. And then she disappeared from sight. I can't imagine what happened to her. I hope she's OK."

She better be hurt or she's gonna get hurt, Ashley repeated in her mind a number of times.

"Me too. Let's see if we can get her on her cell phone."

Ashley picked up the phone next to Megan's bed. Punched seven numbers and the "dial" button. The phone rang.

"Hello."

"Mary?"

"Yes."

"Where the hell are you? I've got Megan here at home and you left her in the park at the lake by herself for two hours. What were you thinking? Where are you and where is the car?!"

"Would you relax? I saw you race Megan out of the park. I was watching her from a bench over on the side of the..."

"You were WATCHING HER? She was by HERSELF for TWO hours. Get back here. NOW."

She slammed the phone down. She was so angry, she thought she would explode… really.

"That woman is maddening."

"What did she say?"

"She said she saw you and she was watching you and saw us leave together."

"See then everything was OK. Thank goodness."

"Everything was NOT OK. You had to go to the bathroom and you had no way of knowing whether she was there or not or how to get her attention… or call her… or anything. She left you out to dry and she'll get a talking-to about this!"

"Ashley, calm down. Everything's OK. She didn't mean anything bad by what happened. I wish she would have been there but everything worked out."

"Everything *didn't* work out. What if I wasn't by the phone? You would have lost it in the park and been a total mess. God knows when Mary would have come by to take you home. And how would she clean you up in public?"

Megan looked down. She was upset that Ashley was upset, and she was upset that Ashley was upset with Mary. She didn't want to make Ashley *more* upset by arguing.

"OK. I understand."

"It's not your fault, honey, it's hers."

Changing the subject was a good idea right now. "Did you call the manager about the people upstairs?"

"Yes. He said that the people haven't moved in yet. Not scheduled to do so until tomorrow. To his knowledge no one has been up there since the weekend. He said he was going to go up, open the door and see if there was anything obvious going on. I told him to fix whatever was going on and get back to me."

"Thank you so much. It's been driving me crazy. I haven't been sleeping or anything."

"I know. That will all change tonight. He has my cell phone number and he's going to call me as soon as he's checked it out."

"They usually don't start making noise until late in the night...say eleven or so."

"OK, well, it's being handled. Nothing more to worry about."

Megan was relieved... at least for the moment. Because as soon as Mary got home, all hell was sure to break loose.

***

She walked in the front door with no evidence or expression that she had just made one of the biggest screw-ups a person can make when caring for someone who can't fend for herself.

Ashley was waiting at the front door and didn't bring Megan out for the welcome.

"What the hell were you thinking?"

"What are *you* getting so bent out of shape for, Ashley? Is Megan fine? Yes. Is she safe? Yes. Was she ever in a bad place? No. Was she...."

"*Shut up,* you stupid bitch! You don't *ever* leave Megan by herself for two hours or even *two minutes* when she can't take care of herself. What do you think your job is? Why are you here? And the cell phone you gave Megan was dead. She had no idea where you were. She was scared. She had to go to the bathroom and she was close to having a terrible experience in the park. My God, Mary. Have you lost your fricking mind?"

Mary simply nodded her head during the tirade, then looked right into Ashley's eyes. She knew she was safe, as Megan would never allow her to be fired, so Ashley's opinion was worth nothing. She had no authority over Mary as long as Megan still wanted her.

"I've got work to do." And she made a path between Ashley and the wall and headed for Megan's room.

"Where the hell are you going?"

No answer.

Ashley simply stood there stunned.

"Hi, Megan." Mary had a soft smile on her face.

"Hi, Mary. I hope Ashley wasn't too hard on you. I know you had family business."

"I did, honey, and I could see you the whole time, but I didn't realize you were so concerned. Well, we're home. Everything is fine and I'm glad of that. Did Ashley take care of the disruptions upstairs?"

By this time Ashley was standing three feet outside Megan's door. She wasn't sure *what* to do or say at this point. She didn't want to upset Megan. Megan was low on sleep and high on stress. Mary was playing this out like nothing big had happened.

I do NOT like this woman. She has GOT to go.

She walked into the room, joining Megan and Mary.

"Do you have anywhere you need to go tonight, Mary?"

"Absolutely not. Everything is fine. If you took care of those noises, then, everything will be fine tonight. You have a good night."

Ashley was steaming. She was being dismissed… and she didn't want to make a scene. She had to look away from Mary so she didn't kill her. Would it have been called justifiable homicide? Probably not, even if such a thing existed.

Calm. Breathe. Composure. Stupid bitch.

"OK, I'm going home. Mary, tomorrow you and I have a talk."

"Anything you want, Ashley."

"Thank you, Ashley." Megan was grateful that there was no more yelling or anything. She hated shouting and mean spirits.

"You're welcome, honey. OK then, I'll see you both sometime tomorrow. Bye Megan… Goodnight Mary."

"Good night Ashley." Mary didn't even bother to look at her when she said goodbye. Ashley was gone. Now everything would be fine.

"I was so upset when I saw Ashley wheeling you away. But at least I knew you were safe. I was talking with Jake in Vegas. He's having some problems but he really wants you and me to come and visit him. He suggested we stay at the MGM Grand Hotel where they have oversized suites that are quite nice."

Megan nodded her head in understanding and she was swept away by Mary's plan.

"Actually, he suggested that we move down there for the winter. I know how frustrating it is for you in the winter with the wheelchair and all. It dawned on me that this was a stroke of genius. You'd be able to recover much faster in warmer weather and a fun atmosphere."

The idea was obviously appealing to Megan, so Mary went on. As Mary spoke of a warmer climate, Megan lit up like the sun. The idea of being outside twelve months of the year made her feel warm inside.

"I told Jake that there was no way we would commit to something as long as six months without first making a short trip to check things out, but that if I got your permission we'd come for a visit in a week or two."

Megan thought it over and agreed. "I think it's a great idea. It would take us out of Ashley's hair and give her a chance to rest for a few days. She's been so busy and working so hard."

Mary nearly gagged over all of Megan's gratitude being heaped on Ashley. But the ends justified the means.

"Absolutely right. Shall we book a flight for, say, a couple of weeks from now?"

"Sure. We have to check with Ashley, but why not?"

"It will be fun, won't it? In Las Vegas they take care of people with special challenges like they are royalty. If you're at a hotel, you get extra assistance. If you want to go to a nice restaurant you get special seating privileges. There are even tables if you wanted to play some games that are designed for people with wheelchairs. I think it's a grand idea. It's settled then. I'll make plans in the morning and of course check with Ashley to make sure everything is OK with her. I think you're right. She needs to take a few days away from us. She was so stressed out today over everything."

Mary's eyes motioned toward the ceiling.

"Quiet up there," she said to Megan.

Megan agreed, it was quiet. But a shiver went through her body. Just thinking about it made her nervous. She didn't quite know why.

"Maybe Ashley has taken care of things."

"You know Ashley," Megan jumped in, "if something needs to be fixed, Ashley's the person to do it."

"And it looks like she did a nice job. Good for her."

***

Ashley sat at her desk at home. The other half of Ashley's mind was back in the park… and at 4190.

Megan had been through so much that being left alone in the park simply didn't feel threatening. Certainly, concerned, but not seriously scared.

Ashley on the other hand had been on the other end of things – the caretaking end – for the last several years. It was Ashley's job to get Megan from Point A to B in life. Megan had become like a dependent. A daughter. She watched over Megan like a hawk.

Now she had to start pondering the possibility of letting Mary go. Firing her. Getting rid of her. Megan would protest vehemently. They had grown close over the years.

Was it really in Megan's best interests to fire Mary?

Ashley was legally responsible for Megan. From that point of view, firing Mary would be logical. From Megan's point of view it would not. She would have to find a way to broach this with Megan sometime over the next week or two.

I hope that condo manager gets back to me. I don't want Megan having any more restless nights. I'm so worried about her. She needs her sleep.

***

It was past midnight. She was reading *A Course in Miracles*. She often did. It helped her feel at peace and helped her make sense of the world. It didn't exactly jibe with her Jewish upbringing but it was something she was able to blend with her beliefs in a congruent and consistent fashion.

The Course simply made her feel better. It made the world seem filled with love. Evil didn't exist. It was only an illusion. The Course made life understandable… at least for Megan.

She glanced at the clock. It was almost one a.m. and she was tired. It had been a long day. She was so thankful that Mary and Ashley hadn't got in a big fight. She loved them both so much. She hated to even see them stare at each other antagonistically.

Everything will be OK. God has a purpose for everything.

There they go. I thought they would take the night off. Ashley must have gotten a hold of the manager...the manager told them to stop and they did...but only for a few hours. Now it's 1:00 and they started up the compressor, probably for the big vibrator.

Maybe I can sleep anyway. Know that it has a purpose and that God is in charge.

The compressor-like sound only got louder. The sound of laughter soon ensued. Then a woman, screaming her way to an orgasm.

My goodness. What kind of people are they? Why can't they have their prostitution at a decent hour of the day? It's the middle of the night.

The compressor sound got louder, the screams became noisier and another sound that sounded like the Emergency Broadcasting System exploded into the night.

Oh my God. They have to stop that. This is terrible. All of this sound. It's terrible. What are they doing up there?

"Mary!" Megan shouted, knowing she'd never be heard over the unbelievable noise that was overhead. "Mary!"

Megan reached down for one of her canes, grabbed it and as quickly as her reflexes had moved in seven years, she rapped hard against the wall. Time and again. She'd either wake Mary up or send a signal upstairs for the noise to stop.

"Mary! My God, Mary how can you sleep through this?! Mary! Please come in here. HELP!"

Mary wasn't coming. The noise was not yielding. It was as loud as a jet engine. The tone. The compressor. The woman.

She picked up the telephone and dialed 911.

"Yes. Please, send a policeman to 4190 Stinson. But it's not here in my condo, it's the people above me. They are making terrible sounds. Prostitution and some kind of a super loud screaming sound like the Emergency Broadcasting System."

"No. Not in my house. It's a condo. Upstairs. I don't know what their address is. Yes. I'm in 4190. My name? Megan Dresden. Yes. Dresden. It just started about a few minutes ago but they've been doing this every night for a week and it's driving me nuts. And they are breaking the law. They have a prostitution ring up there. Can you PLEASE send someone to tell them to stop it?"

"Yes it's LOUD! I can hardly hear you. I can't believe you can't hear the noise on the phone. It's deafening!"

"Thank you."

She placed the phone back on the stand wishing the noise would stop… but knowing that the police were on their way began to settle Megan down. She felt relieved, like justice was going to be done. Finally she would get some peace and the prostitution ring would get busted.

I put my hands over my ears and it makes NO difference. They are so loud.

"Mary!" *Darn. She won't wake up. She can't hear me. How can she sleep through this?*

Megan edged her way out of bed to her walker, then decided on the wheelchair. The hardwood floors made getting to the bathroom easier, but still, walking would take too much time. It wasn't impossible to get to the bathroom and go without assistance, but it was a substantial project. With the wheelchair, it could take a half-hour round trip. With the walker, an hour or more.

Chapter Twenty Two

Later That Night

The lights flashed as the police car pulled up to the front door of the condo.

Officer Anthony Peterson popped out of the car with his flashlight in hand. He didn't have a partner that night.

He traced the outline of the beautiful building with the flashlight, holding it high in the air, a stance which was in vogue nowadays. He wasn't sure when that had changed, but he knew it was cooler than holding it down by your waist. Besides, everyone on TV was doing it and it worked just as well one way as it did the other.

There were two cats over on the north side of the condo and not another sound to be heard.

Maybe the siren shut them up.

He took a tour around the building and found not one person awake in the building, which probably held some twenty units. If anything that was strange, but certainly not a crime.

Rich people go to bed early?

The night had been quiet anyway. Domestics, a few misdemeanors, and that was it. Disturbing the peace was no big deal, but a prostitution ring was something his elite city didn't need. It wasn't so much the prostitution but the drug traffic it brought into the city. People want to pay for sex? Who cares? People want to buy and sell coke, that's another thing.

The problem wasn't that some rich guy was going to get high on cocaine. The problem was that his kids were going to get the cocaine and ultimately O.D. on it. The problem was that drugs were damned expensive and families were wiped out… literally bankrupted because of one person's drug habit. Kids didn't get to go to college because Mom was a junkie or Dad couldn't use recreationally without getting into something much worse. The problem was that because the sale of drugs was illegal and incredibly profitable for dealers, protecting their business often went hand in hand with other violence and crimes. Drugs were just a mess. And it was predictable. For some reason prostitution rings and hard drugs often mixed. Funny thing was the big shots running the show rarely used drugs. They were business men and sometimes business women who weren't stupid. Prostitution usually operated at 50/50 in upper end work. She got half, the big shot got half. He did the marketing. She did the servicing. Normal business, except one thing.

The sleazier types would often encourage the girls to try coke or crack or meth or anything that was incredibly addictive. The addiction helped to solidify the business relationship.

A woman in a high-class business working for Mr. Big Shot would earn half of whatever was brought in that night. Two or three clients could be a couple grand, split out to a thousand bucks each. Not bad for a night's work. Work a couple hundred nights a year and you live in this kind of neighborhood.

Unless of course you became addicted to coke. Coca Cola you could get anywhere. Cocaine wasn't regularly available at Byerly's or Walmart. The girl would likely be on time to work, in order to first engage in the use of her newfound habit. An expensive one at that. It could add another hundred bucks to the big shot's income that night… and if he had a few girls working… he could, and did, make a lot of money.

Fortunately there weren't a lot of those guys around. Most of the upper class girls were smart enough to work on their own, and for that Officer Peterson simply couldn't have cared less. It was a free country. People wanted to have sex. He didn't recall ever raiding a house on a domestic after someone had sex. Murders didn't happen *after* someone had just had sex. Robbery didn't happen after someone had just had sex. If Officer Peterson had his way, he'd probably require everyone to have sex twice daily… and take a Prozac at bedtime. He was sure that this would reduce, if not eliminate, crime.

As he was so often reminded, his opinion was technically not the law – though it often became the law on marginal issues. He could pass on a minor offense, or go down hard on someone who was doing something minor and might get involved in something bigger as a result. He was tough on kids. He hated to be… but he hated the idea of seeing yet another eighteen-year-old end up in prison. That was one benefit of not working Minneapolis. The suburbs had fewer of those problems and he'd had enough of that over the years.

Officer Peterson had met Megan a long time ago at a Minneapolis fundraiser for families of police officers killed in the line of duty. She wouldn't remember him from Adam. He remembered her and her husband. He always gave a lot of money, although Peterson couldn't remember how much. The guy was hated by everyone at The City which probably meant he was a good Joe and sure enough, he cut a big check for some of the families of people he knew. Mr. Dresden was a good guy. That must have been what, five, ten years ago?

He thought he remembered Mrs. Dresden was in critical condition but never heard anything after that. It had been a long time.

The outside of the building was secure. The doors were all locked. The lights were out. There was absolutely nothing going on in here. His instincts were tuned like an instrument.

He rang the buzzer for the manager's office.

"Police."

"What is it? Is something wrong?" The voice sounded stunned or scared, or both.

"Buzz me in."

The video camera pointed right at Officer Peterson and then the red dot indicated a picture being clicked. *Smart company,* he thought. *Good security.*

"I'm in 102. First door on your right."

Buzz.

Officer Peterson went in and was buzzed in a second door.

Security gone wild? Who lived in this place? Rich people. He'd never top $55,000 a year as a cop. But it was a good living. Good pension and at least here, the respect of the community.

The door to 102 opened. The manager was a short guy with messy hair.

"What's going on, Officer?"

"I have a complaint that there is noise on the second floor above 108."

"Let me guess, Mrs. Dresden called."

"That's right. You aware of the noise or what's going on?"

"No. She's a bit weird. She moved in about a month ago and the last week I've had a number of complaints about noise above her bedroom. I've checked. There's nothing."

"Someone living up there in 208?"

"Just moved in this week. Yes. Elderly couple. Sixties or seventies. Retired. Crotchety old guy. Don't know how he can afford this place, but that's not my business."

"Huh." Officer Peterson pondered that for a moment. "Mind if I look around?"

"By all means."

"Are the people in 208 home?"

"Beats me. I'm the manager, not their mother."

"Right. You want to tag along?"

"Sure. What's the complaint?"

"Loud noise. Prostitution."

"What? That's crazy. Yes, I want to tag along. Let's go."

The man in the brown robe led the way up the stairs and they walked down the hall to 208. The flashlight had been doused. No need. The light in the hallway was plenty.

They walked up to 208.

"Their name?"

"Harris, I think."

"You think?"

"Yes. Harris."

Officer Peterson rapped on the door. Police always rapped on the door differently from normal people. The turned their hand backward and knocked on the door with the palm toward their face. Officer Peterson sometimes wondered why police were the only people on the planet to do this.

No one answered at first. Then he heard someone moving in the apartment.

A couple of locks were unlocked from the inside, then a face appeared. Another robed figure. This time a plaid robe. This man had less hair, which was all gray. His face was heavily lined, from years of smoking and sun, no doubt.

"Yes?" The old man looked out and saw the condo manager and a police officer and a look of confusion, anger and fear all rolled into one over his lined features. Officer Peterson had seen the look a million times. Usually it meant nothing was going on.

"Mr. Harris?"

"Yes. What is it?"

"I'm Officer Peterson. I have a call from a tenant indicating that there's been a lot of noise going on up here tonight."

The man's emotions all magnified.

"The only noise in the building came from downstairs about a half hour ago. Someone was beating on the wall and screaming something like, 'idiot'; over and over. We've been trying to sleep, to no avail."

"You look like you've been sleeping sir."

"The noise woke us up about a half hour ago and now you're here."

"Sir, is there anyone except your wife… Mrs.?"

"Yes, Mrs. Harris."

"…in the house?"

"No. What is this all about?"

"Sir, we also have a complaint that there may be prostitution going on in this unit… in your unit. Would you mind if I took a look around?"

"*Prostitution?* Are you nuts? We just moved in this week. We're retired and I assure you there is nothing as exciting as prostitution going on here."

"Yes sir. Mind if I have a quick look around?"

Harris was exasperated.

"Fine. Come on in."

Harris turned some lights on. There were boxes all over the place. Moving boxes that hadn't been opened. Allied Moving boxes. A standard house move. Officer Peterson saw nothing but boxes. No signs of life aside from the old guy.

"Two bedrooms, sir?"

"Yes, two bedrooms."

"Mind if I have a look in that one?"

Vance Harris pointed to the room at the end of the hall.

"Why not?" He went and sat down in the recliner by the TV in the living room.

Officer Peterson nudged the door open. There was no bed in the room. Just boxes. Unopened for the most part. He looked down and saw paperwork for Allied Moving Company. He shined his flashlight on it. $931. Pretty cheap move. Nothing illegal about cheap. Flicked the flashlight off.

"Mrs. Dresden must have been mistaken."

No smell of smoke, perfume, no alcohol present. No bed. He did check to see if there was a bathroom off the bedroom. There wasn't.

Back to the living room.

"Mind if I check in your bedroom, sir?"

"My wife is sleeping!"

"I thought you said the noise downstairs was keeping you awake, sir."

"Awake, but in *bed*, for God's sake."

"You don't have to let me see the room if you don't want to, sir."

"Just a minute." Harris got up. He walked over to the bedroom door and whispered to his wife. Within seconds a woman in her sixties came out of the room. Third robe of the evening. Hair a mess. No makeup. She had been in bed, probably trying to sleep.

"Officer Peterson, ma'am. We had a call indicating a lot of noise up here. Mind if I check your room and a bathroom if you have one in there?"

"That's the craziest thing I've heard. We were the ones who heard the noise. From downstairs. Woman shouting something and beating on the walls."

"Don't hear anything now, ma'am."

"No, it stopped fifteen or twenty minutes ago."

"Mind if I check the room, ma'am?"

"Go right ahead." She motioned with her head. Looked at her husband in near shock. He shrugged his shoulders.

Peterson gingerly stepped into the room. Bed had been slept in. No signs of smoke. Strange for a guy whose face looked like he smoked his whole life. Perfume smell was light. Nothing to get excited about. Turned the corner to a small master bath. Nothing. Two old folks trying to sleep.

"Sir, ma'am. I apologize for the inconvenience. There's nothing going on here. Get some rest."

The manager made his apologies and the two walked out of the condo back to the main hallway of the building.

"Well?"

Officer Peterson was agitated.

"What now?"

"Well, I don't know." The manager didn't want an unnecessary confrontation. There would probably be a price to pay somewhere for management disturbing the residents.

They returned to the first floor hall in front of the manager's condo. Officer Peterson pulled his business card from his pocket and handed it to the man.

"If you need anything else, feel free to call. You can tell Mrs. Dresden that we came out and everything checked out. Give her this card." He pulled another card out and gave it to the manager. "There's nothing going on here. Good night."

He walked out the security doors and back to the car.

"Well, no shit, there's nothing going on here." He slammed the door and decided to try and go back to sleep.

Officer Peterson wondered what Mrs. Dresden had been thinking, but it could have been anything. False alarms. He picked up his radio microphone and got back to dispatch.

"Peterson at 4190 Stinson. Nothing going on here. All clear."

"Copy that, Officer Peterson. All clear."

Chapter Twenty Three

June 4

Day 2448

From the Desk of
Ashley Drexel

Friday, June 4

Mr. Peter Rutherford
Minnesota Capital Development Group
300 West Fifth Avenue SE
Minneapolis, MN 55402

Dear Mr. Rutherford,

I'm the trustee for Megan Dresden. She moved into your 4190 Stinson property this last month and has been having a very difficult time with the neighbors in 208 above her.

The neighbors have been bothering Megan each night with what appears to Megan to be prostitutes and their customers making all kinds of racket. People are apparently having sex all night, making noise, screaming, and there are unusual mechanical sounds, etc. It's ridiculous and must stop now.

We have asked for help from the manager and have had no success in getting him to return my calls or to get the people in 208 to stop disturbing the peace.

For the money we pay to live in 4190, I would think that we could at least get the courtesy of a telephone call.

I'm very disappointed in the Group, your manager and the Association for allowing such behavior in what could have been a nice building.

Mrs. Dresden is significantly handicapped, and recovering from injuries too numerous to enumerate. She was in a car accident seven years ago and we moved to 4190 to help her on her final period of healing.

Please respond immediately by calling me at 763-555-5847.

Thank you for your prompt attention,
Ashley Drexel

Cc: Megan Dresden, Vance Harris, Paul Parks, Mgr., Sandy Davids, Association Director

That should do the trick. If they don't respond to this, then I'll call the police next time. Poor Megan. That useless bitch Mary. I'm so sick of her. Leaves Megan in the park then doesn't answer Megan's cries for help. She's not doing her job. Today I talk to Megan about that woman.

She sealed the last envelope, put on the stamps and readied them for the morning mail.

This is going to stop NOW. Tomorrow all the parties should be reading the letter and then they can call ME to resolve this mess.

She picked up the phone and called 4190. She knew that Megan would be sleeping but Mary should be… *better be* awake.

"Mary? This is Ashley. Do you know that Megan had to call the police last night?"

"What?"

"You were sleeping away while Megan was being driven insane by those idiots upstairs. She cried and cried for you and you never came."

"I don't know what you're talking about. I went to bed at midnight and I got up a half hour ago. You have a problem with me getting seven and a half hours of sleep, Ashley?"

"Mary, we're paying you to take care of Megan."

"Ashley, I'm the ONLY person taking care of Megan. Whatever was bothering Megan last night has stopped and I'll take care of everything here on my end. Now I have to get to work."

Mary slammed the phone down.

She can't do that. She works for us! Who does she think she is? Doesn't she realize we can fire her and she will be out of the best job she ever had in her life? Stupid woman.

Mary walked into Megan's room. She was fine. Sleeping like a baby. She would have a talk with Megan about Ashley's erratic behavior later. Ashley had been losing it. It was high time that Megan put someone in charge of Megan who had Megan and only Megan's best interests at heart, someone who wasn't so stressed.

And we have to make it all seem like it's Megan's idea. She says it has to happen and it probably can happen…have no idea how to make it legal…how to be someone's trustee…can't be that hard. Ashley did it. Weasel. Bet she soaks Megan dry.

Well, two can play at that. We're going to take off for Vegas. That will show the bitch who's in charge.

Mary went into Ashley's office, flicked the computer on and shortly thereafter brought up Expedia.com. Time to see how easy it is to get out of town and to Las Vegas with someone in a wheelchair. People do it all the time, but you don't want to have a wheelchair on board and there is no way Megan could make it down that aisle to a seat in coach… so that means first class and Ashley would freak out at an expensive ticket. *She'd freak out no matter what, of course,* Mary figured.

Sun Country Airlines, a chief competitor of Delta, had some good fares. Whereas Delta tickets cost in the thousands for first class, Sun Country was in the hundreds, and for a nonstop flight.

I don't get it. Why would you fly on a plane that is five times as expensive? OK, we can leave Monday...come back on Thursday...and have three nights at the MGM in that big suite. Wow, it's seven hundred bucks a night. The tickets are only eight hundred and fifty dollars for both of us. Oh well. Not my money.

Ah... "Please enter your payment details."...OK...let's see...her credit cards are in the wallet.

She pushed away from the computer and went into Megan's room. Not sneaking, but not loudly, either. Went to the walker, checked in the bag that she'd made for the walker.

Sure enough here's the wallet...and the credit cards...hmmm... which one? How about...American Express. Sounds good. We'll just put everything else back in there and straighten it up a bit.

Now, back to Expedia.com and see if we can make this happen.

She punched in the numbers, expiration date and the CV code from the front of the card. She'd never seen that before. Hit enter and...

Very nice. Authorization approved. That was easy. Vegas, here we come. She couldn't help but smile, then grin, then smile again.

She flicked off the computer and took Megan's card back to the room. Back to the walker, return the card to the wallet and the wallet to the bag and presto. All done.

Now all there is to do is wait 'til she wakes up, and then tell her the good news. Time to go watch some TV.

***

It wasn't all that much longer until Megan awoke and needed the bathroom.

"Mary." Megan called out, but not so loudly – she never wanted to sound like she was yelling at Mary. "Mary."

Mary heard the cry for help. She used the remote to switch off the TV, and headed back to the other side of the condo.

Megan's hearing was filled with the sound of the compressor. All the rest of the noises had ceased.

There must be some machine up there that they keep on all night. Things had gotten better since the policeman left. They must all go home in the day time after they work. Sleep, maybe? I'm just glad it stopped.

"Good morning, Megan." Mary was rarely so chipper.

"Good morning, Mary."

"Ready for the morning restroom stop?"

"I am. Thank you."

"Heard you had another eventful night in here last night. Ashley called. I told her that we had everything under control."

"You must have been sleeping really well. I couldn't wake you up." Megan wasn't angry; she was just reporting the news.

"Slept like a baby. And Megan, I have some news for you."

She helped Megan into the chair. Megan would have preferred to use the walker but Mary had to have this conversation now, before Ashley called or came over.

"Good news?"

"It is. I've decided that you have been under way too much stress lately. Those people making all that noise up there have kept you awake and miserable for a week. Well, Ashley says she's getting it taken care of, but who knows what will really happen. Then I got to thinking that Ashley has been under a lot of pressure lately as well. She needs a break almost as badly as you do.

"So I've decided you and I are going to go visit in Las Vegas for a few days. We leave Monday, come back Thursday. So even if the next couple of nights are noisy with those mean people up there, there'll be plenty of time for Ashley to get rid of them while we're gone and the best part is, you'll be assured of some peace and quiet.

"So. I reserved a room at the MGM Grand! That big suite I was telling you about where you could either use your walker or wheelchair. It's very big, and it's very accessible. I looked at some pictures online. It's really fancy.

"They have a few of those big suites that are what they call 'wheelchair accessible,' you know, where everything is lower to the ground and so on. So how does that all sound? Exciting?"

Megan was both excited and concerned. "Mary, did Ashley say it was OK? I mean…"

Mary cut her off. Not even going to go there.

"Honey, this is just as much a gift for her as it is for you. You know Ashley, she'll want to work too hard and be too involved, so she won't want you to go. I strongly suggest you tell her to stay here and she can have some quality time with Lauren and Robert. This is a prime opportunity for her to connect with her family for a few nights, you know. Honey, I've thought this all out. She'll be upset initially and we'd expect no less. But that teenager needs guidance from her mom."

Megan's expression changed. *Mary's right,* she thought.

Mary really does care about Ashley and her family. Ashley thinks Mary's abrasive and she can be, but she's always thinking about other people. I can't imagine how I'm going to get on the airplane but I'll just trust that this is part of the bigger purpose. I wish they would turn that compressor off.

"Mary, do you think we can get them to turn that noise off up there?"

"Of course, dear. If we hear it again, I will personally go up there, raise hell, contact the manager and if all that fails, get the police back out here. Now listen, here is the itinerary. You can tell Ashley that you are going to go. Make it sound like it's your idea to give her some time with Lauren. She needs to know you're thinking about her as much as she's thinking about you, OK?"

"OK. I think about her. I worry about her all the time. OK. I'll tell her."

"And you can't take no for an answer. You insist. This is good for you. And it's good for their family. Make sense?"

Mary got Megan back to her bed and helped her up into bed, plumping her pillow just so to make it all nice and comfy.

"It does. Everybody gets to be happy for a few days."

"Wonderful, Megan. Great. Now, I used your American Express Card. I knew you'd want me to put it on there because it's a travel card and just smart to use it for traveling. That's what you would have told me to do had you been awake, of course."

Megan nodded. "Good decision, Mary. You're just like Ashley. Smart. I'm so lucky."

"I suggest you call Ashley soon with your news. Tell her that you are so excited and can't wait to go. Remember, she'll be upset, but deep down she knows she needs the time with her family."

"OK. I'll call her."

"I'll go work on breakfast and be back up in a bit."

***

"Absolutely not!"

"Ashley, you're not my mother. You are my trustee, so don't give me a hard time about this. You need the time off to be with your family, I need to get away from this house, and Mary is willing to take me on a trip. It's going to be fun. I'm going to have fun. When was the last time I had fun?"

Ashley put one hand on her head, and squeezed the telephone with the other. What a turn of events. One minute she's preparing to fire Mary, the next she's trying to deal with a four-day trip to Las Vegas. What a mess.

"Look, Megan, you said the police have taken care of the problem upstairs. Mary hasn't been too reliable this last week and I feel really uncomfortable having you go two thousand miles away with someone who leaves you for two hours at a park."

"Ashley. I'm not calling for your permission. I'm calling to tell you to take a few days off to be with Lauren and Robert and that I want to get away for a couple of days. Can't you be happy for me? I'm happy for you."

Does she have a point? No. This woman will NOT take care of Megan. This is crazy.

"Megan, if anything happens down there, I'm not there to come and get you when Mary leaves you somewhere. You'll have no backup person when something uncomfortable or bad happens. Let's take a day and think about it, OK? Can we talk about it again tomorrow? I mean, when do you want to go?"

"I want to go Monday."

"Monday. Oh my G-, look, Megan, OK, let's talk about this tomorrow so cooler heads can prevail."

"OK, Ashley."

"Talk to you later, Megan."

"Bye, Ashley."

What the hell is that woman scheming? Is she nuts? She leaves Megan alone for hours in a park. She doesn't answer the call of a screaming woman two hundred feet from her door. All in twenty-four hours and I'm going to sanction a trip for four days to Las Vegas. That's NUTS! I don't think I can actually force Megan to not go; and even if I could I'm not sure it would be the right thing.

Goddamn, the world is upside down. Megan, for the first time in seven years, is actually improving physically to where she can get around...a little. What no one sees is this last seven years I've worked fourteen to sixteen hours every day for Megan. There is no, "Thanks Ashley, good job." Nothing. Just getting yelled at by the person who was my best friend forever.

Seven years I busted my ass for David. God love David. What a good guy. But he never took ten seconds off work. He was always on. And then I was always on. And Megan, Megan was out playing.

She was out at a party or putting on a fundraiser. For fourteen years I have totally busted my backside more than any other friend or any employee ever would.

Since the move I've actually had time to spend with my daughter, and my marriage had two good days this week. That would be two damn good days in the last decade. Robert has been so sweet. He gets everything that goes on. He loves Megan too. But he's just about out of empathy for her. I never thought I'd see the day.

And now Megan is hearing things? Or is she? How do I know. When I looked at 4190 it seemed just fine. Had it inspected. Fine. Visited at different times of day and it was calm, peaceful and filled with people well over twice Megan's age. A perfect place for her to continue the healing process, which realistically will never be over.

And now she thinks there's a prostitution ring upstairs. Seriously, how many people could be in a ring that fits in 4190? Five? Three?

But why would she lie? She wouldn't lie. Mary would lie. That woman is a bitch. I wish I never hired her. Megan has no reason to lie. Megan has never lied to me. She never did anything in her whole life except tell me what was on her mind. And now she's acting like a goof.

Why? What is UP with that girl?

The stress is getting to me. Yes. She's there in a chair most of the day and life sucks for her. No doubt. Life has sucked for a long, long time for her. She's had no love or male companionship. Just Grace, then Mary and me. And that is about it.

It's not that people don't love her, it's that it's exhausting just to visit Megan. Every small task is a BIG PROJECT when Megan is involved.

Hookers? Come ON! I just can't see it. I guess maybe...maybe...it's possible. I sure as hell can't go say, "Megan, you are full of shit." There's my best friend, lost forever with that conversation. And more than that. My job, my life, my career. I've invested over half of my life into her family and her life.

No. She is not full of shit. She is a good person. She is a great person. She has always been good to me, loved me, taken care of me and I've done the same for her.

That first day in the hospital, I couldn't do anything but cry and pray.

That's what I feel like now. DAMMIT. I think I'm going nuts. Who's going to take care of me?

***

A nice cool breeze swept through Megan's room. It was midnight. She had watched her nighttime TV shows on cable, including a fifty-year-old Hitchcock movie. She'd also read some pages about Las Vegas that Mary had printed out from the computer.

Computers had changed so much. When she'd had the accident they'd been slow and clunky. Now they were lightning fast. Pretty amazing. She wanted to actually sit behind one and see what else could be discovered. She was praying for the day.

So far, the evening had been rather quiet. The sound of the wind masked the sound of the compressor upstairs. She thought it would be louder when Mary insisted on having the window open but that turned out to be not the case. She had no idea why.

Mary walked in the room with a spring in her step.

"Hello, Megan, I'm up past my bedtime and wanted to see if I could get you anything before I turn in."

"Oh hi, Mary. No. Thank you." She looked over to see if her water and Ambien were by the bedside. They were. "I'll be fine."

"I'm sure you'll sleep better tonight knowing that in just a couple nights you'll be in a luxurious suite at one of the nicest hotels in the world. It's been a while since you were treated the way you really deserve to be."

Megan smiled. "Thank you Mary. I think it will be fun. I'm a little nervous..." she looked down, then back up at Mary, "A lot nervous... but I think it will be fun."

"Can I catch the light for you?" Mary was on her way out.

"Yes. Please. Thank you, Mary, Good night."

Megan's bedside lamp was the only light in the room. She reached for the bottle of Ambien and pondered whether she should take one or two. She decided on two. She wanted to go to sleep and not wake up 'til morning.

She put the pill on her tongue and swallowed two with pride. A month ago, she couldn't even do that. She thought she would sleep well tonight.

On the other side of town Ashley lay awake in bed. Robert was sleeping away, snoring. She hadn't told him about the day's events.

I hope she's sleeping well tonight. It's so hard to believe that all these years of work could be destroyed by that woman. She wants Megan's money? Why take her to Las Vegas? Why?

She knows it's going to be a lot easier to persuade Megan to loosen up the purse strings in her direction now or in the future if she isn't in Edina. It's that simple. Ultimately, all things considered, Megan is safe from anything wild as long as there is no other relationship.

The business. Mary knows that she can't get to that except through me and that IS just about all the money Megan has…Megan has what, twenty thousand in her own account? Everything else in trust. Mary has more money than Megan does. That woman probably has tens of thousands of dollars stashed in a mattress somewhere. No expenses. Nice income.

So, it seems pretty impossible that Mary would be nuts enough to actually kill Megan, even if she was stupid enough to leave her alone for hours. She's an evil bitch but it's a long jump to that scenario.

So the next thing would be to access the money in the company. Megan could probably actually fire me I guess…legally…no matter what David's wishes were. What are the odds that Mary could stand in front of a judge and make him believe that would be the best thing for Megan? Not good.

Any other possibilities? They want to go for fun? To be closer friends? To help Megan be happy? Nope. No other possibilities.

SO, we work under the assumption that some heavy duty brainwashing will be happening in Vegas. And where does that put me? Megan has made so much progress, that this is no time to set her back in any way. She hasn't been sleeping well. Oh God what a mess. You know what the answer is? Megan has to say "no" without me saying "no" because if I say "no" it's like telling your teenager "no."

OK. Plan is simple. Encourage the trip. Cut back on Megan's credit lines for the cards she's carrying. Mary doesn't run off with the money… oh…that's a VERY INTERESTING scenario.

Encourage the trip? It will be four days of hell. And Megan will be at real risk. One screw-up by Mary, and Megan could be harmed or worse.

What a mess. God, I have to get to sleep. Tomorrow is going to be a long day.

Ashley fell asleep. Five hours later her world would take another turn and she wouldn't even know it.

***

"OH GOD! OH JESUS!"

Terror.

Megan shot up in bed. It had never dawned on her until now that her body had the ability to do that.

Violent shakes and quivers pounded through her body. She couldn't steady herself or stop the shaking and body spasms.

She looked up. She could see the ceiling moving. The noise was horrific. The compressor was at full blast. The Emergency Broadcasting System couldn't have been louder and there were screams from at least two or maybe three women. She heard a sound like a jackhammer.

"MARY, MARY, HELP ME!"

Mary heard the cries from her bed. She bolted out of bed and raced into Megan's room.

"Megan, what's wrong?" Mary was alarmed. Megan looked white as a ghost and Mary was scared by how scared Megan was.

"Mary, tell them to stop! I'm shaking so bad. I feel like I'm going to fall out of bed!"

Mary saw that Megan was shaking, but not violently… but Megan *thought* she was shaking violently. Instinctively she grabbed the bottle of Ambien and gave Megan two of them. She put the Ambien in Megan's mouth.

"Drink it down." She had no idea what she was doing. Megan would need to calm down and the Ambien might help.

She set the glass down and then sat right next to Megan. Put her arms around her and held her tight.

"Calm down, honey."

"GET THEM TO STOP ALL THE NOISE MARY. GET THEM TO STOP IT NOW!"

Mary thought fast. There was no noise. The window was open. There was a nice gentle breeze. The neighborhood was silent.

Jesus, what the hell do you do?

"I will honey. I will, but first we need to calm you down. No matter how loud someone else is, you can calm down."

She had no ideas where those words came from. Megan started to breathe more regularly as if the words were an incantation.

"Oh Mary, I can't handle that noise. You have to stop them. Please, go up there and stop them and come right back down. Please don't leave me."

Mary wasn't sure if she wanted her to stay or go.

"You want me to go up there, stop the noise and then come back right away? Is that what you're saying?"

"YES. Now please go get them to stop."

"OK. I'll be right back." She went for her robe, put her slippers on and bolted out every door between her and the stairs heading up to 208. As she hit the final stair she didn't know what to do next.

Like a dream but being awake. Dammit. Do I wake these people up? DAMN.

She put her ear up against the door. Nothing. The halls were silent.

Either Megan was nuts or she was. *DAMN.*

The last thing Mary wanted was to stir up any trouble before their trip. In forty-eight hours they'd be in Las Vegas.

She raced back downstairs and was literally out of breath as she got back to Megan's room. Megan wasn't in bed. She was in the wheelchair, wheeling herself to the bathroom and weeping. Mary grabbed the grips on the back of the chair and pushed her along.

"How are you, honey?"

"Did you tell them to shut up and stop it?" She was focused on getting to the bathroom. Her bladder wouldn't hold much longer. Mary maneuvered her and got her up.

"How are you, honey? I want you to answer me, without asking me a question." Again she had no idea where that came from. But it was the right thing to say strategically to help Megan calm down.

She had no idea if Megan was still hearing things or if she wasn't. Not a clue. She didn't know how to tell Megan that it was silent in the apartment upstairs. God, this was strange… at least she had stopped shaking. That was good news.

"I, I, I, they are still making some noise. I don't think you got all of them to stop."

"Well honey, I yelled at 'em when that door opened and I said, 'Y'all have two minutes to shut up or I'm calling the police.'"

"Who was in there?"

"I have no idea. I beat on the door. It opened and I yelled, then I raced back down here to make sure you were OK."

"Oh, thank you, Mary." She put her head down as she sat on the stool.

The noise began to subside. Mary saw that the color was coming back into her face. At least she wasn't going to die.

"How are you, Megan?"

"Better. Not as scared."

"Well, nothing to be scared of really. Just some stupid people making noise, if you think about it."

Megan did think about it as she nodded. Megan signaled that she wanted to get her back onto the wheelchair. Mary got her off the stool and moved her quickly back to the chair and toward bed. Megan put her hand on the bed, and Mary instinctively knew that Megan wasn't ready to get into bed yet. That was fine.

"Mary, this has to stop. If this happens again, we have to move."

Mary's heart lightened and the wheels in her brain started turning at full blast. Better than she could have ever hoped for.

"Darn right. What a terrible place Ashley put us in here. What was she thinking? I can't imagine. Well, how about we figure out where to sleep? We don't need to deal with these crazy people anymore."

"OK. That's right. We have to get out of here."

"We will, honey. We will."

Mary put Megan back in bed.

The next day Megan called Ashley immediately upon waking and told her what had happened. Ashley insisted on talking to Mary, who verified everything Megan had said. Ashley knew the letter would arrive that day at all the parties' doorsteps.

She called the police to stop in and check again. No one was home and in fact, the manager said that the Harrises were having their mail held for the weekend. No one was even at the condo.

It couldn't be stranger. Maybe there was a prostitution ring based in there, who knew? It just didn't add up. Something was definitely screwy.

The next night Megan heard the racket again. Even louder and with more people. In the morning she called Ashley, who was now at her wits' end. She finally decided to spend the night there with Megan and Mary and get to the bottom of things.

When she went upstairs to knock on the door of 208 at about ten p.m., no one answered. She had no idea what she would say had the Harrises actually opened the door, and she was relieved no one was home. Then she double-checked with the manager, who was growing more annoyed by the day. The Harrises were out of town and wouldn't be back until Monday night.

Back to 108. The guest room was taken up with her office and as a space for extra storage, so she removed the rollaway from the closet and decided to sleep in Megan's room.

Mary loathed Ashley but this was the night before they were leaving for Las Vegas. Nothing would be said that might stop the trip. She went to bed, and all was peaceful.

Ashley said goodnight to Megan and they both fell asleep. It was about eleven. Ashley wasn't a night owl like Megan.

At about 4:30 Megan started talking and then shouting in her sleep and then opened her eyes, wide awake.

Ashley watched, confused, then chilled, then terrified.

My God.

She jumped off the rollaway.

Megan knew Ashley was there, but all she could do was look at the ceiling, raise her right fist and yell at the ceiling.

"SHUT UP, STOP IT. GO AWAY!" She looked at the ceiling and wept. No tears. There never would be again in her life. She sobbed loudly. Megan was clearly being terrorized.

Ashley looked up. Speechless, for the first time in her life not knowing what to say or do.

"Megan, Megan, Megan. Listen, honey. It's OK."

"It's NOT OK, they're driving me insane. I can't take it! There are three of them having sex and the compressor is full bore and the Emergency Broadcasting System is full blare. Can you PLEASE go get them to stop?"

Ashley didn't know what to do.

"OK, Megan, I'll go see what I can do." She got up, put on her robe and shoes and headed up to 208.

What if there was a noise but I didn't hear it? No, that's not possible. I watched Megan going crazy.

She got up to 208. It was silent. She rapped on the door. Nothing. She rapped again. Nothing. She waited. Nothing. As she already knew, no one was home. She went back downstairs. Back into the bedroom. She went to Megan, who had her face in her hands sitting on the bed.

"Did you tell them to stop? Because they're quieter but they still are making noise."

"Honey, listen to me." Ashley tugged at Megan's hands. "Listen, Megan. Listen."

"What?"

For Ashley, this was as hard as seeing Megan immediately after the accident. Her best friend in the world was having hallucinations or delusions or something. Because what she was saying couldn't possibly be real... could it?

"Megan, honey, there is no one there. They are out of town until tomorrow night."

There was a long pause. Ashley held Megan tight.

Mary arrived on the scene. She knew what was going on right away. She simply stood in the doorway.

Megan looked at her hands. The ceiling. Mary. Ashley… her eyes stayed with Ashley. Ashley held her breath, waiting for a sign that her friend was not lost to madness.

"Then they are radioing me to get me back for sending the letter ratting on them about the prostitution ring. Ashley, they are radioing me. They're doing this to punish me. Ashley, you have to get them to stop."

At this point in Megan's life, Ashley was powerless to stop her going to Las Vegas. But she was very, very worried.

Chapter Twenty Four

June 11

Day 2455

The service on Sun Country Airlines was really pretty good. It had been years since Megan had been on a plane. She felt heartened that she hadn't received many "looks" from other passengers. The flight attendants didn't seem to find her repulsive, either.

Maybe this trip will be fun after all.

She certainly had wondered.

Mary was fast asleep in the seat next to her. Megan was glad to see her resting. They would arrive in twenty minutes.

As they flew in over Lake Mead she craned her neck to look past her sleeping caretaker at an array of blue and blue green colors in a lake that looked like it had been drying up or losing water somehow.

It is the desert after all.

She could see people waterskiing and boating on the lake. It was really quite beautiful, like all the views out the window for the past hour and a half, since flying over the Rockies. This was also where she encountered something she had happily forgotten about long ago. Turbulence in the air.

It dawned on Megan that in the "unlikely event of an emergency landing" of any kind, she would never get off the plane, and neither would Mary, who was pinned in the window seat. Those fears and that scenario were soon allayed as the descent brought the city and "The Strip" into full view. Like a theme park for grown-ups, there was a huge pyramid and a castle next to it, a Statue of Liberty, a huge Space Needle similar to the one she had seen in Seattle years ago. There was an enormous castle, and not far away was the Eiffel Tower! She had been to all of the "real" structures except the cartoonish looking castle, in real life before the accident. It brought back memories. Lots of memories.

And then there were buildings, dozens of enormous buildings that must have been fifty stories or more, each, in the middle of the desert.

Numerous helicopters could be seen in the air. And the traffic on The Strip could be seen from where she was. It looked like 35W and Crosstown at rush hour.

The pilot had indicated moments ago that the current temperature was 97 degrees and that within a couple of hours the city would reach its day's high of 104.

Not a cloud in the sky. So picturesque.

As the plane touched down, the entire cabin applauded. She didn't remember that ever happening before. Maybe gamblers were appreciative people, or maybe they didn't fly much. After the bumpy Colorado part of the flight, she confessed that she wanted to applaud as well.

The touchdown was what woke Mary up. The brakes were on and Megan wondered what would happen if they stopped working.

I'd never get off the plane, would I? Well, we're here, and it seems like a fun place.

The mood on the plane was giddy now. As people stood to get their baggage from the overhead compartments, all she could see were smiles. People talking about sports and blackjack, craps and roulette. Megan knew nothing about these games; she had never been much of a gambler, and neither had David. He used to say he worked hard for his money and wasn't going to "piss it away" gambling. She always hated that phrase. David rarely cursed but that theme was common with David. His mom must have drilled it into his head early. "Waste not, want not." That was another. Megan's Mom and Dad had no such phrases that she was aware of.

After a hundred people squeezed by her, ramming their luggage into her left arm, occasionally hitting her in the head with handbags… they were the last ones on the plane. The flight attendant brought a wheelchair to Megan's seat, where, after much trouble, Megan was able to get into the chair, with some assistance from Mary.

From here, Mary would wheel her through the "D" Gates, as they were called. There were slot machines clanking not long after deplaning. Mary moved pretty quickly as she was going to have her luggage picked up and delivered to the hotel. Megan had no idea you could do that. They walked past a Cinnabon, Ruby's Diner, an eating spot that looked straight out of the 1950s, and a store that sold DVDs and what appeared to be portable DVD players. That was definitely new and interesting. Then they got to the escalator. That would have been impossible, so they located the elevator straight ahead and took it down one flight. Just as they wheeled off the elevator a tram was arriving. The doors opened, and Mary pushed Megan onboard.

"How do you know where to go?"

"Used to live here. Fun town. We'll check in downstairs."

"You can check in for the hotel at the airport?"

"Yep. There'll be a place to register for the MGM. They'll get the luggage and bring it over. All we have to do is have them bring up the limo once we get our room keys."

The elevator pinged. It was empty. Mary wheeled Megan on and hit the "1" button. Megan listened for noise.

The elevator was quiet but the noise was here… following her. How strange.

It's that compressor. How can that be? We are all the way across the country.

"How ya doin', honey?"

Megan looked up and paused. "I'm fine. Are you glad to be here, Mary?"

"Oh, honey you don't know the half of it. We are going to have a great time."

The door pinged, and they were on the baggage claim level.

Mary was right. There was the MGM Hotel Registration. Right here in an airport. What a strange thing.

"Can we get a limo for you?"

"That would be nice."

Mary reached into Megan's bag and snapped out a MasterCard. They were next in line, and Mary had them checked in, while a bellboy arranged to have their luggage delivered to their hotel room.

How will he know which luggage is ours? This airport is like magic. Wonder what the hotel will be like.

Megan wasn't sure what she was excited about, but she was excited. It had been years since she had ridden in a limousine. They could be so nice, so spacious, and glamorous.

The bellboy directed them through the baggage area, taking the claim tickets from Mary. He brought them straight to a line of limos, and his signal was met with an instant response.

In seconds the driver was out of the car and ready to help Megan out of the wheelchair. With the bellboy's help she was delivered right into the car. Megan wasn't sure how they maneuvered her that quickly, but they did. Mary entered on the other side and sat a few feet across from Megan. The driver slid the wheelchair into the trunk and was quickly back inside the car. It was graceful and seamless, and she felt happier than she had in a long time.

"Water's in the cooler on the sides, ladies."

Mary reached in and snatched two. She unscrewed the top of one, handing it to Megan and making sure it was steady in her hand, then opened one herself.

The desert heat certainly was that and more, but when the driver closed the door, the car almost instantly cooled.

They were off.

The driver followed Mary's instructions. She told Dan not to go straight to the hotel, but to the end of The Strip first, and then to turn around and drive all the way back down so Megan could see up close the sights she'd seen from the air. She wanted Megan to see the pirate ship in the lagoon at Treasure Island, the volcano in front of the Mirage, the Eiffel Tower in front of the Paris, and the Statue of Liberty, standing tall, in front of the New York New York.

They didn't drive past the giant pyramid at the Luxor or the castle at the Excalibur but they could see both. It was strangely beautiful, and a lot to take in. Megan commented excitedly on each of the hotels and their main attraction The Strip. She really liked the dancing water fountains in front of the Bellagio Hotel. She wanted to see them again for sure.

And here was the MGM Grand. Not as amazing from the outside as so many of the other hotels on the strip but it was enormous. Maybe Dan was right and this was one of the largest hotels in the world.

Five thousand rooms? How can anything be that big? I wonder why Mary wanted to stay here instead of at one of the other hotels. Doesn't matter. This is exciting!

As quickly as the driver and bellboy had gotten Megan into the limo, another bellman and Dan got her out and back into the wheelchair. Before she knew it she was in the spacious registration area. The first thing she saw was the array of enormous, super-sized TV screens on the walls over the registration area. The first video she saw was of a magician she recognized but whose name she couldn't recall. The next video clips were from what looked like the Crazy Horse in Paris. They were showing clips from other attractions at the hotel as well. She had been around the world and never seen anything so big… and this was only the registration area. She suspected this was going to be quite a stay!

They were destined for what was called a "Marquee Suite." Eight hundred dollars a night seemed rather expensive for two people but the suite would be wonderful. Two bedrooms, completely handicap accessible with a whirlpool, complete living room and 1700 square feet of wheelchair freedom. There was a big TV in each bedroom and a giant TV in the living room. What more could anyone want?

That was important because tonight *CSI: Crime Scene Investigation* would be on, and Megan never missed an episode; it was one of her favorite shows.

She had grown to love mysteries of all kinds in the past several years. But *CSI* was special. She often imagined that someday when she was able to walk again, she'd like to be an actual crime scene investigator.

The show was always exciting in a methodical kind of way. The show was in the top 20 most watched shows since the crash. It made her heart race every week

As they wheeled down the long corridor on the twenty-eighth floor toward the suite, Mary's heart jumped when Megan announced her plans to stay in and watch *CSI*.

"Are you sure?" Mary prayed that Megan was sure. A night out in Vegas with Megan's credit card and no time limit could be great fun, and it would give her a chance to see her cousin earlier than she had originally planned.

"I can't wait to get out and play, but tonight I just want to stay in and watch CSI. You go on, see a show, have fun. We can go out tomorrow. I'm tired from traveling anyway. I'll have more energy tomorrow."

They arrived at the double doors at the end of the hallway. Mary stopped the wheelchair short of the door, slid the key card down the slot, and the indicator flashed green. In they went.

"This is so beautiful." Megan was thrilled. She felt so at home. It was so meticulously decorated and in some ways reminded her of the home that had been taken from her. Mary had calculated that it would have the desired effect.

She had no problem giving Megan the master bedroom. They were both gorgeous and the only difference was the whirlpool.

I'll be gone anyway, what do I care?

Within seconds the doorbell sounded.

"What's that?" Megan was startled. She then realized she was still hearing the compressor sound and didn't like it.

"It's just a doorbell. Someone is at the door, come on."

She wheeled the chair around, went past the wet bar into the living room, and answered the door.

It was the man from room service. Strangely, he had their baggage, along with a basket of fruit, and a bottle of wine to boot.

Mary immediately went to the bag on Megan's wheelchair and grabbed a $10 bill, handing it to the man.

"Can I put your bags in your rooms?"

Mary liked that idea.

"Yes, please do. The big one goes in the master bedroom, the small one goes in mine."

"Very well."

Megan couldn't believe how fast they had gotten here with the bags, and of course she saw the fruit and wine, which the man carefully placed on the enormous dining room table.

"I am leaving a corkscrew and two glasses for you as well. My name is Roberto and if there is anything I can do for you, please push 7 on your phone, and I will be here for you immediately."

Mary and Megan thanked him in unison.

Then Mary opened the drapes along the perimeter of the room. The view of The Strip was magnificent. When the sun went down, it would be a spectacular sight.

"Mary, you were right. This is wonderful."

There were only a few places the wheelchair would fit between furniture to get up close to the window, but Megan immediately laid her paths. She loved the view.

"What should we order for dinner?" Mary wanted to get food up here and then get out.

"What time is it?"

"It's six-thirty."

Megan wasn't used to having things move this quickly. In what normally would have been an all day and night experience, perhaps ten hours, she had just gotten from the airport to her hotel room in less than forty-five minutes.

Mary snatched the room service menu off of the desk, and noticed that was where they could connect to high speed Internet access. They wouldn't be using that perk. No way was Ashley going to have any chance to contact Megan without Mary being aware of it.

"They have Prime Rib, New York Strip, Porterhouse, Tuscan Halibut, Herb Grilled Organic Salmon, and Pesto Sea Bass. My goodness, they have everything. Are you sure you'll be OK here by yourself?"

"I want to be here by myself. I'll be fine."

"Are you sure you want me to go out and leave you here?"

"Yes, Mary, I'm fine. I want to watch *Survivor* and *CSI*. You said that *Survivor* starts at eight here so that means I'll have plenty of time to see what's happening on the island while I get ready to watch *CSI*."

"Get ready to watch TV" was an unusual statement for some, but not Megan. It took time, a lot of time, to get to the bathroom and back. She moved like a snail, and it would take about an hour for her to get to the bathroom and back into the living room.

"Well then, we need to get you a nice dinner and soon."

"What would I do without you?"

"Oh, you know I hate to leave you by yourself, but I know you want to start becoming more independent; I know how important that is to you."

"It's so important, Mary."

"You do need to be independent, don't you dear? There's a phone by the toilet in the bathroom and there is one by the bed and there is one on the desk and the table. If you need anything, remember to call Roberto. I'll order you a New York Strip and then take a shower and get changed."

Megan nodded and started wheeling herself slowly around the suite, getting used to the terrain. It wasn't the same as hardwood floors, but she could manage. Mary had set the walker by the desk, so Megan could use it if she decided to get out of her chair.

Mary knew that Megan could only be about as independent as a ten-year-old, but it was, after all, her idea to stay in alone, and she would tell Ashley that. On her way into the bathroom, Mary opened the doors to the television housed inside an oversized entertainment center.

Megan had figured out the remote control by the time Mary returned. It was just about seven o'clock. The doorbell rang.

Again Megan flinched. Again, she was hearing the compressor sound. Where was it coming from? She wished she could figure out how the sound from 4190 could be here. It made no sense.

Mary turned the door handle and Roberto wheeled in an elegant table and setting that was exquisite, almost regal, she thought. Megan would be able to eat while sitting in her wheelchair. There was enough food for an army.

"Just the one meal this evening?"

"Yes, just for Megan. I'm not hungry, thanks."

Not in a million years would she tell someone else she was going to leave Megan alone for the rest of the night.

"Very well. May I open the wine and pour you both a glass?"

That sounded good to Mary.

"Yes, that would be wonderful." Mary was sounding as sophisticated as she possibly could. She generally hated the wealthy, but she was in this elegant suite and she thought she should act like she fit in. She no more belonged there than the man on the moon. But there she was, she tipped well, and Roberto had learned long ago that in Las Vegas, appearances are deceiving.

Mary nabbed another $10 out of the wallet in Megan's bag on the back of the wheelchair and gave it to Roberto.

"Bill this to the room?"

"Of course." Mary thought that sounded right.

Roberto poured, and made eye contact with Megan. He was an attractive man, she thought. Probably Mexican; she wasn't sure. He reminded her of the gardener.

"Will there be anything else?"

Megan finally got in a few words. "Thank you, Roberto, no."

"Very well then. Remember, I'm number seven on your telephone."

"Thank you, Roberto." Megan was finally regaining her assertiveness.

"You're welcome."

Mary slid yet another $10 into Roberto's hand, as he turned for the door. And now, Mary was ready to get out of there.

"OK, Megan, what else can I get you before I go? Are you sure you want me to leave you to your independence and not stay here with you to watch *CSI*?"

"Definitely. I want to manage on my own. "

Mary feigned a sigh, as if she had given up.

She wheeled Megan up to the table Roberto had left and made sure she was set straight on, facing the television. She looked to make sure the walk to the bathroom was clear.

"Megan. That door goes straight into the bathroom." She opened it and showed Megan the six-foot journey from where she sat. She went over to Megan's walker, leaned it against Roberto's table, and removed a door stop from the bag on Megan's wheelchair. She slid it under the bathroom door.

"Can I take you in there now or do you want me to get out of here?"

"I'm fine Mary, why don't you go and have some fun?" Megan thought she was being forceful. Mary never ceased to be amazed at how suggestible Megan was.

"All right, well dear, I'm off then. I've got my cell phone. You know the number. I charged your cell phone, and I'm leaving it here on the table. If you need anything call me or Roberto. He seems like someone you might need to call for help once or twice in the course of an evening."

Megan couldn't have agreed more. If she could figure out a way to pay Roberto to spend the evening with her, she would. But it wasn't likely. More likely was a good dinner, *Survivor, CSI,* and then to bed as that would be about eleven p.m. Minnesota time. Megan was tired.

"Your medication is here on the table. I also put some by the nightstand in your room in case you end up there and don't want to come all the way back out here. OK, I guess I should go now."

"Yes. You should go now."

She kissed Megan on the cheek. "Enjoy the show and call if you need me to come home."

"OK, but I'll be sleeping. Go have fun."

As the door closed behind her Megan flicked on the TV. She didn't really want to watch local news but that was the choice. No use getting involved in a movie you weren't going to finish watching.

***

Jake was a country hick, pure and simple. He and Mary sat down in a corner in the back of Buca di Beppo's restaurant. It was a hole in the wall Italian place behind the Flamingo with good food and photos of every celebrity that had ever visited the place from the '50s to now. Ernie, who was about seventy years old, played the accordion for tips, or not.

They both lit up cigarettes. She smoked a Newport and his was a Marlboro. Both of them were happy, relaxed.

"So what do you think? Is this going to be the week to finally make this happen?" Jake's voice was hopeful.

"I think so. She's REALLY happy to be here and she's loving me right now. Some of it's because she's away from that loon, Ashley, I swear. God, I hope so. I am so sick of hearing my name over and over. Mary this, Mary that. Mary would you please. Mary thank you. Mary Jesus Christ – forget my name already. Yes! This is the weekend."

Jake was all of fifty years old, but with his yellowed teeth and weathered face he looked like he belonged in an old Western movie. He could pass for Ernie's age in most people's eyes. He pulled an oversized envelope out from underneath his shirt. Why he had the envelope in his shirt was beyond Mary. Jake was quirky, and she simply wasn't going to ask.

"I had the lawyer draft the document. He says it will be legal in Nevada but won't carry back to Minnesota."

"So if we want to control things, it has to be from here?"

"That's what the man says. Now that she's functional, she has the right to appoint whomever she pleases to take care of her affairs. 'Course she could do it all herself, but you'll get the Power of Attorney and all the rest of the fancy legal lingo and we'll be set for life."

"Do I need to go before a judge?"

"Manly says ya don't. Says all ya gotta do is get her to sign the papers in front of a notary, get them to sign, and as long as you're in Nevada, you'll be running the show."

"After slaving for half a lifetime it's nice to know there's still justice in the world."

The irony of the statement wasn't lost on her, but it was on Jake.

"You want me to set up an appointment at the bank?"

"No… uh, yes. Go ahead. Day after tomorrow. Lunch. Wells Fargo downtown. I'll figure out a way to get her there."

"Good. Ya don't think she'll be any trouble, do ya?"

"Not a bit. I think I've got it all figured out."

She reached for the envelope, and he handed it over to her. She flipped the clasp open and pulled the papers out. There were a lot of them. Scanning through the bunch, she saw the agreement between her and Jake.

"50-50?" she snapped.

"Ya goin' back on your word to the family? We always said if anyone makes it, we split it equal."

"But you haven't slaved for years taking care of this."

"You want to go back on your word now?" His eyes flashed an angry warning she knew she should respect.

"No. It's fine." She clipped the fuse right before the spark hit the dynamite.

Arriving at their table, Ernie squeezed his instrument and sang for them.

At first they were both clearly and obviously annoyed by the intrusion, but after a while the distraction served to calm Jake down.

Mary took a dollar out of her purse and set it on the table for Ernie.

Ernie finished his song and trekked a couple of booths away, where he played another upbeat tune, from the '40s this time.

Mary reached into her purse again and pulled out a twenty and laid it on the table. The waitress hadn't even come for drinks at this point, but she didn't want to stay. She kept trying to calm herself thinking that the difference wasn't that big of a deal. But of course for Jake, it was.

“The waitress gets twenty just for letting you sit here?” he asked her.

“Yeah, why not. It’s Vegas. I’ll see you at noon at Wells Fargo, day after tomorrow. I’ve got tickets to a show. Gotta run.”

“OK, see you then.” She turned and walked out. He grabbed the twenty off the table, and waited for the waitress to come. He was going to eat. Mary might have been living high on the hog, but he had not. In the trailer park, there was no hog.

***

The previews for *CSI* were showing on the television. Then the theme song played.

The Who. *Who are you? Who, who?*

Tonight’s episode would affect Megan in ways she couldn’t have even imagined. Gil from *CSI* had been called in on a case to investigate the murder of a woman who had not let her murderer in… or out... of the apartment. The crime scene was bloody and scary looking, and Megan shivered as she watched.

The compressor sound had been bothering her ever since Roberto left. She wanted to know how she could still hear that sound in Las Vegas. It made no sense. And it was so loud.

She didn’t have this episode figured out early on like she did many others. She had to see Nick being watched through the small circular holes in his ceiling, before she had it figured out. It was the cable guy. Of course. He didn’t go out the front door or the window, because he went up into the ceiling. Brilliant.

Who would ever have thought of that? What a sicko.

Gil found all the bullet-sized holes in the ceiling and investigated the attic of the victim’s home, while Nick was being threatened across town. Gil seemed surprised at how many holes were in the ceiling and how well they were concealed from being seen from the apartment below. This guy was a pro; of course that’s what cable guys do all day. They make holes in floors and ceilings and track wire from side to side, so there are no cables visible. The cable guy had her every move down pat. He could terrorize her with phone calls from inside of her own house…from the attic…and she would think he was psychic, while she went psychotic.

The killer knew every step and breath the victim took. Every fear she possessed. She was a fish in a fishbowl just for him.

In the attic he had video equipment, high tech sound equipment, a tap into the phone line, and everything he needed to eavesdrop, spy on her, and torture her with scary calls and noises. No one would solve this kind of crime except Gil Grissom, of course.

To kill her, he would come down through an attic opening in the ceiling, as he did earlier in the show to attack Nick at his place.

Had she only been nice to him the day he installed her cable, he would never have killed her. It gave Megan the creeps. What was particularly disturbing was that the other team members, investigating his apartment where he lived in the attic, found dozens of video reels, camera equipment, and even more sound devices. He had everything he needed in his own attic.

What if that happened to me? I couldn't fight back! I'd be killed, too… and it's funny because all of these CSI's are based on true stories, I think. So this really happened to someone…maybe not in Las Vegas where the show is… but somewhere. What if that's why I hear the compressor? What if someone is eavesdropping on me? What if someone is watching me and torturing me with all of these sounds? There are holes in my ceiling!

She slowly poured herself another glass of wine, as she watched the final scene of the show. They got the bad guy. They usually got the bad guy.

She took her medications in one hand and sipped them down one by one with the wine. She wasn't supposed to mix alcohol with her medications, but it didn't make much difference one way or the other to Megan.

Maybe they're filming this week in Vegas, and I could meet some of the stars from the show. I wonder where they film it. They always talk about the Tangiers, but I don't think it's a real hotel.

Previews for next week's show looked exciting, and she would make sure that there was time to watch it. The show had been on forever. David had loved it too.

What was it about Gil Grissom that she liked so much? Warrick and Nick were much better looking and her age. But Gil was more interesting – more intricate. Sure sign of not being twenty-two any more, when you like the interesting fifty-year-old guy instead of the hot young ones.

I think I'll go to the bathroom and call it a night.

She grabbed her walker. She needed to get up and get at least a little exercise. She had been sitting all day. She hated the wheelchair but had to admit that today it really got her around, and she was happy about that.

Mary will probably be out for hours, which is fine. She wasn't going to use Mary's bathroom, she would use her own. The walk over there would be a long one. Forty feet, probably. So that meant about a half hour from here to there. She could wheel herself there in half the time. But she needed the exercise. After that, of course, she could plop into bed and call it a night.

The cell phone rang. It could only be Ashley or Mary. She bent over to pick up her phone and saw Ashley's number on the caller ID.

"Hello, Ashley. Did you see *CSI* tonight?"

"I did. Excellent show." The connection wasn't that clear, but Ashley could hear Megan.

"I didn't think you'd catch it this week."

"Why?"

"Because I figured you and Mary would be out at a show or something tonight. You know, getting wild in Las Vegas and all that."

"No. I told Mary she had to get out and see her cousin. I wanted to watch *CSI* and then go to bed."

"So what did Mary do?" Ashley got that uneasy feeling in her stomach.

"She went to have dinner with her cousin and then go to a show, I think."

"So...you...are there all alone?!" She was suppressing the anger, which she knew she couldn't contain for long.

"Yes, and I'm just fine. I've had dinner – steak and wine...and Roberto... he's the butler or room service guy or whatever they call them here in Las Vegas...and..."

"You mean to tell me that you are all alone?" It was as if she hadn't said the same words ten seconds ago.

"Yes, Ashley, and everything is fine. I need to establish my independence. I need to..."

"You need to *establish* your independence? Megan, you're doing that every day. You get a little better each and every day. You're doing great. But Mary has no right to up and leave you."

"She didn't up and leave me. I *told* her to go."

"This is ridiculous. OK. I'm calling Mary."

"Ashley, don't do that."

"Megan, just relax, and I'll get Mary back there."

"I don't want Mary back here."

"I want Mary there, Megan; that's why she works for you. She's supposed to take care of you."

"And she's doing a good job."

"She's having dinner with her cousin somewhere. You probably don't know where or when she'll be back. And if you fell or if there was a fire in the building, you'd be all alone and probably dead. No Megan, Mary is behaving irresponsibly *again*, and I am *sick* of it."

"But, Ashley..."

"Listen Megan, I love you. I'm not mad at you. I'm going to call Mary and get her butt back over there where she belongs. Call me if you need anything, OK?"

"OK." Megan didn't know what to say. She felt defeated. Ashley meant well, but she didn't need a mother. At least, she didn't think so.

"Talk to you later." Ashley ended the call and immediately punched in Mary's cell phone number.

Across town, Mary was walking out the door of the restaurant when her cell phone went off. She instantly hoped it wasn't Megan... and... it wasn't. It was worse. It was that bitch in Minneapolis. Oh, was she going to be surprised by the events that would take place in the next couple of days.

Why should I answer the phone? Who needs the stress? She turned the cell phone off and slid it back into her purse. To hell with you, Ashley. To hell with you, you first-class bitch.

Back in Minneapolis, Ashley was beside herself. She could call the hotel, but needed to think what the ramifications would be. She had no idea that Mary would pull this kind of stunt.

After much thought, Ashley figured it out. In about an hour, she would have a message delivered to the room, have housekeeping open the door so the messenger was able to get the message to Megan. That would keep it simple and not so loud that Mary had to hear much. Housekeeping or Roberto or whoever would be able to report back to let her know that Megan was OK. She couldn't send messengers all night long, but she could send someone once, or twice.

***

As Mary got into a taxi, she found herself more than happy to be seeing the late show all by herself. She was sick of all of them. She was sick of Jake, and of Megan, but mostly of Ashley. She was tired of being a slave. But that would soon change.

At the Monte Carlo, the theater began to fill and soon every seat in the house was packed. The magician's six curvaceous female assistants were all lovely. And that worked for her. Mary hadn't been with a woman in years, but she couldn't stand men. Jake she tolerated. Her friend in Owatonna back home was nice, but all the rest of the men dotting planet Earth were slime. She had realized early on that she preferred women, something that most people still didn't get. She was older, but she wasn't dead.

She was not fat, but she was twenty pounds overweight and would never look like a pretty magician's assistant again. Her face had plenty of lines and hard knocks beaten into it. She wasn't ugly but neither was she attractive. For years she had buried her desires – who would want to be with her? Perhaps she thought, in Vegas, anything was possible, even magic.

And here she was, coming to see a magician. Cute enough guy in his forties, but he did nothing for her. She had never been attracted to men and didn't figure that would ever change. She simply wanted to escape reality for a couple of hours and knew this show was highly touted, and promised to do just that. She reached into her purse to make sure her cell phone was powered off. It was nice not to have to worry about Megan or anything for a while.

And there he is, the Master Magician. Nice smile. She would take any of the girls in a heartbeat though, and she knew that most of the rest of the adult audience would do as well. That was what the girls were there for. Feeding the fantasy.

***

Megan made her way back from the bathroom toward her bed with about four steps remaining, which meant four minutes to go. She opted against the wheelchair. Independence didn't come without cost.

The doorbell rang.

She smiled.

It rang again. There was nothing she could do except to keep walking toward the bed. Whoever it was would assume they were out for the night and leave her to sleep.

Strangely enough she heard the door open.

"Hello? Hello? Knock knock?"

It's Roberto, and he's just walking in?

"Yes?" Megan tried to be as loud as she could, but she simply didn't have the capacity to yell or to be loud enough for someone to actually hear her.

"Miss Dresden. It's Roberto. I have a message for you. May I come in?"

Why not? Maybe he could flip the switch for me when I get in bed and get me a glass of water so I can take my medication. One step to go and I'm in bed.

"Yes, come on in!"

Roberto came around the corner into the master bedroom. Megan, in her old-fashioned plaid flannel pajamas. She had just sat down on the bed. Such a shame that such a young person had to live like this, he thought.

"Miss Dresden, I have a message for you. Would you like me to read it out loud or give it to you?"

"Bring it here. I'll take it. Thank you, Roberto. Can I tip you in the morning? My purse is about fifty minutes away."

He handed her the envelope, and she gently and slowly began to open it. Something seemingly simple like opening an envelope was never easy for Megan. It required dexterity that she didn't have.

"Of course, that will be fine. Can I do anything else for you?"

"Would you get me a cup of water so I can take my medicine?" She pointed at the pills spread out on the table. She felt so old, when she looked at all the medication she was on. But they were all absolutely necessary.

"Of course."

He gave a slight bow and walked into her bathroom and poured her a glass of water. He brought it back, set it on the table by the bed, and made himself ready to be dismissed.

"On your way out, would you turn off this light for me?"

"Certainly. Are you sure you're all right here by yourself? Should I check in on you later?"

"Thanks Roberto, no, I'm fine. Will you be working tomorrow?"

"Yes, ma'am."

She hated being called *ma'am.*

"I will see you then. Thank you for everything, Roberto."

"My pleasure. Sleep well."

He turned the light switch off and exited the suite knowing that Ms. Drexel in Minneapolis was quite right. Mrs. Dresden should not be left alone. But she wasn't in any real danger.

At least not yet.

Roberto contacted Ashley to tell her that her assessment was correct. Megan was fine, but she should not be left alone. He could not believe that Miss Mary left her there alone like that. He would think of an excuse to call on her in an hour or so. He told Ashley that Megan had a phone within arm's reach and that it appeared that she was taking her medication. Ashley told him that she would make sure his concern was rewarded and that she would send him fifty dollars that very evening.

***

Megan took one pill at a time; it was a project that took quite a while. She had done it numerous times in the dark at home, but it seemed even darker here, which didn't help. There were two sets of blinds, both heavy. There was *no* light in the room. It was so dark that the infrared motion detector (at least that's what Mary called it earlier) on the ceiling kept blinking. Megan had no real idea why anyone would want a motion detector in the first place, let alone a hotel.

The last pill was an Ambien. She had considered taking two, but it had been a good long day; she was exhausted. There didn't seem to be a need for two.

The Ambien tumbled down into her stomach, and she lay back in bed. She moved her arm to touch her walker, to make sure it was there. It was.

She lay in bed thinking about how nice the trip was so far. The limo ride, the delicious steak, Roberto; it was all wonderful. The hotel was so nice. She only passed through part of the casino, and it looked enormous. She couldn't wait to go out tomorrow night. Mary said she had something special planned.

I have got to be the luckiest person to have Ashley and Mary. They both care so much.

As she pondered some of the commercials she had seen on TV for more things to do and see in Las Vegas, the air conditioning had succeeded in reaching the set point where it shut off automatically. The room was cool.

But when the noise of the air conditioning subsided, she noticed that the compressor sound was here.

How can that be? They're in Minnesota. It's over a thousand miles away. There's no way that they can be upstairs here as well. Or could they? The cable guy on CSI *was upstairs…but he was quiet. In fact he was very quiet. But he also came down through the ceiling. No, it isn't as loud as it is in Minnesota. It's like because they are so far away the sound is quieter. Why's that?*

They're either upstairs or they're somehow getting the sound into the room. But why would they be upstairs? Maybe they wanted to get away for a few days? There's a lot of sex business in Las Vegas. Prostitution is legal here, I think. Or somewhere in Nevada. Oh, I wish Mary was here. She would figure it out and get them to stop making noise wherever they are.

Megan turned on her side and the sound only got louder. She now wanted to ignore the noise. She heard people walking in the hallway; she heard people in the room next to hers having sex. It was torture.

I want to have sex! I'm sick of hearing other people having sex. The woman is moaning. My God, what is he doing to her? She's screaming or something. God, is it some kind of kinky thing?

The noise of people having sex and the compressor sound was something she needed to get away from, but there would be no getting away from it tonight. They had come to Las Vegas and rented a room next to hers.

How impossible is that?

She covered her head with the pillow, but the compressor was still running and the woman was having sex again. *Does she ever quit? Maybe it's a different john?*

Dear God, please let me sleep. I really need rest. I'm so tired and I want these people to leave me alone. They are driving me crazy with their sex toys and noises. Please let them stop.

God had no response, and the woman kept moaning and coming, over and over again. She was some kind of nymphomaniac. And the loud compressor running their sex toys was pushing her to the brink.

How big is that vibrator?! My God, they need a machine to keep it powered?

The people having sex, whether it was one, two, three, four… she didn't know how many, but they made a lot of noise; it was agony.

Just like the victim in CSI. *There's no way I can get away. She couldn't either. Someone is trying to drive me crazy.*

She pulled the pillow off of her head. She reached for the bottle of Ambien and after several attempts at the childproof top, it came open. She poured a bunch into her hand, returned all but one to the bottle, and took her second Ambien in less than a half hour. The half hour had seemed like an eternity to Megan. She was going crazy and needed to sleep. A good night's sleep, and this would all be just a bad dream.

Back home it's the same time they start every night. But they are here. And that means they have one of these suites at $800 per night; they must be doing a GOOD business. That girl is working all night; she's got to pay for that expensive suite, or maybe there is another girl in the same suite - one in each bedroom. I bet that's it.

She wanted to cry.

Soon the second Ambien overcame the noise of sex toys and orgasms and she finally was pushed into a deep sleep.

"Megan…Megan…Megan."

Mary tried waking her.

It must be a helluva nightmare. She's crying in that way of hers… no tears. That's just SO weird.

"Megan…Megan…Megan!"

Megan's eyes popped opened, and she startled awake. There was a look in her eyes like that of a deer before it gets hit by a car – pure fear.

"Megan? Megan? Megan? Are you OK?"

She blinked several times. It was Mary.

"Where am I?"

Mary backed up. This better just be a bad dream.

"We're in Vegas, at the MGM Grand. It's nine a.m., and you've been crying in your sleep. Are you OK?"

Megan looked around the room as she listened. Just the air conditioner pumping cool air into the room.

Maybe all the sex has stopped for the day. Makes sense. It's morning. Maybe it was all a dream.

"Good morning Mary. I need the bathroom right away."

"I'll grab the chair for you." Before Megan could say anything, Mary was out the door. Megan looked at the clock; it was almost nine. She had slept nearly ten hours – not unusual for Megan; her body simply needed more rest than most.

Megan was almost standing as she slid out of her bed. Mary parked the wheelchair right by the bed. Megan carefully sat down in the chair, and Mary whisked her to the restroom and helped Megan onto the toilet.

Mary seemed especially happy – almost ecstatic. "I'll be back in a few minutes for you. I'm going to go clean up in the other room."

Megan would never make it in here, but I should put these documents somewhere out of sight. D-Day is almost here. I just have to get a "yes" vote from Megan, as far as signing is concerned.

Just minutes later, Mary helped Megan back into the bedroom and helped her get dressed for the day.

"I need to get some sleep, honey. I need a few hours before we go out sightseeing. I'll either put something on the tube for you or get you a good movie."

"Thank you, Mary."

What if she won't sign? What if she decides that even Ashley doesn't need to be her guardian anymore? What if she wants to hire an attorney and prove she is now 100% capable of taking care of herself?

"You're welcome, honey."

Megan debated whether she should tell Mary about last night. She'd probably had a nice time out, and this would spoil it. No, no need to tell her.

"Do we have plans for today?"

"Do we ever!" Mary looked up and smiled. "Megan, we are going to take a limo to the Venetian and visit the Egypt exhibit at the Guggenheim Art Museum there. Then we are going to go to Caesar's Palace and spend a few hours looking at some of the most luxurious shops in the world – they're called The Forum Shops. Then we're going to come back here for you to nap and rest. And yes, I have a fun night planned for us as well. We'll have dinner at the Sea Blue downstairs and then we have reservations to see one of the greatest magicians in the world. How does that sound?"

"Wow!" Megan was truly excited. It sounded so wonderful.

Chapter Twenty Five

That Night

The day went as Mary had told Megan it would and they returned happy. Megan had a great time and absolutely loved the Forum Shops. Arriving back at their home away from home, Mary pushed Megan into their suite. Yes... *Home Sweet Home.*

"Here we are. I'm going to take you into your bathroom, and I'm going to mine. I'll be back in a minute."

Mary was on fire. Her plan was working. Megan was experiencing more than quality time with her. She was experiencing life with her. Fun. Excitement. It was almost surreal. It was Vegas – of course it was surreal. What better place to hypnotize someone into doing pretty much anything you want them to…and…tomorrow was going to be big. Very big indeed.

Megan was probably a little wired, too, but Mary knew that Megan would need a good night's sleep if the plan was to continue on schedule.

Mary got Megan up, back into the wheelchair, and over to the shower. Getting her cleaned up wasn't terribly difficult, as the shower here was quite spacious. Her pajamas were on the fifteen-foot-long vanity. It was ridiculously lavish. Then over to bed. Megan had told her she wanted to take either a quick nap or go to bed for the night; she wasn't sure. Mary knew it would be bedtime even though it was earlier than Megan's normal two a.m. bedtime. They'd had a long, eventful day – most enjoyable.

Once Megan was in bed, Mary sat herself down in the oversized chair a few feet from the bed. She put her feet up on the ottoman and put her hands behind her head.

"Did you have fun tonight, Megan?"

"I did. It was a great day. And the magician was just amazing."

"I'm glad you had a good time. I always try so hard to make sure you have fun. You know, I've been thinking...but I...don't know – "

"What is it, Mary?"

"Well, hon, I've been worried about Ashley. She's been under so much stress, and I'm afraid that she's starting to lose control with Lauren and Robert."

"Is she really under a lot of stress?"

"Megan, it's evident. She is always flying off the handle. She's not being her old, sweet self. She used to be so mellow and happy," Mary nearly choked on that, "but these days she's so angry and upset all the time."

"What do you think is causing all of this?"

"I think she feels like what happened to you was in part her fault – out of loyalty to both you and David. She's always putting you and your needs ahead of her own and her family's; it isn't natural. She wouldn't even consider allowing someone else to take over as your guardian, because she's such a good person and I think she'd go on doing it forever – no matter what the effect on her health and family. Don't you ever wonder what it does to her family? Can you imagine the stress? The fights? The loud arguments? How bad Lauren must feel every day, without the love and support of her mother at home? Ya know? You always tell me that Ashley wants to adopt another child. Well, how is she going to do that and remain your guardian? I can't imagine how she takes all that pressure!"

"I don't know, I guess I never thought about it like that."

"Well Megan, forgive me dear, but you need to. Ashley deserves a life, too."

This was all painfully slow, but in a few hours the papers would be signed and the drama would be over and it would all have paid off. Or at least that's how Mary thought it would go. Little did she know that

Megan would not absolutely require a trustee to make all her decisions now that she was regaining her independence.

There was a very long pause. Megan did a lot of soul-searching. "You're right. I think I can take care of myself now."

Mary laughed.

"Well, let's not get carried away. You've improved so much in the last few years, that's for sure. But there is still quite a way to go. You still have lots of therapy and doctor visits to go to. But you're right, we do need to let Ashley have fun, adopt another child, and enjoy her life more. You're right; you've hit the nail on the head."

"Then what do you suggest?"

"Well, I suppose, someone else could be your guardian. You know I'd do that for you. Well, just until you are walking and moving at break-neck speed again. I'd be willing to do it…I guess…only until you are back to normal."

"Oh, I couldn't ask you to do that. You never get a break from me as it is; I wouldn't want to add to your stress."

"Good point. But, who else would do it, except for me? I do see your point, but who else is there? You know, if we did do that, would we have to make it legal and all that? I can't even imagine what would have to happen."

Megan paused. She had never thought about the process before, either. Before Megan could think of a reason why this wouldn't work, Mary piped in. "I guess we could put it in writing with someone official, so you could let Ashley get back to living her life. How long has it been since she's had even a day or two off? Seven years? That's just too much."

"Sure, we could do that."

"Are you sure? And when do you want to do it?"

"When we get home?"

"Sure, or you know what, honey? My cousin Jake has a good friend who's an attorney. I bet he'd be willing to do it while we're here, so Ashley wouldn't have to deal with the stress of making the change when we get home. We could make it a surprise. Then we would buy her and Robert and Lauren tickets to fly to Paradise in Mexico!"

"Oh, that would be nice!"

"So, are you sure you want to do this, Megan?"

"Definitely. If you are willing to help me by becoming my guardian, then Ashley can spend some quality time with her family and adopt another child, just like she always planned. I think this is what's best for her."

"OK, fine. You convinced me. I'll talk with my cousin in the morning and see if his friend would be willing to see us. And boy, do I have a day planned for us tomorrow!"

After the day's review and a little chitchat, they were both happy and completely exhausted after the exciting and eventful day that had just passed. Mary, too, apparently was going to bed now. Megan's medications including an Ambien were all set out on her end table. Megan had thought about telling Mary about all the ruckus of the previous night, but decided not to spoil such an exceptionally upbeat day.

The air conditioner kicked off, and as if on cue, she heard them starting up again upstairs. She lay down on the pillow and thought she should ask Mary to stop them before things got any louder.

Mary closed the drapes, shut the door to the bathroom while leaving the light on, and stood by the light switch at the entrance to the room.

"Mary?"

"Yes, Megan?"

Megan paused. She appreciated everything Mary had done that day, and didn't want to make her play policeman again, if she didn't have to.

"Thank you for such a fun day. I can't remember the last time I had so much fun."

"Sleep well, Megan." She turned the lights off and left the door half open.

Megan's head hit the pillow snugly after downing her various medications. The Ambien would help her sleep, even if they got wilder upstairs.

She heard a woman moan with pleasure and, though it wasn't all that loud, it was all too frustrating. It had been so long since she had touching…even a glance from any man. She ached for someone, anyone She needed affection. It was maddening to live with the thought that she would never be desired again. *That couldn't be the case,* she thought to herself.

I just want to know if I can ever feel pleasure again.

The woman moaned again and again. Soon she heard the bed rattling upstairs. Her body started to shake from the vibration that came through the ceiling and the walls.

My God. What are they doing? I'd hit the stupid ceiling, if I had anything long enough to reach it. That vibrator must be as big as the bathroom. It vibrates so that it almost shakes the room. I wonder if this bothers the other hotel guests who have rooms that connect to theirs? Please stop the racket. Dear God, please let them stop the racket.

She shook and shook all the way down to her toes, but the compressor just got louder and louder. *Oh my God!* They cranked it up a notch, and now the pitch was even at a higher frequency than before. Finally, the woman stopped moaning. Maybe he was done…or she was…or the hour was up. She didn't care. She was just glad that the woman had shut up.

Megan began to cry her peculiar cry, without tears. She sobbed noisily. Part of her hoped Mary would come in; part of her was glad she didn't. Part of her wanted to call Ashley; part didn't. She cried louder, and unlike other nights, she fell asleep feeling completely helpless.

As Megan exhausted her emotions into sleep, Mary hit three 7's on the dollar slots – the $240 jackpot. She had only put in five rolls of silver dollars, so she had profited to the tune of $140. Slots weren't exciting when you were losing, but they could be fun when you won. The change girl came by, gave her a bucket to pour her dollars into, and congratulated her on her winning. Mary didn't tip her; she had no reason to. The change girl hadn't helped her win the money.

Megan's credit card wasn't like her debit card. It seemed to allow unlimited cash advances. She knew that couldn't be right, but she'd take what she could get from the ATM machines.

Taking her now-filled bucket to the cashier cage, she felt rejuvenated. Soon she would need to go check on Megan.

She's tired; she'll be fast asleep. She looked at her watch and saw that the MGM's show "Crazy Horse" would start in about fifteen minutes.

"Crazy Horse" was touted as one of the best topless shows in town. *That must mean classy, whatever that means. Straight from the Crazy Horse in Paris, huh? Well good, and why not. Go to the show, then call it a night. God knows, if anyone deserves to relax and unwind it's me.*

***

The clock changed the time to 10:59, and Megan's eyes opened, even her right one, which often took some effort.

That woman is screaming again. God, what is happening up there? The compressor is full blast, so they must have a bunch of them up there at once – maybe three girls and three men. Why not? Anything's possible! I can't believe they followed me all the way to Vegas. They're making thousands of dollars, while torturing me all at the same time.

Soon the walls started to vibrate again, and then her bed as well. And then Megan started to vibrate.

Oh my God! What is happening?

Mary!

***

Lasers tracked the girls' bodies on stage. It was like something out of another time. There were all kinds of colors and images reminiscent of the psychedelic era. It was interesting enough, though, that she could have done without the classy part; she enjoyed watching the girls dance. As she watched she committed herself to losing a few pounds. If there was ever going to be a return to normal life, she needed to look as good as she could.

At least these girls are working for a living. Not everyone gets to sleep away on a free ride in life.

***

Upstairs, Megan pushed her hands against her ears. She didn't want to hear that woman screaming and moaning anymore. No matter what she did, she couldn't stop hearing that horrible noise or stop her body from quaking. Her hands trembled; her heart fluttered.

Oh, I think I'm going to die.

As she bent over to reach for the telephone to call for help, she lost what little balance she had left and fell to the floor, hitting her head hard on the floor. She lost consciousness instantly.

***

About 12:30 a.m. the show let out. Mary thought it had been a good way to pass an hour or two. And it was time to call it a night. Tomorrow would be a big day, very big. Tomorrow, Ashley is out and Mary is in, and ultimately, she would end up filthy rich.

She swiped her card in the lock and the door opened quietly. She knew Megan would be sound asleep and didn't want to disturb her. That would mean a trip to the bathroom, a glass of water and probably another Ambien.

She almost tiptoed like they do in the old movies. She opened the door to her bathroom and went straight in. It was completely silent. Even the air conditioner had stopped blowing for the night.

Megan awoke first. She opened her eyes slowly. It was just after nine a.m. She found herself startled by a spider on the floor, which she instinctively swatted away with her free arm. Her legs tingled in a painful way, like pins and needles.

She couldn't tell if she was dreaming or not. She couldn't be dreaming – her head hurt too much – her whole body hurt.

Who gets a headache in a dream?

The compressor was still going, but she didn't hear any people. Maybe they were done for the night.

Getting up from this position would prove to be very difficult. She somehow needed to use her arms to push herself up and grab the end table to get some leverage. What a mess.

As she found her way to a kneeling position the pins and needles feeling became increasingly painful. At least she was moving, and the vibrating call girl had stopped her shaking.

We've got to get out of here. They're here; we're going home.

She fell back to the floor and soon fell asleep, exhausted.

***

The phone rang. Her hand was two inches away; she decided she could grab the phone while on the floor.

"Hello?"

"Hi, Megan, it's Ashley. Listen, I got a letter from the attorney for the people upstairs; they claim they've made no noise at all since they've been there. So what I'm going to do is write their lawyer back and tell him we're not going to press charges, but we are going to have the police stop by regularly to make sure everything is on the up and up, up there. Is that OK with you?"

"Ashley?"

"Yes, honey, how are you doing?"

"I have a bad headache. I fell out of bed last night."

"Oh, my God. Are you OK?"

"Except for the headache, yes."

"Put that woman on the line."

"She is sleeping, I think."

"Figures. What are you doing?"

"I'm sitting on the floor."

"You're what?"

"I was trying to get up when the phone rang. I was tired of trying to pull myself up, so I decided to answer the phone instead of getting back in bed."

"Oh Megan, you should have let it ring; it would have gotten Mary up and off her butt."

"I didn't think of that."

"That's OK, Megan, it's not your fault."

"What caused you to fall out of bed?"

Mary stood in the doorway.

"Megan darling, what in the world?"

She grabbed the phone from Megan and hung it up.

"I was talking to Ashley."

All the more reason to hang up. That bitch.

"Are you OK?"

"Will you call Ashley back?"

She lifted Megan to a sitting position on the bed and checked her head, which now had a raised bump the size of a marble.

"I'm sure she'll call back later."

The phone rang.

"I bet that's Ashley."

"We'll call her back; let's get you fixed first. I'll get some ice out of the freezer."

She steadied Megan back against her pillows and went for some ice.

She opened the little refrigerator/freezer under the wet bar and grabbed the ice cube tray. She clicked out a half dozen cubes onto the counter and went to the bathroom for a washcloth.

The phone finally kicked over to voice mail. She made a makeshift ice bag with the washcloth and brought it straight back to Megan and held it for her on her head.

"OK, this will help the swelling go down on that nasty bump. You must have fallen pretty hard."

"They were driving me crazy. They were shaking me so much; they shook me right out of bed."

"Who was?"

"The people upstairs."

"They're here too? Can't we ever get any peace?!"

"Oh, they are driving me crazy. They run the compressor all night and that woman just moans and screams. They must have a few women working up there."

"Well, it is Vegas, Megan." Mary smiled.

"No, these are the same people that have been driving me crazy at 4190."

"What makes you think that?"

"They have that compressor going. That's why I ended up on the floor."

Mary was thinking about that for a moment when the phone rang.

"Damn her." She picked up the phone with her free hand and glanced at the caller I.D. "Here. It's Ashley." She handed it to Megan without answering it.

"Hello? Yes. Sorry. Mary had to help me get up and back in bed. She's got ice on my head now. I'm feeling better."

Ashley was so angry Megan could feel the vibes coming over the phone. Ashley was telling Megan she wanted to talk to Mary.

"No, you're really stressed out right now. Besides, I'm coming home and I might be leaving for some other town somewhere else very soon."

"What?" Ashley was beside herself and so was Mary. In fact Mary's jaw dropped and stayed that way for nearly a minute.

"They've come here to get back at me for having you write that letter. I know it's them. They brought the compressor and that woman. They're the same people. I'm positive."

Ashley tried to calm down on the other end. Then in her best and most soothing and calm voice she said, "Megan, coming home is a great idea, but once you're back, we need to get to the bottom of this. There's no sense in running off again."

"I'm coming home, but if they try and bother me again, I'll go somewhere they won't find me. I'm not going to let them get to me. I want you to book us the first flight home. Can you look on your computer and see when that is?"

Mary was watching her plan fall apart before her eyes. She had to think fast and figure a way around this. She closed her mouth – clenching her teeth and put the ice pack more firmly against Megan's head.

Ashley was busy running her fingers over her keyboard to delta.com. They'd have several flights back from Vegas, she was sure of it. Sun Country only offered intermittent flights and that just wouldn't do. She wanted Megan back now where she knew it was safe.

"There is a noon flight out of Las Vegas, and it arrives at 4:57 p.m. Minnesota time. Let me check seating. There is a first-class seat open that we could get you with a ticket upgrade. Mary will have to fly coach."

"She won't mind." Megan was sure of herself. She was leaving, and she was also leaving that compressor sound behind that was driving her mad. They're here but she was going home and who knows where to next. "Please book the flight. We'll be there. We have enough time to get there."

"OK, you'll both have e-tickets; all you have to do is check in when you get there."

"Thanks, Ashley."

"I'll be at door six outside the baggage level to pick both of you up."

"See you there."

Megan hung up the phone. Mary was dumbfounded. She hadn't ever seen Megan take so much control, not ever. She was slipping from Mary's grasp and that couldn't happen.

"I think it's a fine idea to get away from these idiots. We can always come back later in the week, right?"

"Or go somewhere where they won't bother me. I'm not going to let them drive me crazy."

"No, you aren't. We'll fix everything. I promise."

She had no idea how her plan would play out. They were going home. It was insane, but she had no choice. Megan was determined, and she didn't need to add fuel to this fire. Too much was at stake.

Packing was something Mary didn't want to do. Packing meant leaving and leaving meant losing… if she didn't play her cards right.

Chapter Twenty Six

Later That Morning

The ride to the airport was quiet if not uneventful. They arrived at 10:04 a.m. and had to check in, take the elevator up to the next level, and finally clear security, which would be a real inconvenience. Ever since the accident Megan had to be wanded and patted down; she had pounds of metal in her body – a real-life bionic woman. Finally, security had finished with her, and they proceeded onto the tram, over to the D gates, and up another elevator arriving at the gate with no time to spare.

If Megan would cooperate by staying in her wheelchair, they'd make it just fine. The bitch booked her in coach and Megan in first class. Mary went to Vegas in style but was going back like a beaten dog with her tail between her legs.

The fact of the matter was that Megan had said that she wanted Mary to take over the guardianship. Now there were a couple of choices: Mary could fight Ashley in Minneapolis for Megan's guardianship, if Megan would allow it, or she could wait until they went to another state or country where she would have a better chance, though proving residency might be difficult, but necessary, according to the attorney back in Vegas. And perhaps that was the answer. Establish residency. Get Megan some kind of government issued ID. It would be years. if ever, before she would drive a car again. No driver's license was forthcoming. The most obvious strategy was to continue to get closer to

Megan… to support her against Ashley. That was the key. Every time Ashley said something to upset Megan, no matter what it was, she would take Megan's side. Support Megan. Unfailingly. Then, when the chips were down it would be an easy choice. Mary would be the clear-cut choice for friend and guardian.

The flight touched down at 4:46 PM. It was a little early because the jet stream was shooting from southwest to northeast. Being last off the plane was the only option. It would take quite some time to get their luggage and meet Ashley. Just over an hour, as it turned out.

Ashley was there with the trunk open, like a chauffeur. Mary loved the idea. She would join Megan in the back seat and let Ashley drive them home. Megan was visibly relieved to see Ashley as they came out through door six. Ashley raced up to Megan and bent down to give her a big hug and warm welcome home. She had only been gone for a day and a half, but it seemed like a long time, for both of them.

Neither Mary nor Ashley heard as much as a "hello" from each other. Neither had anything to say to the other at all but they both succeeded at helping Megan into the Mercedes and getting her belted in. Within minutes, they were on the road and headed home.

"How was your trip, Megan?"

"Those people were horrible. I couldn't believe they followed me to Las Vegas to make all that racket. They must really hate me."

Ashley found it hard to believe that the tenants upstairs who claimed innocence would follow Megan to Las Vegas. It seemed all but impossible.

"Mary, did they bother you?"

"They drove us both nuts."

"The moaning and the screaming? The vibrating sound?" Ashley inquired.

"All of it. It was terrible. Couldn't believe the MGM would let people like that in their hotel."

"Huh. OK, well, you're home now and they aren't, so tonight will be peaceful, and you can catch up on your sleep, Megan."

"It wasn't all bad. We did have a nice trip, too. It was just at night that it was unbearable."

"Well, you're home now, and we'll see to it that things quiet down here." Ashley was firm in her resolution that Megan wouldn't have any more bad nights.

Once they arrived at 4190, Megan was actually glad to be home. Leaving for Las Vegas seemed like a million years ago. She had almost forgotten the torture of her recent nights in her bedroom here.

Ashley didn't know if she should offer to stay the night or not. Mary had screwed up in Las Vegas, but here Ashley was only minutes from Megan, if Mary took off on one of her excursions. She had just about had enough of Mary, that was for sure.

Yes. Tonight she would stay.

Mary couldn't have been more perturbed. The last person on the planet she wanted to be around tonight was Ashley. But that was Ashley's plan.

Megan agreed that it would be a good idea for Ashley to sleep in the bedroom with her. Ashley would use the rollaway. That would make for an uncomfortable night's sleep, but she would be close to Megan. And unless something bizarre was going on, they would both sleep just fine.

Mary brought Megan all of her medications and some water to her bedside. She asked Megan if she needed to use the restroom, if she wanted a snack, if she wanted to see the paper. She was in and out, in and out. Ashley wondered if she was this solicitous every day. Impossible. Every other day she was leaving Megan in the park or in a hotel room alone. Mary must be politicking to keep her job. *Good. Maybe a little pressure will keep her in line; it certainly can't hurt.*

Mary turned the lights off and went to her room.

Megan was lying calmly in bed, but she heard the compressor going upstairs. It was not as loud as usual, but it was definitely there.

There is no way they could be up there. Of course it wasn't that loud. Maybe they had a main compressor and a compressor they can take on the road with them. Maybe they have more going on up there than meets the eye. How did they get home so fast? They couldn't have known we were going to leave...or that we actually did...the only way they could have gotten home at the same time is if they heard us talking about it and took the same flight home. Or maybe, Sun Country had a flight about the same time... or earlier. They heard us talking, then took home the flight right before ours?

But how could they hear us talking at the MGM? There couldn't have been holes in the ceiling...or...microphones...or...listening devices. I was there most of the time. It just makes no sense.

"Good night, Megan." Ashley was exhausted, and she turned over and would be asleep in no time.

"Good night, Ashley." Megan was nervous. She didn't want them to start the racket again. She didn't want them to know she was home. She just wanted to sleep. She was going to be quiet and invisible.

She took her various medications and was starting to doze off, when the compressor kicked in loudly so loudly it startled her.

Why doesn't Ashley wake up? It's so loud! Is she deaf? Does she sleep so soundly that an earthquake could hit, and she'd snore the time away? What about Mary? This doesn't bother her, either?

Oh God, there she goes screaming again! They DID follow me home. They are so EVIL. I can't believe this. It's all because of Ashley's letter. That is the thing. It's either on purpose to drive me crazy, or they have two locations for their prostitution ring. Or BOTH. Maybe they want to drive me out of here, so they can operate their business without interruption. They must be very upset with me. I would be right? I mean, Ashley sent the letter to EVERYONE. Everyone knows how loud they are and what they are doing.

And now again!

And the ceiling began to vibrate...and the walls...and Megan in her bed...and she let out a scream and almost sat straight up wailing.

"Ashley!"

Ashley was up on the scream and didn't need name recognition.

What is it?

Mary raced to the room and stood at the door.

"Megan?"

"Mary, did you hear them? They were so loud. That woman was screaming and moaning again. It was terrible."

Mary paused and looked at both of them, then back at Megan.

"I think it's disgusting that they are as loud as they are. It's maddening. If they don't quiet down, I'm going to call the police." She folded her arms against her stomach. She'd had her say.

Ashley looked away from Mary and back at Megan.

"What noises did you hear, Megan?"

"I can't believe you slept through it. If you listen you can still hear the compressor."

Ashley listened and heard nothing, except the fan that circulated the air.

"You mean the fan?"

"No, the compressor upstairs."

"You must have hearing like a dog," said Ashley, "because I didn't hear anything."

"Figures." Mary hit that hard and then turned to Megan "See, no one believes you but me! Megan, I'm going back to bed. If you need anything, let me know. Good night, honey."

Mary again turned and walked out.

There was an uncomfortable silence in the room. Neither knew what to say to the other. Megan was scared and Ashley was perplexed… dumbfounded…and speechless.

"I'm going upstairs. I'll be back in a few minutes."

"OK. Thanks, Ashley." Megan was heartened. If anyone could make them stop; it was Ashley. There's no way they could cover up everything now.

Ashley stepped out in her pajamas, climbed the stairs two at a time, and came to the door of the offending apartment. She knocked. The old man came to the door.

"Yes? Ohhhh, it's you." He started to close the door, but she got her bare foot in the way and winced when the door hit it.

"What's going on in here?"

"What are you talking about, Miss Drexel? We are sleeping. We are *trying* to sleep. And if you don't leave my property, I will call the police and have you removed from these premises."

"Oh, you will. I don't know why I doubt that. What's all the racket that's been going on up here?"

The old man's patience was wearing thin. "Miss Drexel, get out."

"Fine." She peered around him and saw nothing but a nightlight. No noise. No smell. Nothing. Just a disgusted old man.

She turned and walked slowly back to Megan's place.

What is going on? They hear all this noise. Sounds of machines and people moaning and groaning. There are vibrations strong enough to shake Megan out of her bed, but I hear absolutely nothing. Am I going nuts? Are they going nuts? How can TWO people go nuts at the same time? None of this makes any sense.

I think what I have to do is have that place upstairs investigated. We have to find out if anything is going on up there once and for all. Calling the police is out, but a private investigator...

So first thing in the morning, I'll call a private investigator to find out: who these people are, where they work, what they do and how they spend their nights. Because this is all crazy.

She leaned against the door to Megan's place and put her hand on the doorknob. She turned the knob and went in. All was quiet. She went to Megan's room. Megan was still awake, just sitting there, probably waiting.

"Hey, how's it goin'?" Ashley tried to sound upbeat, with only marginal success.

"They aren't screaming any more. The compressor has been turned down to a dull roar, but I can still hear it up there."

Ashley wasn't going to discuss quality of hearing issues. Instead she told Megan her new idea.

"Tomorrow we're going to get a private investigator to check the place out. Try and figure out who these people are, what they do, what's causing all the noise, everything. For tonight, I'm going to stay in here with you. OK?"

"OK." Megan felt defeated, hopeless. Just the idea of trying to go back to sleep scared her, but she felt better knowing Ashley was there. "What did you find out upstairs?"

"Megan, the old guy answered the door. I peeked in his place while I was talking to him. He was mad as heck that I woke him up. There was no noise coming from his apartment, there was no sign of a party or any other people. The place didn't smell from cigarettes or perfume or anything."

"Did he let you in?"

"Megan, I couldn't go in. I'm not a police officer. I can't exactly say, 'Can I look around?' can I? I didn't even ask to go in. I asked him to keep it down, and he told me that if I didn't leave he was calling the cops."

"The girl is directly above my room and so is the compressor. You couldn't have seen it from the front door. He must have known you were coming up, so he straightened everything up real fast to make it look like nothing was going on."

"How would he have known that I was coming up there? I didn't even know I was going up there until a few minutes ago."

"Maybe my house is bugged."

"Oh, come on. Why would anyone do that?"

"To get back at me. You know people bug other people's houses. It's not all that unusual."

"But why do that to you? You aren't a threat."

"We already sent a letter to everyone telling them how loud they were with all the sex noises and equipment and all that."

"And you think someone would go to the trouble to bug your house for that?"

"I'm not sure."

Ashley looked up at the ceiling, then stood up, walked around the room, poked her nose in corners, moved stuff around, but all she saw was a normal room in a nice condo.

"They're sneakier than you are, Ashley; it's criminal. They hide their equipment and work under the cover of darkness. It's not going to be out laying around for everyone to see."

Ashley didn't know what to think. They heard them up there, she didn't. She was resolved to fix this mess, though. "Tomorrow we'll get the professionals to work on this. You ready to go to bed?"

"Sure, why not. Do you think it's OK if I take another Ambien?"

"Don't see why not, as long as you don't do it often."

"OK."

She reached over to the table and struggled with the childproof top on the bottle and finally got it. She flipped off the top and got one tablet out of the bottle. She resealed the bottle and set it back down. A couple of gulps of water and the pill slid down her throat.

"Good night, Megan."

"Good night, Ashley."

Megan fell asleep quickly. Ashley didn't. She listened and listened for an hour until she realized that she wasn't going to hear anything, and then she too went to sleep. She assumed now that Megan was home, and she was here, that everything would be fine.

She assumed.

***

"Megan, Megan, Megan." A male voice laughed in a rather sinister fashion. And it woke Megan up instantly.

"Who's there?" Megan's eyes opened, and they darted around the room. Ashley was fast asleep. The clock read 5:33 a.m.

She had to go to the bathroom and didn't want to wake Ashley, but she *really* had to go. The compressor was on but there was no moaning or screaming woman. The voice must have been a dream, but it seemed very real.

Bathroom.

"Ashley? Ashley?"

Obviously disoriented herself, Ashley didn't know which way to look. Then she saw Megan sitting on the bed in the darkness. "Megan? You OK?"

"I'm fine. I need you to help me to the bathroom. I really have to go… now."

"OK." She jumped out of bed, grabbed the wheelchair, helped Megan in, and hustled her to the bathroom. Megan could now take care of the rest of things on her own. For years that had not been the case. It still took a lot of time, even with the wheelchair assist, but that was nothing compared to the old days.

Ashley gave Megan her well-deserved privacy. She looked around the bedroom. Saw nothing. Heard nothing. She had slept hard and surprisingly well for being on a rollaway bed. She'd like to get another ninety minutes of sleep. Boy, was she tired. She figured that Megan must really be exhausted.

"Ashley? Can you help me back to the wheelchair?"

She got back up and opened the door into Megan's bathroom. She was still making progress – trying to stand up on her own. Ashley helped her and didn't bother to ask if she wanted to do anything herself. It was time to go back to bed.

"Thank you."

"No problem."

Ashley moved Megan back to the bed and helped her in, gave her a sip of water and offered her an Ambien. Megan nodded. Ashley had no problem with that, as a sleep-deprived Megan was certainly worse than a groggy Megan.

For just a moment Ashley looked at Megan through the dark and remembered back to when she'd had to feed Megan through a straw, helped her take her first baby steps, and tried to teach her to say "hi" and "bye" and "cat" and "dog." Ashley loved Megan and had been a dedicated friend, always and forever. It was just tragic to think of the changes that had ravaged this once vital and beautiful young woman.

"Rest well, Megan, at least for a couple more hours."

"Not just a couple. I'm going to sleep in until noon." Music to Ashley's ears.

Megan listened with frustration to the compressor hiss but went back to sleep surprisingly quickly, and just minutes later Ashley fell back asleep, hearing nothing but Megan's breathing. Everything was fine.

At least for now, she thought.

***

Knock, knock, knock. "Megan…Megan…Megan!"

She shot up.

"What!"

Ashley sat up straightaway.

"What's up, Megan?"

"Did you hear that?"

"Hear what?"

"Three knocks and my name. Some guy was saying my name over and over again, and he was laughing at me."

Ashley breathed easier. A nightmare.

"Megan. You were dreaming. Some kind of a nightmare. Don't worry about it. Everything is just fine."

Mary walked in the door.

"How did you two girls sleep last night?"

"Mary, did they wake you up last night?" Megan wanted to see if Mary was as bothered as she had been.

"They bothered you, too?" Mary asked.

Ashley couldn't figure it out.

"The compressor was so loud, and this morning someone was calling out my name and laughing at me."

"You're kidding!" Mary looked shocked.

"No, it was terrible." Megan looked down at the floor. The more noises she heard, the more sleep-deprived she became. She looked beaten. Shattered.

"Well, maybe Ashley didn't get the job done. I'll go see what I can do later on. I've got to work on breakfast first, and I'll see you in a bit." Mary left for the kitchen.

Ashley rarely had moments where she didn't get words in, but they were coming more often these days.

"I think they're trying to get back at me for sending that letter to the association members. The one that said they were 'loud and disturbing.'"

Ashley didn't know what to think.

"Well, like I said, we'll hire a private investigator today and get this thing resolved once and for all. It's all starting to get to me as well."

Ashley stood and walked around the room, looking everywhere, in corners, opening closets, looking behind nightstands. She still saw nothing.

"If someone is bothering you, Megan, I'm going to find out who and why, and see to it that it doesn't ever happen again. I can't imagine why this is happening, but we will figure it out."

Chapter Twenty Seven

A Few Hours Later

Ashley arrived at the office of John Wagner, Private Investigator. His office was located in an old building on First Avenue in downtown Minneapolis. She half expected to see a bimbo in a tight skirt at the reception area, smoking a cigarette.

Instead what she found was a generic office, as if he were any ordinary CPA. Utterly disappointing.

There was no secretary at the front desk and Wagner's office was just behind the next door. She bypassed the vacant secretary's desk and tapped on his door.

"Come on in." John Wagner was tall, nice looking. He looked tired, and a bit stressed out, but nothing that signaled she had made a wrong choice.

John had twenty years on the police force when he retired early. He could have had more money and retired later, but he'd had it. There was no reason to take any more punishment. Being a cop made you see the world in a particular way. Everyone was a bad guy.

Being a P.I., on the other hand, you tended to find it about 50-50. Half the people you saw were bad guys and the other half were basically good guys. It made for a better world. And the business was consistent and predictable. Find this missing person or that runaway, or keep an eye on my cheating spouse, or investigate this employee's past. The former was more difficult and had more risk involved. The latter was typically less interesting, rarely dangerous in any way and always paid very well. His fee was $600 a day. That could be a few hours a day for a few days, or one full day.

Ashley thought he was a bit expensive, but the guy seemed legit. That he was a former Minneapolis cop helped her believe that he could be trusted to do good work. He seemed to be OK as far as she was concerned, as far as her instincts were concerned.

"So, what can I do for you?"

She grilled him about his experience, and having exhaustively explained his credentials, he was anxious to get started on paid work.

"I need you to check to see if the people living above Megan are running some kind of prostitution ring, what their source of income is, what they do, who comes and goes, especially late at night – after midnight. I also need you to scan Megan's condo and check for any surveillance equipment that might be hidden."

He stroked his chin, kicked back in his chair, and looked at the ceiling. He was adding up the hours in his head. "Twenty to twenty-four hours of work. I'll charge you a flat fee of $1,500, including equipment. You will have a definitive answer on all of this. I'll get you everything you asked for and more, down to the size of the old man's underwear."

Ashley almost thought that response was too much – a little over the top, but she felt like it meant something to him – pride in his work or something like that.

"Deal. I'll give you $500 today." She pulled cash out of her purse and handed it to him. "I'll pay you the rest when we have the information we need. Fair enough?"

"That's fine. We'll figure it out, Miss Drexel."

"Mr. Wagner, what's the crime involved if someone is bugging Megan, figuratively or literally?"

"Frankly, nothing too impressive unless there is videotape involved. Sexual stuff always gets more attention from the courts and cops. But putting a bug in someone's house…or a microphone…or frankly even having a hooker working in your building is all pretty uninteresting stuff. Court? Yes. Sentence? Not likely; it's a petty misdemeanor. A slap on the wrist and a fine is about the most you'd see out of it."

"That's what I thought. Well, here's my card. Call me as things progress, would you?" Ashley was relieved to have the process started and to know that it wasn't on her shoulders to solve this one.

"You have a good day, Ms. Drexel… and get some sleep. No offense, but you look pretty tired."

"You should see Mrs. Dresden; she's a wreck!"

"I'll do the computer work this morning, public records search this afternoon, DMV search after that, and I'll have all the tax records, county and state, by the end of the day. Tonight, I'll be outside your friend's house with scanning equipment. I'll have a good picture by this time tomorrow. All the details will take a few days to fill in, but we'll get to the bottom of it soon enough."

"Thanks. Talk to you soon." She got up, saw herself to the door, and returned to her car, wondering what would happen next.

Private detectives see the world a bit differently from the rest of the world. A police officer arrests people all day long for doing things they shouldn't be doing; it's all they see. They investigate. They arrest. They go to court. They testify. They watch the criminal they risked their life arresting go free. The police officer sees nothing but bad people and injustice. Every day, five days a week. Police officers die seven to nine years earlier than the average person, and even younger when they walk the beat.

Do it to serve? Not when it comes down to it. That was part of the initial impetus, of course, the rationale, if you will. But it was also the adrenaline rush of the chase, the risk involved. Life is filled with stories and every police officer has thousands of them. It was about risk and personal pride.

Wagner found being a private detective different, even though he still carried a gun. You investigate. But you don't put your life on the line. You don't care if the person goes to court or jail, as long as you get paid, and you've done your job. You are often (but not always) looked down upon by the cops on the beat… if you are looked at, at all. The P.I. doesn't see everyone as evil or bad.

There are two people involved when a P.I. goes to work. There's the person paying you to hunt, and the hunted. The risk level is low, and the boredom can be maddening. The worldview of the hunted is like that of the police officer. The "hunted" is evil. The hunter, paying the mercenary to dig up dirt on the hunted, is only evil about half the time.

Often the work they're hired to do is an invasion of personal privacy. In other cases, it's about seeing if someone really is stealing from the hunter. It has its purpose.

This case was a strange one.

It sounded like these people upstairs at 4190 were perverts. The idea of harassing a handicapped woman seemed about as sick as you could get. If they were guilty of this, he'd love to get the evidence to nail them to the wall. He still had friends on the force. If he needed any information, the kind of information that only a cop could get, he'd get it.

The first thing he did was boot up his computer. He did searches for the address and came up with the owner's names associated with that address; then he went to the county record to find out what the house was worth, when they moved in, how much they paid, what it was taxed at, if there were levies or assessments due, all of that general information. Nothing of interest to report here. Total time invested: twenty minutes. Total operating cost: zero.

Next he took that data and went to the various "Find People" websites where he had memberships. There were the White Pages on line where you got their phone number, whether it was listed or not. Then to a source where you input the data, get their e-mail address, and any other little tidbits of information. Total time: five minutes. Total cost: zero.

Then to court records with the county, state, and federal websites to find out about major convictions, marriage and divorce data, birth records for their children and grandchildren. Total time: ten minutes. Total cost: still zero.

Once all of that was accumulated, he went to the various class reunion type web pages and found out the name of the high school and year each person graduated. School attendance is documented and has been for a century. Total time: two minutes. Total cost: another zero.

Next up: Using the main search engines combining words and interests with the person's name to find all references concerning them on the Internet. It's rare that someone can't be found on the web. Very rare. They usually have to be in the technology business or the security business to know how to stay off the radar. Total time: forty-five minutes. Total cost: still zero.

Within an hour he had collected more data than the average person could have in a year. Just twenty years ago, P.I. work began on the computer. It made their work at the data collection stage very cheap and fast, compared to the traditional ways.

The man's name was Vance Harris. He was married. Had been for forty-six years. Hailed from Scottsdale, Arizona before it had become a haven for snowbirds. Guy owned a commercial building in Arden Hills valued at $350,000. It was rated "low industrial." Could be offices, could be a warehouse. It wasn't manufacturing. Mr. Harris and his wife had just purchased the condo at 4190 and had closed on April 19. The place was empty, since the original owner had passed away.

Mr. Harris had an email address, and Jeanette Harris did not. Her records were sketchier as everything was in the husband's name. He did find a record of some volunteer work she did in 1998 with MDA. Aside from that, nothing. She was sixty-seven years old. He was sixty-eight. Probably. People in this age bracket often got away with lying about their age. No judgments. No criminal record. No DWI's. No nothing. Pretty boring American couple. Didn't really seem like the kind of people who would be involved in a prostitution ring and the harassment of a handicapped lady, but who knew? And ultimately, who cared? He was getting paid and getting paid well to find out just what exactly was up at 4190.

It was just before midnight the same night. Ashley opted to return home. She had been all too happy to spend the night with Megan, but it would be nice to be back at home with her own family.

Outside, across the street from 4190, sat a 1999 Toyota Camry. Inside was John Wagner. He had a number of interesting gadgets in the Camry with him. After sundown he placed listening devices outside of Megan's room and five on the outside of the condo above hers.

Fortunately she was on the first floor, so it only took a stepladder and the appearance of being a painter doing touch-up work to get the rest of the listening equipment in place.

In addition, he placed a small video camera outside the window on their deck. It pointed in through some blinds, which seemed likely to stay "cracked" and the camera could be operated by remote. It was focused at a wide angle and had a built-in audio, but that wasn't its purpose. He wanted a visual, and he could record as much as ninety minutes in high quality HD, and that was precisely what he intended to do.

The camera would register date and time, and the battery might allow up to the entire time to be used. The less he used the remote, the more likely the battery would hold its charge for several hours. He would retrieve the camera and microphones before dawn. He'd be there for the next six hours, following his usual procedure. It would be boring.

The camera could easily be discovered if Mr. or Mrs. Harris chose to take an evening stroll onto their deck. It would be hard not to spot the camera. In the event it was discovered, though, it wasn't traceable to John Wagner. It had been purchased on the street, as part of a shipment shortage from Sony to Best Buy. Essentially, it didn't exist.

At about 12:14 a.m., the microphone on his client's condo picked up a loud screaming noise. It was a woman and she was sobbing. Saying things like, "turn it off," and "why are they doing this to me?"

He hit the record button on the remote, which was aimed at the deck of the Harris' condo. A single light appeared to be on in the Harris' home. There seemed to be a flickering source of light as well, probably the TV. He'd know for sure when he saw the video in six hours.

Certainly the woman screaming would be Mrs. Drexel's "Megan."

Another female voice was picked up by the same microphone. This one was quieter. The microphone picked up a few words but not much of the second voice. Probably standing or sitting too far from the window.

Expecting something to happen upstairs, he focused his attention on the second-floor condo. All was quiet. Oddly quiet. If the secondary light was from the television, why wasn't he hearing sound? He should be picking up something. The equipment wasn't state of the art, but it didn't need to be. He'd tested it before coming out and all was in working order.

Occasional door closings, toilet flushes, and feet scraping the floor were picked up and that was it.

The woman on the first floor finally stopped sobbing and screaming about twelve-thirty a.m. Then some quiet talking from the other voice, probably the person who soothed the screamer and then evidently returned to bed, as the lights were now all off again.

Now all six microphones were silent. They remained that way until six a.m., when he collected his video camera and all six microphones before the sun hit the horizon. It had indeed been an uneventful evening. He'd check out his video when he got back home, then call Mrs. Drexel's cell phone to leave a message with his findings.

He connected his camcorder to his television.

Almost immediately he watched a man, retired-age, sit down. The man sat and stared, probably watching TV out of view of the camera. Most of the time his face was expressionless. About every fifteen minutes the man would get up, go into the hallway, disappear and return a couple of minutes later. Couldn't tell for sure, but it looked like he was watching television and leaving his chair during commercials. No sign of any other life in the house, *not a creature was stirring, not even a mouse.* About two a.m. the man did something that caused the light to darken, and he walked out of the camera's sights.

The guy watched TV and went to bed. He watched TV without the sound on, but he watched TV. Go figure. Screaming woman below, nothing above. What the heck is going on?

He turned his own TV off and slept about four hours until noon.

He got in his car and hopped on Highway 35W north up to Arden Hills. He made his way into town and found the location of the building Mr. Harris owned.

Professional Building.

Shit.

Not what he was expecting to find, if the guy was harassing Megan. You expected something, but not this.

He parked in the lot. Looked like dentists, eye doctors, attorneys, standard stuff. He sighed.

It was a two-story building; that was it. There were nine small businesses listed on the directory and none of them seemed out of the ordinary.

He found the building fairly quiet. Normal people walking around doing their thing. He peeked in the optometrist's office and found that it was just that; then he walked up the stairs until he hit the law offices.

He entered. "Mr. Harris in?"

"I'm sorry sir, there is no Mr. Harris here," the receptionist smiled.

"OK, thanks. I'll find it." He left just as the woman was going to ask if he wanted help. That was the problem with Minnesota. Everyone was nice and everyone wanted to help you – even when you didn't want it.

Next office over was a dentist's office. Drills were whirring. He cracked the door and asked the receptionist for a Dr. Jackson. No Dr. Jackson worked here.

Kids were waiting impatiently in the chairs reading Highlights magazine.

Hey, I had a subscription to that when I was a kid. I didn't know they made that anymore.

Downstairs he found other offices, stopped in, glanced around, smelled, and listened for appropriate or inappropriate sounds; there was simply nothing strange about this building in any way. Nothing.

Turning for the door he noted no camera. If you operated a prostitution ring, you'd have a camera to warn you of a bust. Nothing here. Outside, he went around the building to make sure there was no basement and no offices or rooms he missed.

Everything was in order. Just the wheels where hamsters came every day to run in circles for nine hours. Nothing. Nothing at all.

Wagner turned the key and started the car. He pulled the video camcorder out of the trunk and recorded each car in the lot and on the streets around the perimeter of the building on tape, paying special attention to license plates.

Coming up with a quick thought, he turned the ignition off, opened the door, and headed back to the building. He walked into the optometrist's office.

"Hi, I'm John Wagner. I run a small business from my home, and I understand that there will be an office opening up here soon. I'm seriously thinking of leasing space. I'm wondering if you guys like the place enough to renew your lease."

The women stared at each other, not sure what to say.

The first one to pipe up said, "Sure why not. I don't own the place, though. Dr. Burndt does."

"Owner come down a lot and bug you guys?"

The other woman decided to take this one. "I wouldn't know what he looked like, and I've been here a few years."

"Thanks ladies. Much appreciated."

"No problem." He turned and walked away. The owner rarely came in. No house of ill-repute here.

Driving south on 35W, he hit traffic, and slowed down to a near-standstill at the University of Minnesota exit. He simply couldn't make heads nor tails of this whole thing.

These people were spending good money to find out nothing, or at least, it certainly seemed to him like nothing was going on. This afternoon and evening he would watch for an opportunity to follow the elderly couple, to see if that might lead to something. When it came right down to it, John Wagner didn't believe these people were anything more than two fairly wealthy retired folks. And of course you could make money in prostitution, but the fact was that most of those types didn't make as much as people thought. When drugs weren't involved, it was basically a benign activity, and generally not typically run by couples who'd been married over forty years.

Strange case.

It was six o'clock, and Ashley couldn't wait anymore. She called Wagner's cell for an update. She had been chomping at the bit all day, but knew she had to wait to call until he'd at least had some time to investigate.

"So, Mr. Wagner, what do we know so far?"

"They're a married couple in their late sixties. Been married for nearly fifty years. They own a small office building in Arden Hills, a typical professional building – their tenants include an optometrist, doctor, dentist, attorney, and a hairstylist. Reasonably well kept-up. Nothing special. No extra space for illegal activities to take place. Probably makes a thousand a month, if that, on the property as an investment, certainly not much more, and it's filled to capacity. That leads you to believe the people are happy there."

"As far as last night goes, there was a scream at the main level 4190 bedroom around midnight and the guy upstairs was awake, almost certainly watching television, without the sound on. Maybe he was wearing earbuds. He seemed unaffected, and then about two a.m. he turned off the lights and went to bed. There was no activity in the building, except your friend's place, that was of any interest. Quiet building overall. I only had the two places hooked up with microphones but the entire building seems benign. Most residents are probably retired. Any idea if that was your friend who screamed? It was pretty high pitched, and the woman seemed very frightened."

Ashley was silent and a bit sad. It certainly seemed likely that the screamer was Megan, and it seemed that it was a repeat of the previous night.

"Did the screaming last long?"

"No ma'am. About twenty seconds, and then there was another voice in the room. The lights switched on briefly, then back off. Seems they went back to sleep."

"OK, thanks, Mr. Wagner."

"I'll get back with you as soon as I find anything else. I've been watching the place today. Nothing going on. Maybe tonight we'll see some activity. I'm going to set up again and this time follow the traffic in and out of 4190."

"Thanks again, Mr. Wagner."

Ashley just couldn't figure it out. The investigator seemed to be doing a decent job, and there was not much to do until he found something one way or the other. She decided to head on over to 4190 and talk to Megan. She could call her, but then Mary might answer and derail the conversation. And Ashley wasn't up for Mary.

***

Megan was watching the weather on channel 11 when Ashley arrived. Mary heard her arrive, but didn't bother to meet her at the door, or even say hello at all.

"Hi, Megan!" Ashley spoke loudly. It was often hard to tell if she was just talking loudly or shouting or angry or all three. Ashley could be difficult to read.

"Hi, Ashley." Megan put as much as she could into it. She was in bed being informed that the weather was going to be rainy with a chance of thunderstorms, some severe, tonight.

"Whatcha doin'?" Ashley came into the bedroom, purse in hand.

"Seeing what the weather is going to be like tonight."

"Got plans?" Ashley hoped not. She really wanted Megan to stay put here at 4190, and not jet off on another plane ride bound for who knows where.

"Nope. Just watching."

"OK. Hey, have they been noisy since yesterday?" She pointed up, knowing full well that there'd been no noise last night.

"Yes. There were horrible noises last night and this morning when I woke up, too. I didn't sleep much. Maybe five hours."

Ashley was expecting a better report, because she knew better. Wagner told her that nothing had happened last night. Nothing at all.

"What time did you get up?"

"The first time, about six, the second time about nine."

"And when did you get to bed?" She put her purse down and sat on the edge of Megan's bed, as she so often did.

"Early... about eleven, I think. Everything was fine; then they started that stupid compressor, and the johns came. It was so hard to get back to sleep. They kept me awake until about one o'clock."

She has no reason to lie. None. Why would she? It makes no sense. Clearly she was shook up, and she's getting more shook up every day.

"Did Mary hear them?" Ashley figured that Mary was standing in the hallway, probably with her shoulder against the door, listening in.

"Yes. They didn't wake her, though. But, when I called for her to come and help me, she was quite upset with them, too."

"Huh. Have they been quiet today?"

"Well, they never turn off that compressor up there." She pointed at the corner of the ceiling where she heard the noise. Ashley didn't want to say anything. She was more confused than ever. "Did you hire the detective?"

"Yes." *And what do I tell her now?*

"When does he start working for us?"

"He did some preliminary work yesterday. I guess the people upstairs are a married couple in their late sixties – they've been married forever. They own an office building in Arden Hills and that's about it so far."

"Did he get over here and see what they were doing last night? They were so loud; there must have been ten people up there. It sounded like an orgy."

Ashley paused. She didn't want to lie to Megan. She also didn't want to tell her anything that would cause Megan to believe she thought Megan wasn't being truthful. Ashley and Megan had been close friends since high school. Ashley trusted Megan and the opposite was true as well. Megan wouldn't lie to Ashley. So it was clear to Ashley that this was all real – it was either all real in Megan's mind, or it was real in the real world.

"I think he stayed outside. He didn't have much to say about it."

"That's too bad because if he would have been here, he would have seen these sleazy men entering the building like Mary did. The entrance is videotaped at all times. Maybe he can help us put them out of business."

She could hardly say that the only thing Wagner heard all night was Megan screaming.

"I'll ask him to watch extra close tonight. He has listening devices, you know."

"Good! Well, he'll see what they're up to then. I want them thrown out of this building, and fast."

"We're going to figure out who they are, what they're doing, and we'll get them to stop."

There was a long silence in the room. Outside, Mary had a smirk on her face that Ashley couldn't see, but sensed.

"I don't want to live here anymore, Ashley."

Ashley placed her hand on Megan's knee. "I know they're driving you crazy, and it wouldn't be quite like home even if they weren't. Let's see what the private investigator can find, and then we'll work through the police or whoever, to get rid of them."

"I think it's personal now. I think that they're doing this on purpose to hurt me or to drive me insane, something to make me leave the condo."

"But why would they do that, Megan?"

"I mean, I think they're doing this because of the letter. I think they want to drive me crazy and get me out of here."

Ashley had heard similar thoughts in the past from Megan, but she thought them off the cuff and impulsive. It became clear now that Megan had been doing some thinking, and she was changing somehow. Megan really believed the tenants upstairs were doing something very strange and trying to drive Megan and Mary to the brink. But from Ashley's vantage point, nothing was happening.

She would know more soon.

***

The detective had found that the old couple owned two luxury cars. One was a Lexus and the other was a BMW. Both were less than a couple of years old. Mrs. Harris had driven to the grocery store today, and Wagner followed her closely enough to know that she had bread sticking out of the top of one of the grocery bags and some Raisin Bran topping the other bag. She had gone straight to Byerly's grocery store, and then straight home. About sixty minutes. Now, Mr. Harris was heading somewhere.

Wagner put his sandwich away and fell in behind Harris on the highway. Harris pulled into a Blockbuster Video. Old people do things the old way, no streaming-online video for the Harrises. Wagner went inside shortly after Harris.

The employees greeted Mr. Harris by name, and didn't even notice Wagner. They obviously knew Harris. Wagner didn't even register on the employees' radar. Wagner stayed about a dozen feet to the right of Harris as he went down the New Releases aisle. He picked up a couple of action flicks. One with Nicolas Cage. The other was something about cowboys and aliens. *The stuff that people watch.* He went to the checkout counter.

Harris checked out and paid his $6.39 with tax, and was out the door. It appeared the Harris couple was going to be watching action heroes tonight. Outside, the elderly gentleman headed for his automobile. Meanwhile, Wagner hustled to his car and returned to 4190 to set up some additional audio and video devices. Tonight he would have the entire building covered.

The gadgetry he got to use on the job was neat. Not quite James Bond, but definitely high-tech. The tedium, and in this case the wild goose chases, were getting him down. He wanted to help the handicapped girl, but the fact was, he suspected he was going to fail to do so.

Stopping at an Exxon station, he popped into the bathroom and changed into painter's garb. He had painting gear in his car; he was only going once or twice to most places he staked out, and no one ever noticed the lack of a painter's truck because no one ever thought of stuff like that. It was amazing. You could walk down the street with an axe in your hand and people might idly notice, but it wouldn't draw as much attention as you'd think.

Slipping back into the car he was off to 4190 at high speed. He'd set up from the Harris side of the building first, then work his way around the front, to the opposite side, and finally the back. There would be a camera focused on the door of the Harris condo and any doors to the building; the cameras would be recording. Whatever happened was going to be on tape. Today, if these people were there, he'd get them all in crystal clear HD.

Peeking into Megan's place, he noticed no one was home. Had Ashley said something about a therapy appointment? Perhaps. He took advantage of their absence by installing a microphone immediately outside Megan's bedroom window. Today, no stone would be left unturned.

***

Mary drove carefully and quietly. Megan sat in the seat beside her. The Mercedes Benz was a convertible, a rarity in Minneapolis. Megan loved it. Each year it was becoming more collectible. Candy apple red. She'd never seen one like it anywhere – in that way it was like the clothes she used to wear. And she liked that.

I wonder what would happen if I tell Mary I want to leave? She must be going crazy with these people, too. I wonder if she'd want to drive to Chicago or Milwaukee or anywhere to get out of here and get a few days of peace.

Ashley would worry of course, but she'd worry more if Megan didn't start getting some sleep. She tried to think of how to be firm with Ashley without hurting her feelings. No one on the planet meant more to her than Ashley. Mary was close. But Ashley was special. Always loyal. Always there.

"Mary – I want to go to Chicago."

"You *what*?"

"I want to go to Chicago. Tomorrow."

"Why would you want to go to Chicago?"

"Because those people are driving me crazy. If we leave, then they won't be able to bother us. They haven't been keeping you up, have they, Mary?"

"No dear. They are a little noisy but I think you get most of the noise, because they are directly above you. It's dreadful how they behave."

Megan was nodding her head. She was going to Chicago.

"So, let's leave tomorrow. Can you get us a room at the W downtown?"

"Of course, dear. We'll do that. If we can leave tomorrow, we will."

Megan was getting to be full of surprises. Mary wondered what it would be like to drive for eight hours to Chicago in a car with Megan, because it wouldn't actually be eight hours. How would she deal with gas station pit-stops? Walking would take a couple of hours, and just because you got to the bathroom didn't mean you could actually get into the bathroom when a wheelchair was involved.

The idea of getting away from Ashley kindled hope in her, but the idea of dealing with a road trip with someone whose bathroom breaks could be ten times daily didn't seem tolerable. Yet, once in Chicago or wherever, she could get back to work on her master plan, and that was promising.

Ultimately, getting Megan away from Ashley was the hinge on the door that her whole future opened or closed on. It was decided. They would go. Megan would tell Ashley the news and Mary would appear to be an innocent participant, the observer in the whole thing.

"Yes, we'll leave tomorrow if we can."

Once home, they pulled into the underground garage across from the leader of the prostitution ring. Megan was just getting out of the car door as the man emerged from his vehicle.

"Is that him?" Megan was loud. Very loud.

Harris looked at her, wondering, then figuring it out.

"It's you. The one who wants me to stop disturbing my neighbors. I'm so noisy, huh?"

He started to walk toward Megan's car. Mary didn't like the looks of this. It could get ugly and that was the last thing she wanted. Nothing good was going to come from this confrontation.

"Hello, sir." Mary didn't know his name and didn't know how to address him. Her greeting seemed weak, but it would have to do.

"And who are you?"

"I'm Megan's caregiver, Mary Burnett. And who are you?"

"I'm Vance Harris. I live above your condo. And you folks have a habit of being mighty loud and you seem to be pointing the finger in the wrong direction."

Wagner was watching, and noted that both cars went into the underground garage at the same time. This was going to give him ample time to finish his work and find a nice, cozy place to tuck himself into for the night. He hadn't thought of putting a camera in the underground garage. And it just might be a good idea. If he was still on the job tomorrow, he would do that.

"Mr. Harris." Mary was trying to figure out how to get Megan inside without further confrontation. "I need to get my friend into the building, so she can get to the bathroom. She isn't able to get around, as you can see. So if you please, we need to get moving. We don't want any ugly incidents here."

Harris was upset. The letter from Ashley had pissed him off. He'd done nothing and was being made to look like a villain, picking on a defenseless, handicapped person, in front of all the residents in the building.

"Well ladies, stay away from my unit, and I'll stay away from yours. If you try any more shenanigans, I'll make your life a living hell. I'm warning you: stay clear."

He turned and walked away.

"Asshole." Mary couldn't resist. He turned and looked at them. He did nothing but scowl, turn, and continue on into the elevator, taking it to the second floor. It would be some time before Megan and Mary would get there.

"He's so mean-looking and nasty with that stubbed-out cigar hanging from his mouth. I don't like him. You can tell he's the kind of guy that would run a prostitution ring or deal drugs." Megan was angry, but she didn't have the physical ability or energy to express it the way Mr. Harris did.

"Well, we won't have to deal with him tomorrow. We'll be on our way to Chicago."

"He's just so mean! I don't like him and now that he's seen me, he's going to want to make my life even more miserable."

"Now Megan, that's not necessarily so."

"I'm telling you, he is going to make life terrible for the both of us. He knows that we know about the prostitution, his girls, and his compressor. He knows that – "

"Megan!" Mary needed to think and the underground garage was not conducive to thinking. "If he does run a prostitution ring, the detective that you hired will figure it all out. No one knows we're going to Chicago, so he won't be following us. We'll get in the car tomorrow, and it's off to Chicago."

She slid Megan into the wheelchair and pulled the walker behind her as she pushed the wheelchair to the elevator.

Megan heard the compressor noise there too. She had grown to abhor that sound.

That thing must be LOUD. My God, what kind of vibrator does it power?

"Do you hear that? They are already getting ready for the johns up there!"

"Yes, Megan, yes. They are absolutely rude and crude." Mary didn't quite understand everything Megan was concluding, but she wasn't going to argue with her. She was going to support her. Period. No exceptions. Mary: *support*. Ashley: *enemy*.

***

Once in the apartment, Megan's internal rant began.

It's either I go or they go. He knows it. Harris is evil; I can feel it. He's running that ring, I've found them out, and now they'll do whatever they have to do to drive me from my home. They've figured out how to keep the police off track, but they won't get away with this forever.

I want to get out of here. I want to leave town now, tomorrow. I've got to get out of here. I can't handle it anymore. I know Chicago is the answer. They won't go to Chicago.

For now, I need some earplugs or headphones to drown these sick people out.

"Mary?" Mary came into Megan's room.

"Yes? What is it?"

"I want to go to Chicago right now. I can't wait!"

"All right. I'll book the W and pack. We'll leave in the morning."

***

A pretty blonde knocked on the door. She was tall, maybe five foot ten, and wearing a very skimpy halter dress. Mary answered.

"Hi, I'm sorry, I must have the wrong unit. Can you tell me where the Harrises live?"

"One floor up."

"Thanks so much. Have a nice day." She walked away. Mary's heart pounded.

It was one of the hookers, and she didn't even know where to go. On the job training? Guess so. Everyone has to have their first day at work or at the new office.

"*Megan!*" Mary went running into Megan's room. "Megan!"

"Listen honey, one of those prostitutes just knocked on the door asking where the Harrises live. She was dressed like Britney Spears and she's in her thirties. She's obviously new, so they must be hiring new girls. My God, Megan, this is getting crazy. We're definitely out of here."

Megan nodded her head knowingly. It was time. They would head to Chicago. No one would know. They wouldn't even tell Ashley; they couldn't risk being followed. They needed to get cash – a lot of cash. They couldn't use credit cards, because she knew how easy it would be to be tracked by the authorities that way – or by anyone. Megan knew Ashley would be upset, but she just couldn't risk anyone finding out where they were headed.

Wagner brought his family SUV that night. It had room in the back for all the equipment he needed to monitor the 4190 building . Eleven microphones and four video cameras in all.

He heard the knock on the Harris's door, and with his remote he turned on the video camera he'd set up on the deck. It would start taping right away, and continue until he turned it off.

"Who is it?" The old man could be heard easily on the microphone.

"Jenna."

"Jenna who?"

"Jenna... Jenna!"

"Come in."

The door must have opened, because Wagner heard it close. The old man spoke. "So what are you doing here today?"

"Nice place. I wish it were mine. I, um, I need money. A loan. Not a lot, just enough to get me by 'til the end of the month."

"Jesus, don't you make enough money? Haven't I given you...?" The voice trailed off and Wagner could only hear some sobbing.

"All right, all right." There was silence for a minute, and then he heard the girl.

"Thank you. I really appreciate it. I'll have it back to you by the end of the month."

"Uh huh. OK, you do that."

"I'll be leaving." Those were the last words he heard, because the inaudible mumble Harris gave simply couldn't be picked up.

I'll be. He said it out loud, though no one was there to listen. Maybe there was a prostitution ring here and maybe this girl was one of the new ones or someone who hadn't been to this location yet.

Through the feed from one video camera he watched Jenna come to the door, and he couldn't help but stare. Most hookers weren't this good-looking. This girl was fit, healthy, and tan. She oozed Minnesota. But Wagner didn't judge her beyond that. She could be a hooker. And because she was quite attractive it made sense she'd be working the high-rent district, even if it was the suburbs. He had a lead. It was about time.

At 11:54 p.m. his cell phone vibrated. He'd told Mrs. Drexel she could call anytime of the day or night, even if he was on watch.

"Hello."

"I just got a call from Megan, and she's frantic. Says that they are upstairs in droves – maybe twenty people. What's happening?"

"The only significant noise is coming from Megan's unit. The people above did have a visitor earlier. A woman who certainly could pass for a hooker, but right now, that unit, and all the units for that matter, are pretty much silent. It appears that Harris is watching TV again without any sound, but I can't be sure until I check the video in the morning."

"You're telling me that the only unit making noise is Megan's?"

"Yes ma'am." The old policeman in him was coming out.

"But they're telling me that there are twenty people shaking the ceiling and that there is so much noise the bed is vibrating."

"Mrs. Drexel, there is nothing going on and no one awake in the building except your friend, who's now calming down, by the way. I have her room, their kitchen and a living room all wired for sound. The two women are talking and that's it.

"There's no other noise and certainly no sign of any parties or people having sex or even midnight snacks. The place is pretty dead."

There was a long pause that seemed to last forever for Wagner.

"Hang on, will you, Mr. Wagner?"

"Sure thing."

Ashley got on her cell phone while keeping the connection to Wagner. She called Megan's number, and Megan picked up. Wagner could overhear Ashley's side of the conversation.

"Megan, are you OK?"

"They're driving me mad?"

"Right now? Well, is Mary there?"

"Yes. She's right here."

"OK, well, that's good. I promise, honey, I'll check with the investigator in the morning and see what he has found out. I really want you to get some sleep, take an Ambien, and call it a night."

"I know you'll do everything you can to get them to shut up. Love you."

"Love you, too. I'll see you in the morning."

Ashley turned off her cell phone.

"Mr. Wagner?" Ashley wanted to finish up for the night.

"Yes, Mrs. Drexel."

"Let me know what you find on the video, send it to me tomorrow, and of course call me if anything comes up tonight. You can email or fax me an invoice, and I'll get you squared away."

She sounded exhausted and exasperated. There was no explanation for what Mrs. Dresden was hearing.

"Silent except for Megan's unit?"

"Yes ma'am. Harris is almost certainly watching TV, but that's about it. Like I said, there's not another person in any of the other six units that's even awake."

"You're certain of this?"

"Positive."

"Thanks, Mr. Wagner."

"Good night, Mrs. Drexel."

Wagner played with the dials on the equipment, trying to raise the gain on all the microphones. The fact was that there was nothing going on. No one making any noise, and nothing suspicious was going on. At least not now.

A shame. That poor woman has been through hell, and now this. Again, he repeated the obvious to himself.

He'd be there for six more hours then call it a day.

Chapter Twenty Eight

June 21

Day 2465

Ashley got out of bed knowing a tough day lay ahead. She was going to have to talk with Megan about seeing her ENT doctor and a shrink. She was hearing things, or so it seemed. Nothing wrong with hearing things, but she didn't need to have something driving her crazy, if it could be fixed. Megan would, of course, be an unwilling participant in any such conversation. But she would have little choice in the matter.

At ten o'clock, after about two hours of considering how to communicate with Megan, she picked up her phone and called 4190.

Megan picked up on the third ring.

"Hi Megan, did they bother you last night?"

"Ashley, I can't take it anymore. Mary and I are moving out of here. They kept us up all night! I'm going far away. They were so loud last night; I only had two hours of sleep."

Kept us up, what does that mean, us? Mary was hearing this, too? Seems unlikely. Or you never know, maybe the private investigator is in on the whole thing. No, that's crazy. I hired the guy. That was too random, for him to be in cahoots with Mary.

"Megan, today I want you to see Dr. Anderson. I think you might be hearing things."

Megan had no idea what Ashley was talking about.

"What do you mean?"

"I mean the private investigator called a half hour ago and went through the happenings of the entire night at 4190 with me."

"Well, there you have it then. You know what they were doing. Does he have video, too?"

"Yes, he does."

"And what's on the video?"

"Harris was up until two a.m. watching something on TV. No one else was in the unit with him who was awake between eleven at night and six a.m. The entire building was quiet."

"That's impossible. There were a ton of people upstairs making noise, having sex, running the compressor at full blast. It was so loud it made my bed vibrate."

"Megan, no one was upstairs except the old guy, Harris. That's it."

"Are you saying I'm a liar, Ashley?" Megan was furious. Never in her life had Ashley not been on her side.

"No, Megan. I'm not saying you're a liar. I think you're hearing things."

"So now you're saying I'm crazy, too?"

Megan stopped talking as she heard Mary, clear as a bell, yell, "If she doesn't believe us, to hell with her. You and I both know it's real."

Ashley had no idea what to do with this conversation. Better to talk in person and have the private investigator bring his findings and evidence to 4190.

"Megan, I'm going to have the investigator bring the audio and video recordings over around lunch time. We'll go through all of it then."

There was a long, long pause.

"Ashley, we're leaving for Chicago. We're going to stay at the – . Never mind. We'll call you when we get there. We can't handle all of this noise, and now your betrayal as well. It's just too much for one person to take. Bye, Ashley."

The phone went silent.

Ashley simply looked at the phone. She was stunned.

Chicago.

She put on her shoes and raced to the car. She was going to stop this trip right now.

Back at 4190, Mary had finished packing the red convertible Mercedes. They were going to be on their way as soon as Megan was seated in the car.

"I can't believe her. She says she's your friend, and she calls you a liar right on the phone. Says you're what? Hearing things? She's no friend. What a bitch. I would never stab you in the back. I believe you, even if no one else does."

"She didn't exactly say I was lying."

"She said you were hearing things, and she took the word of someone she's known for maybe all of five minutes over yours. There's no loyalty there. I don't think so. She doesn't deserve your friendship, but I'm not going to say anything else. Let's go."

Megan slid into the wheelchair, and Mary brought her to the underground garage. Mary wheeled Megan over to the car and gingerly eased her into the passenger seat. She pushed the wheelchair to the back of the car and put it in the trunk along with her walker and all kinds of other travel items like a cooler and suitcases. Mary was amazed she could fit so much into the trunk.

Stupid bitch. God I hate her. Megan will see who her friends are now. She'll never question me again. Ashley calls her a liar, and I'm there for her – to pick up the pieces.

She slammed the trunk shut and slid into the driver's seat. She *loved* driving this car!

With luck, the trip would be fruitful, and might even be fun.

The seat belt automatically belted her in. "How you doing, Megan?"

"The noise is driving me nuts, but I'm fine. Doesn't it bother you?"

"Oh it does, but I try to ignore it."

"*How* can you ignore it? It's so loud."

"I just don't think about it."

That was dumbfounding to Megan. And so was the fact that she was hearing the compressor in the garage. That didn't make any sense. How could that be? She didn't want to think about it, at least not yet.

"Let's go, Mary. Chicago, here we come."

"Good idea." She revved up the engine, and they were off. Soon they were on Highway 94 heading to Wisconsin. It would be a long day. Leaving at ten-fifteen the way they did would put them in Chicago smack dab in the heart of rush hour – assuming they made the trip in eight hours, which wasn't likely. They'd probably be much later than that, so it should all work out just fine, as far as the traffic was concerned.

"Megan, when was the last time you drove all day in a car?"

"Eight years ago."

The compressor was still running as they hit the Wisconsin border. How could she hear the compressor sound in Wisconsin? Megan knew it wasn't *that* loud, but there had to be an explanation. It wasn't as loud as when she was home, but it was still there in the background. She thought over the past week or so and realized that in fact sometimes it seemed quiet, but it kept coming back. It was odd – very odd.

Either the compressor sound is somewhere in this car somehow or it's being transmitted to the car from 4190. Harris would do it just to get revenge. What a mean SOB! I want him to go to jail – to pay for his criminal activities. I want to see him behind bars – to pay for driving me crazy. HOW can I hear the compressor when we are sixty miles from home? It's not possible. Could they really be transmitting a signal to my head somehow?

What about my cell phone? They could be transmitting this through my iPhone!

She reached into her purse and pulled out her iPhone. It was powered off. She returned it to her purse and let out a sigh.

If I cover my ears the compressor seems louder. I take my hands away, and it gets quieter. I plug my ears with my fingers, and it gets louder. The sound IS inside. Now, that is strange. So you leave the house where they are making all the noise and then they somehow send it to you, but not on the cell phone.

How then?

Radio waves? How does that work? And how does Mary hear it? She must hear out here from what I hear in here, or something like that. Maybe she can hear it through me?

This is crazy. It's so crazy. Why would they do this to me? Because we told everyone in the building about them? They would transmit radio waves into my brain because of that? And how does my brain hear it?

OK, it doesn't. It can't. I went to college. It can't happen. I'm not stupid.

The radio waves are going to the metal bone in my ear from my surgery in my left ear. Must be like a radio receiver or something. A walkie- talkie.

But we're sixty miles from home. But of course you can pick up radio a hundred miles away from the station, I think. Something like that.

Obviously you can't hear what's going on in a condo two hours away from where you are unless it's being transmitted. Technology can do some pretty amazing things nowadays.

This can't be that hard.

Maybe the cell phone doesn't have to be powered on to carry a signal.

No, that doesn't sound right. I think Ashley told me once that to "keep your life private, keep your cell phone off." She was watching that Person of Interest TV show or something.

The surgeon!

The stuff they put in my ear was to help me hear after all. Maybe Harris figured out that I had surgery there and knew how to take advantage of me, or maybe they knew the doctors and the doctors told them about me. Or maybe this happens to a lot of people, but no one ever talks about it.

What sick people. Why did we have to move to 4190 in the first place?

It was almost as if Mary were reading Megan's mind.

"You know Megan, when you think about it, if we hadn't moved into 4190, those crazy people upstairs would've never bothered us. They'd have never met us. If Ashley had done her homework on this place, you wouldn't have had to be put through this. But no, she does what's easy, takes the first thing that comes along, and poof! Off to Chicago we go because the people upstairs have made our lives in Minneapolis impossible. It's such a horrible thing."

She looked over at Megan and saw that Megan was staring straight out the window, her gaze fixed on something about a mile out. It looked like a radio tower.

It was beginning to come together for Megan. They were radioing to her – like a cell phone but not the cell phone. In fact, it was the same thing as a cell phone, except for the fact it was being radioed into her head. She didn't want to talk to Mary anymore about it, just in case Mary might think she was going crazy, too.

Megan's cell phone rang.

"It's Ashley."

Mary said nothing and Megan pressed "talk" and put the phone to her ear.

"Hello?"

"Megan, where are you?"

"We're in Wisconsin on our way to Chicago."

"You guys need to turn around and come home."

"No, Ashley. We're going to Chicago to get away from the crazy people upstairs."

"I'm here at your place right now; there is no noise and there are no crazy people upstairs."

"There will be tonight," was Megan's instant retort.

"Megan, please, tell Mary that you want to go home."

"But I don't want to go home. They're there, not here."

"Megan, this is ridiculous. There's no one here doing anything to you."

"Ashley, I think they're radioing to me, now. I hear them right now."

Ashley decided not to comment. There was no reason to. "Look Megan, I can't help you if you leave town and don't let me know where you're going."

"Don't you think you've helped me enough? If we wouldn't have moved into 4190, this never would have happened."

Mary looked over at Megan and back to the road.

There was silence. Mary couldn't believe what she was hearing, and she was joyful. Ashley couldn't believe what was happening, either. She was heartbroken and dumbfounded at the same time.

"Ashley, I'll call you when we get to Chicago. Bye." Megan clicked the phone off then turned the power off.

On the other end, it took Ashley a while for everything to piece together. She had to get Megan to a doctor and away from Mary as soon as possible.

***

Mary had taken the top down so the wind was in their faces and in their ears. They were halfway to Madison when Megan stopped noticing whether the compressor was running or not. But Megan couldn't fully escape the terror, even if it stopped for a while.

It's such a pretty day out. So nice to be able to drive with the top down. It's been forever.

They are buzzards. Aren't buzzards the birds that fly around and look for animals that are dying or are dead and then they swoop down and have dinner? Well, I'm dinner. I am a sitting duck.

Chapter Twenty Nine

Late Afternoon

Once in Chicago they paid a valet to park their car, because there was no parking lot at the hotel. The bellman helped Mary set Megan in her wheelchair, promising to deliver their luggage upstairs shortly.

Mary and Megan checked in to what promised to be the biggest suite in the place.

Arriving on the seventh floor, they found their room, which was very nice indeed. A five-star hotel not far off Lake Shore Drive, it was probably one of the best places to stay in Chicago. It wasn't the MGM, as far as size, but it certainly would do for a few days, Megan thought. They weren't there to see the sights; they were there to get away.

Unfortunately, the compressor was still running.

It's got to be radio. There's no other way, unless they are here with us, had the car bugged to send the sounds of the compressor, and then sent them here. But how would they know that? Do they know what we are talking about?

Oh my God, that could be it. If they can send the message here, why wouldn't they be able to hear what we are talking about back there?

She gingerly got up from her wheelchair, pulled herself up with her walker, and decided to exercise a bit by walking around the room. She hadn't been getting her normal amount of walking done, and as a result she felt some pain and creakiness.

Just as her fear peaked, the compressor stopped. Completely stopped. No noise whatsoever.

They stopped! They stopped radioing to me? Why? Why would they stop? Are they playing with me? Did they go out for dinner? It's about nine o'clock, maybe that's it. Maybe they turned it off until later, when the girls get there – about eleven o'clock or so.

But why not keep it on? Does it run on a battery? No way. Not something that big and noisy. No, maybe they decided that I'd suffered enough for the day? They'd give me a break?

"Whatcha thinking, Megan?" Mary appeared from the bathroom with a towel in her hands.

Megan was lost in thought.

"What do you think of the hotel?" This time Megan looked up at her and cracked a smile.

"It's quiet."

"It's very quiet up here. Seven floors up. Traffic– you can get a dose of it but not this time of night. Probably in the morning at rush hour. Maybe we'll go shopping tomorrow. We're only two blocks from Michigan Avenue and if you look out the window, you'll see plenty of shops out there to find you some nice, new colorful clothes!"

"That would be very nice, Mary. It's quiet, Mary. It's really quiet."

"Well, that's because we are away from that horrible 4190."

"I just don't understand."

"You know what I understand, Megan?" She didn't give Megan a chance to answer. "Pizza. Chicago has great pizza, best in the world. I say we get a pizza. "

Megan wasn't certain what to think. She was loosening up and walking a bit better than when she first stood. She felt good, and it was *quiet*. Maybe something good was about to happen to change things for the better.

"Why not have pizza? That would be nice. Can we get a cheese pizza? No pork?"

"Of course we can. Let me find the phone book."

There were several brochures from local stores and shops on the desk, and next to those was a bottle of red wine that also looked inviting. Mary shuffled through the brochures and found a couple for pizza. She picked one and dropped the rest of the brochures. She picked up the telephone and called out for pizza delivery.

"They said they'd be here in twenty-five minutes. That seems like pretty fast service, doesn't it, Megan?"

"Sounds good. I'm really hungry."

"Should we open the wine?" Mary was already at work on it. Must be an amenity for people who are crazy enough to spend this kind of money on a hotel.

They both smiled at the welcome sound of the cork releasing from the bottle, and Megan turned her attention back to the street below.

It was getting dark. The sun behind the buildings was not quite down yet. The streets below were virtually deserted. It didn't seem like one of the biggest cities in the world.

"Here you go." Mary handed Megan a wine glass.

Megan took one hand off the walker and held herself up with the other. She had a sip of wine, very slowly. She didn't want to spill. She felt steady, better than she had in days, but she knew better than to use her feelings as a guide. What she felt and what the reality was in her body weren't always the same thing.

"Cheers," Megan said. Mary clicked Megan's glass, and they both took another sip.

"Want to sit down?" Mary asked because she wanted to, and she sat.

"No thanks. I'm going to stand for a while and sip this wine and enjoy the view."

Megan could handle a wineglass and standing with one hand on her walker for a few minutes, but probably not much more without running the risk of falling. She could see Lake Michigan off to the left. It would be nice to take a stroll down Michigan Avenue again. She hadn't been there since she was young. Such a long time ago, it seemed.

"Mind if I turn the TV on?"

"Go right ahead."

Mary did. She flicked through about twenty channels, finally settling on Channel 9, the WGN Superstation. When she saw that the news was on, she immediately clicked over to AMC to see what movie was playing. The last thing she wanted was to watch the news, because that pretty much meant of course, bad news. She wanted Megan to stay upbeat, since she seemed to be feeling better now.

The show was *Mad Men*. She'd watched it a few times. Looked like it was half over – that would be fine.

Megan continued to sip her wine and was finishing the last drop in that glass as their food arrived.

Mary hopped up from Mad Men and opened the door. The delivery boy was wearing a bike helmet. Mary didn't ask. She just wanted food. She handed him a twenty, told him to keep the change, and closed the door behind him. She opened up the pizza box on the desk.

It smelled wonderful. This wasn't just pizza, it was pizza. Real Chicago-style pizza, much better than anywhere. There were some spices in the box as well. This was the life.

"Should we go in the other room and sit at the table?"

"There's another room?" Megan hadn't known that.

"Right there. It's got a table with fruit on it."

Megan might never have seen it. It would take her a while to get there as it was twenty steps away, but she had time.

"Sure, you start without me. Can you take my glass?"

Mary did, and Megan was on her way. She'd be in the adjacent room in about ten to fifteen minutes. Mary sat down, poured herself another glass of wine, and ate and drank while Megan walked over.

"Sure you don't want me to get the chair for you?"

"Definitely. Just eat and enjoy."

Just what Mary wanted to hear. Exactly what she wanted to hear. Meanwhile, Megan enjoyed the walk across the suite and the sound of silence mixed with *Mad Men*, a show Megan loved. Megan's cell phone rang. Mary got up and dreaded answering it, knowing who it had to be.

"Hello? Yes, she's here. She's walking over to the table to eat some pizza. We'll call you back." She clicked the phone off and sat back down.

Megan knew it was Ashley, of course. She'd call her back after she got seated.

Mary saved Megan a few pieces of pizza and sure enough, Megan arrived and seated herself in just under fifteen minutes. That was progress. A few weeks ago that would have been a twenty-minute trip.

"Would you call Ashley back, so I can talk to her?"

Mary pulled out her cell phone. When it started ringing on the other end, she placed the phone into Megan's hands.

"Hello, Mary?"

"No, this is Megan. Yes, Ashley. How are you?"

"I'm fine, Megan, the question is how are *you?*"

"Ashley, it's quiet here." There was silence from Ashley for a few moments.

"Megan, that is very nice to hear. How are you feeling?"

"I feel better than I've felt in weeks. It's nice to be here. I just had a glass of wine and now I'm going to have some pizza. It looks so good."

She certainly sounded better than she had this morning. No need to rock the boat. She was OK.

"Did you pick the Westin or the W?"

"The W, of course."

"How was your trip down there?"

"It was fine. Long time to be sitting in the car, but it was fine."

Realizing Megan had food on the table, she wanted to let her eat. God knows if Mary would have another meal for Megan in the near future.

"OK, well, I'll call you again in the morning, OK?"

"OK, Ashley. Thank you for calling. Bye."

Megan set the phone down slowly and then aimed for a piece of pizza to put on her plate.

"It sure is nice to be here, Mary. Chicago was a great idea. Thanks for bringing us here. It's so nice and quiet."

"I'm glad. You eat, and I'll pour you another glass of wine."

She hadn't planned for this adventure but being in a nice suite at the W in Chicago wasn't all that bad. But it wouldn't be so wonderful for long. Hotels are nice, but even suites can get old after a few days. So what would happen next? She really didn't have any idea.

Megan did her best to eat the pizza, something that realistically she could not have done at all not long ago. She was making real progress in her rehab. And Megan did worry about rehab. She knew she needed to be doing therapy every day, and that wasn't going to happen in Chicago or at 4190.

But more important than physical rehabilitation was the fact that things were *quiet*. Maybe they couldn't get into the hotel anymore via radio; she was too far from the signal. Maybe that was it. She had no idea. She was just thankful for the silence that she was experiencing.

It wouldn't last long.

Chapter Thirty

June 22

Day 2466

No one was having sex in adjacent rooms that night and that helped Megan fall asleep and sleep hard for nearly fifteen hours. When she awoke in the master bedroom, she could feel that the sun was high in the sky, though in downtown Chicago, you couldn't actually prove such an assertion.

The restful peace was met with great appreciation for God and the Universe.

Dear God... God, I don't know how I've endured all of this, but I thank you for helping me.

She took her time in getting to a sitting position. She had not been in a rush for a decade, so the desire to race up was simply bred out of her by the nature of her circumstance. But getting to the bathroom had been a big problem for years and years, one that would often cause embarrassment and humiliation. Here she could get to the bathroom in fifteen minutes – about twenty steps. She simply had to wake up and then move quickly. Most of the time she made it.

Mary emerged from her room and told Megan that she had fun planned for their day. They were going to get the wheelchair and walk Lake Shore Drive and Michigan Avenue, stopping off at Grant Park and maybe the Field Museum. Chicago had a wonderful art museum, as well as the Adler Planetarium and The Museum of Science and Industry. But most importantly it had shops – lots and lots of shops. Today they would visit clothing stores, jewelry stores, shoe stores…. and do some retail therapy and credit card damage.

The streets of Chicago were packed with people bustling to and fro. Lots of businessmen, shoppers, tourists, and panhandlers. And Megan was surprised to see a lot of people in wheelchairs and an assortment of other disabled people.

First stop, Macy's, which would keep them busy for a couple of hours. Each bought an outfit, Megan's colorful and bold, even for her, but especially for a woman in a wheelchair. Mary settled for gray and black. They each got a new pair of shoes as well. Total bill, just under a thousand dollars.

It was about two-thirty when they found a sidewalk café on a side street. They sat for an hour having a quiet lunch and watching the people go by on Michigan Avenue.

Megan simply loved the area. It was alive with people and lots of fun.

After leaving a hefty tip that was greater than the price of the meal, they returned to Michigan Ave. and strolled until they came to a shoe store. Megan's feet never were the same after the crash. Back then, they had swollen up to three times their normal size. When all was said and done, her original size 7 shoes would no longer fit her now size 9 feet. They both found comfortable walking shoes and left about $200 with the store. Mary was carrying a lot of bags as she pushed Megan, but it was worth it. It was like Christmas come early.

Their last shopping stop was at a jewelry store. Megan wanted a necklace. The store owner personally helped her find just what she was looking for, once she became aware of the kind of money that Megan planned on spending. She made sure Mary walked out with a beautiful bracelet, too. The total tab was just under three grand. As the hour approached five, they began to head back to the hotel. The walk was invigorating, the air was fresh, and there was nothing but a single cumulus cloud dotting the sky.

Megan didn't think of anyone back in Minnesota even once during the day. She was having what seemed to be the best day of her life, except for, well, maybe except for her whole life before the crash. But that was another world. Another time.

Back to the hotel they went, calling it a day. Megan needed to use the restroom and she was exhausted, even though she was quite happy.

They ordered room service: Teriyaki salmon for Megan and a ribeye for Mary.

The food was delivered on a large silver cart. The butler set everything on the table in their "dining" room; he was prompt, efficient, and quiet. Mary handed him five dollars and saw the door close as he left.

They sat, ate, and talked about the events of the day. As they were finishing, the hotel phone rang. Mary picked up, and it was Ashley. She didn't even say another word after "hello," but simply handed the phone to Megan.

Ashley attempted to persuade Megan to come home, but Megan declined. Megan told Ashley that the night before she'd had her first good night's sleep in weeks. Then Ashley made what Megan would later consider to be a big mistake. Ashley asked Megan how she liked the W, Chicago style. Megan told her that it wasn't the Ritz Carlton, her favorite, but it was very nice. And best of all, it was peaceful.

Megan told Ashley she'd think about when she wanted to come home, and they could talk more about it tomorrow. For tonight she simply wanted to enjoy the evening and relax.

Both women fell asleep around eleven, after sipping a few small glasses of champagne.

Chapter Thirty One

Sunrise

Tap. Tap. Tap. It was the familiar noise.

"Megan...Megan...Megan. Get up!"

The shouts from the man blew her eyes wide open. She sat upright and looked left and right. There was no one there, but the compressor was on and pumping.

Gunshot!

Glass shattered throughout the room and ricocheted into the ceiling. The explosion was loud, but she had no idea where it had come from.

Megan hadn't moved so quickly in years. Adrenaline shot through her body, as she bolted up out of bed, grabbed her walker and stood up, screaming for Mary. She wanted to run, but couldn't. Her body flushed with fear, and her limbs felt tangled. She was up and then she was down, collapsing in a heap on the floor.

Mary raced out of her bedroom and over to Megan.

Mary was terrified. "What the fuck is going on? It came from *that* room!"

She pointed to the room next to theirs, but Megan had another story to tell.

"He woke me up, told me to get up! When he fired the gun. The bullet's in the ceiling. *Look!*"

"Who did? OH MY GOD." Mary saw the bullet hole in the ceiling. She turned and saw the shattered glass and went to look out the window. She could see two men running away from the hotel.

"I don't know. The people running the compressor, the buzzards. What do you see?"

"I see two people running. Two men. They're headed down an alley across the street. Let's get the front desk to call 911. Maybe we should just get out of here!"

Mary picked up the hotel phone, pushed the zero button, and waited six or seven rings before a rushed voice answered the phone. "Hello. Mrs. Dresden? We have a situation here. Please stay in your room. It may not be safe to leave your room. We'll call you back when everything's OK."

Mary began to speculate silently on what was happening. *Megan's friends had found them again. How did they DO that? Did they follow us all the way? Even stopping at the rest stops and gas stations for an hour each? Or did they come down later?*

Mary got the courage to go to the window again and scope out the street below.

"It may not be safe to leave, Megan! There's a bullet hole in the ceiling and shattered glass all over the place. The two... the two buzzards just ran into the alley across the street. Get the police!" Mary was both furious and scared to death. She was in survival mode. She hung up. It was 5:35 a.m., almost dawn. The sun would be up in about a half hour. Mary looked at Megan, who was already preparing to leave, packing things into the bag hanging from her walker.

"They want us to stay in our room, Megan. Something about it not being safe to leave."

"*Oh noooo.*" Megan's heart pounded, and Mary's began to race. "They're after me!"

"You think it's them?"

"I know so. He shouted at me and told me to get up. Mary, I need to go to the bathroom."

Mary didn't bother to speak; she simply helped Megan into her chair and over to the bathroom. She returned to the living room and peered out between the curtains. She didn't have to sneak around. She'd seen them head between the two stores across the street. But she didn't see anything now, and she was terrified.

"Somebody has a gun somewhere around here. We have to get out of here. Maybe they're after you. Oh my God! What do we do? Damn it!"

Mary started packing as well. She raced around without really accomplishing much – like the proverbial chicken with its head cut off. She packed their bags as quickly as was possible, given her current state of mind. Realizing there was too much for her to carry as well as helping Megan, she had to get someone up here straight away.

Less than fifteen minutes later they were ready to go; Megan appeared at the door of the bathroom in the wheelchair.

"Megan, we're getting out of here." She picked up the phone and called the main desk.

"W Hotel…" She cut the receptionist off, before she could say another word.

"Send up a bellman to get our luggage and have the valet bring our car to the front of the building. We're checking out."

"That won't be necessary Mrs.- " Again cut off.

"Car and bellman, now; no questions please. There's no time; we're ready to go now."

Within minutes, she had all of the remaining items packed and ready to go. The bellman knocked on the door.

"May I…" The bellman got cut off by Mary as well.

"Put the luggage on the cart and make sure our car is waiting for us in front of the hotel. We'll meet you down there." She handed him a twenty, hoping it would motivate him to move quickly without speaking.

"But ma'am, you don't have to…" the bellman was flustered and frustrated, obviously trying to convince the women to stay, but there was nothing he could say that would stop them leaving.

He took the luggage down and easily beat them to the valet, who did indeed have the red convertible ready and waiting.

As Mary passed the front desk with Megan in what looked like a scene out of a Woody Allen movie, Mary shouted at the front desk staff as they passed, "705 checking out. Put it on our bill. We left the keys in the room!"

And out the front door they went. The bellman helped them into their car. This time there was no additional tip, because as soon as Mary was in the car, she had her foot on the gas and they headed toward Lake Shore Drive and then north.

Another gunshot rang out. Mary pushed the accelerator in terror. She was doing eighty in a 45 mph zone, but still noticed a van and an SUV following closely behind them. Megan pulled her visor down and flipped the mirror open. Terrified, she saw the van and the SUV right on their tail. She trembled with fear.

Mary saw an exit sign for Wrigley Field, took the exit, and then raced through the stoplight taking a sharp right. In no time they were in a densely populated residential part of town; there was no way you could go faster than 30 or 35 mph. She drove as fast as she could without hitting cars on either side of the narrow streets, reminiscent of European streets, or some parts of New York, or even Boston. They passed the ballpark. Everything was still around the park. People came from all over the world to watch baseball here. They would drive as fast as they could to get out of this neighborhood.

"Stupid narrow streets. Stupid people. Stupid cars parked on the side of the road. Get out of my way!"

There was some moving traffic now that needed to be dodged as well. She had to get out of here.

"Move it! Step on it!"

Megan looked into the visor again and saw the SUV close behind them. She knew they were in deep trouble. They were driving a red Mercedes convertible in Chicago with the top down. They were easy to follow and an even easier target.

BANG! Another gunshot.

The buzzard had decided to act instead of radio. The radio transmissions were just Act One.

"Mary, the compressor is so loud! My head is screaming! They're shooting at us! What are we going to do? They *are* the buzzards! I knew it. Ashley thought I was crazy. Oh my God! How are we going to get away?"

"We have to find a police station or a police officer or a highway patrolman or *something*. I need to get back on the interstate. Eventually we have to run into 294 if we keep heading west and if we don't get shot first."

She drove faster and almost recklessly. It wasn't as easy as it looked in the movies.

Two more gunshots rang out.

This time the shots hit the car, but no glass broke, no windows were shattered.

"OH MY GOD!" Megan was starting to hyperventilate. What are we going to do?"

Mary was now ignoring Megan completely. 294! The interstate. This is insane. Why the hell would anyone do this? She pushed the accelerator to the floor and raced up the ramp at an insane speed, throwing them onto the highway.

Within seconds, she saw a sign: "Pay Toll Ahead 35 cents each axle." Run a toll booth, and they HAVE to send a cop to arrest you. Run it – driving recklessly, and you might get the entire Chicago police force on you.

And that's exactly what she did. She picked a lane that had no cars in it, but the crossbar was down. She accelerated to 80 mph and drove through the bar. The wood splintered in front of them; they swerved. Other cars around them virtually stopped in shock and confusion.

A siren blared.

Finally!

She looked and saw the SUV, but it wasn't moving forward. They'd finally stopped. Her plan had worked.

The cop pulled them over. Mary explained how it all started back at the hotel, that she was doing the crazy driving on purpose. They both described the van and SUV to the officer, who took careful notes. He found the story hard to believe, but the bullet holes in the fender were pretty compelling evidence. A phone call to the W confirmed that they had indeed departed in terror from their suite, where a shooting had taken place. Apparently, whoever shot at them was just aiming to scare them, as there would have been no way to ensure accuracy of the shot from the ground below. It would miss... or hit.

Mary gave the officer her cell phone number, their address, and all the information requested. She said they'd come back to the police station if needed. Megan insisted they should do everything they could to find the shooters and put them in jail. After questioning them for some twenty minutes, and making a few more calls, the officer decided to let them go. What else could he do with them?

They hadn't seen any faces. Just two vehicles on the road and two men running from the W Hotel. Nothing else. The officer had offered them refuge at the police station, which they both declined. There was no sign of the SUV or the van. They were still scared, but no longer in a state of panic. They promised to drive carefully and avoid all lunatics with guns, as if they could control the psychos who were shooting at them.

The sound was being pumped into Megan's head from somewhere, but she hadn't wanted to say anything about it that might aggravate the situation.

Finally, by ten to seven they were headed north on the interstate, and in desperate need of a plan as to what to do next.

They decided to stop and use a bathroom and get some food; they were starving. Since the cop had pulled them over, nothing else had happened; they seemed to be safe.

They found a suitable exit about thirty minutes later in Gurnee, where they saw signs for Six Flags amusement park. They figured they would stop there to eat, fill the tank, use the facilities, and get off the road. Mary thought they should duck inside the amusement park once it opened to mix in with the crowd; this would give them a chance to think and plan what to do next.

She didn't consider that the apple red Mercedes convertible was something that a person could spot from an airplane at 34,000 feet.

At the Truck-stop Café, they simply didn't feel comfortable talking about the recent events. Megan was panicking again because the compressor sound was screaming in her head. She whispered, "They are radioing to me. It's driving me crazy."

Mary assured Megan that they would talk about it later. Megan looked around and saw suspicious looking men everywhere. Could one of them be the one who told her to get up this morning, and then shot at her? The one making the compressor sound in her head? The one trying to drive her crazy?

They took their time with breakfast. They certainly weren't going back to Minneapolis, where the buzzard was based. They weren't going to go back to the W in Chicago where the shooting happened. They decided during the short drive over to Six Flags that they would simply stay there in Gurnee until things cooled off.

Gurnee, Illinois was a growing city and had been for over thirty years, since the building of the amusement park, which way back in 1976 was called Marriott's Great America. Marriott was the Midwest's answer to Disney World. It was an enormous park with fast roller coasters, enormous log rides, and shows to treat all ages. It was just nine a.m., the place had just opened, and the parking lots were already packed. Thankfully, handicapped parking spaces were taken seriously in Gurnee and there was a spot for them less than a hundred feet from the front gate.

After getting Megan into her wheelchair, the two of them went to a ticket window and bought all-day passes.

Beyond the handicapped equivalent of a turnstile, they entered another world. Megan couldn't have been more relieved. The hustle and bustle of people and the music playing overhead and all around almost drowned out the compressor noise that the buzzard was sending,

How many others have those cruel people tortured? Or is it just me?

Megan wanted some reassurance. "Mary, you think we're safe here?"

"Honey, I thought we were safe at the W."

"They're going to chase us everywhere we go. They found us in Vegas. They found us in Chicago. They're going to find us anywhere we end up."

"They can't find us everywhere. How could they find us here in the park? Even if they saw us come in, they're going to have a hard time finding us among twenty thousand people."

"How many of those twenty thousand people are in a wheelchair?"

"Hmmm, maybe twenty," and they both knew it was true. The fact that Megan was in a wheelchair made them easy targets.

That bitch sent the letter and we've nearly been killed for it.

They'd lost the bad guys for now, but clearly they would be located soon.

"So what happened this morning, Megan? What did you hear?"

Mary pushed her through one of the themed areas as they talked, both facing forward.

"Well, first I heard the tapping sound…like someone knocking on a door. Then I heard someone tell me to get up, and then I heard the gun shot. BANG!"

"Huh."

"Did you hear the guy who was talking to me?"

"I heard the bang. I nearly hit the ceiling I jumped so high."

"Of course, you couldn't hear it, he was in here with me." Megan pointed to her left ear.

"What did he look like?"

"I don't know. I mean, maybe he wasn't really with me. Maybe he radioed to me and told me to get up."

"Maybe. Whatever, we have to find a safe place to stay where people with guns aren't going to find us."

"Should we call Ashley?"

Mary sighed. At this point, maybe the bitch could help. Maybe she could do something for them, even though she was four hundred miles away.

They walked around the park for a while, watching people and theme characters interact. Kids rode the roller coasters, their parents ate popcorn and snacks while they watched their kids having fun.

For Megan though, it was only nice to be here because she felt safer in a crowd. If she had to face reality, though, she figured they were no safer here than they were at the W. She was so easy to spot. It didn't take a rocket scientist to figure out where the handicapped lady was. The wheelchair was a dead giveaway. The style of clothing Megan wore – well, that was the other thing that drew people's eyes to Megan.

Listening to the background music, they wandered through the park without saying much. Finally Megan came up with the answer.

"We're going to rent an apartment."

"We're what?"

"We're going to rent an apartment in the most secure building we can find. I want to live somewhere that no one can find us, or radio to me, or shoot at us."

Mary couldn't argue. Being shot at had changed her thinking. She looked at her cell phone; there were four bars. Good enough for Megan to call Ashley and give her an update.

Ashley picked up on the fifth ring. "Hello?"

"This is Megan."

"Oh, hi, Megan. Why are you calling on Mary's cell phone?"

"Well, I'll tell you. I've got a story for you, Ashley. This morning an old man told me to get out of bed, and I was really scared. All of a sudden, there was a gun shot."

"What!"

"That's right, a gunshot at the W."

"What are you talking about?"

"They chased us out of the W, through the streets of Chicago, and onto the highway until we came to a policeman who helped us out – "

"You got *shot at?*" Ashley was beside herself. *What was going on?* "Megan, is Mary there?"

"Yes, she's right here."

"Can you put her on?"

"Sure. Mary, she wants to talk to you."

Mary looked more than a little surprised.

"What do you want?"

"Mary, did you get shot at?"

"Several times this morning. At least four or five?"

"Where?"

"In the hotel, in the car. It's those people upstairs. If you had done something sooner, none of this would have happened. The car is a mess, but it still runs."

"You mean you know who shot at you?"

"The crazy guy upstairs from 4190. And someone else was with him."

"You were shot at by the guy from 4190?"

"Bunch of times. Thanks for nothing, Ashley. Real good job of taking care of everything. You know, I will take care of Megan; you just keep yourself safe back there while we're getting shot at here, why don't ya? Megan wants to get an apartment here, where we're safe and out of trouble. They must want her dead real bad."

Once again Ashley was dumbfounded. Nothing was going on at 4190. Nothing ever had been.

"Are you two all right? Where are you now?"

"We're at Six Flags Over America. North of Chicago. We came here to get out of sight of these buzzards that are gunning for us."

"OK. Well… you're OK then?"

"Sure. Sure. Yes. We're great. Megan will be traumatized for life, and I enjoy getting shot at. Two bullet holes in the Mercedes. Yes, we're doing just grand."

"OK, I'll call you right back." Ashley hung up before she had to listen to Mary's voice say another word. She just didn't like that woman… at all. Unfortunately, she had to deal with her.

She shook her head a few times. *There is no way this could be real. There was NOTHING going on upstairs. The detective said there was nothing. Nothing on video. Nothing on audio. Nothing in real life. There's nothing there. I'm calling the W.*

She found the paper she had written the W's phone number on. She quickly punched up the 312 area code and number.

"Hi, this is Ashley Drexel. Megan Dresden and …"

"Ah, Ms. Drexel, I'm sure you are worried about your friends, but they are fine. They left very quickly this morning, though. Their suite was involved in a shooting, and they raced out of the hotel before we could tell them that the shots were fired by random street thugs. I can assure you, they were completely safe in the hotel room."

"They said that there's a bullet hole in the ceiling! And they were *fine?*"

"Yes, that is true, but they were unharmed. I am sorry. I apologize. It was one of those things that was beyond our control. They were a bit rushed, but they were fine. The valet brought up their car, and they took off rather quickly."

"Do you know what happened to them after that?"

"No, I'm afraid I don't. They were very frightened, as were many guests, but they were never in any real danger. I assure you."

"That's not how I hear the story. I'll be calling you back later."

Ashley hung up and looked at the phone.

"What in the ..." She mumbled to herself. Her heart was beating wildly. Megan and Mary were at an amusement park 400 miles away. They were going to get an apartment. They were shot at four times? What the hell was going on?

She dialed Information in Chicago.

"Hi, can you connect me with the police department, please? No, not an emergency."

Finally, a sergeant on duty from the north side answered. The officer pulled up the morning's reports.

"That's right ma'am, red Mercedes convertible. I've never seen one of them before. Two bullet holes in the back end. Two women from out of state, they were held roadside until it was determined they had done nothing wrong."

"And you just let them go?"

"Well, ma'am what would you have had the officer do? They were the victims, not the perpetrators."

"Well, I don't know. Did they find the person or people who did the shooting?"

"Doesn't look like an arrest was made."

"And what are the police going to do about it?"

"Frankly, not likely anything, ma'am. No one was hurt and shootings are part of everyday life in a big city. Looks like the hotel will have to replace a window and make some minor repairs to the ceiling. No other major damage reported."

"That's terrible!"

"Yes ma'am, it is."

And she was off the phone. They had been shot at! They could have been killed!

Time to call John Wagner and have him check the unit over.

"It's getting scarier," she mumbled to no one. She rang his cell.

The PI wasn't thrilled with getting a last-minute call to go over to the condo, but Ashley had to know for sure. "The old man and his wife are in their condo and their cars are in the garage. You sure she said she heard his voice?"

"I think that's what Megan said. Yes, I'm pretty sure."

Wagner made his way to 4190, did some looking and listening, then called Ashley back.

"Well, he's here, and unless he's a hell of a ventriloquist, she didn't hear *his* voice."

"OK, thanks. Put it on the bill."

"Will do."

The PI was more than curious, and he decided to hang around for another hour or two to see if anything interesting might happen. His client, a handicapped woman, got shot at in her car in Chicago. Coincidence? Not likely. *What the hell IS going on?*

***

The amusement park was the distraction they needed after a bizarre and very scary morning. Neither had ever been shot at before. Neither had ever been in a car chase and the one accident Megan had been in years ago didn't end up well at all. Both were shaken, although Mary tried hard not to show it.

"OK, we'll find a place to stay."

"Mary, not just a place to stay… a safe place to stay with security and – well, a really secure place. We have to hide!"

Mary's instinct was to tell Megan to shut up, but two bullet holes in their red Mercedes suggested a different tack for their communication. Their nerves were really frazzled.

"We'll do that after lunch. We'll find a safe place, I promise. We'll get a newspaper and we'll find a furnished apartment. That should be the best way to do it. Yeah, that's what we should do."

"Good idea." Megan liked that.

The shooting seemed further away in time now. Neither of them could remember anything about the vehicle or the people driving it. It had all happened so terrifyingly fast.

They wheeled their way to the parking lot and saw their car only about a hundred feet away. The red Mercedes with two bullet holes in the back.

They stopped at the 7-Eleven about two blocks from the park and picked up a detailed map of the area as well as *The Waukegan News Sun* and the North Metro edition of *The Chicago Tribune*. One of the papers would likely have some ads for places to live. They stopped at McDonald's to peruse the papers and the map.

Mary decided they'd try and find a place right here, nearby. There was something about the park that made Megan feel safe. She wanted to stay here. She didn't want to go back to Chicago or Minneapolis.

Megan called a couple of complexes and used price as a guide, selecting for further consideration the highest priced rentals they could find. They drove past two, but on the third one, they found a gated community with walls ten feet high.

They parked near the office and wheeled in. It was nearly three o'clock.

It was probably unusual for someone to insist on taking possession of an apartment on the same day as the first look, but Megan appeared about as non-threatening as you could get. Mary had a pile of cash and that didn't hurt, either. Cash always raised eyebrows, but people had their quirks.

The sales girl wasn't a cop; she didn't care. Whatever...whoever...if they have the money, they can live here.

They had a place picked out by dinner time. It was a two bedroom, two bath place that was in move-in condition and fully furnished. It had been another insane day.

The main floor apartment had a nice sidewalk that Megan could navigate easily. The best part of the apartment was the fact it was in a gated community, literally. All the way around were ten-foot high walls. Private and secure. There were two entrances, and you had to have a key *and* approval by a security guard to get into the community of twelve townhomes.

The furnishings were upscale but still not up to Megan's standards. Even so, they made themselves at home fairly easily and soon clicked on the remote control. Megan flipped over to the news, which would begin in a few minutes. She was curious if the news would cover the shootings.

After settling in, Megan became very disturbed that the compressor sound was louder than it had been, and that there were other sounds in the background, too. And there was also a sizzling noise accompanied by the sounds of crickets.

What are they trying to do to me?

"Two eighteen-year-old men were arrested this morning racing northbound on I-94, after their high-speed pursuit of a red Mercedes Benz. Witnesses saw the young men shoot in the direction of another young man in the Loop this morning, and then watched them take off after the red Mercedes, which it appears they mistakenly took to be the gang member they were chasing. The two women driving the Mercedes convertible were unharmed and released after questioning by a highway patrol officer. The two young men were taken to the Cook County Jail and are waiting to be charged.

"In other news, it's going to be a sizzler tomorrow. Stay tuned for Mike Caplan and his weather forecast."

Mary watched Megan watching the news. Megan was shaking her head. More like one young man and one old man. She was sure the news people had the story wrong; otherwise, it made no sense – no sense at all.

The man had told Megan to get up. She did. There was a gunshot. That's what happened. There were no gang members anywhere. This was the buzzard and an accomplice. No doubt about it.

"Can you believe that, Mary? The reporter said that the shooter was a young kid, and he's in jail…and they were in some kind of gang-related activity. That can't be right!"

Mary didn't know what to think. She was confused. They probably just got the information wrong from the police, or maybe the old man was involved in more than just a rinky-dink prostitution ring.

"Megan, that makes it sound like the shooting outside our window and on the streets was a coincidence."

"Mary, I don't believe in coincidences."

"Me neither."

"I'm scared, Mary. Really scared. Mary, when you go out tonight to get dinner would you pick up a few things for me?"

"Yeah, sure. What do you want me to get you?" Mary was lost in mental space. She couldn't figure out any of this.

There was a long pause as the two women stared at the TV screen.

"I want a police scanner."

"A what? A police scanner? Where do you get those?"

"Probably a store like Radio Shack, I guess."

"OK, I'll pick one up."

"And a microphone and a digital voice recorder or something we can record sounds with."

"A microphone and a digital recorder. Anything else?"

"Nope, that should do it."

She was going to ask but decided she really didn't want to know. She needed to get out of there to do some thinking. Something scary *was* going on, and she needed to figure it all out.

"I'm going to stop at an auto parts store or somewhere and see if there's anything they can do to cover up those bullet holes. And you know, we might not want to be driving the red Mercedes any more –

too easy to track us. We stick out like a sore thumb. We should probably stick to taxis or get a rental car."

Megan nodded. No question about that. That was why they bought it ten years ago, to stand out in the crowd. Now Megan thought it might get them killed. And Mary who once couldn't wait to get in it and drive hesitated for the very same reason.

"OK, call me if you need anything. I'll be back in a few hours."

He's not in jail. The TV people were lying. Maybe the cops are in on it, too. Tonight or tomorrow when that old man talks to me, I'm going to get him to talk so I can record his voice. Then, I'll have them all thrown in jail. And then I can live in peace.

They must have some kind of a radio set up, or somehow use a cell tower where they send out signals to me…to the bone in my ear. I wonder if this was done on purpose so anyone could radio me? I'd hear anything.

The police scanner should take care of that. Right? Doesn't a police scanner pick up all that kind of stuff?

Megan stood up from the wheelchair and grasped her walker. She wanted to look around their little apartment. Ultimately, she'd end up in the bathroom. She saw the cell phone on the table and decided to take it with her on her tour around the apartment.

As she walked into the kitchen, she took a rare glance up from the floor and saw a bunch of magnets on the refrigerator. Letters and numbers of all kinds of primary colors. Red, blue, green, yellow and the rest.

That gave her an idea as she walked toward the refrigerator.

Magnets… Magnets are powerful. What if I used the magnets like an MRI scanner? Then no sound could get into my head from anywhere. Nothing could penetrate that kind of a thing.

If I put all the magnets on my head, then the sound won't be able to get in my head, especially to the metal bone. I'll use the magnets to change the frequency of the waves that it picks up.

It makes sense. It should work. Make a mini-MRI. It will keep the radio waves out of my head. It will work; I know it will work.

Question is, how will I keep them on my head. Glue? No. Tape? No. Hat? No. Scarf? Yes. Sew them into a scarf, and I can wear them directly over my ears that way. Then, I won't have to hold them with my hand but they'll just stay there blocking the transmission.

Then I'll find out what wavelength they're transmitting to me on using the police scanner and I can tell Ashley to call the cops. They won't ever be able to hurt me again.

Megan put all the magnets from the refrigerator door into her pockets. She had no needle and thread at the moment. She would have to call Mary and tell her to buy a needle, thread, and a scarf. Megan called her as soon as she thought of it.

Mary returned with bags of groceries, scarf and needle and thread, the police scanner and the microphone and voice recorder. Several trips to the car and finally she was finished. She put everything away and brought Megan her things.

She told Megan that the bullet holes in the red Mercedes got the attention of everyone in the store and while one of the guys in the store offered to patch it up, he also laughed at the strangeness of what he was doing. Not every day you saw bullet holes in a car, a red convertible Mercedes, driven by a woman twice his age. She had tipped the guy, figuring she might be back for some reason.

She gave the needle and thread to Megan. Megan didn't have much dexterity, but she was sewing.

She watched Megan work with needle and thread and the magnets and had no idea what she was doing, and didn't ask. She was still in shock herself. She'd been shot at. She might have been killed. She was no Hollywood stunt driver. Mary considered herself very lucky to be alive.

She didn't feel comfortable in the apartment they were in, but, it was secure, secure like a fortress. Nothing was going to happen in that place.

Looking out the front window, she woke up from her daydream. There was a cable truck parked in front. She hadn't noticed it when she came in. She hadn't seen anyone on the street at all.

"Hey, Megan, was there a cable guy here when I was gone?"

"Nope. Just me." She continued to work with greater anticipation of completing her task.

"OK, just that there's a cable truck in the front and I didn't see him come in or out."

"What do you think he's doing?"

"I don't know. Doesn't everyone in the complex have cable? Didn't the manager tell us that the apartments were all cable ready? I think that means that all you have to do is hook up your TV set. There shouldn't be any need for a cable guy. But there's the truck. A white truck. Lake County Cable Installers."

The intensity of the compressor sound had increased. It was loud now. Megan had a hard time concentrating, it was so loud.

"Hey!"

Megan looked up.

Looking out the window, Mary saw something that made her jump. She retreated back into the living room. That Harris guy had just walked in the main entrance! Mary was sober, straight and stricken with terror.

"Megan! Harris just walked in the front door."

"You mean, Harris the buzzard guy? What's he doing here?"

"I don't know. But you know it has something to do with us."

"Should we call the police, Mary?"

"And say what?"

"I don't know. Tell them that the buzzard is here."

"Now why would the police care about that? And why is the buzzard *here* if he was supposed to have been put in jail four hours ago?!"

"I don't know. Just that – they might do something. But you're right. The police are in on it. What are we going to do?"

"Be ready to get out of here at any minute."

She went into the kitchen and looked around. It was well stocked. She opened and closed drawers. *Knives equal protection.* She grabbed the biggest one and put it in her purse.

"How did he get here so fast?"

Mary came back out of the kitchen and looked at Megan. "I don't know. I really don't."

"I do."

Again, Mary simply wasn't going to ask. There was so much to think about. Megan sat tensely looking at the TV.

They are not only radioing me, but I act as a beacon or a signaling device somehow. Somehow they know where we are. Like with some kind of GPS or something or maybe they hear us talking about where we are going. That's the only way they could know where we are. The satellite. That would be expensive, probably, but if I had a microphone on me, then they could hear everything I'm saying to Mary and probably everything she is saying, too.

"Mary, could you get me a piece of paper and pen?"

Mary didn't speak. She simply did as Megan requested.

Megan didn't write much; she hadn't for years. She had some practice in the last year, but not a lot. She began to scratch notes on her pad. Methodically. Slowly.

She wrote: *Mary, the ear surgery. They implanted a microphone. They can hear me. They can hear you. We shouldn't talk about where we are or where we are going. Then they won't find us.*

It took about ten minutes to get that all written legibly.

"Mary?"

Mary was in her bedroom on the bed thinking. Wondering. Not panicking, but not feeling good.

"Yes, Megan. I'll be there in a minute."

What is Harris doing here? Why is he shooting at us? Dammit, this is Ashley's fault of course. BITCH.

She got up and strolled into the living room.

"Yes, Megan. What is it?"

Megan said nothing. She simply held her notebook up for Mary to read or take from her.

"My God. I think you're right."

Megan nodded her head. She knew she was right.

Chapter Thirty Two

June 23

Day 2467

Wagner hated doing stuff that was completely and obviously illegal. When he tapped into the phone line at the Harris condo posing as a phone repairman, he knew he could lose not only his license but his livelihood as well, and maybe his life. He'd tell Ashley about this later and bill her.

It took him only minutes to fix the phones, placing a microphone in each phone in the unit. There were three. In seven minutes he was out of there, very apologetic and leaving a bogus work order on the counter for Mr. Harris as a receipt for his work. Paid for by the building manager, of course.

He went back to his truck and checked to see if his equipment was picking up the signals and it appeared it was. He wouldn't be absolutely certain until someone actually used the phone. He set up voice-activated digital recorders on each receiver to catch every word.

No one was going to outwit him.

***

The buzzard was in Illinois so it was obvious that Megan and Mary couldn't stay at the new apartment. They were going to have to pack up, yet again, and get out. They wouldn't tell anyone and would leave the almost $9,000 in cash they'd put down as a deposit, first and last month's rent, to be dealt with later. A month's rent. These people had guns.

I can't believe I thought Megan was full of shit. These wackos are real and they are out to kill. My God, what did Ashley put in that letter?

The next morning, Mary packed up everything including the new scanner, recorder and microphone she had bought for Megan. She got everything and put it all in the car. The red Mercedes had to go. It was so obvious. Today they would rent a car, a big car, and then head somewhere, anywhere that no one would find them. They stared at the cable truck which had been parked there for hours. No one in or out of the truck. Just sitting there.

Megan knew full well that it had to be where they were signaling her and tracking her voice from. They might hear her talk, but she'd never say anything about their location again. She wouldn't make that mistake again. This time when they drove away, they'd get a rental car and head as far away from Minnesota and the buzzards as was humanly possible. They'd head out and keep going... to where, no one knew, including them.

Mary helped Megan into the passenger side of the Mercedes. Today they would dump it. The beautiful convertible Mary just loved to drive, had to go. She didn't actually know what to do with it. At the moment, she didn't really care. She wanted to make sure that this time they weren't followed.

As if she couldn't keep the thought inside her head another second Mary blurted out, "Megan, Ashley has done a terrible job watching out for you. Oh, sure, at one time she was helpful, but you know, you and me have been through a lot lately. Ashley hasn't been any help; she just makes it seem so trivial – like being shot at and nearly killed is no big deal. She just doesn't seem to care about you. You know I believe you, even though no one else does. If she loved you, she'd believe you. I love you, and I believe you. If you would like me to, I'd be honored to be your trustee, or whatever it's called."

There was silence.

Mary drove north. They headed for the City of Waukegan, intending to find a rental car there, which they did. It wasn't difficult to persuade the manager on duty to fix the Mercedes in exchange for letting him use it free of charge, while he made the necessary repairs over the next few months. They certainly had no desire to continue driving it anyway. They headed straight to the rental car counter and ordered a beat-up old Chevy for a week. Of course none were available, since even low-budget rental places had decent cars these days.

The guy on duty thought to himself, "What suckers! I've got a couple of live ones here; no way am I letting them go. I'll let them rent my old Buick and charge them a grand."

They had a fistful of cash that needed to be spent. And the charge didn't even seem to faze them. The big Buick was much roomier than the Mercedes, though nowhere near as sleek or stylish. Heck, who was kidding who? It was a junk heap, a rust bucket with wheels. But they didn't care as long as it started, and it did. No one would expect to see them in this car; they were unrecognizable. Mary hated to see the Mercedes go as much as Megan did, but they both knew that if the Mercedes was here and they weren't, the chances of getting found again were not as great. It was a good plan, and after the manager had some of his employees transfer all of their possessions from the Mercedes to the Buick, they were on their way.

They both breathed a sigh of relief as they drove north on 41 toward Milwaukee. The fact was they hadn't decided where to go. Vegas, Chicago, Minneapolis. None of which were any good. But as far as Megan was concerned, it made no difference as she was still getting radio transmissions pretty much everywhere.

They decided they would stop at a Motel 6 west of Milwaukee. They wanted to discuss their strategy for escape. The entire two-hour drive they mouthed to each other everything that had to do with direction and location. They occasionally winked and said something to misdirect the buzzard like, "Indianapolis is a safe place, then we'll go to Pittsburgh."

The buzzards might be able to transmit to Megan and make her life hell, but they weren't going to get Mary. Not a chance. Shortly they'd work their way back to Winona where Mary had an old boyfriend who was still a friend after all these years. Probably the nicest man she'd ever met. She didn't really want to see him again. He was too nice. Too kind. Made her feel like she was a bad person. She never could tell him some of the things she had done or planned to do. He was the only person whose opinion she cared about. Besides Megan, of course.

Mary figured if Megan would sign over the guardianship of herself to Mary, then she would essentially run Megan's life and that meant she'd buy them a place that was beautiful. Not some stupid condo with nutjobs in it.

She also knew she had to fix this problem. She thought about killing Harris. If she got caught she'd go to jail. She didn't want that. She just wanted to be away from them and safe. They weren't transmitting to her, thank God, just Megan. She wanted to keep it that way.

They pulled into the parking lot of the Motel 6 and the first thing they saw by the front door to registration was two girls with halter tops, baring their belly button rings and tattoos to the world.

"Tramps." Megan said. "Hookers. The old man probably owns this place. Let's make sure we don't let anyone know who we are. Pay cash, just like the customers, and write a fake name down. Like Catherine Grissom. Catherine and Grissom from CSI. I like that. You can be Ashley Stokes for Ashley… and Stokes."

Mary smiled a genuine smile. She liked it.

Mary made her way from the car into the motel registration area.

"Stokes. Ashley Stokes. Two nights. How much for your biggest room? I have a handicapped friend in the car who has a hard time getting around. Need a main floor."

"Two nights? That'll be $137 plus 14.5% tax."

She pulled out her credit card and then remembered the plan. She put it back in her purse and placed two $100 bills on the counter.

"I'll need a driver's license, please?"

"It's in the car. Look, just keep the change, OK?"

It worked. That would be almost a fifty-dollar tip.

"Thank you, Ms. Stokes. Room 113, around the corner. There's an accessible ramp there. Vending machines right by your room."

"You have breakfast in the morning?"

"No ma'am. Sorry, we don't."

"OK, thanks." She grabbed the key – a real old-fashioned key, not a credit card type key.

"Good night, Mrs. Stokes."

Mary put the key in her purse and saw a man trying to work the girls. They were young. Maybe eighteen or twenty. What the hell were they doing hooking at such a young age? Motel 6 didn't seem like a good place to procure clients, either.

She told Megan about the girls inside and they were sure that the old man owned this entire stretch of hotels in the Midwest. Either that or he had paid off the managers. One thing was for sure, no one knew they were here. No one.

"Radio?"

Megan nodded. It hadn't stopped.

"OK."

Megan didn't think it was OK. Once situated in her bed she pulled out the police scanner first. She was going to find the frequency the old man and his people were transmitting to her on and then call the police, or the FBI or whoever wasn't crooked, and get them stopped.

Mary walked in, a puzzled look on her face. "Whatcha gonna do with that thing?"

Megan didn't look up. "I'm going to find them."

"I hope so." She left the room without so much as another word. She didn't understand everything that was going on. But she couldn't get what she wanted if people were shooting at her and Megan. The buzzards had to be stopped.

Megan finally got the scanner working and began going from frequency to frequency. She couldn't believe how many there were. It wasn't like TV or radio where you have maybe a hundred choices. It looked like there might be a thousand or two thousand. Didn't matter. She would find them all and as soon as she found the one transmitting the compressor sound – the one that they used to torture her in the morning…well, then she would have them.

Megan's cell phone rang. It could only be Ashley. She looked at it and then picked it up. Even though Ashley had somehow screwed up lately, she was still her friend. But she couldn't let Ashley have any information because somehow the buzzards knew where she was going.

Maybe this thing in my head sends sound too. That must be it.

"Hello."

"Where are you, Megan?"

"I can't tell you. The old man might be able to hear us talking and I don't want them to come and try and kill us again."

"Well, where are you? Are you in a restaurant, a hotel, a…"

"We're fine but they keep radioing me that compressor sound."

"Listen, Megan, about that…"

"No! Don't talk about it! I have to figure out how to communicate with you without them having any way of knowing where I am and I don't want to make them angrier with me than they already are. They tried to *kill us.*"

"Megan, that wasn't the people upstairs, it was…"

"It was the Harris people. It was that ring of criminals and they even have part of it here where we are now."

"What?"

"I can't talk about it. I'll write you a letter and tell you where it is. I'll have Mary send it out in the morning for fast delivery. Express mail. That will tell you where we are."

"Megan. I really wish you would come home. I'm very concerned about you, honey."

"I know you are. So please get them to stop radioing me. That's how you can help. Get them to stop! Now I have to get to work on finding these guys. I love you."

"Megan, we need to talk."

"I have to go, Ashley." And she hit END on the keypad. She was starting to become more adept at using this tiny little phone. Not so long ago she couldn't even pick it up. Now she could actually finger a specific key. She was getting better. Slowly but surely.

Megan grabbed a note pad and pen off the end table and wrote down each frequency. She made notes of anything she heard on that frequency that was suspicious and she wrote down those frequencies where she heard sounds that weren't static.

After four hours of that she fell asleep, the notepad in her hand.

***

"Megan, Megan, Megan…ha! Ha! HA!"

She opened one eye. The other followed. The compressor was loud.

What time is it?

6:11 a.m.

Shouldn't they all be sleeping? How are they signaling?

"I know you can hear me, you sick buzzard. I know you can!" The compressor got louder. "Stop it." She was shouting at the scanner now. "Stop it! STOP IT!"

It didn't stop. She started to shake but she had to get to the bathroom. She would wheel herself over because the walk would take forty-five minutes. She wished they had gotten a room with two beds instead of a two-room suite.

Megan made it to the restroom and back to the bed. She climbed up on it. She hadn't slept enough and they were torturing her again. The noise was deafening.

She looked down at the wastebasket she had thrown paper in all night and got back out of bed. She picked it up, shook out the paper, got back in bed, and grabbing the pile of magnets she now kept on the night stand, put them all inside wastebasket, which she then put over her head .

"Stop it, you buzzard!"

The volume was getting louder and louder. She couldn't bear it. She started shaking, and then she started vibrating.

"PLEASE STOP IT! What do you want! LEAVE ME ALONE."

Mary came into the room and raced over to Megan, pulling the can of magnets off her head.

"What's going on?"

"They are laughing at me and they turned up the volume on the compressor. It's so loud. You wouldn't believe it."

"I do, honey. We've got to get them to stop this."

"They're driving me crazy! We have to do something."

She wept but no tears came. As much as Mary felt for Megan in this moment, she had always been repelled by the sound of her tearless weeping. To her, it seemed showy and overly dramatic. Like intentionally loud sneezes.

She sat down by Megan and put her arm around her and held her close.

"Stop crying, Megan. We're going to get through this."

Chapter Thirty Three

June 24

Day 2468

The phone rang in Ashley's bedroom. 7:14 a.m. She would have had to have gotten up in sixteen minutes to go to work anyway. She looked at the caller ID. It was Wagner.

"I put a microphone on all their phones yesterday and monitored them with different digital voice activators overnight. They didn't take but one call and that was around nine p.m. It was the daughter hinting that she needed money, and Dad didn't go for it in a big way, apparently. Aside from that there were no phone calls in or out and the apartment was pretty dead all night."

"Isn't that illegal?" She was starting to wake up and as she did, she realized how thankful she was to him for doing this.

"Probably. Listen, whatever they're doing to your friend, it isn't coming from this house and it isn't coming from this building. These people are old and boring. The most exciting and high-tech thing for them is a TV on with almost no sound… or maybe silent… maybe headphones. That's it."

"OK, I suppose I owe you something for this."

"You do and I'll put it on the bill."

"Thanks."

She hung up and the phone rang just as she set it back down.

"Hello?" She picked it up before the caller ID kicked in.

"Ashley, you have to make them stop!"

"Megan? What's wrong? Where are you?"

"They're torturing me! They woke me up laughing at me and then they turned the compressor all the way up."

"Megan there's nothing happening upstairs at the Harrises. I got off the phone with the private investigator and he said that he checked all their phones and there was nothing there or anywhere in the building."

"But there is! Can't you hear it?"

"Well, no, but you are calling me at home, honey. I'm in bed."

"You have to get them to stop."

"Megan, I want you to come home today and I promise we will make them stop."

She had to regain some control of things as life was definitely getting out of control for Megan – and that meant Ashley's own life was out of control as well. Megan was suffering. There was no doubt about that.

***

Megan sat in the passenger seat. The rental car was packed and ready to go. Her persecutors had stopped the high intensity noise and taunting, but they continued to punish her. She was unable to find the frequency on the scanner but she would work on it all the way back to Minneapolis.

In no way did Mary want to head back to Minneapolis. There was no doubt that Chicago was a scary place and the buzzards were definitely there, but weren't they back in Minneapolis as well? Wasn't the headquarters of these wacko ringleaders right in the room above Megan's?

No matter, she had to figure out how she was going to get Megan out of Minneapolis for good as soon as possible. Maybe she would be OK with going back to Vegas or to somewhere else. Minneapolis was where Ashley was queen and that wouldn't do. No, they would return.

And then Megan and Mary would leave very soon, and she would have it all planned out.

***

The instructions were simple. Ashley wanted Wagner to put a listening device and recorder in every room of the condo and record everything. Every sound. Every whisper. Everything. Megan would be home in a few hours apparently, though Ashley wasn't sure exactly, because Megan wouldn't say exactly where they were. She only agreed that she'd be home "soon," and told Ashley to please not ask where she was.

She also agreed with the detective who wanted her to let him have a colleague in Chicago check out what happened at the W Hotel, and report back to the PI as soon as possible.

She knew the wiretapping was totally illegal, and she was normally as straight as an arrow when it came to the law. Fifty-five meant fifty-five, and the speed limit was the speed limit. But there was nothing "normal" about this – it was scary and no one was doing anything about it.

Even if she didn't have the answer by the time Megan walked in, she would have at least set those wheels in motion.

Then came the more difficult task of setting an appointment for Megan with a psychiatrist at Hennepin County Medical Center (HCMC). Obviously Megan needed something for the anxiety she was suffering. Clearly Megan was suffering badly. She sounded crazy on the last phone call. Was she hearing voices? Was she really being radioed? What was the compressor noise that was supposedly being transmitted to her?

She had worked with the psychiatrist through Megan's healing process from the accident, so it wouldn't be that big of a slap in the face when she told Megan, "Tomorrow we're going to HCMC to see the doctor." She didn't look forward to telling Megan that, but Ashley had to figure out every angle.

Fact: There was a shooting. Mary and Megan were almost killed. There was nothing going on upstairs at 4190. There was nothing going on at the building in Arden Hills. Megan said she'd heard the people upstairs talk to her immediately before the gunfire.

All of that led to absolutely nothing.

The idea that someone was radioing Megan seemed absurd. Absurd, but possible. Could the metal plate in her head act as a receiver, or even crazier, as a transmitter? Didn't she see that on TV once? *Gilligan's Island?* That was it. Gilligan acted as a radio and the Professor thought he could get it to send transmissions, or that's how she remembered it. But that was ridiculous. *At least I think that's ridiculous.*

But Megan had been shot at and that wasn't crazy, it was terrifying. Whatever Megan was experiencing from all this, she couldn't be any better since the shooting, and seeing a psychiatrist simply made good sense.

***

Ashley made sure that she was at 4190 when Megan arrived. She met them at their car as they drove in and parked. She gave Megan a big hug while Megan wept. When Megan calmed down Ashley said she wanted to take them all into the unit so they could sit down, and calm down.

Mary and Ashley barely acknowledged each other. Mary grabbed a bunch of bags, then Ashley did the same. Mary and Ashley brought the first round of bags to the unit, and then went back to get Megan and the final set of bags.

By the time Megan got out of the bathroom, Ashley had unpacked and put away all of Megan's stuff, taking most of her clothes to the hamper. They hadn't washed in a while. She left the police scanner, the microphone, the pad and pen and the tape recorder on the foot of the bed as Megan made progress back to the bed. Ashley was about to burst inside with the massive rush of adrenaline coursing through her, but she didn't want to rush Megan. It could all wait a few more minutes, and it was clear that Megan was very distracted, more than Ashley had ever seen.

Megan dropped onto the bed, exhausted.

"I'm really glad you're home. I missed you and I was so worried about you."

"They won't leave me alone, Ashley. They're driving me crazy. All day and night, and then they taunt me every morning. They say my name over and over...sometimes they laugh at me...and then they turn up the compressor and shake me out of bed. Ashley, they know where I am. Now you told them I'm home! Please don't ever, ever, say where we are again. It has to stay a secret, so they don't kill us all."

Ashley didn't know what to say. She wasn't the one who had been shot at, Megan was. And Mary was nowhere to be seen. She'd probably gone straight to bed. Who wouldn't?

"Megan, we're going to do everything we can to stop this. No one's going to kill you here. I think that what happened in Chicago was not about the buzzards. I think it was a random act of violence for you guys – "

"Random? Random? Ashley – *random?* He woke me up. He said my name. He laughed at me and then *shot at me and there is a bullet hole in the ceiling of the W Hotel in Chicago to prove it!* There is nothing random about any of this. We have to find them. They're out to get us!"

"Then why aren't they killing you here?" Ashley bit hard on her lip after she let that fly. Megan didn't need that, and she didn't need it herself.

"You always were *good* at consoling, weren't you, Ashley?" Mary was standing in the doorway. "The reason they aren't killing us here is because they live here and they would be arrested, you idiot. Here they just drive us crazy. In Chicago they want to kill us. Don't worry yourself, Ashley. You won't need to fret for long."

She turned and walked away.

"That woman." She kept the anger in and focused on Megan. It was going to be a long night.

Chapter Thirty Four

Minneapolis

Dr. Berkowitz walked into the room with a smile on his face.

"Nice to see you both. It's been a few months, hasn't it?" He looked at his file but he didn't need to. He'd been working with Megan for years. He was there from almost the beginning.

Megan and Ashley were seated and it was apparent that Megan was disturbed. She fidgeted nervously with her cell phone.

"Doctor, I'm not crazy."

"Megan, my dear, I do not think you are crazy. Just tell me what you have been experiencing lately that brings you in this way today."

"A while back the buzzards started making noises in the room above mine at the new condo. They were having sex all day and night, and I figured out it was a prostitution ring. They were making such a racket that I couldn't sleep. And then it got personal."

"Who are the buzzards, Megan, and can you take me through this a little more slowly?"

"OK, the buzzards are the people on the second floor. They have a prostitution ring that they run out of their house and they have a bunch of hotels where they also have girls working for them. When we complained that they were making too much racket upstairs they started to radio noise into my head, and wake me up in the morning and laugh at me and taunt me. Then when Mary and I got to Chicago, they shot at me!"

He raised his eyes and looked at Ashley.

"They did get shot at in Chicago. Yes. The police said it was a random shooting. The bullet ended up in the ceiling of Megan's room and they were both very scared. Then they were chased through the streets of Chicago all the way onto the interstate. They must have been terrified."

Berkowitz uncrossed his legs and sat back.

"And the noise upstairs and the radioing to Megan?"

"The private investigator I hired has gone over the building with a fine tooth comb. There is no prostitution ring at the condo or at the office the guy owns. The PI can't figure out what the compressor sound Megan is hearing is, or how it's being sent to her, if that's even possible."

"It's not."

"What do you mean it's not, Doctor? I hear it 24/7. All day and sometimes it's so loud it shakes me out of bed and makes my whole body vibrate."

"Megan, I've known you for a decade. I care about you. I'm listening to you, and I'm listening to Ashley. We both want you to feel better.

"I can't feel better if you don't stop them from transmitting to my head!"

"OK, listen, Megan, do the voices ever tell you to do anything like hurt someone?"

"No. I'm not crazy."

"Do the voices ever tell you to hurt yourself?"

"NO!"

"What do they say, Megan?"

"They say my name over and over. Almost every morning they wake me up. Then they laugh at me or turn the compressor way up so it explodes throughout my head. Sometimes when they really want to punish me, they turn it up so it shakes me."

"What else do they say?"

"They laugh at me. They say my name in a mean way. Sometimes they send the sound of a girl screaming while she's having sex. Everything else is kind of muffled and hard to hear."

"And what Ashley described about the gang members. Is that correct?"

"NO. She wasn't there. The buzzard woke me up. He said my name three times and then laughed at me and then *shot at me.*"

The doctor was clearly perplexed.

"And the police report?"

Ashley cut him off. "The police and the hotel both confirm the shooting. And the car they drove away from there was hit by two bullets in Chicago as well."

"And how did all this happen, Ashley?"

"It was a gang shooting. They weren't aiming at Megan; they fired wrong or something. Then when Megan and Mary left the hotel the bad guys followed them. They were driving a red convertible and maybe the gang kids wanted it or whatever, no one really knows. "

"*I was there and I know what happened!* The buzzard tried to kill us!"

"OK, Megan, let me ask you another question. What do you hear right now?"

"They are radioing the sound to me. It's loud."

"Is anyone talking to you?"

"Not now, no."

"Megan, I think you have tinnitus. The sound you hear is sometimes described as ringing in your ears. Happens to all of us. Sometimes it's a momentary noise, a ringing or whooshing that then goes away, but unfortunately for some people it stays for the rest of their life. It's benign and can't harm you. It doesn't mean you have a brain tumor or any other kind of disease. The voices are probably dreams or hallucinations and while I am concerned about that, we'll figure it all out one way or the other.

"You think I'm crazy?"

"No, Megan, I don't. I think you have been under a great deal of stress and I would like you to trust me and allow yourself to be admitted to the hospital here for a week or two."

"You want me to stay in the crazy people joint because they are trying to kill me?"

"No, Megan, and if indeed they are, they will not be able to get in here. There is no way to get in or out of the psychiatric wing without my permission or a tank. There are guards. There is staff. It would be impossible. You will be completely safe here. I guarantee it. You will not be disturbed by anyone. That doesn't mean the sound or voices will go away right away though. There are some medications that I think can help you – "

"You want to drug me!?"

"Megan, please, no, of course not. I want to give you some medication to relax you and help you think clearly."

"This is stupid. I've been shot at! A bunch of times. That's no delusion! They're radioing me right now! I can hear it! That's no delusion!"

Megan began to weep. Ashley put her arm around her and pulled Megan's head to her shoulder.

Dr. Berkowitz breathed a heavy sigh. The pain was evident on his face.

"Ashley, why don't you believe me?"

"Honey, I do believe you."

"You believe the old man is doing this to me?"

"No, honey, but I believe you hear the sounds and voices and I believe you were shot at."

"But can't you see? It's them. Do you really want to put me away in a loony bin?"

Now Ashley started to well up inside.

"Megan. No one is going to put you in a loony bin. Dr. Berkowitz cares about you and wants to let you spend a few days resting where you won't be bothered by anything."

"But the buzzards are still sending me the compressor sound. Nothing will change here."

Dr. Berkowitz decided that was the place to come in.

"Megan, one thing changes."

Megan's weeping calmed a bit. She looked at him. "What?"

"No one can hurt you in here. There will be no guns. No shooting. I promise you that you will be able to relax at least a little bit. Please,

Megan. I strongly suggest this. Whether the buzzards are there or not. Please admit yourself for a week."

None of them spoke for the next two minutes, which seemed to take an eternity to go by. They all looked at the floor as if an answer was down there.

"OK. I'll stay here for a week. Then I want to get out and go somewhere that the buzzards aren't."

"Fair enough."

"What do we do?" Megan was scared.

"I'll fill out an admit for you. You've been a patron to the hospital and your husband before you for many years – at least a decade. I would imagine that would warrant you VIP treatment. In fact, I'll see to it. We'll get you your own room, if you like."

"I do like, yes. My own room."

"Then I will make sure you get three square meals each day, a healthy snack at night and everything you need from reading material to a TV that works."

"But I can't get out?"

"You'll admit yourself for one week and Ashley is your trustee so she could order you out at any time."

"Will I have a phone in my room?"

"No, but there are a few pay phones in the Community Room. The room where people go to play games and watch baseball and so forth."

"Where all the nuts are?"

"No, Megan, just people who need a break."

"OK. OK. Let's do what you want. At least the buzzard can't get me in there."

***

"You stuck her in an insane asylum?"

Mary threw her arms in the air. Ashley wanted to tell Mary face to face that Megan would be in the hospital for the week and then be released. Ashley never said so out loud, but she definitely thought that

Megan would be better off for a week without Mary around her. Might help her.

“It’s not an insane asylum. She’s at HCMC under the care of Dr. Berkowitz.”

“Can she go home in the morning by simply walking out the front door?”

“No one can go home in the morning from any hospital simply by walking out the front door.”

“You know what I mean, Ashley. You’ve had your friend put away. You should be ashamed of yourself. These nuts are out to get us and now you make us an easy target. You make me sick.”

“You know, Mary – I don’t care.” She got up walked to the door and left. The entire conversation was one of several that night that would be recorded by the P.I.

One thing was sure. Megan was safe from anyone who might shoot her, whether randomly or with intention.

***

“Megan, Megan, Megan.”

She opened her eyes. It was pitch black. It took her a minute to realize she was in a hospital room. She remembered now. The medication they gave her the night before, Seroquel, had simply knocked her out. But now they were back.

“Go away! Leave me alone!”

And the compressor sound was loud. A digital clock sat by her bedside with all of the things that Ashley had gone home and brought back for her. It was 5:48 a.m. As soon as her eyes adjusted to the dark, she slowly slid out of bed, grabbed her walker, and walked toward the room with the night light beckoning. It had better be a bathroom or she would be in trouble. There wasn’t much to see except the shadow of the light. A staff member had put her bed close to the restroom – good thinking on their part.

She took an Ambien and swallowed it with a sip of water.

"At least you can't get me in here, you buzzard!" She talked to the room in general, knowing that the buzzard would hear her. *Sick people. Why do they do things like this?*

Forty minutes later, her business accomplished, she was back in bed, the compressor sound hissing in her ears. She hated the sound. That's why they transmitted it, of course. It was torture.

"Tomorrow, I'll find you!" She knew her police scanner and notepad were somewhere nearby. She wasn't going to be a sitting target. No matter what Ashley thought, she was going to find these people on the scanner and have them arrested. Maybe they weren't transmitting from the room overhead at 4190, but one thing was sure, they *were* transmitting.

Why doesn't she believe me? She believes some private detective who is probably working FOR the old man. How could she be so taken in? I know she cares, but look where I'm at. The loony bin. I guess if there is ONE good thing, it's that they can't get me here. They can make all the noise they want, but they can't get me.

Of course Berkowitz thinks I'm nuts too. Doesn't he realize that Mary and I were both shot at? That we both have heard and seen the buzzard? Is it really that complicated, Doc? LOOK AT THE STUPID CAR with the bullet holes in it.

Oh, man, that's back in Illinois.

I wish Mary would call. Of course, it's only six o'clock in the morning. Oh, I hope this medication works soon. I just want to sleep and try and ignore the buzzard. Don't they ever sleep? Is all they do all night and day have sex?

It's like...

...and the medication quickly took effect with the Seroquel still at work in her system. She would sleep for some time.

***

"Megan? Megan? Megan."

Megan's eye popped open, and then her other one. She was startled quickly and thought she'd heard a gunshot…when she saw a woman dressed in white. The nurse. The hospital.

"You OK, Megan? I'm Patty, I'll be around today 'til five, so if you need anything let me know. Can I get you some breakfast, or would you like to go to the Community Room and eat down there?"

"You mean with all the fruit loops?"

"Oh come on, there's no fruit loops down there."

"They're all crazy, that's why they're locked in here, like me."

"Are you crazy?"

"Well, isn't that what it says on my chart you have in your hands? Look and tell me."

Patty read the notes.

"Says you are suffering from what might be post-traumatic stress disorder with possible delusions and tinnitus. I don't know, you might be crazy, but in need of some R and R is more like it as far as I can tell. Should I bring you some breakfast?"

"Yes, thanks, Patty.

"See you in a bit."

Young. Pretty. Probably ten years younger than me. Just out of nursing school I bet. Or maybe not even. Maybe this is nursing school. God knows. I wish I was that pretty. I used to be. I bet she has sex all the time. God, am I obsessing about sex again? Seven years. Anyone would be obsessing.

I bet she goes home to the boyfriend or husband and right to bed. God. Why me? I guess I'm not supposed to ask that question. But why not? Is it self-piteous – is that a word, piteous? – to wonder "why me?" I mean it's NOT Megan and Ashley and Mary and Berkowitz. It's ME that's in here.

The medicine. Seroquel. That stuff knocks you out.

I wonder what you do here all day. Play checkers…play video games. Stare at a white wall. Watch One Flew Over The Cuckoo's Nest? *I mean what do you do in the nutbin?*

***

The third day she ventured out of her room at noon. Each morning she had awoken to the buzzard taunting her, sometimes whispering her name, other times shouting. Then the buzzard turned the compressor way up. In the evenings the buzzard would put the volume on high so Megan could hear one of the girls having an orgasm. But in the last few days two things had been somewhat different. She had not spoken with Mary, and she had not been shaken or vibrated by the buzzard. She missed Mary very much.

Ashley had stopped by each day after work at the new office in Megan's shopping center. Ashley would relate what the private investigator was finding out – absolutely nothing – and each time Megan would cringe. How could Ashley take the word of a complete stranger over her own? It made no sense. The bullet holes were *still* in the car. The bullet hole was in the ceiling of the hotel room in Chicago. How hard was it to put two and two together?

And of course Dr. Berkowitz turned out to be correct. She was safe in the hospital. And for that she was thankful to God. She prayed every day. Today was Shabbat. She would pray a lot today.

Megan would go to the Community Room for lunch and meet some of the people. Crazy or not, they might be nice or even conversational.

Refusing her wheelchair from the nurse, she decided to make an afternoon of it. She would walk the distance to the Community Room. It was maybe eighty feet from her room, and it might take about an hour to get down there. She was getting faster as time was going on.

She passed people in the hall! Most people walked slowly. Everyone looked pretty normal. Megan observed that she was one of the youngest people there. Some smiled at her and said good morning. Some just looked at the ground as she passed. At first she thought that was rude, and then she realized that she looked at the ground as people had passed for the last several years. The hospital wing seemed like an office building, she thought. No one had hospital gowns on. Everyone seemed… normal.

Well, almost everyone. There were a couple of nonstop talkers. People who just talked to themselves. One woman shouted at no one in particular. Megan determined she would stay away from that one.

Lunch was scheduled for one o'clock and she was making splendid progress with her walker as she trekked the journey to the Community Room. She started seeing some of the faces pass her again… both ways. She didn't know whether those people worked here or just were out for exercise.

Finally she arrived at her destination. There was a television on in the corner. It looked like there was a baseball game on but she couldn't see over the heads that were in the way. She sat down at a table that had four chairs. She thought maybe someone would join her.

A nurse stopped by almost immediately and asked Megan if she would like soup and salad or a sandwich and piece of fruit.

Not much of a choice. She ate better in her room, actually. But she asked for all four items and the nurse grimaced but then nodded her agreement.

There were thirteen tables in the Community Room. Hers was the furthest from the TV and closest to the hallway leading back to the room.

Today was day three. Three down, four to go. And then where would she go? She wondered if Mary had any ideas.

Megan had been working the scanner day and night looking for the frequency the buzzards were broadcasting to her on. No luck so far. But obviously they were broadcasting and she wouldn't quit. Not in a million years. She wanted them to be punished for what they were doing to her. If it weren't for them, she wouldn't be here.

"Hello, young lady, may I join you?"

Megan looked up at the man. Mary's age. Probably sixty. Blonde hair with patches of gray. Clean shaven but plenty of wear and tear on the face. He was nearly twice her age, and then she realized how she must look to him.

"Yes, please sit down."

"Name's Peterson."

At that moment the same nurse who had taken Megan's order delivered it to her along with the necessary silverware, and placed a napkin on Megan's lap… and smoothly shifted her attention and looked into Mr. Peterson's eyes.

"Hi, Mr. Peterson."

"Hi, Patty. The usual."

"I'm sorry, I forgot what the usual is. You're looking good today sir."

Patty was about the same age as Megan. Maybe thirty-five. Just as trim and blonde as can be. What was she doing there? She was pretty too. That's a pretty nurse and a pretty food service gal. Two for two. Who did the hiring here?

"Nice big Caesar salad."

Patty nodded, looked at the two of them, then walked away.

"She's one of the nice ones. She's on our side."

"Oh?" Megan hadn't a clue as to what Mr. Peterson was talking about.

"That's right. Say, what's your name?"

"Megan."

"Hi Megan, I'm David Peterson. From Washington, D.C. I'm on assignment here in Minneapolis. Long story."

"So you aren't a patient here in the hospital?"

"Well, I am, but I'm not, if you know what I mean."

"I'm not sure that I do. Tell me."

"I've just met you. I'm not certain I should. If you were one of the bad guys, I'd pay the price."

"Do I look like one of the bad guys?" Megan didn't know why she said that, but it seemed appropriate.

Mr. Peterson took a serious look at Megan… distrustful and serious, both. Then he laughed.

"Nah. You're clean."

"I'm clean?"

"You see, Megan, the United States government has been doing experiments on people with mental illness for fifty years. Before you were born there was a movie called *One Flew Over the Cuckoo's Nest* with Jack Nicholson. Good example if you ever saw it."

"I was just thinking about that the other day. Yes, I've seen it."

"Everyone does here. You aren't alone. Anyway, one thing that was secretly sponsored by the government a long time ago was lobotomies. In the old days they used to do lobotomies on people in these kinds of wards."

"What's a lobotomy?"

"That's where they, the government doctors, take out part of the frontal lobes of your brain to cause you to behave better. They don't do as many nowadays. Not considered politically correct."

"That's disgusting." Megan put her soup spoon down.

"It's nothing compared to other stuff they do, but I can see where you might find it distasteful. Because of legislation, you aren't supposed to do them anymore, in this country, anyway. Now the CIA is testing all kinds of new drugs on people who have requested the wrong kind of information in the Freedom of Information Act."

"What's that mean?" Megan was fascinated.

"Well, say you wanted to know something about a relative. Maybe they were part of a terrorist group in Afghanistan. Now, you request information on your relative and it sends up a red flag. The Feds want to know why you are requesting information about someone in a terrorist group."

"OK."

"So now you get your information mailed to you, and the government searches the national computer tracking systems and puts a tracer on you."

"What's a tracer?"

"It's a digital tracking device. It goes on all your credit cards every time you buy gasoline, groceries, anything. Big brother is right there to watch you. You ever notice that strip on the back of your cards?"

"Yes. I have."

"Well, think about it. When you slide it in the grocery store card machine..."

"The what?"

"You don't know what a card machine is?"

"I haven't shopped for groceries in ten years."

"Huh. How do you eat?"

"I have a helper; I'm a little slow getting around because of a car accident I was in, but I have been shopping for clothes and jewelry at a mall a few times."

"OK. When you give the girl your credit card she slides it through a machine or on the cash register there is a place she can swipe it. Sound familiar?"

"Yes, I've seen that. I know what you're talking about."

"OK. Now, the back of your credit card has a lot of information about you hidden in the magnetic strip. Stuff no one should know. Secret stuff. Your driver's license has tons more data encrypted on it.

"Everything about you is there. Everything. As soon as you use the credit card or a police officer scans your driver's license, the government can find .you."

"I knew it."

"You knew what?"

"I knew they could find us if we used our card at the motel!"

"Yes, well, everyone who takes your credit card is running this information. The banks get it, the government, everyone and anyone can get access."

"Oh my God." Megan now knew how the buzzards were tracking her. It was the credit card usage. From now on it would be cash only. *Wait 'til I tell Ashley. NOW she'll believe me, and not her stupid private detective.*

"You paying attention? I'm not talking for my health, here."

"Yes. Yes. Please go on."

"So anyway, that's just one way the government and big brother keep an eye on you. They know everything you buy, from guns to toilet paper. They have instant information as to where you are because you are the only person, theoretically, that can use your card."

"Wow, I can't believe it."

"It goes deeper than that. Your cell phone can be used to pinpoint your exact location. So when they're trying to find you, you can't hide.

There's even a micro-chip in your passport. So, for example, here you are, a potential terrorist, or someone who the government doesn't like; and now they know where you are and what you own and how to find you, in seconds, and that's just one way of tracking you and me."

He paused and looked around, making sure no one else was listening.

"Soon as they think you're a subversive element, someone who's a threat or who's going to harm the government, in some way, well, they start coming for you."

"Coming, how?"

"At first, if they're getting fairly certain you're one of the bad guys, they raid your house or your place of business and grab you. Put you in a psych ward like this one, and test new drugs that do some pretty nasty things to people. Here's an example: they use truth serums to find out what you know, who you're working for, why you're getting sensitive information, what you were going to do with that information and so on. Then they give you Rohypnol – "

"What's that?"

"You don't know what Rohypnol is?"

"I'm not up on all the drugs. I've been… incapacitated for almost a decade. Can't you tell?"

He looked at her. He looked at her like she was a boring magazine. "So you have. Rohypnol is a drug that makes you forget everything that's happening. So, if you had Rohypnol in your soup there, you'd forget this entire conversation, this entire afternoon."

"Are you serious?"

"You bet. College kids use it to get girls to have sex with them and then of course, the girls forget everything that happened. It's called the 'date rape' drug."

"Oh my God, I've seen stories about that on the news."

"Well, where do you think the college kids get the drug?"

"The government?"

"Where else? The government needs to know if this stuff works, so they test it by watching these kids at their parties. Who cares if a few babes get banged, as long as they actually forget? That's the part that's so beautiful for the Feds. They watch other people test the various drugs before they ever touch them. Rohypnol is important for a lot of reasons."

Megan was riveted.

"So last winter a bunch of us at the *Post*..."

"The what?"

"The *Post. The Washington Post.* Newspaper. Biggest in D.C. Everyone reads it. So, we get a lead that this is happening and that not only are babes getting raped, that's nothing new – but that the guys who are giving the drugs to the girls are either becoming mysterious accident victims or they're disappearing into thin air."

"I don't get it."

"It's simple. Some of these guys with the Rohypnol pose as college kids or just a guy at a bar on a Saturday night. They are CIA. Get it? They are CIA. They are part of the government. They are personally testing the medication on college girls to see if they work. Then they finish their testing and they disappear. Head back to HQ at Langley."

"To where?"

"To Langley. CIA Headquarters."

"Then what do they do?" Megan was magnetized to the story.

"Then they take all the information they got from the babes. They take their phone numbers, license numbers, their address, and they have them participate in a health survey later on, maybe a couple days later. They figure out a way to get the babe to go to the doc and tell the doc that she thinks she was raped at a party."

"OK."

"Then the doc contacts the CIA and confirms or denies whether the babe remembers anything or not."

"Oh my God. There are doctors in on this?"

Peterson laughed so loudly that it drew the attention of others in the Community Room.

"Maggie, dear."

"Megan," she corrected him.

"Yes, of course. Megan...Megan...Megan...then what happens is..."

He said her name three times so he wouldn't forget. He didn't care what her name was, at all; he just didn't want to look stupid.

His words seemed to disappear into thin air. She felt hypnotized. His lips were moving but she couldn't hear what he was saying. Then she snapped out of it.

"And the CIA sends a few bucks to the docs to keep them part of the team."

"That's disgusting!"

"It gets better. Some of the guys with the CIA started selling Rohypnol to the kids to make some extra bucks. Government doesn't pay all that well salary-wise, even for CIA. Lots of cutbacks, you know? So they sell the stuff to some of these college guys, let the guys use the stuff, follow them back to a hotel or apartment, they have sex, they're done and the CIA guy whacks the guy he sold the stuff to."

"*Whacks* him?"

"Kills him."

"You are *kidding!*"

"Not at all. News won't report it because they are being paid off by the feds to keep their mouth shut until things are under control."

"Oh my God."

"You got it."

"How do you know all this stuff?"

"I'm an undercover reporter. I faked that I was mentally ill to get into this place. Flew in from D.C. last month. See, a lot of the women end up going nuts. In the rape exam sometimes there are signs of sex with multiple partners but they don't remember anything. I guess rape is a big deal to them. So they get this post-traumatic stress disorder and some get admitted here, and there are more in other wards all over the country."

"So what do you do?"

"I interview them. Try and find out if they were one of the people involved, and then I look for leads to find out who specifically is behind it all. I'm working the bottom of the chain right now. Pretty soon, I'll be working the top of the chain. But right now, I want to nail these guys who are whacking the college kids. I want to nail the CIA. If I get this, I get the Pulitzer Prize."

"Wow. That's amazing. And some of those girls are here?"

"I've seen four so far this week. I'll talk to each of them, real subtle, they'll never know I was here. In a week I disappear back to D.C. with a bunch of leads on these guys and then we play detective and nail these bastards."

"Wow. Wow. That is just so amazing. It's incredible. I never would have thought any of that stuff was going on."

"Only problem is that the CIA is starting to get smart to what we're doing and they have a few of my buddies on the run."

"You mean they found them?"

"No, they're trying. They're on to me, too. So, I might never get back to the *Post*. I might end up in Panama or something. Better than getting whacked."

"You mean they want to kill you?"

"You got it, babe."

"That is so scary."

"Well, while you're here, keep a low profile. You never saw me. You don't know me. I don't exist."

Megan had no idea what that meant.

"OK, I will. I won't tell anyone that I saw you here."

"Good. Then maybe I live to see another day. If I get out of here, I'm free, but I still have to get a little more information before I hit the road."

"OK, well, I won't tell anyone."

"I might need your help while I'm here. If I do, I'll let you know. For now, I gotta get out of here. I don't want anyone to see we've talked this long."

"Wait, before you leave, I have a question for you."

"Sure."

"Could anybody find out where you are, when you use that credit card?"

"Anyone with a contact at Visa or MasterCard or whatever, sure. Of course. It's all in the computer the second you use the card. Anyone can hack your account online and see where you just made a charge with your credit card."

"Can they find you by other means?"

"Sure, there are lots of ways. What are you wondering about?"

"Like implants to send and receive radio transmissions… like having a microphone and a speaker inside your head."

"They've been doing that for fifty years. Where have you been?"

"So they do that?"

"Of course."

"And those radio waves can find you anywhere?"

"Anywhere."

"I knew it!"

"I have to run."

"But what about your lunch?"

"You eat it. Looks like you need it. I'll see you around." He pushed himself away from the table and headed down the hall.

At first Megan was in shock. Then she just shook her head. She was right. Ashley was wrong. She wasn't crazy. Mary wasn't crazy. Ashley just didn't know what she was talking about and the detective guy was being fooled. Unless he was in on it too!

Of course. How would Ashley know if he was in on it or not? There was no way she could know.

She's got to get rid of that P.I.! Her head was spinning from everything that she had just taken in. Then it hit her. *That guy doesn't work for the newspaper. He said, "Megan, Megan, Megan." He's one of the buzzard's men.*

Her heart began to pound really fast. "Oh my God!" She said it so loud that everyone turned and looked at her. Megan got up and walked without alarm but quickly enough, for Megan.

A nurse followed her, then approached her. "You OK, Megan?"

"That man that was here."

"Yes, Mr. Peterson."

"He's one of the buzzard's men."

"He's a bit weird but I'm not sure I'd call him a buzzard." She looked down at Megan and was concerned. Megan looked frightened.

"No. He's one of the buzzards that's been following me across the country. He's been torturing me and trying to drive me mad."

The nurse felt pity and sadness. Not this nice girl. "I'm sorry to hear that."

"Where is he staying?"

"He's in one of the rooms down the hall, one of the ones past yours. Don't let anything he said scare you, though."

"He's already been doing that for quite some time. How long has he been in here?"

"I think he's here for a month altogether, and he's probably been here maybe two weeks so far."

"Maybe he's just part of a team of them."

"Megan, are you OK?"

"I want to call my friend Ashley. Right away. Is that OK?"

"Sure, there's a pay phone over there. But I think Ashley said she'd be here today sometime. She's your trustee, right?"

"Yes."

"Do you want me to get you some change?"

Megan reached in her purse. It had quarters and dimes in it. She was already prepared for such an incident.

"No, thanks. I've got change." Megan got up again and started her long walk across the community room to the pay phone.

About half way across the room, she ran into Ashley.

"Hey, Megan, it's nice to see you came out of your room! How are you?"

"The buzzard man is here."

"What? What are you talking about?"

"He said his name was Peterson. Told me a story about how he was working for the *Washington Post*. But then when he said, 'Megan, Megan, Megan,' I knew exactly who he worked for. And we have to get rid of the private detective!"

"Megan, let's sit down, OK? And can you quiet down so everyone here doesn't see us making a scene?"

"OK, let's sit down."

Ashley moved a small table about four feet away to where it would be close to Megan. Then she pulled up a couple of chairs and they both sat down. "OK, what's going on, Megan?"

"The buzzard is here."

"He can't be, I saw him at 4190 this morning."

"No he is here."

"Megan, that is ridiculous. No one is here."

"Peterson. His name is Peterson. He came up to me and told me he was working with the *Washington Post.* "

"You think the *Washington Post* is involved with this?"

"Of course not. Don't be ridiculous. That was the story he was telling me."

"Then why do you think he's working for the buzzard?"

"He knew about implants, and about radio transmission, and he said, 'Megan, Megan, Megan.'"

Ashley could only sigh. "Megan, I don't want to argue about this."

"I want you to fire the private detective. He's part of the whole thing."

"Megan, he's been doing extra work just to help you."

"He's in on it. He's telling you that there's nothing happening at 4190 and we know that's totally wrong. Remember, there are bullet holes in the car to prove it to you. That's the only way he would tell you that nothing is happening. It's not just the car. Remember, I've been shot at too, you know. Does he tell you that was my imagination too?"

"Don't be silly, Megan."

"Ashley, you've got to get me out of here."

"Look, I'm going to talk with the doctors about this Peterson guy."

"Doctors? You trust them? How do you know that the doctors aren't part of the whole thing?"

"Megan, why would the doctors be part of it?"

"To get paid off. Money."

"Megan, doctors make plenty of money. They don't need to be paid off by a buzzard."

"I think I know what's going on here and when I have it all figured out, I'll tell you. But for now, fire the detective."

Ashley felt that the subject needed to be changed or she would be the next admitted to the ward. "Listen. I have some news. The buzzard is suing you."

"What!"

"He's suing you for telling everyone in the condo that he was making noise, spreading the word that there is a prostitution ring going on in his place, and he wants a lot of money."

"That's crazy. How can he be suing me?"

"I talked with him and told him to withdraw his lawsuit. Explained you'd been through hell, but he was not even thinking about it. He filed a suit against you."

"How much is he suing for?"

"Five hundred thousand dollars, Megan."

"Five hundred! How dare he! Let him go ahead. Once we get to court the judge will find out what he's doing and that'll take care of the whole thing."

"Megan, he's very serious. He knows what family you belong to and I think we should offer a settlement. I've contacted an attorney and he thinks that we can minimize the damage, but that there probably will be damages awarded."

"You tell the attorney that we are going to countersue."

"For what?"

"For the torture they've been putting me through!"

"OK, Megan, I'll talk to the attorney."

"I want you to get me out of here."

"Megan, that's not a good idea."

"Why?"

"Because you're safe in here."

"The buzzard has Peterson here."

"Look, I'll talk to Berkowitz and find out about Peterson, OK? I'll do it now. He's probably in. You trust, Berkowitz don't you?"

There was a long pause. Megan looked at the table and tried to find the right answer to that.

I've known him for ten years. I think he really cares.

"I think so."

"He's helped you, Megan. He cares about you. You've known him forever."

"OK, talk to Berkowitz. Tell him I want to leave."

***

An hour later Ashley and Megan found themselves in Berkowitz's office.

"Apparently Mr. Peterson was in the employ of *The Post* some five years ago, but has been unemployed for the last couple of years. He was staying with relatives when they finally decided he could use help here. I really can't share more than that with you."

"Why can't you share more, Dr. Berkowitz? Afraid that you will expose the whole thing?" Megan was furious.

Berkowitz sighed.

"Megan. I can't share your case with anyone and I can't share anyone else's with you. It's the law. I'm bound by doctor-patient confidentiality. However, I will work it out that Mr. Peterson doesn't disturb you, if you like. I can have him put – "

"No thanks, we're leaving." Megan was steadfast.

"I think if you finish out your agreement to stay here for a few more days you would really feel much better. You were doing pretty well until today. Your chart indicates you were upset a few times at night and in the morning, but during the daytime you were fine."

"They usually turn the compressor down in the daytime. Not too busy in the escort business in the daytime, Dr. Berkowitz."

"Ashley?" Dr. Berkowitz deferred.

"Megan?" Ashley deferred.

Megan didn't defer. "We're leaving, now."

"All right, Megan. I'll have one of the nurses get your things and bring them down here and help you take them out to the car. You drove, Ashley?"

"Yes. The car is in the lot outside."

"Fine then. Megan, I'm going to have a script of Seroquel for you to take with you so you can have it at night to help you sleep. Might make you feel better. Three hundred milligrams at bed time. All right, then?"

Megan looked at Ashley then back at Dr. Berkowitz. There was no compelling need to keep her in the hospital.

"OK. Three hundred at night."

"I'd like to see you back in a couple of weeks, Megan."

"Maybe." Her reaction was almost instant… like a reflex.

Megan had no intention of coming back to this ward, ever.

***

Things had been tense the last few weeks. Megan only really communicated well with Mary. She had refused to talk to anyone else. Not her aunt, her cousins, not anyone.

The last thing Ashley had wanted to do was argue. To debate and fight about what was happening to Megan was not going to get either of them anywhere. Megan had made her decision. She was leaving with Mary and that was that. But first there was the matter of settling the lawsuit with Harris. Ashley wasn't up for giving in to their proposal by settling, but she was concerned that if the suit went to trial, anything could go wrong and it could cost Megan everything she had left. Ashley had a clear vision of the courtroom: Megan telling her story of the buzzard, the psych ward, everything else. And nothing good was going to happen. *Settle*, she thought.

"I want Judge Eller to mediate this."

"You really want me to contact Judge Eller about this?"

"I do."

Eller agreed to the mediation just nine days later. He said he'd take an hour with the two parties.

It was extremely unusual to ask a judge to mediate a settlement but that was the advantage of being Megan Dresden and not Joe Blow. Megan thought she remembered meeting a Judge Eller, and she had a lot of confidence that he would not award anything to the Harrises, but that he would reverse the entire thing and make them pay her. She was certain.

Chapter Thirty Five

Hennepin County Court House

The mediation with Judge Eller occurred in his chambers. Eller was well known as a fair but tough judge. Everyone knew the Dresden name in Minnesota, so Eller would too, but it would not likely bias him.

The moment Ashley had suggested mediation to the Harris family, they instantly agreed. They knew they were going to get something big… maybe even hit the jackpot.

Both attorneys spoke before the judge. Ashley spoke at length, not about how the Harris family was guilty, but that they should let this go because of Megan's emotional, physical and mental state. That tack didn't sit well with Megan, but thankfully she was quiet throughout the mediation.

"Mrs. Dresden, you've heard the claim against you. The Harris family has shown that you have indeed offered comments that could be construed as slanderous and arguably libelous. The damage, frankly, appears minimal but their statement and evidence including your written letter and public verbal comments indicate that they have a point to be made in favor of an award for damages. What do you have to say about all of this?"

Ashley started to talk and then Megan immediately stopped her. Megan looked the judge straight in the eye. She trusted him and believed that he would exonerate her. There was no doubt in her mind. To do anything else would be criminal.

"Judge Eller. These people are running a prostitution ring at 4190. It's a big one. They have girls working all over the country for sure, maybe all over the world. When we moved into 4190 they were really loud. The girls would scream, and the ceiling above my bedroom would shake. My body would shake, too, and we couldn't get them to shut up. This went on for quite some time. Then I asked Ashley to put a stop to it and she sent the letter to everyone thinking it would get them to stop… stop that and stop them radioing to me with the compressor sound."

"Radioing to you?" The judge's forehead crinkled as he took notes. The Harris family simply smiled. Mary had her hands over her heart, sitting at the back of the room. Ashley had her head in her hands at this point.

"Yes, sir. They have been transmitting their compressor sound to me all over. In Las Vegas, Chicago, everywhere. Sometimes they laugh at me. In Chicago they said, 'Megan, Megan, Megan,' and they laughed and then they shot at me."

The judge's eyebrows raised.

"Yes, sir, they shot at me and there is a hole in the W Hotel ceiling and two in my car to prove that they shot at me! Mary, my caregiver back there, she can tell you exactly what happened."

"Mrs. Drexel?" Judge Eller was perplexed.

"Your Honor, Megan was shot at in Chicago by gang members. It was a terrifying experience for Megan and Mary. The police report is in the file."

"It was *not* gang members. It was *them*!" She turned and pointed to them, and the Harris family simply sat confidently.

The judge thumbed through the police report that Ashley had handed him.

"Mrs. Dresden, it says here that the people who shot at you were gang members."

"Then how did the gang members know how to wake me up, to use the compressor? They said my name and as soon as I woke up, BANG. They shot through the window. They saw me sit up. Mary was there."

The judge stroked his chin.

"Go on with your story. Tell me what this compressor is."

"The girls use the compressor to power up their vibrators."

"Their vibrators?"

The Harris family laughed in unison. Ashley's heart sank.

"Yes sir. Their vibrators. They have these huge vibrators upstairs that the girls use when they are having sex."

"And you have seen these vibrators?"

"No sir. I hear them and I've felt them."

"Go on."

"Well, the kind that vibrate chairs and beds. They track my location with radio waves and they send sound to my brain with radio waves. They are mean and nasty and I want them to stop and if they would stop, I wouldn't have to write another letter asking them to stop."

"I see. Go on."

"That's it, Your Honor. They have tried to kill me. They have tortured me. They have made my life hell. You can ask Dr. Berkowitz. They give me medication just to keep me stable. I've been through hell, Your Honor. The accident I was in killed my husband and left me like this. I lost my home because the City is shutting down our four stores because of politics."

Eller looked at Ashley. Ashley nodded. It was true.

"Then these people got mad at me because I sent a letter saying they needed to quiet down. I didn't do anything to them. Nothing. I didn't even know them. I just wanted them to quiet down so I could heal. Can you please ask them to stop? That's all I ask you sir. I just want them to stop torturing me."

The judge looked at Megan with great sympathy. Megan was obviously telling the truth. Judge Eller saw it. The Harrises quit laughing, and they sat still, believing that in minutes it would be over, and they would win.

"Mrs. Drexel, you said there is a psychiatric report from Hennepin County?"

"Yes, Your Honor. It's in the file." He turned to it and spent some time reading the report. It seemed like an eternity. Everyone was silent.

Finally he looked up. "Mrs. Dresden, I'm familiar with Dr. Berkowitz. He is a good person. The sounds you have been hearing are tinnitus and the voices are part of an illness called schizophrenia. It's something that can be treated."

"I am *not* crazy." Megan was firm and angry.

"No one is saying that you are, Mrs. Dresden. No one."

He looked at the Harris family, who looked a little too smug for his liking.

"There is no question you have been through a great ordeal. I know you've been shot at, several times. It is horrible. I know about your accident. But, Megan, these people had nothing to do with it."

Megan was ready to speak again, and the judge raised a finger to silence her.

"Mrs. Dresden, these people have not suffered greatly but they have most assuredly been slandered and libeled. That means that you, either on your own or through your trustee, have said defamatory things verbally and in writing that aren't true, and which might cause members of the public to think differently about this family now than they did before.

"Megan, I believe that you believe what you are saying is the truth. Do not think for one second that I think you are lying. I simply believe you have mixed events and the causes of those events into one cake mix, and they simply don't all go together.

"I also don't believe you intended for those things to happen and I think the damages, while modest, are real. I want you to get help Mrs. Dresden. You are a good person. You are honest and you are kind and you have suffered like few other people I've seen in my life. I feel terrible for what has happened to you. I know everything you are experiencing is real.

"Megan, my mediated ruling for the plaintiff is in the amount of $35,000, and the case is closed and may not be reopened in the future.

Neither party is permitted to exercise any retaliation or further aggravation from this point. Further, Mrs. Dresden, you and your housekeeper may have no contact with the Harris family. Mrs. Dresden. Megan. I have an uncle with schizophrenia. He got help and he lives pretty much a normal life. I want you to get help. I don't think you are crazy. I think you have been hurt and are hurting. You have done a great deal of good for the people of our State and my understanding is, around the world, as well. This ruling is not a reflection on you in anyway. It is only about the real damage that has been done to the Harris family. Good day, everyone."

The Judge rose and everyone silently exited the room, with Megan leaving last.

She looked at the Judge with the saddest and most disappointed face he had ever seen.

She whispered to him. "Why don't you believe me?"

"I do believe you believe these things are happening. Please get help."

"Come on, Megan." Ashley touched her hand and they slowly made their way out of the judge's chamber. Not a word was spoken until they left the building.

***

"That's what you get for having Ashley handle your affairs. You pay $35,000 to the buzzard. It's disgusting, and I can't believe it."

"Mary, how could he do that? He seemed like a good person."

"I don't know."

"Could he be in on the whole thing too?"

"I don't know. He must be. You get shot at, and then you give them $35,000? Makes me sick."

They sat at the dining room table and ate their bacon, eggs and toast. It had been two days since the decision, and Megan was still reeling.

"Why doesn't anyone believe me when I talk to them about this? They all think I'm nuts?"

"You're nuts because you let that bitch run your life."

Megan was silent.

How could Ashley not believe me? She knows everything that happened. She knows the truth and she still sides with the private detective and the hospital.. .and the judge.

"Look Megan, they are all against us. The judge, the cops, the detective, the buzzard, the prostitution ring, everyone. We've got to go somewhere where someone is on our side. Somewhere we have friends that we can trust."

"Where?"

"We go to..." and then Mary mouthed 'Vegas' so the buzzard couldn't hear her through Megan's radio transmitter.

"I couldn't be crazy, could I?"

"If you're crazy then I am too. And I'm *not* crazy." Mary was sure of that. "We've got to get her off your back so you can make all of your own decisions with someone who is on your side. Someone who's looking out for your best interests. It's a big responsibility and you don't screw the person you're responsible to."

Megan thought about it and gently nodded her head.

"But how do we get rid of the old man?"

"We're two people against a whole ring and who knows how big it gets. They got into the hospital, and that was supposed to be a safe place. They shot at us in Chicago. I don't know. But I know if we sit in one place for long, we are going to be dead ducks."

"They can hear us right now, you know."

"I know."

"I want it taken out."

"We'll get it done...there...by someone we can trust."

"OK, Mary. That's a good idea. I've been scanning the frequencies on the scanner. So far I haven't found them. I've written it all down. There are a few frequencies that they might be using but I can't pin them down."

"Huh. Well, maybe a police scanner doesn't pick up everything. It doesn't pick up the satellite radio."

"That's true. Maybe they don't use police frequencies, or the frequencies that criminals would normally use."

"They are smart cookies, Megan. Very smart."

"You want to leave tomorrow?"

"Yes…no. I have to see the doctor tomorrow."

"Friday?"

"Yes. We leave Friday."

And they did.

Chapter Thirty Six

Day 3349

It had been nine years.

And they would leave and return, and return and leave. Over the next seventeen months they would move from hotel to motel to apartment to hotel. The buzzard always found them. Megan heard them everywhere. Mary saw them everywhere. They found out how big the prostitution ring was, and that there was no stopping the old man from torturing Megan, particularly at night and early in the morning.

Every morning she would awake to, "Megan, Megan, Megan." Sometimes they would be laughing at her. Sometimes they would be waking her up, and she would hear the door of the condo at 4190 being knocked on. She deduced it was the manager at 4190, who was covering for the buzzard.

Mary regularly saw the buzzard and his girls. She watched them closely every time they entered or left the building Megan and Mary were living in. The buzzard was relentless. When he was being particularly cruel, he would turn up the volume to an unbearable level. He would turn it so high that Megan would vibrate, and sometimes it was so bad that the bed she was in would shake.

Mary tried to pursue the change of Megan's trusteeship, putting herself in the driver's seat, but Ashley wasn't about to let Mary do that.

Each day Megan became more fearful than she'd been the previous day. All attempts at writing messages on paper instead of talking out loud failed. The buzzard always found them by radio, and usually the same day or within two days of their finding a new place to live, the buzzard or one of his employees would be seen by Mary entering the same building they were in.

Megan would use cash. A fake name. They would buy new cell phones. They would buy pay-per-use cell phones. They tried everything they could think of to elude the buzzard, and they always failed.

Megan couldn't pinpoint the source of the radio transmissions on the police scanner, and after filling hundreds of legal-sized pages with her notes, she gave up on that course. She always had the scanner with her but she had given up. He was smarter than she was.

Sometimes, often on Mondays, the buzzard would lighten up on the torture. Megan thought that maybe he would come into periods where he was thinking of changing his mind. Sometimes on the Sabbath, when she would pray, he would turn the compressor down. But never was there a failure to be awakened by the "Buzzard Wake Up Service."

Knock, knock, knock. Megan, Megan, Megan. Laughter. It was almost identical every single day. On occasion there would be muffled sounds in the background like he was talking to someone else or others were talking, but rarely could she make anything out.

Fortunately the buzzard had a business he had to tend to, so the knocking and taunting would usually end after he woke her up.

Mary kept a piece of cutlery in her purse at all times. She had seen the buzzard or one of his men and his girls at every location they went to. She didn't experience the morning routine of being awakened by him, but then, she didn't have an implant.

And the implant was apparently going to stay, because seven different doctors in as many cities told Megan that there was no implant, and that they couldn't take out the surgical corrections and reconstruction she'd had after the accident, without causing permanent deafness. She told them she'd rather be deaf but no one would help her. No one would help her and no one believed her story, except Mary. Mary was loyal and true. She cared. She watched out for them both. When they were on the run, they were on the run together.

Except for Ambien to get to sleep, Megan took no medication.

Back home, Ashley did everything she could to keep up with Megan. She carefully watched the now-rare credit card usage, getting hints from Megan in their sporadic phone conversations about where she might be. She kept an eye on Megan's investments and made sure that when Megan came home everything would be in good condition. But she couldn't do much for Megan's state of mind. She couldn't have Mary fired, and she'd tried. It didn't work. Megan had that right, and only Megan.

After spending some time, including a Thanksgiving holiday at a complex in Scottsdale, Mary and Megan felt that the place they had found with round-the-clock security and the option of hiring in-house security worked for them. It was another gated community with tall walls, and they decided to move there for good. Ashley had Megan's important possessions: her CDs, her DVDs, some jewelry and a police scanner shipped to their new place.

Ashley needed to get Megan to come home, and for more than just a day. Everything she had tried had failed at keeping them in Minnesota for more than a day at a time. Her legal options were few. She loved Megan and she would never intentionally do anything that might damage their friendship, at least what remained of it.

Ashley would cry some days but she would cry while she worked on helping Megan in any way she could. Other days she was like a general involved in combat. Some days she was like a cyber spy, hunting down the location of the two women so she could keep tabs on them. She worried about Megan around the clock, as she had for the last decade.

And each day she dreaded thinking about what Mary's role in all of this was. Mary would rarely communicate with her. Ashley knew that Mary was responsible for much of the misery – but to what end? There was a lot that didn't make sense.

Unfortunately, all her efforts ultimately failed. Megan's Aunt Rebekkah and Megan's other friends had largely given up hope on her. Everyone pitied Megan, but after being told to back off by Megan and Mary, every one of their family and friends stayed away. Everyone except Freddie – and Ashley, of course.

Freddie would try and see Megan whenever she was back from one of their trips. Aside from Robert, Freddie was the extent of Ashley's support at this point in her life, and she needed him.

Robert had known Megan forever, it seemed. He had loved her for years and he was deeply concerned for her, but more than anything, Robert just wanted his wife back. Yet the last two years had been even crazier than the preceding seven. Robert was determined to have Ashley home for Christmas and to focus on their home this year for the first time in a decade. He had a plan.

He was going to make space for Megan in their home, but he would not invite Mary. She could stay at 4190.

Robert was one hundred percent military. He was disciplined. Focused. And now he was going to take charge of this mess. He had felt resentment filtering through the love and admiration for years. It had to stop. Megan was going to move into his family's house next week, for the Christmas season, and if he had to go down to Arizona and get her, he was willing to do that.

Ashley arrived home at seven, after working at the shopping center office all day. Between the two of them, she and Robert generated enough income to live very well indeed.

During dinner Robert made an announcement. "Megan's coming here next week, and she's going to stay with us through the first of the year."

Lauren and Ashley looked up from their plates. Ashley seemed to understand as much as Lauren, not much.

"What?" Ashley couldn't read Robert at the moment.

"I'm calling Megan tonight. I'm clearing out the guest room downstairs and Megan's going to have full run of the basement. It's nice down there. She'll be comfortable; she'll be safe. I have most of the month off, and if she doesn't come up here with that leech 'friend' of hers, then I'll go down to Arizona and get her."

Ashley kept quiet for once. She didn't say a word. If Robert was one hundred percent military, then Ashley was the general of the house.

But when Robert got like this, it was the final answer. And she didn't object; she was simply stunned.

"We're going to call her. I'll talk to her. We'll book her on a flight Sunday and she can fly up here with the nutcracker. Mary can stay at 4190. Megan's moving in here and she'll have limited contact with Mary during that time."

"We'll debrief Megan every day to make her realize that no one is chasing her and Mary. Further, we're going to call her aunt, her cousins, her brother, Freddie and all of her friends, and they'll meet us at 4190 when Megan arrives. We're going to do an intervention."

"You mean like for alcoholics?" Ashley got it, she thought.

"Yep, except I'm thinking more along the lines of a cult member deprogramming intervention."

"You know those things always end up with the person hating the people that they love."

"She already hates everyone that loves her and if she doesn't get some real help soon, all of those people are going to forget about her forever. Christmas is her favorite time of year and she's going to have a good Christmas."

"OK."

"One more thing. We're going to be with her as much as we can. We know that the worst part of the day for her is from bedtime 'til the voices wake her in the morning. I can't say I understand what's going on, but I want to see it all. I want to get her better and I want us all to be able to move on with our lives."

Ashley was a bit offended at the possible implication that she hadn't done enough to succeed, but she knew she had. The living situation that Robert proposed was something that she wouldn't have asked him for. Robert truly was an amazing man and as lucky as he was, she was lucky too.

An hour later the plates were cleared, and all three of them helped with the dishes and the after-dinner cleanup. They cleaned until the house was spotless. Robert pulled the cell phone from his pocket and pushed buttons. He waited for Megan to pick up.

"Megan! Yes. It's me. How's Scottsdale? Good. You have a nice place there, do you? Great. She always does a good job at finding you a nice place, yes, she does. Yes, just like Ashley. Yes. Now Megan, listen closely. You know I have connections that lead all the way up in the Department of Defense. I'm sick of seeing you suffer and I'm not going to stand for it any longer. You need more help and support than you're getting and I'm going to make some things happen here. Yes, really.

"Like, you are going to stay here with us beginning Sunday. Yes, you're going to stay through the fourth of January when I have to fly to Baghdad. Yes. I *have* to go. No, I'm not afraid. The war is over and I don't want you to be afraid for you *or* me, because we're going to take care of you right here. Christmas is going to be real special for all of us and I'm going to make sure we make progress at getting these torturous sounds to stop.

"Megan, who cares how or who? I will personally stop everything. No matter what it takes. I'm going to get them to stop. Yes, Mary will fly home, too, but she will stay at 4190. She'll have the run of 4190 by herself. Nobody will bother her, I promise you. I'll take care of that, too.

"Ashley will call you with your itinerary and so forth. We'll have the entire downstairs ready for you when you get here and I have a bit of a surprise for you when you arrive. We'll talk more about that later. Yes, a surprise for you. You're welcome .No, don't worry about it. I love you too. Yes, she's fine. She's healthy and she'll love to have her Aunt Megan here for a month to hang out. She really misses you. Yes, I really want you to come. Of course I do, and it's not what I want, it's what is going to happen. Do you want me to come down there and get you or can you get on the plane? OK, great. You know how to get a hold of me. No, the plan will NOT change. You are our guest for December. Yes, the whole month. We can't wait. It's going to be fun. OK now, we have much to do. You have a good afternoon out there and Ashley will get back to you guys tonight when we have everything set up. You're welcome. Yes, even if I have to ask President Obama himself. I've met him and he would help if I asked him. We are going to make some headway on this problem. All right then. I've got a lot I need to do. Ashley will call you in a few hours. Love you. OK, bye."

Ashley watched her husband, feeling smart, lucky and appreciative all at the same time. She didn't think he had a clue as to what December would be like, but Robert operated with a ferocious resolve, and right now Ashley needed that.

"Call Freddie and get him to set up the intervention – the party – for Sunday at Megan's. Have everyone be there sixty minutes after the plane lands. I'll pick up Megan and bring her back to 4190. Everyone comes. This is not a request. This is the way it is. Anyone that hems or haws, have them call me. Megan has taken care of all these people for her entire adult life, now it's time for some reciprocation."

"You know it's going to be tough, Robert, and it's going to be humiliating for her."

"The toughest things in life are what make you strong. Megan is a fighter. She'll survive."

***

No one except the buzzard scared Mary. Well, the old man, and Robert. She never liked running into him. The world was even blacker and whiter with him than it was with Ashley. She didn't like him, didn't want to go along with his demands of bringing Megan back. But he was threatening to come to their new place in Scottsdale, and that was even worse.

He had gotten a special security clearance with the airport and met the women at the gate. He arrived with a wheelchair and a cart for people with disabilities to fast-track them to baggage claim.

He got a big hug from Megan and a handshake from Mary. He couldn't care less how Mary was. He was here for *Operation Recovery*.

Everyone from Megan's aunt to her most distant cousins were waiting at 4190. The place was packed. He had a local church bring in chairs. He had everything under control… except one thing. No one knew if this might be too much. It could be too much. But he had Megan's very best interests at heart. If he didn't change something, nothing would change. He wanted his wife back and he knew he wouldn't get her back until Megan was better. The *Operation* began today. He was doing it for Lauren, Ashley, Megan and himself. It was time to experience some short-term pain in exchange for some long-term happiness and sanity.

***

"Surprise!"

"Welcome home!"

"Hi, Megan!"

Three dozen people gave Megan room to make her way into her home.

"Hi, Aunt Rebekkah. Hello, everyone. Isn't this nice. It's not my birthday, though."

Streamers hung from the walls and a "Welcome Home" sign hung from the ceiling. Mary looked and only grimaced. She said hello to no one, but a number of people said hello to her.

Instead of making her way to the bedroom, Megan took the first chair she came to and then looked up at all the faces. She looked at everyone, wondering why they were all there.

"OK, everyone, sit down."

Robert was ready to go right to work. And like good soldiers, everyone listened to him. Ashley was in the kitchen working on snacks with one of Megan's twin cousins. Silence filled the room. Robert turned to Megan as he stood.

"Megan, for almost ten years you've been through hell. David was killed. You nearly died. Your body was crushed, and thanks to Ashley and some great doctors you came back from the dead yourself. You walk, but you weren't supposed to. You talk, and you weren't supposed to. You can do everything anyone else can, and we all know that you were simply not supposed to make it. And you did. Here we are on December second. We all want you to have the best Christmas ever, but this is not a Christmas party or a birthday party.

"We know that you have been running for almost two years. Hotel to hotel. Apartment to apartment. Condo to condo.

"We know that you feel we've all turned our backs on you, not believing that your adversary the old man is torturing you or even bothering you every day. But that isn't quite right. We DO believe you. We know you hear these things. And we know that you were shot at in Chicago. The only thing is, the people in this room agree with doctors, that the noises and voices aren't the old man but they're sounds that are heard only in your head, and not transmitted from some other location.

"We all know that lots of people experience things like this. We wanted to let you know how much we love you and support you in getting well. After our gathering here today, Ashley, myself and your book club partner over there," and Robert pointed to Lauren. "Well, we're excited that you'll be spending Christmas with us – an old-fashioned Christmas.

"Now, this speech took me almost a week to put together. But it all boils down to this. We all want to help you."

Robert sat down and everyone in the room applauded and smiled. Robert had done a wonderful job and everyone knew it. Everyone except Megan and Mary.

Megan looked up and around. Mary was at the back of the room. It was very quiet. This was the part where Megan was supposed to cry,except she was physically unable to cry and she wasn't feeling tears of joy. Everyone including Megan wished that she could cry real tears.

Instead, in the deafening silence and anticipation of her reaction, she heard the buzzard transmitting the compressor sound and an assortment of other noises to her.

As she looked around, she realized they were here to tell her she was crazy, but in a nice way. Megan felt no compulsion to speak, but she had a chance to explain what was happening to her and Mary, and to ask for help in getting the buzzard.

She stood up, and as always was a little hunched over when she got up, like a woman twice her age or more. Expectations filled the room.

Megan looked at Freddie, her aunt, cousins and her lifelong friends.

"The buzzard started this whole thing when we moved in here. He had been running a prostitution ring up there. When the girls would have sex they used this big vibrator that shook the ceiling. It shook the floor and it shook me out of bed sometimes. The noise drove me crazy. But I'm not crazy!

"Mary helped me. She got me out of here after we wrote the letter telling them to stop. Then they sued me saying that I hurt them! And the judge bought their pack of lies. It was terrible. But Mary took me everywhere trying to escape the buzzard. None of you believe the buzzard is real but there is a bullet hole in the hotel room in Chicago where the buzzard and his men tried to kill me. The police covered it up saying that it was gang related, but it wasn't. He woke me up and made fun of me then shot at me. I don't know how I'm alive today.

"I wish you all would believe me. You say you believe what I say but not what's really happening to me. So you *don't* believe me. Not even Ashley believes me. And if they aren't stopped, they're going to try and kill me again and again. They've shot at me. They've shot the Mercedes up. I have a picture to show you."

She reached in her purse and slowly pulled out a photo of the Mercedes and the bullet holes.

"This is real! They are trying to kill me! Call the body shop in Chicago! It's real! Every single day they torture me. They laugh at me. They have an implant in my ear and they use it to find out where I'm at and transmit all these terrible sounds. And you don't believe any of this. Only Mary believes me because she has seen the buzzard and the bullet holes and the prostitutes. She drove us through Chicago while they chased us. She hid me anywhere she thought would be safe for me. She is the only person who cared enough to believe me and do something to help me. She doesn't think I'm crazy because she is living in fear for our lives, too.

"If you would have believed me, no one would have shot at me or the car in Chicago. But you didn't and it almost got me killed and they will try again and we'll keep running until someone stops the buzzard. You're supposed to be my friends and family and you let me out there to get tortured and shot at. I can't believe that you just go about your business while we're being hunted like animals. I can't understand it and it hurts me so much that you think I'm crazy when the bullet holes are in the car! I can hear the buzzard every day! And no one stood up for me at the mediation and we had to pay the buzzard all that money. It's sick."

And Megan sat down. From the back of the room Mary hit the wall with her hand. Everyone turned around and looked at her.

"You all should be ashamed of yourselves. You lie. You don't give a shit what happens to us and then you throw a party to tell Megan she's crazy. You're all a bunch of traitors, sickos and liars. You have no idea the hell we've been through for the last two years. Megan calls this guy the buzzard because when you think of a buzzard that's what this nut job does. He waits for Megan to be at her weakest and most defenseless moments and then he attacks. He's sick. He's disgusting. He tortures this woman and he's waiting for her to die. I've seen them follow us. I've been shot at by his men. We barely lived to be here today to watch you all show how much you really don't care."

She began to cry.

No one expected that.

She stormed off to her bedroom, slamming the door behind her.

There was a painful, uncomfortable silence in the room that no one broke. Finally Megan spoke again.

"I've got to go to my room and get packed. I'm staying with Ashley and Robert for the next few weeks where they can keep an eye on me. I can't believe you think I'm lying. All I've done for years is try to help you all as best I could. All of you."

And Megan walked toward her room. It was done. It was over. The intervention had been beautifully planned, perfectly executed. Robert had done a wonderful job, but it had all fallen flat. He was angry with himself. He wondered what he could have done differently to get Megan to understand how much they all cared about her. Ashley walked into the room and to Megan, whom she kissed on the cheek. Now she would save her husband.

"OK everyone, sandwiches and drinks are ready. Everyone can go into the dining room and get something to eat. We won't be leaving for an hour, so make yourselves at home."

Finally people started whispering, then talking.

"Ashley?"

"What is it, Rebekkah?" Megan's aunt was fighting back tears.

"She really has gone crazy, hasn't she?" She spoke so softly that Ashley could barely hear her.

"She is *not* crazy. She just hears these voices. That's all. We're going to get her help." Ashley's voice boomed above the room. Megan hadn't made it to her bedroom yet.

"I don't need your help, any of you." And she opened the door to her room and crept along until she was inside and shut the door.

***

That night Robert showed Megan and Ashley the surprise he had arranged, and how his device scrambled frequencies from getting in or out of the house. He turned the TV on first. Then he hit the scrambler and the TV just put out static. Then he did the same thing with a radio. Then he did it with Megan's cell phone.

The device created static where there was once radio, TV, or cell phone. He showed them how the device stopped the Internet from working.

He brought Ashley and Megan to the garage, turned on the cars, let them fiddle with the dials. All static. Inside, Megan turned on the receiver to the stereo system. Then the device. Static. All static. Her police scanner: no more police calls. All static.

From the time she got in bed at night until she woke up, she would have control over the ability to receive or send any kind of message, radio wave or phone call, in or out. He set up the device and put it next to her bed that night. It was easy to operate but it must have taken hours to hook up.

It was U.S. Military issue and it was a device that no one else on the planet would likely be able to access without being in the military. He knew Megan believed that the buzzards were sending her radio transmissions and he wanted to prove to her beyond a doubt that the house was one hundred percent secure. And he did.

They tested it on every piece of electronics equipment and every battery-operated device there was at the Drexel home. If the machine was on, nothing that got near the machine worked. It was that simple.

That night Megan got in bed and asked if she could call Mary. Robert agreed, noting that the cordless phone would only operate as long as Megan left the machine off. As soon as she turned it on, then everything would go to static. What would work? She could talk on the phone using a land line, which they still kept in the house, despite nearly always using their cell phones.

She called Mary and told her what Robert had done. Mary wasn't all that happy with the news. She wanted to know who and what was going to protect her at 4190. Megan hadn't thought of that. Midway through the call, Megan wanted to secretly test the scrambler. She flipped it on and Mary's voice immediately went to static. The TV on the other side of the room worked fine, but when she turned the radio on, it was all static. The police scanner was devoid of activity. The remote for the TV didn't work. All static.

She called Mary back and apologized. Shortly thereafter she hung up and again turned the scrambler on. Two Ambien later, she was sleeping like a baby.

The next morning Robert knocked on Megan's door.

"Megan? Can I come in? Megan. It's Robert. Megan?"

Her eyes popped open and fear rushed through her body.

"Robert?"

"Yes."

"Come in."

He did, and he had a soft smile on his face.

"How'd you sleep?"

"Just fine. I can't remember when I slept so well."

"Did the scrambler make a difference?"

Megan closed her eyes and listened. There was no noise.

"Yes. They're gone. There is no noise. It works. Wherever I move I have to get one of these if we can't put those buzzards in jail."

Robert was flabbergasted. She heard nothing?

"You really don't hear anything?"

"Not a thing, Robert. Thank you. You are the greatest. When I yelled at everyone yesterday at 4190, I shouldn't have included you. I know you care. I'm very sorry."

Not having a plan for this scenario, he simply gave her a kiss on the cheek and got up from sitting next to her.

"No problem. I'm glad we got you some peace. I'll bring breakfast down after you clean up. Say, an hour?"

"Thanks, Robert. That will be fine."

Finally, someone believes me and is doing something about it. I should call Mary and tell her. But if I do that then I have to turn the machine back off and they'll come back. I'll talk with Mary later. I want to just enjoy this silence.

"It went away." He said it with a stunned expression as he hit the top stair and walked into the kitchen to kiss his wife on the cheek.

"*What?*" Ashley turned to Robert and prepared to let the eggs burn.

"It's gone. The buzzard isn't there. The scrambler worked."

"That's *not* possible. There is no buzzard. It can't have worked. It's tinnitus and schizophrenia."

"I haven't seen her this calm in a long time. She looks at peace. I don't know what to make of it."

"Maybe she thinks she doesn't hear it, but she really does."

"Ashley, I don't think that makes any sense. Either she hears something or not."

"I've got to think about it."

And she did. For the next three days, morning and night there was no noise. There was no noise at night, none upon waking when Robert came and got her each morning and none at night as she was dozing off. There were brief moments in the daytime where she said the compressor was turned on and that was during times when the scrambler was off, but Megan was thrilled.

She told Robert at least two hundred times in three days how much she loved him and appreciated everything he had done.

Ashley and Robert couldn't have been more surprised or shocked. Certainly the silence that Megan was experiencing was a blessing, yet it also convinced Megan even more strongly that the buzzards were out there. The device was scrambling signals to her brain, just like it was creating static for the radio, cell phones and cordless telephones.

"I'm going to call some of the specialists in communications and see what they make of this." And he tailed off, realizing that he didn't quite know how he was going to explain everything, only that he would.

This is not possible.

That night Robert tucked Megan in as he had the previous three nights. He watched her turn the scrambler on and Megan was smiling and content as she began to drift off into sleep.

Robert had been up late studying electronic advances and schizophrenia and tinnitus. He was trying to piece all of this together. He wasn't a doctor but he was no dummy, either.

That night Megan had a horrifying dream.

The woman had dark hair, full lips and a figure made to order by God himself. Her dark brown eyes were almost black and could be seen in the dim light that was on at the back of the room. She smiled a devilish smile and licked her lips as she straddled the man.

He put his aged and worn hands on her shoulders. He sat himself up and she bent forward so that his face was buried in her breasts. She moved back and forth as she found just the right angle for their pleasure, and soon she moved faster and more rhythmically.

"Megan, Megan, Megan. Ha, ha, ha!" He laughed as she rode him. She grinned as she arched her back into a posture where he could barely see her face. Only her breasts, two peaks on an otherwise shimmering smooth body.

Then she showed him her face again, and with her right hand she reached down between the two of them and turned the vibrator on.

"Oh! That's good." She was back in rhythm.

"Aren't you glad I found you? Where have you been hiding? I'm so glad you are back."

It didn't take long. She was beyond excited and moving toward orgasm herself, or so it seemed.

"Oh! Oh yes!" She was not shy, and she was loud.

With her right hand, she clicked a button on the vibrator and it got louder and more vigorous. She started to shake and let out a scream of ecstasy. She turned it up to the highest level possible and it shook the bed. Her breasts bounced and her body was most violently shaken left, right, up, down, as if she were riding a mechanical bull.

"Oh my God!"

Then he came. He screamed for her to stop. But you could see that she was going to come too, whether he liked it or not. He was past done and needed her to stop, but the vibrator continued to shake her.

"Stop!"

And she reached down behind the gigantic vibrator for a gun which she pointed into his face. She was shaking so badly she might miss, from even this point-blank range.

"Megan! Megan! Megan! Stop!"

She pulled the trigger and a deafening bang echoed against the walls.

***

Megan was shaking. Her bed was shaking. She had seen it all. They were back. She let out a scream.

Robert immediately ejected himself from his chair and was down the stairs and in Megan's room in a matter of six seconds. Megan lay there screaming, eyes closed.

"Megan!"

She opened her eyes and looked at Robert. Panic filled her body and filled the room.

"Are you OK?"

"They're back. She has the vibrator on high and she shot him and she's shaking me and laughing at us. I think she might have killed him. Robert, the compressor is so loud! Please, please make it stop! Oh my God! Make it stop."

Robert was used to being in panic situations but nothing had prepared him for this. She was evidently hallucinating.

"Sit up, Megan, come on, let's get up, out of bed and get you in motion."

She closed her eyes and wept. Tearless weeping, fear and agony. The noise was horrifyingly loud. But the woman had stopped screaming. She couldn't see the man anymore.

"Open your eyes Megan, *now*."

She did, and she found herself standing. Robert flipped on the light and she winced.

He turned on a radio and held it by her, moving the digital selector up and down, showing her there was nothing to hear except for static. He put the phone up to her ear and it only hissed like the compressor.

"The scrambler's on. They can't signal you whether they're there or not, Megan."

Megan looked at the phone and radio, confused. She looked at the scrambler and sure enough it was in the "ON" position.

The screaming had stopped and the compressor was much quieter, but not completely gone.

"Robert, they've got to have bugged the house. They know I'm here and they've got to have speakers here in the room where they're piping in the sound. I've been found. Robert, what are we going to do?"

"Megan, no one has bugged the room. There are no speakers here that weren't here before. Nothing's changed."

"I heard them. They were having sex."

"Who?"

"I think the old man and a hooker. Only she was beautiful, like a movie star. Oh God, what are we going to do?"

"Megan, it was a *dream*. There is nothing going on here. People have dreams like that all the time."

"Don't you see? Nothing ever happens when you are in the room. No. They don't want to let you hear them or see what's happening to me. It's so everyone can think I'm crazy."

"Megan, no one, *no one* thinks you're crazy. Let's get you to the bathroom and get a cold washcloth on your face. We're going to inspect this room for you inch by inch, even if it takes the entire night."

"OK, Robert, thanks. Thank you. You're saving my life."

Robert searched every inch of the room as Megan watched and directed. About a third of the way through the task he realized how ridiculous it was. Ridiculous and necessary. He had to show Megan that no one was in the room.

She was satisfied that there was nothing in the room, now, but that there definitely had been at other times. She rejected any other explanation. Robert didn't want to fight with her. He didn't want to argue and he would not do so. Eventually he would finish the inspection with her and he would stay with her until she got back to sleep.

***

The drive back from Dr. Berkowitz's office had Megan and Ashley in a heated debate about how they should proceed. Berkowitz gave Megan another prescription for Seroquel, which Megan had been taking but had run out of; she'd never bothered refilling it. Berkowitz reiterated his previous diagnosis of tinnitus and schizophrenia. He told Megan and Ashley that Megan was supposed to take the medicine at night so she could sleep better.

And Ashley knew that wasn't enough. It was a start, perhaps, but reinforcements were needed.

Once home, Megan played video games with Lauren. That gave Ashley a chance to do some Internet research. She Googled "Minneapolis, tinnitus, schizophrenia."

One of the top results was a Marc Daniels. He had a long FAQ page on his website about tinnitus and it seemed to match Megan's experience. Ashley called his phone number.

He agreed to see Megan for a tinnitus consultation. He didn't work with schizophrenia. Did anyone? "Too damned complicated. Like putting a jigsaw puzzle back together."

Ashley told him that she didn't want him to help with the schizophrenia, but with the tinnitus. Daniels didn't utterly buy it, but he did agree to see her for a consultation.

Two weeks later they arrived at his Apple Valley home. They were expecting a clinic or something similar and Megan only rolled her eyes as they pulled into the driveway of a modest home in the suburbs. He met them at the door. He learned that it would take Megan a while to get to the den by herself, where Daniels would hold the session.

Daniels spoke with Ashley while Megan made it slowly down the hallway to the den he used as an office. The den was separated from the dining room by a partitioned wall. An Italian leather sofa hugged one wall, and the love seat, where Megan and Ashley would sit, was adjacent to the sofa. The surface of the coffee table held glasses of water, magazines, notepad and pen. The wood-burning fireplace had a brick surround and created a pleasant, relaxed feeling. The overall ambience was cozy and professional at the same time.

Daniels listened carefully to Megan's story and jotted notes on his legal pad. Other than that, it was obvious from the outset that Daniels was not your ordinary therapist. He reacted to everything Megan said in a completely nonchalant fashion. Everything Megan said, whether it was about the buzzard, shootings, car chases, moving from place to place, or radio waves, the whole kit and caboodle didn't raise so much as one of his eyebrows. It appeared that he thought that all of those things were normal and fine, and what was the problem?

"Megan, the problem is that people invalidate other people based upon their own beliefs about reality. There are a lot of people who think you are nuts. This matters? Really? Who cares? Maybe they're all nuts. Weren't the people who blew up the Twin Towers nuts? Those are the real nuts. They hurt people. So let's assume you are right or sane or pick a word, any word, and let's assume they are nuts and who knows, we might throw in people who think you're nuts...into the nuts category, but we'll give them a chance."

"You're just saying this to try and get me to talk."

"Megan, I couldn't care less if you talk. I get paid the same one way or the other. I had a lady who sat and stared at me right here for two hours straight. She had a point to prove. I had no such point. I worked answering my email until she said goodbye. What the hell do I care. I'm seeing you once. That's it. Once. Every day people call me saying they're going to kill themselves. Tell me they are going to OD on Valium. Idiots. You can't kill yourself on Valium. It's a benzo. Now, try the SSRI's? Now that you can kill yourself on. Serotonin – almost like an explosion in your brain if you OD on that. You'd have an electrical feeling through your body for a few hours and your face would light up like a Christmas tree and eventually you would die. OD on Valium and you sleep…a really long time. No, you can talk as much or as little as you wish."

"Well, I'm only here to please Ashley."

"Good. I do dumb shit like that too. My kids say, *'PLEASE, Dad…'* and I'm like …ugh…OK fine. Whatever, let's go. You have to do stuff to please the people you love. You love her?"

"Well, yes."

"Well, then, you should do this to please her. That's what life is about."

Megan told Marc her entire story from beginning to end.

"You have one assignment. Write down all the arguments for and against the radioing theory. That's it."

And two hours from the time they arrived, they were out the door.

The next day was R Day... restraining order day. Ashley had been working on this for some time, with Robert's support. It was going to be as big a shock to Megan as it would be to Mary.

I can't imagine how I'm going to tell Megan that we now have a restraining order against Mary. Megan is going to lose her mind.

Ashley watched the drivers on the road as she went to pick up Megan on what would be Mary's last day of work. Mary would now have to take her money and find somewhere else to live.

Megan's Aunt Rebekkah was going to move into 4190 for an undetermined period. Megan had lost her father years ago. Since the intervention, Megan had refused contact with her aunt, and everyone else, for that matter, except the Drexels. The only person who really understood, in Megan's mind, was Mary.

But Mary had become too big a part of the problem. When Megan was looking for some lipstick in Mary's bag and found the knife, she didn't know what to think. The handle had been taped and then string had been wrapped around the tape. Anyone on the receiving end of the knife wouldn't have a story to tell later. It was more than scary looking.

Mary had recently begun to talk more about "the buzzard." She would call Ashley at all hours, yelling at her to get the buzzards arrested. Megan and Mary led a strange life together. Megan heard the buzzard, and Mary would see the buzzard and his men… and women. But Megan never saw much of anything except the floor she was walking on.

Mary couldn't have a telephone conversation with Ashley without screaming obscenities at her. It had become obvious that Mary had tried to get Megan to sign over rights to her person but the timing was never right, and Megan hadn't done it yet. Even if she had, it was questionable as to whether it would have stood up in court. Mary wanted it all. After having spent every day of the last several years with Megan, she had come to the realization that she really wanted to be Megan. The wealthy celebrity socialite.

She'd even started telling Ashley that she was far more deserving of wealth than Megan ever would be. Yet, she also claimed her allegiance to Megan as Megan's only true friend.

Apparently Megan had told Mary on more than one occasion that they were "friends to the end, through thick and thin" and no matter what happened, Megan would take care of Mary.

Each time Megan had an appointment with a psychiatrist, Mary created a ruse to get Megan somewhere else so that they would never get there. The one time Ashley did get Megan to the doctor's office, Dr. Berkowitz told both Megan and Ashley that Mary was essentially "brainwashing" Megan.

Clearly, Mary had developed a kind of schizophrenia as well. But it appeared that Mary's schizophrenia was far more of a danger to Megan, than Megan's own blurring of fiction and reality.

Mary and Megan spent a night in Rochester at an old high school friend of Mary's. The next morning, Mary was found sleeping with a butcher's knife in her hand. Her entire body was covered in aluminum foil. She told those who listened that it was a way to stop the buzzard from hearing their conversations, thinking their thoughts and sending radio transmissions.

When their friend Bill found Mary that morning, he gently plied the knife from her hands, moved several paces back and called for Mary to wake up. He was very glad that she no longer held the knife in her hand because she swung that hand wildly. Her old friend Bill would not have survived her attack if she'd still been armed.

Bill called the local hospital asking for instructions on how to commit her, knowing that Mary would never go willingly. Under the pretext of getting some tests he needed urgently, he asked Mary to go with him to the hospital for support. That day, Mary was committed. Bill felt terrible but knew it had to be done.

Mary would be in the hospital for a week until Ashley could arrange for her to move to the apartment Megan was going to buy her in Arizona, a long way away.

Ashley had nearly fallen over when she heard about the condo, but the price was more than worth removing some of Mary's influence over Megan. With Mary around, Megan would never get well. She would never be "normal" again.

Ashley didn't want to admit it, but she had run out of options and alternatives to get Megan well.

The drive to Daniels's house for their second weekly session couldn't have been longer.

"Ashley, I can't believe you encouraged this. Poor Mary."

"Megan, look, she needed to be committed. She was obviously a danger to you and Bill and herself."

"But why?"

"Megan, I'm not the one who committed her. Bill did. I was up here in the Cities, you guys were in Rochester."

"But we could get her out so she doesn't have to suffer."

"No, Megan, we aren't doctors. She'll get help there. Bill wouldn't have brought her in if he felt like everything was OK. But, it's not. She was holding a knife and you said she had aluminum foil all over. That's a little scary. So, no, we aren't going to get involved."

"You're actually glad she's in the hospital – a psych ward, because you think she's crazy."

"She's going to get help. She *needs* help."

"She needs help because she believes in the buzzard, right?"

"Megan, she needs help because she is a danger to herself and others to the point where Bill became really concerned. She's obviously delusional. She's seeing all kinds of things that simply aren't there. And then she's making up stories. "

"Just like you think I make up stories, right?"

"You don't make them up, your brain does, and that's different from your mind. Ask Daniels again, he'll tell you."

As Megan so often did, she shifted from one emotion to another, one subject to another, very quickly, especially under stress.

"I think he might be a gigolo."

"Who?" Ashley looked at Megan in the passenger seat.

"Marc."

"Marc who? The therapist guy Marc?"

"Yep."

Ashley laughed hard as she drove.

"You're laughing at me."

"Yes, I am. That is the funniest thing you have ever said."

"I'm going to ask him."

"You're actually going to ask Marc if he's a gigolo?"

"Yes, I am." Megan nodded with certainty.

"You do that, honey. I can't wait to hear what he says."

They arrived at his home on time. Ashley had spoken to Marc earlier in the week, asking for his take on the situation, and if there was any realistic hope. His response was not overly optimistic about the schizophrenia. However, he was quite certain that the tinnitus, which covered the compressor sound and most of the auditory hallucinations, was not going to be all that hard to bring down in volume, given time. He also indicated that he wasn't looking for any long-term clients, and he didn't want to see Megan more than one or maybe two more times. Being in the midst of divorce had sapped the therapist of his once boundless and captivating energy. Today he was a shadow of his former self. The only thing that remained was his certainty about getting his clients well. He was their warrior, no matter how many battles he would personally be crushed in.

"So Bill committed Mary, and Ashley won't do anything about it."

A sense of relief coursed through his entire body and spirit. At their last meeting it had been clear that Mary was more than a bad influence for Megan.

"I think for some period of time it is a very good idea for you two to not see each other."

"Well, Ashley made that clear when she took out a restraining order against Mary."

"Really? Huh! Well, Megan, that's probably a good thing. She has a very unstable edge about her that is not conducive to you getting well. I think that once *you* are well, it would be great for you guys to do lunch and stuff, but I think that it's probably best for now. She'll be able to do other things when she gets out of the hospital. She'll be able to get away from you for a bit. So let's not say this is a disaster but actually a good thing. She *does* need help."

"Now you think *she's* crazy?"

"I think that she's afraid of what she sees in life and how she interprets it. And, frankly, she has a very angry side to her. Remember I have actually talked to her, and she isn't always the nicest person .I think for a while, this distance is a good thing."

This was more than true. Megan had given Daniels Mary's phone number and he spent a lengthy evening speaking with her about the buzzard and her version of the story.

"But don't you think we should get her out of the hospital?"

"No. She needs help and she'll get it there until she heads off to Arizona. They'll help her calm down, and if they have some kind of a program she'll be helped even more. I don't know anything much about that, though."

The reality was simple. Megan had several reasons for hope that no one else with schizophrenia or severe tinnitus had.

First, she had financial resources. Truth be told, the schizophrenic wouldn't likely be "cured" in a hospital or institutional setting. It would require hundreds of hours of piecing a human puzzle together. This wasn't going to be a twelve-session experience. If Daniels were to take the job it could be a solid twelve months of once or twice a week, if everything else went right.

Second, Megan had Ashley. Whatever Ashley's motives, it was obvious she was determined to do every single thing possible to get Megan well.

Third was Daniels. He believed and practiced that given the right environment, the right context, the right people, the right medications, the brain could be changed enough to where you could shift just enough to go from living in hell to living in heck.

Any missing piece of the puzzle meant that Megan would be another case with schizophrenia or severe tinnitus that would simply live the rest of their life in hell and then die.

Daniels was not so forthright about Mary. He felt bad for Mary. She would never get well. She had no resources. She had no chance. There was nothing he could do about that. He couldn't tell Megan that. It would have sealed her to the same fate.

If the therapy with Megan were going to happen, it would require walking a tightrope as Ashley had done for some time, and taking calculated risks on Megan's behalf.

What would that mean?

There was an abrupt change of subject. Where it came from, Marc had no idea.

"Are you a gigolo?"

He didn't miss a beat. "A gigolo? No. But I'm willing to learn."

Ashley burst into laughter and Megan gave her a look.

"I think you are. You're a Scorpio and I'm a Scorpio and I know how Scorpios think. Sex all day long."

"Well, that's true Megan, but I don't have time to be a gigolo. I'm pretty busy. Therapy, kids, writing, it's a lot to do. But maybe in the future."

"Well, if you ever do…"

"You'll be the first to know."

"Thanks."

And another switch in subject.

"I think that you don't believe me, Marc."

"What don't I believe?"

"You don't believe that the buzzard is radioing me and torturing me."

"Megan, do you like it when people question whether what you're saying is true or not?"

"I hate it." She gave Ashley a look.

"Do me a favor, then, would you, and don't tell me what I think. I'm already in the midst of a divorce from one woman who thinks she can read my mind. Please, don't you follow in those footsteps."

"Do you talk like this to all your clients?"

"Only you."

"Well, do you believe me?"

"Does what I believe really matter? There's a big asteroid headed for earth. When it hits the earth, it will destroy all mankind in an instant. I don't believe it's there. It hits. Oops. I was wrong."

"I don't get it."

"What does it matter what I believe? All kinds of people believe all kinds of things. The people that are the closest to reality have the fewest problems."

"Well, if you want to be my therapist, don't you have to believe me? Do you think the buzzard is radioing me?"

"First, I do believe you. I believe you one hundred percent. It's possible the buzzard is radioing you. We have cell phones. Have you ever seen *Person of Interest*? I remember once on *Gilligan's Island* they used this idea as a plot, so why not? It's possible. It hits my radar."

"Really?"

"Really what, Megan?"

"I mean, you believe he's radioing me?"

Marc sighed. "I mean it's possible. How the hell do I know what he's doing? And do I really care? No, I don't care. You didn't ask me to give you opinions on what is possible in the universe but to physically reduce your tinnitus. So whatever this buzzard is doing is meaningless if we can just turn his volume down, right?"

"What?" Megan was incredulous.

"Look, our job is to get the volume of the tinnitus, the compressor sound, so quiet that it doesn't bother you. Or maybe make it go away. If we do that, what do we care if it's real, whatever that means, or not?"

Megan thought about that. It made sense. If the compressor sound was gone, it really wouldn't matter. Except…?

"What about the fact that they were trying to kill me? Do you believe that?"

"Not for a second. For that to happen would be instant prison for the retired guy, so I'll call him 'the buzzard,' too. And he took *you* to mediation to resolve his issue. You laid it all on the line before the judge. The buzzard didn't try and kill you."

"So you don't believe me?"

"I've never gotten really upset with a client, but... there you go again, talking about what I believe! It doesn't make a lick of difference whether I believe something and whether it might be real. Who is to say that I have a monopoly on the interpretation of reality?"

"I don't understand." And Ashley hadn't said a word since they arrived. Marc couldn't remember if she could speak.

"Everybody believes different stuff. Everyone remembers things differently from the next person. We disagree about whether someone else was in the room at Christmas or whether the person was invited that year. People argue about who was right, and people kill each other over arguments about who is right or wrong, and about what they remember or believe. Are you saying that when you believe something you are automatically entitled to it?"

Megan shut up. She looked down. She looked back at Marc then spoke.

"That sounds like a lot of crap."

"Of course it is, if that's what you think it is. See how this works. I respect what you say about yourself, your opinions, your beliefs, your morals."

"Can the buzzard hear our conversation?"

"Not possible."

"How do you know that so fast if you don't know anything else?"

"Because he'd have to have a radio transmitter in your ear and that would have to have been inserted during your surgery years ago, years before there ever was a buzzard or a compressor or a huge vibrator. And you'd actually have to be able to put a radio transmitter in a human head that could transmit all around the world without being picked up in the airport screening security system. 'Ma'am, I'm Jack with TSA and we see you have a radio transmitter without a power source in your head that might interfere with the navigation of the plane you'll be flying on today. We need you to remove it.' Did that happen to you on your last airplane ride? No.

"Is it possible? No. Doesn't hit the radar. TSA. Gotta love the government. They find *everything*. They are in the finding business. They find the most dangerous toothpaste known to mankind.

"Everything else you 'believe' could be true, Megan, but this is simply not possible. I wish it was. That would be pretty neat technology. But it's not, so you have to come up with another way for the buzzard to be picking up on your conversations.

"You told me that these people have followed you from Chicago to Vegas. How do they get through security with all that stuff? How do you get through security? Not gonna happen.

"How are you going to turn off that transmitter once you get to 10,000 feet when you're on the airplane, then turn it back on as you come back down on descent to land?"

"But you think it's possible that he's transmitting and torturing me?"

"Sure. It's possible. Why not?"

"OK."

And there was a long silence. Marc reached down to his coffee table and took a sip of his Diet Coke. He heard an email come in on the laptop sitting next to him and he turned the sound off.

"I think that he can hear what I'm saying."

"No, you don't."

"What do you mean, I don't?"

"You want to believe he can hear what you're saying but you know it's not possible, so you have to have faith that he can. So, if you ever want to come back to me for therapy, you have to go home and write up fifty different ways he could hear your conversations in Vegas or Wisconsin or Chicago, here or wherever, but radio transmission ain't one of 'em. You need to believe that to keep the rest of your life experience, your storyline, if you will, intact.

"Either you are an intelligent thinking person who shifts your beliefs when you learn new information, or you are a politician. Have you ever dealt with those corrupt people?"

"Oh, do I have a story for you..." She almost launched into it but she jumped back a thought. "You think I'm making this up like a story?"

"Not in the way you mean the question. We all make up stories of our life. What happens. What means something. What means nothing. It gives us meaning. It's how Viktor Frankl survived the Nazi concentration camps at Auschwitz and Dachau. It's how we all make sense of life. You simply need to change this part of the story. You aren't anyone unusual. You are a person who is hearing people have sex with big vibrators. Big deal! If that's the worst thing that ever happens to a person, well, what a life. I wish I was either having sex or hearing someone have sex. I'd be having a better day."

Ashley laughed.

"I think you're making fun of me."

"That's OK. Let me ask you a question, Megan. Why did you come back? Why come back to see me again? You don't need to be here. Why come back?"

She paused. "Well, because you were funny and you are cute. I don't mean to be offensive."

"Wait, you mean you like me because I'm cute?"

"Well, yes."

"Thank you so much! I have waited my entire life wishing someone would like me for my looks."

Ashley broke out into laughter again.

"OK, listen, at some point, we should really get to new business. What meds are you taking?"

"I'm taking 300 Seroquel at bedtime and an Ambien."

"Ten?"

"Yes. Ten milligrams."

"Seroquel doing anything for you?"

"It helps me sleep."

"Good. Since you started that med, has the number of times you've heard the buzzard talk to you decreased at all?"

Megan rifled through her memory.

"Yes. I think that's right. How did you know?"

"Just a guess. Let's keep doing that. No change there and by the way, I can't prescribe medication. I only make suggestions on how to use it, so you have an informed opinion when you talk to Doc Berkowitz. How about the Ambien?"

"It seems to help me get to sleep but it doesn't help me actually sleep for very long."

"Anything else?"

"Not much anymore."

"OK, well, if we're going to bring the tinnitus volume down and reduce your anxiety and depression levels, we'll probably need to bring in some help. Write this down…"

Ashley snatched a pen from her purse and wrote in her Day Runner.

"How about one and a half milligrams of Klonopin divided into three doses. When you wake up, at dinner time, and at bedtime. So half a milligram, three times daily…and…let's go for fifty milligrams of Zoloft either at bedtime or in the morning.

"The Zoloft is an antidepressant which will do a few things for you. First, it will help you reduce your attention to the sounds and voices in your head. It's sort of an anti-OCD-for-tinnitus fighter."

"You think I'm OCD?"

"Did I say that? Hello? Did you go to the same school as my wife?

"I didn't say anything of the sort, Megan, but if you give me twenty seconds I can say something, and then you can tear it to shreds, OK? Are you sure you aren't a mom?"

She was silent.

"When you have tinnitus or voices or whatever in your head, it's hard to not pay attention to them. Our brain tends to compulsively check the volume levels, what they are saying, and ultimately we obsess about the tinnitus and voices whether we want to consciously, or not. The Zoloft, most SSRI's, will help a bit with both. Bonus. It will also help eradicate some depression."

"Oh, OK…but I'm not here about depression."

"Really? You aren't depressed? You've been shot at and tortured and you aren't depressed?"

"Well, yes."

"And back in the days when David was around, were you depressed?"

"No."

"And were you hearing tinnitus in those days?"

"No, but they weren't radioing me either."

"OK, fine. But you were fine in those days right?"

"Yes."

"So all I want to do is get you to *not hear* the buzzard and his compressor."

"How can you do that when he's radioing me all day long?"

"Well, that's the beautiful part of the brain. It can only pay attention to so much stuff in the course of any discrete period of time. We make other things more important to the brain than some idiot with a ham radio kit and all of a sudden, you can't hear him anymore. Have you ever turned the volume on the TV down? Does it mean the people are no longer speaking because you can't hear them?"

"Well, of course not."

"Just a minute ago you said I thought you were OCD. Your brain was so busy trying to fight me that you didn't even listen to what I said. You couldn't have heard it because you were focused on your thoughts about what you were going to say next. Humans do this all day long. No one listens to anyone, they just pretend they know stuff. Megan, didn't you tell me that you hear him less than you used to since you started the Seroquel?"

"Yes, but that's because he's had trouble with reception and sending."

"How do you know that to be true? That is a guess, right?"

"Well, no. The buzzard is having troubles."

"OK, how do you know that?"

"Because I hear shouting in the background. They're yelling about the reception and transmission problems."

"You heard them say that?"

"Well not exactly. I hear them shouting, but the microphone is muffled so I only pick up part of it."

"OK. I'll write that down. Now. The Klonopin is a good medication for tinnitus. It will reduce the fear response, reducing anxiety. Without getting technical, it helps about seventy percent of people reduce tinnitus volume as well."

"Isn't that addictive?"

"Breathing is addictive. Drinking water is addictive. Yelling at an ex-husband is addictive. You can never give up any of these things or you go crazy and then die. Meanwhile Klonopin, you can give up and it costs you nothing when you get divorced or die. At a dose this small, there is little if anything to think about. But if you'd like to be scared of some more stuff in life we could make some shit up. Your choice.

"You talk to your doc about using these meds for twelve weeks. At the end of that time, we reevaluate where you are. If you use them for twelve years and you can't hear the buzzard, how are you feeling? Not terrible? Simple enough. Each day you track your tinnitus and your emotional response to your tinnitus in a journal of your own creation. You write down how loud it is and how you feel about it. Then if you come back and see me again, you'll know if you are getting better or not."

"So you think I'm crazy."

"Jesus. Did I say that? Never tell me what I think until we get married. Until then just ask. I will always tell you what I think and you'll never make stuff up out of thin air. Did I say you were crazy?"

"Yes. You said the medication would make me better. It won't because they are radioing me."

"I don't care if the buzzard is radioing you. It doesn't matter. He can sit at that ham radio 24/7 for all I care. He can use the vibrator 24/7 for all I care. *You don't care either.* You don't want to *hear it* or *feel it.* You don't really care if some nut job is sitting around playing with his radio equipment, do you? Really?"

She said nothing.

"The medication will cause you to pay less attention to the compressor and buzzard and keep it out of consciousness, so that any stimulation they are giving your brain will eventually become secondary to everything else going on in life. Eventually it won't matter how hard they try to radio you, or how high they turn the volume up, it just won't work.

"Megan. Look. This is simple. Imagine that you are watching a hundred TVs at the same time, like you do at a Best Buy store. Now imagine that they're not tuned to the same channel, but each is different. Some are on the Animal Planet channel, some are on the History Channel, CNBC, MSNBC, Nick and so on."

"OK."

"Now, they are *all* on and all the hundred TVs are on *different* channels, right?"

"OK."

"How many do you think you will be able to tell me about what happened on the show, after a half hour of watching?"

"I don't know, maybe ten?"

"Exactly. Ten out of a hundred."

"So I don't get it."

"Our job is to teach your brain to pay attention to the other ninety sets. Not the ten with the buzzard on it."

"But his is the loudest!"

"Ever been in a romantic conversation?" Marc leaned over the shoulder of the chair and looked Megan right in her eyes as he tilted his head.

"Ever notice how the world disappears and doesn't reappear until you are done talking?"

"Um, yes… I suppose."

"That's what we are going to do with the tinnitus and buzzard 24/7. Doesn't matter if he's really there or not!"

"Really?"

"Really."

"You ever had tinnitus?"

"For two and a half years. Loud as a vacuum cleaner for the first year and a half. I hated it."

"You hear people talking?"

"Nope. I heard the UPS guy at the door though."

"What do you mean?"

"I mean I'd wake up to the sound of the UPS guy knocking on the door, delivering a package. We've always had a small business in the house."

"And the UPS guy was not real?"

"Well, he was real. But he just wasn't at my door when I got up to go and check."

"Did you think you were crazy?"

"Nope. I was too sane to be crazy. I wished I had been crazy. Simple auditory hallucinations. No big deal. Everyone has them."

"Everyone?"

"Yep. Everyone."

"Ashley? Robert? Mary? They all have auditory hallucinations?"

"You left out Barack Obama."

"So you think I have auditory hallucinations?"

"I am absolutely positive you do. I don't know whether the buzzard is causing them or not though. That's a different issue. The buzzard *could* be radioing you. But I won't know for sure until we progress in our work, which I said I wasn't going to do, so you should give me a good reason not to do it right now. "

"Marc, did they scare you, the hallucinations?"

"Nope, they pissed me off because I could have gone back to sleep but instead they got me up and I stayed up. Happens right before you go to sleep and right as you wake up. The fancy words are hypnagogic and hypnopompic states…and that just means that we are at our most suggestible and confused right as we wake up and go to sleep. We can't tell right away if we are sleeping or are awake. It can be very annoying."

"I'll bet."

"Anyway, don't worry about my hallucinations. Don't worry about any auditory hallucinations. Everyone has them. What I want you to do is intelligently figure out how the buzzard is hearing our conversation because there is nothing in your head that is transmitting anything to him. Everything else you are saying could be 'real,' so to speak, but the transmission element is faulty. I need you to figure out how he is hearing you. That's your homework again for the week, and this week you actually *do it*. Figure out how he's getting that signal from you."

"Homework?"

"Yup. Don't come back unless your homework is done. You said you've been to eighteen different hotels and motels all across the country. OK. Then investigate and see how the buzzard heard you and Mary talking. Find out how he knew you were wherever you were at the time. Investigate the rooms of the local hotels you were in. Look around your old house and your new condo. Don't stop searching until you find the answer. *How* did the buzzard know where you were going to be?

"A few practical tips to get you past the tinnitus life. First, buy a baby soother. Something that can sit next to your bed that has the sound of rain or a babbling brook. Something environmental that has a broad band of frequencies. Then, when you go to bed at night put the soother on a volume where you can hear it and your tinnitus. That way, when you wake up your brain will have a sort of 'split attention.' It won't know whether to listen to the ocean or the tinnitus. Part of getting better is to start confusing the brain.

"I wouldn't turn the volume louder than your tinnitus unless you're having a real bad night. Masking the tinnitus is OK for short periods but I'm not convinced it will get you well and certainly not as quickly."

He snatched a sip of his Diet Coke as Ashley chimed in.

"What about these tinnitus retraining generators?"

"Better for people who have moderate tinnitus and people who aren't freaked out by what they are hearing. The generators look like hearing aids but they send a constant single sound into the ears all day long. I've never seen a reason to use them rather than an iPod or any mp3 player, with music you like. Lots of my clients can't stand having yet another tinnitus sound in their head and they end up blowing thousands of dollars for nothing. Listen to music you like, or learn to like some classical music, or music with a lot of high frequencies. Or buy some environmental CDs and download them into your iPod."

Megan put her hand to her ear.

"What about my hearing aid?"

"Make sure it's programmed correctly so you have just the right amount of sound entering and the least possible distortion, and avoid that hollow sound."

"Anything else?" Ashley was taking notes.

"Well, there's a lot of stuff to do. The most important is to stay absorbed in your work. Be involved in things outside of your head until you can be in your own skin without fear when you hear the sound. So watch movies that are exciting. Watch mysteries, read mysteries. Go shopping. Go to the park. Do things. Have a rich schedule of things to do and give all of them one hundred percent of your attention.

"Measure your tinnitus volume exactly five times every day as we discussed last time, and then don't measure it subjectively or objectively aside from those times. Part of getting well is breaking the obsession to listen to tinnitus and the compulsion to see how loud it is. These are normal things to do, but they are not good things to do, and will undo most of the good work you might be doing.

"When I say you'll get better, I specifically mean, if you follow what I suggest, you will hear the buzzard less and when you do hear it, it won't be so damn loud. Perhaps, eventually never. Just don't tell the buzzard that. That way he'll sit at his radio 24/7 trying to freak you out while you go about living a fun life in a bikini on a beach. Make sense?"

"Why haven't any doctors suggested all this?" Ashley was rather incensed.

"Because they don't know. And because those that do have some knowledge of tinnitus, they go with what the current treatments that have had some research and seem 'sensible.' Unfortunately most of the research is thin, not compared to placebo groups and that is bad for people who are suffering. Very bad. I think the last thing is that the things that work are very inexpensive. See an osteopath for strain/counter-strain therapy, intracranial sacral therapy, take a benzodiazepene like Klonopin or Xanax. Take an SSRI antidepressant. These are all cheap. Not much profit in this area. And because the response time is so long before people get well, most people give up on doctors and most doctors give up on their patients."

"OK, well, we'll get to work on all of this, and our homework."

Chapter Thirty Seven

Three Hours Later

The ride home was very quiet. Megan felt like she had just been disciplined by her mother, not gone through therapy. Ashley didn't know what to think.

He didn't say I was crazy. He yelled at me like he was angry at me, not like I was sick or crazy.

"See Ashley, Marc doesn't think I'm crazy."

"I know he doesn't."

"He believes me about the buzzards. He's the only one aside from Mary."

"Well, he doesn't believe there are really buzzards. He's speaking hypothetically."

"No, that's not what he said. He said he believes that the buzzards are transmitting to me."

"No, Megan. He's saying it's remotely possible. One in a million. He doesn't think there are buzzards doing this to you." Ashley was getting loud.

Something about being yelled at by both Marc and Ashley got Megan's energy going.

"I want to go to the Belmont."

"The hotel?"

"Yes."

"Why?"

"I want to see if we can find any holes in the walls to see where they put the wires to the speakers so they could hear me."

"Megan, that's just…"

"Don't say it's crazy. Marc said I had to do my homework or don't come back. Well, I want to investigate."

That meant Ashley would investigate and like always, it would only be Ashley's word for what she saw. Megan probably wouldn't be able to walk around the hotel, go to the window of her old room and investigate. She probably couldn't navigate the hotel grounds. Ashley wasn't optimistic but they took the next exit and got back onto 494 heading east toward the airport. To the Belmont they went.

They pulled into the oversized parking lot and Ashley stopped at the front door.

"What do you suggest, Megan?"

"I want to look for holes."

"*Where* do you want to look for holes?"

"In my old room."

Ashley looked at her watch. 1:15 p.m. It was right between check-out and check-in. Why not? "Sure. Let's go. You get out and work your way in and I'll park and be back in a minute."

Megan was out of the car and on the sidewalk. It would take fifteen minutes to get to the registration desk, if she moved quickly. And by comparison to two years ago, she was moving much more quickly. Ashley parked and walked briskly back to Megan. She met her inside the doors and they moved toward the registration booth together.

The two approached the front desk and the hotel clerk immediately recognized them.

"Welcome back to the Belmont, Mrs. Dresden. Will you be needing a room for an extended period of time again?"

"No, we uh…" Ashley stuttered. "We need to have a look at a room Megan stayed in once before. We need to take some pictures for her scrap book. I know it sounds kind of odd. We'd be happy to pay you for the night of course."

The clerk looked confused but immediately smiled. He hit a bunch of keys on his computer trying to search for Megan's old room and then seeing if it was available.

"Excellent. Would that be one night then?"

"Yes." Megan got into the conversation.

"Two keys?"

"Yes please. And can we have the key to the room above the room we had before?"

"The room *above* your old room?" He was curious to say the least, but counting the extra dollars in his mind. "One moment."

He hit some more keys.

"Would you like that for one night also?"

"Yes." Megan was back in charge.

"Two keys?"

Megan looked around the lobby. It was empty. No prostitution ring. Maybe they were all at lunch or working. Ashley answered instead.

"Yes. That would be great."

He inserted the cards into the key making machine and handed the ladies their key cards.

"Enjoy your stay."

"Thank you."

"Thank you."

And they were off on their own private investigation.

They checked both rooms inside and out. They got a ladder from housekeeping to use outside and also to check the ceiling for wires, holes, patched holes, and anything else that looked suspicious.

Ashley felt like she had lost her mind, with all the climbing she was doing.

The ceiling in both rooms showed signs of no attention or maintenance. When it was all said and done, clearly there was no wire or sound system going from room to room or from the outside in. There were no holes, patched or otherwise, in the walls between the one adjoining room and Megan's old room.

After four hours of searching every square inch they returned to the room that Megan had stayed in with Mary. Exhausted, Ashley took a seat at the foot of the bed.

Megan was both satisfied and puzzled.

"There's nothing here. Nothing. It's impossible."

"Megan, there's nothing here because there is no buzzard." Ashley was always patient but she was tired. She hadn't been up and down a ladder this much, ever.

"How did they hear what we were saying?"

"There is no buzzard, Megan."

"But that's not possible. I hear the compressor right now."

"You hear your tinnitus."

"Do you think I'm crazy?"

"No, honey. But I think I am. We've been here a long time. We've checked everything from the inside of the toilet to the bathtub faucet. We've taken apart the air conditioners and pulled out the sprinklers in the sprinkler system. We've pulled up carpet and all we have found is how tired we are."

"You're right. There's nothing here."

"You're sure, Megan?"

"I'm sure. There is nothing here. You think we can look around 4190 today?"

"No. How about tomorrow? Robert and Lauren will be waiting for me. And I want you to come with me for dinner tonight."

"What about Mary?"

"We'll talk about that on the way home."

Playing detective was interesting for about ten minutes. Then it became dull, frustrating and anger provoking. Ashley had held it all in, but now was a perfect time.

"I had a restraining order placed against Mary. She can't come back to 4190 or come within fifty feet of you."

"What? That's crazy. Why?"

"She's a potential danger to herself and you."

"She would *never* hurt me." Megan was angry and loud.

"I know, but we have to let the doctors decide about that."

"Ashley, who is going to take care of me? When can Mary come back to work and when can I talk to her? She must be terrified."

"For right now, she can't come back to work. You can talk to her later in the week and you're probably right. I imagine she is scared."

"Can we go see her?"

"No. They won't take visitors at this point." Ashley had no idea if this was true but Ashley wasn't going to let Megan visit and that was certain.

Megan began to cry with her pitiful tearless weeping. It was always hard for Ashley to listen to Megan cry. She rarely cried. When she did, she was really hurting. But Ashley couldn't stand Mary. She fervently hoped she would never see her again, but clearly, Megan was devastated.

"Ashley, who is going to live with me?"

"Your aunt is going to move in for a while."

"My aunt? Oh God. She probably thinks I'm crazy too."

"No one thinks you are crazy. Everyone understands that you're simply suffering from tinnitus and auditory hallucinations. There are lots of people that deal with these things every day."

"I can't believe all this is happening to me."

They pulled in the driveway, got Megan out of the car and into the house. It would be a difficult evening.

***

Arriving at 4190, they were back to being detectives. They had called the manager, who had left a small ladder in Megan's condo so they could inspect the ceiling of the house. Ashley didn't tell the manager what it was for. The manager was not too happy with Megan any more. Megan had been the source of a lot of controversy in the condo and had long since become the least liked person in the building.

The condo was quiet when they opened the door. Two kittens scurried by on the floor as they walked in.

"What's that?"

"They're kittens. My mom and your aunt picked them out a couple of days ago. My mom stayed here last night while you were at my house and got them litter box-ready for your place. Rebekkah's going to take care of them. They're for you. They need names, by the way."

The kittens tumbled and played in the corner of the living room, every now and then racing from chair to couch to the top of the table.

"You've been saying you wanted kittens so I thought this would be great. It's been a while since you've had a pet."

"They're so cute." A smiled stayed on her face as she tried to follow the kittens around to pet them. But she couldn't even get close. They were too fast and having too much fun to be cuddled or caught.

"Their food is in the laundry room. That's where their bowls are. We set it up so that their food dish is on the left side of the counter. That way you can feed them if Rebekkah's out for the afternoon."

"What should we call them?"

"That's up to you! Look at them. They *love* being here with you."

For a few minutes thoughts of Mary were pushed aside by Megan's new friends. She loved cats and this had definitely softened the blow about Mary.

Chapter Thirty Eight

One Week Later

Marc was in a surprisingly good mood and they both recognized it.

He wrote notes furiously as Megan recounted the events of the last week.

"…and we couldn't find anything. So it's a mystery."

"Where did you look?"

"At 4190, the old house, and a hotel Mary and I stayed at."

"So what does that cause you to think?"

"It makes me think that they have some other way to hear me talking other than microphones and wires."

"What would those options be?"

As always, Ashley sat back, supremely enjoying the fact that Marc was as focused as she was at getting Megan back to normal.

"I don't know."

"Did you check the phones?"

"Ashley took them all apart."

"Did you check the walls and the places where the cable is wired for TV?"

"Yes, we did that."

"What about all the ceiling stuff like lights, light bulbs, sprinklers…"

"We checked everything."

"The cars?"

"We checked them too. Completely."

"You missed something, Megan."

"What?"

"You tell me."

"How do I know? We checked everywhere. There is no radio equipment."

"I don't believe it."

"It's true. There's no receiver or transmitter in any of the places we went and looked at."

"You're positive?"

"I'm positive."

"Fine."

Marc smiled inside and bit his tongue so he wouldn't burst.

"All right. So we can conclude what?"

"They can't hear us talking. But I think they have something set up somewhere so they can hear us at 4190."

"So move."

"Move where?"

"Anywhere that has no microphones. Somewhere that has thick walls. Check the place out before you move in."

"OK, We'll move. Can we do that, Ashley?"

"Why not? We've done it before."

"When can you move?"

Ashley spoke up, considering it was going to be a lot of work for her, and her opinion counted.

"If Megan wants to move, we can move tomorrow… somewhere."

She soon saw even more upsides to Megan moving. Mary wouldn't know where the new house was. She'd have no idea about the changed phone number either. In effect, she'd never be able to find Megan. That would make the restraining order a moot point. The move would be a pain but it would ultimately be perfect. After all, Megan was going to stay at Ashley's until further notice anyway. This way they'd just pack everything and move to a new place. Of course, where? It didn't matter. This would be perfect.

"Great. That's your next assignment. Before you come back to see me, you need to be in a new place. Somewhere that you determine in advance is safe. Secure. Bug free. Buzzard free. Don't move in unless that is the case. Perhaps Robert would be generous enough to sweep and OK the space for you before you set foot inside?"

"OK. That's what we'll do. Ashley, is that OK?" Ashley was still entranced by the whole idea, thinking of how many problems this would actually solve, and how to make sure that nothing would go wrong. No forwarding address for the management. Nothing. Clean break.

"Yes. Fine. Whatever Megan wants, we'll do it."

"Wonderful."

"So let's go back to the investigations you did this week. Megan, are you absolutely certain that there are no bugs in any of these places?"

"Yes. I already told you we looked everywhere."

"What about something that might have been there, that might have been removed?"

"It's hard to imagine. There was no new paint in any of the places we looked and there were no holes or anything, so I don't think so."

"Did you figure out how they could hear you then?"

"I don't think they could at the places we searched."

"Are you *sure*?"

"Yes. Positive."

"And did you think of an alternative? What about the cars?"

"I already told you! We checked there too. Nothing."

"OK, so you are telling me that there is no way they can hear you, is that what I hear you telling me?"

"I don't think they could hear me."

"No. I need you to tell me something as a fact. Something that you're absolutely certain of. So you'll also need to come up with a solution as to how they heard you if it wasn't through transmission or microphones and wires in the various places."

"What if I can't think of anything?"

"You need to have the answer to this question the next time we see each other."

"OK."

"How has the noise been the last week?"

"Better. It's still loud but not as horrible."

"Do you ever have times when you don't notice the noise for a few minutes?"

"When we were investigating there were some times when I didn't notice it…until I noticed it…and then it was back loud."

"Understood. That's a good sign."

"How come?"

"Because the volume is to the point where you aren't always one hundred percent focused on it. Your attention can be elsewhere part of the time. That's one of the first steps in getting better."

"But I'm not sick. The buzzards are transmitting the sounds to my head."

"That's a hypothesis. An idea that we have no evidence for yet. It might be right, no one has a clue yet. So, let's say it this way. The noise level has reduced and you are gaining more control of your mind. You are starting to run your brain instead of outside influences. Is that fair enough?"

"OK. I think so. I mean, you're saying that I'm ignoring the buzzards even though they are transmitting to me?"

"Sort of. Based on what you've told me you did this week as far as searching, I don't think the buzzards are transmitting or receiving but I'm open to them transmitting, and yes, you are starting to run your brain. Starting to ignore the tinnitus by focusing on other things."

"What about the voices?"

"Are you hearing them a lot?"

"Every morning he wakes me up. He's so mean. *Megan, Megan, Megan.* Always three times. Sometimes he says other stuff but it's muffled and I can't hear it. He's always laughing at me and sometimes he turns the compressor up to hurt me."

"OK. So he wakes you up. What do you do when he wakes you up?"

"I get up and go to the bathroom."

"And what if you didn't wake up?"

"I guess I'd never get to the bathroom."

"So the buzzard is actually working for you for free."

"What do you mean?"

"I mean if he doesn't wake you up, you have sheets to change."

"Ye-es, that's true."

"He might be a jerk, but he's saving you a lot of laundry time."

Megan looked down and then nodded her head.

"Does he ever say *Megan, Megan, Megan* at any other time?"

"Sometimes when I lie down to go to sleep."

"When people lie down, that's when their tinnitus is worst. There are a lot of different reasons but it almost always is quieter when people get vertical, when they sit up, get up and move around. Do you notice that things are quieter when you get up and move around?"

She thought and thought.

"Well, it used to be loud all the time but now he talks to me only to wake me up or once in a while late at night. But the compressor is always on. Sometimes he pumps other noise into my head."

"But it's almost always quieter once you're out of bed."

"Yes."

"Excellent."

"Marc, did you know that Bill put Mary in the hospital?"

"Yes, you mentioned that. And what do you think of that?"

"She was just trying to keep the buzzard away from her."

"How would aluminum foil help do that?"

"Scramble radio signals going to her ear."

"She had a surgery too?"

"No. She never had a surgery."

"Then how is the buzzard contacting her?"

"I don't know..."

"Is it possible?"

"I don't know."

"Think about it for a second. The aluminum foil is to scramble messages from the buzzard's radio but she doesn't have anything in her head that could be a receiver. How is this making sense?"

A long pause. Ashley and Megan exchanged looks.

"I don't think it is."

"So how would you explain her behavior?"

"She's scared."

"I know, but why the aluminum foil if she can't hear the buzzard? Why the knife?"

"I don't know. It doesn't make any sense. She never heard the buzzard. She only saw him."

"So if someone wakes up wrapped in aluminum foil and has a knife in their hand, what would *you* do? Would the aluminum foil help her visually? I mean, if they were spying on her would they notice the aluminum foil?"

"Of course they would."

"So she wasn't hiding. She was stopping them from radioing her, right?"

"I guess."

"Don't guess. Be *certain*. Is there any other reason?"

"No. I can't think of any."

"Do people wear aluminum foil in general, anywhere, for anything?"

"No."

"So she was behaving a bit unusually?"

"Yes, I think she was."

"And if you were Bill, would you be worried about her?"

"Yes."

"Did Bill do the right thing?"

"Yes."

"You sure?"

"Yes, but she's not crazy! She's the only one who believes me."

"I don't think she is crazy. I think she genuinely hears the buzzard."

"But she can't hear the buzzard, Marc. You said so."

"No, you said she can't hear the buzzard. I'm not convinced yet."

"Well, she can't."

"You are one hundred percent positive?"

"Yes. So what are you saying?"

"I didn't say anything. You are telling me everything. I'm just sitting here taking notes. I'm just glad she's safe where she is."

"Ashley has a restraining order so she can't work for me anymore."

"Yes, you mentioned that before."

This time Marc paused. He and Ashley had spoken about this possibility a number of times but he didn't know she had acted on it. This was good news for Megan long-term but it could be tough on her short-term.

"Megan, when someone has a knife in their hand in their sleep and they're wrapped in aluminum foil, that's a good reason to be concerned about the people you love. I think Mary can get help at Mayo. Someday maybe that order can be changed. Who's taking Mary's place for now?"

"My aunt."

"There ya go. That'll be OK."

He paused and thought.

"Listen, Megan, over the last several weeks you've really started to improve. At some point, when you are better, quieter, when the buzzard doesn't bug you as much, you are going to have a story to tell. You will be able to help people with tinnitus. I hope you do that, because you are improving."

"If this noise ever goes away, and I pray every day that it does, I'll help as many people as I can."

"Good. I remember saying the same thing. Be careful what you pray for!"

Two more hours of therapy in an extended session finally ended with Marc rubbing his eyes, not in as good of a mood as he had initially been, but still happy.

"Why are you so happy today?"

"It looks like my family is going to get back together."

"Oh, good. I'll pray for you."

"Thanks, Megan."

They said their goodbyes and Megan made the journey to the front door. Quicker each week. Maybe five or six minutes this week. She was getting better.

On the ride home they got stuck in traffic on 494. It was a standstill. Unusual for midday – an accident, no doubt. Ashley put the car in park.

"You know Ashley, it's to the world's benefit if I have tinnitus and the buzzard isn't doing this to me anymore."

"What do you mean?" Ashley looked at Megan inquisitively.

"If this is tinnitus and the buzzard isn't doing all of this anymore, then I can help more people. If this is the buzzard hurting me and it isn't tinnitus, then no one will ever be helped."

"You mean you want to help people with tinnitus?"

"Yes. Just like Marc said. I want to help people. This is terrible. And I do feel better. There aren't as many horrifying days as there were before. I am getting some better."

Ashley smiled.

"I want to show God I appreciate him guiding us to Marc."

"I'm sure he knows."

"You know Ashley, this traffic jam was sent by God."

Ashley again looked over at Megan, the car still in park.

"You think so?"

"If it wasn't for God causing this traffic jam. I would never have figured out that this is just part of God's bigger plan."

"The traffic jam?"

"The traffic jam, and everything about all of this."

"OK, honey." Ashley didn't know what to say. She was a Christian and believed that God intervened in lives – but in traffic jams? Maybe if it helped Megan, it would be just another one of those things you let go of and let her think. She could be right after all.

Week after week Megan and Ashley would take two hours and spend them with Marc. Sometimes Megan's tinnitus was louder, sometimes softer, but the trend was unmistakable. She was really improving.

Marc had often told her that tinnitus is nothing more than remembering sound – 24/7.

Like horrifyingly vivid memories, sensations, emotions and visions for soldiers or rape victims with PTSD, except it's sound, and not alleviated. But Marc had also told her that, like PTSD, it could improve, the noise could reduce in volume and then instead of being one loud 24/7 siren, it could become episodic as the neural pathways carrying tinnitus in the brain atrophied. It would be a process. Nothing would happen quickly, but she would get better if she followed her "life instructions" from him to the letter.

Each day Megan did exactly as Marc had told her. Five times each day she listened to the noise in her head for the purpose of measuring the volume subjectively. She wrote down how loud it was on a scale from one to ten. Each day she wrote diary-like comments about what happened that day so just in case the buzzard wasn't real, she'd have a record of the things that made her better and the things that made her worse.

Chapter Thirty Nine

Megan's Condo

Mary got out of the hospital before Megan moved.

Mary paid no attention to the restraining order given to her upon her release from the hospital. Instead she returned to 4190, arriving while Ashley and Megan were packing. She walked in the door, furious.

"What the hell are you doing? Where are you going?"

"Megan's moving. And you aren't supposed to be here."

"You can't keep Megan and me away from each other. I'm the only person that understands her."

Megan continued to pack while watching the two of them fight over her. It was heartbreaking for Megan. She wanted everything to be normal again.

"Look Mary, get out of here."

"You can't kick me out."

"You have to leave because we are *moving*. I'll have all of your stuff sent wherever you go. It will be in storage until you call me at the office."

"I'm not going anywhere!"

"Yes, you are. You have been brainwashing Megan and undermining her sanity. It's time for you to leave. The judge issued the restraining order because you are a danger to Megan."

Megan looked up but still said nothing. What could she say?

"Megan, I'm not leaving!"

She walked over to Megan and looked her in the eyes. Megan started to weep. Ashley's heart fell.

"Talk to me, goddammit."

"This isn't my idea, Mary. Ashley says you are fired and that you have to go. There's nothing I can do about it. I want you to stay. You are the only one who believes me. You see the buzzards. You've been through everything with me. There's nothing I can do."

"You said you would always take care of me."

"I will Mary. I promise."

"Well, how the fuck are you taking care of me by kicking me out?"

"I can't control this situation but I can make sure I always take care of you."

"Are you going to buy me a place to stay?"

"Yes, of course I will."

Ashley had had enough.

"OK, Mary. Out. Or I'm calling the police."

"Where will I go?"

"You have a pile of money and you can go anywhere you want. *Now leave.*"

"Fine, you bitch. I will leave and see you in fucking hell."

She slammed the door so hard it made the room shake. Megan immediately wept louder. When Ashley went over to comfort her she simply pushed Ashley away. The only person who understood was gone.

Ashley had a flashback. It was a moment with David, in the drugstore. The office.

"Now, listen Ashley, if anything ever happens to Megan, you make sure she's taken care of. She's a smart girl but not the kind who could take care of herself, you understand?"

"Oh David, don't be stupid, nothing is ever going to happen to you. You are young. You're going to live forever."

"Well, just so you know."

And then she was back in the present.

"You know, she had a very hard childhood."

"What?" Her trance was broken.

"If you were nicer to her, maybe things would be better." Megan was angry. "She raised her brothers and sisters, you know."

"Oh come on, Megan. So did I. Let's not go down this road. Some people go through horrible childhoods and it drives them to do great things. Some people go through horrible childhoods and they use it as an excuse to do nothing, have nothing and be nothing. And that's Mary."

"She has been a friend! Are you saying that's not important?"

"No Megan, I'm not saying that's unimportant. I'm only saying that she wallows in her own self-pity and it makes me sick. I don't trust her. She is constantly doing things to you that are scary and I don't like it."

"Scary like what?"

"Scary like leaving you in the park about a half dozen times while she goes off and has coffee. Scary like that."

"That was a long time ago and I asked her to leave me alone."

"Oh, please. You are standing up for someone who abandoned you time after time while she went shopping."

"I told you I asked her to leave me alone all those times."

"Megan, I'm not going to argue today. We have a lot of work to do to get you to your new condo."

They worked in silence for an hour.

***

The next day, they went to see Dr. Berkowitz. Ashley needed to have Megan talk to Berkowitz about all of this. His appointment book was filled, but for Megan, he'd do anything he could. She didn't like revisiting the hospital, but that's where he was working today.

"Dr. Berkowitz, we finally ditched the wheelchair this week."

"Excellent. I'm very glad to hear it, Megan. So you're using the canes or the walker most of the time?"

"Both. I want to get rid of the walker as soon as I can. I'm doing a lot better."

"That's really good to hear."

After some pleasantries Dr. Berkowitz broached a sensitive topic.

"Megan, what you and Mary have been experiencing is a fairly unusual delusion. The French refer to it as *folie a deux.*"

Megan looked away, uncomfortable.

"Megan, it's not all that unusual. It happens when two or more people live together and experience the same delusions. Take one of the people out of the environment and very often they both improve. It often works that way with paranoid schizophrenia."

She looked to the doctor who had been so gentle with her for so many years, her mouth wide open.

"And you still think I'm crazy? Well, I'm not crazy. The buzzard is transmitting this noise to me and Mary has watched it all happen now for a long time. I am not paranoid. And I'm not schizophrenic. That means you're crazy and I'm *not* crazy."

Berkowitz took his glasses off and looked her in the eye.

"I thought you said the buzzard wasn't transmitting the sounds anymore!" Ashley was loud and certain.

"Well, it would serve no purpose if the buzzard was sending the signals. That's what God said. He said I'd be OK." Megan's resentment dwindled as she remembered her conversation with Marc. "Or, he could be transmitting some of the time and talking to me some of the time or I could be remembering it all. I don't know."

Berkowitz wasn't going to attend to this part of the discussion. It was difficult enough to tell a patient they suffered from schizophrenia. His experience was that no one wanted to hear those words and he wished there were a politically correct, more delicate, way to say them.

"Megan, it's a good thing that the two of you are separated because the delusions you share would only have gotten worse. Now you both have a chance to get better. I'm sorry it had to be so painful for you. You know, Megan, we have known each other a long time. You aren't crazy. I know you are suffering. Ashley knows you are suffering. I'm sure others do as well and we all want you to get better, and you can get better."

"Dr. Daniels believes me. He believes the buzzard is real. Is he crazy too?"

Berkowitz looked at Ashley. Didn't she just say that the buzzard was no longer transmitting? Or was she saying that the buzzards had once transmitted?

"Just this week, Megan and I thoroughly inspected a number of places that she has lived. Megan determined that there was no way the buzzard could hear her or anyone around her. She determined that there was no way she could be transmitting messages to the buzzard at all. This was all part of a homework assignment that Daniels gave Megan. But because Megan believes that something might have been implanted in her ear during ear surgery, she still believes it's possible that they can and do transmit to her."

"Go on."

"But yes, Daniels did say there was a remote possibility she might be able to receive something from the buzzard, but he by no means believes it's likely. He's not dismissing a tiny possibility, but having us carefully evaluate our beliefs about the buzzard and replacing the beliefs with facts, which is what we spent this week doing. He's offering very few opinions as to what he thinks. This last week Megan had to prove to him that the buzzard was not indeed sending or receiving."

Megan looked indignant.

"You were in the room with me and he said it was on his radar. He believed me. He said he did!"

"Daniels believes you. He doesn't find it likely that people radioed you because you told him there was no way they could."

"Well, we're going to get this straightened out when we go back to see him."

Berkowitz put his glasses back on and turned to Megan.

"And Ashley is correct? You looked for ways that you could be transmitting to the buzzard and found nothing?"

"There was nothing, but that doesn't mean they aren't transmitting to my head. And they *are*, at least sometimes I think so. Or they were until recently. It's hard to know exactly. I think they stopped but I know they're real. They've been driving me nuts for a long time."

Ashley had to chime in.

"Megan, you said that God ordained the traffic jam so you could help people with tinnitus because all of this would mean nothing if the buzzard was real."

Megan looked down and began to weep. She had forgotten that somehow. Ashley knew the "buzzard being real" meant that the elderly couple were intentionally transmitting.

"I know. But they are there. I don't know how it all works but they're trying to drive me crazy."

Berkowitz put his hand on her shoulder.

"Megan, we all believe what you're telling us. We simply know that no one is trying to destroy your life and make you go crazy. It's simply a shared delusion and I truly believe that with therapy you'll improve."

She raised her head and looked at him.

"I wish you'd believe me."

"I do believe what you're telling me. I want you to understand that I know you're hearing these sounds and words. There's no question. Our objective now is to make them go away. The Seroquel will help. Promise me you'll keep taking it."

"OK. I will."

"Thank you Megan. Please come back in a month, or sooner if you like. Let me know how you're feeling. I understand you've moved into a new place?"

"Yes, today's our first day there."

"Wonderful. I believe things will begin to improve. It may take some time but you will get better."

***

The new place was a twin home. Only one set of neighbors and Ashley had found out the husband was gone quite a bit on business. The wife was almost always home and had spoken with Ashley in detail about the neighborhood. Mostly upper income retirees. Nice people, the lady said.

Ashley was relieved to get there. She didn't like the silence in the car on the way over any more than Megan did. Ashley was so tired of this situation. She wanted Megan to get better and soon. Maybe the Seroquel would work. Maybe Daniels would be successful. She had never failed to be an optimist in life but even her optimism was fading.

Megan's eyes showed glimmers of hope as they walked in the front door.

"This is pretty. Wow. Very nice. Much nicer than 4190, Ashley. Don't you think?"

Ashley was taken aback by Megan's mood swing. And she wasn't going to fight it. They both saw a note from Robert on the counter that said, "Cleared by Drexel."

"It's very beautiful, Megan, and you deserve the best. I'm glad you like it. Should we look around, then start unpacking?"

***

Two weeks later they were back at Daniels's home for therapy. He always seemed glad to see Megan. Did he see her as a challenge? Was he flattered by Megan's flirtations? Was he simply thrilled to see her improvement? He was tough to read. Robin Williams, Dennis Miller and Kelsey Grammer rolled into one, he could be as cynical as other comedians – and that was a big part of why Megan was willing to come back week after week – she had fun, because he was funny. And on the less funny side, like most comedians and a lot of therapists, he suffered from chronic depression, and certainly Megan's situation was one of the more complex of his therapeutic career. Having suffered from severe tinnitus himself, he knew the temptation of attributing the cause to external factors, something outside a person's own brain. Because it seemed so foreign; it *did* make you feel like you had no chance of regaining control of your life.

Today Megan was upset.

"...and he didn't believe me. And then Ashley said you didn't believe me. And then..."

"Hold it!" He'd never sounded this mad. Like he was going to hit her and then put her back in the hospital.

"What?" Even Ashley's smile disappeared, for a moment.

"You told Berkowitz I didn't believe you?"

"Ashley did, yes."

"I told Berkowitz that you didn't believe that the buzzards were transmitting to her and that you told Megan that they might be to help you build rapport."

"OK, let's get this straight and settled so there is never a miscommunication again. First, I've always believed you, Megan. I always believe you. You would never lie to me. Would you? I didn't think so. Secondly, I said it is remotely possible that you could somehow receive radio transmission if there was a receiving device somehow implanted in your surgery to repair your hearing. But it seems extremely difficult to piece it together as that surgery was years before the buzzard even knew you existed. Additionally you couldn't have passed through TSA without setting off all kinds of alarms, thus rendering the original notion highly unlikely.

"I've let that go, and then told you it is *remotely possible* that you are receiving some transmissions from the buzzard. You can construct a scenario. That makes it possible. But plausible? Probable? No. Ten percent chance? No. One percent? No. Less than one percent chance, yes."

"So you don't believe me either." She was now angry.

"*I didn't say that!* Megan, I said that I always believe you. Just because you say God exists or Jesus didn't or whatever you think at the moment, doesn't make it a fact. I can disagree with the content and still believe you. There is a huge important distinction here. And Megan, you are going to *drive me insane.*"

"You don't believe in God?" She was very curious in a worried way.

"Now, let's not go there. The point is, I can disagree with your belief and still believe *you.* I can believe you are honest, trustworthy, credible. And I do, and I have never questioned that for a second. I am positive you will always tell me the truth."

There was silence while everyone processed all of this.

"It's very hard for me to understand how you can believe me but not that the buzzard transmits to me."

"Didn't you tell me that God told you that this was without purpose if the buzzard was transmitting? That you have a role to play in helping people? That if the buzzard is transmitting you can't help people with tinnitus? Did I not get that? It's right here in the notes, in your notes that you took over the last two weeks. I didn't make this up. Did *you*?"

"No, that's all true."

"And God was *wrong*?" He was really upset now. His voice got louder.

"Of course not."

"*So set me straight right this moment. Is the buzzard transmitting any more or not?*"

He looked her right in the eyes. His face had reddened with what appeared to be anger. Ashley was frozen. Megan looked at him and then answered carefully.

"I don't think he's transmitting any more. But he was."

"Are you *sure* he's not transmitting anymore?"

"Yes."

"And he's not receiving information from you now?"

"Yes."

"And he can't hear you now?"

"Yes."

"And you can't hear him but only the memory of what you once heard, whether it was the buzzard or some voices from a TV show?"

"Yes."

"Now *you* tell me what you believe so I can write it down and understand it myself, and as I write down what you believe I need you to write down what you believe."

She felt very pressured but she wanted to comply.

"I believe that the buzzard was transmitting to me but he isn't any more and no, I don't think he can hear me."

"Write that down."

"OK, then from now on, when you think the buzzard is talking to you or transmitting horrible noises, what are you going to do?"

"I'm going to say, 'You're not real.'"

"And *who* are you talking to?"

"The buzzard."

"So you are going to talk to the buzzard, who is not real?"

"No. I mean, I'll say, 'He's not real. It's just my memory playing a sound loop.'"

"And how will you feel?"

"I'll be a little upset, I guess."

"Will you think your life is in danger or that someone is following you?"

"No, not since Chicago. No. I don't think so."

"Well, if he isn't real, then how can he follow you?"

"He can't."

"Then write that down. OK, so tell me about how you feel your life is threatened."

She thought for a long time. Ashley sat silently, looking across at Megan from her position on the loveseat.

"I can't. I'm not threatened at all."

"Now, are you saying that to appease Ashley or me?"

"No."

"Are you positive?"

"Yes."

"Write that down." He breathed a heavy sigh of relief and mental exhaustion. Today's session had been a grueling two hours of reorganizing Megan's beliefs and feelings, and he was wiped out.

Before they left, Megan took a restroom break. Ashley became inquisitive.

"You know Berkowitz doesn't yell at Megan. In fact, no one yells at Megan,"

"Have all of the gentle approaches with Megan been helping? One piece at a time, we're pulling the old programming apart and replacing it with new possibilities. As long as she makes each conclusion herself it will continue to reduce the noises and the voices and someday, she'll be normal again."

"How long do you think?"

"Well it's been about seven months now. And we're probably halfway home. Today was big."

Megan exited the restroom and said as loud as she could, "Are you guys…?"

"Yes, Megan, we're talking about you. I guess we'll have to finish this later. Ashley was just telling me that Dr. Berkowitz doesn't yell at you."

"It's true. He's a very nice man."

"...and that the sounds and voices you hear are going to continue to reduce in volume over time."

Ashley looked down, processing all this information about her friend; she looked back up and winked at him. She understood. All the other approaches had failed, and that's why Megan kept coming to see him. Orthodoxy had gotten them nowhere. Clearly Megan was getting better. At last she didn't believe some of the things she experienced to be real. By no means was therapy over, but unbelievable progress had been made. They'd come a long way. One mercilessly slow footstep at a time.

Megan no longer had a shaking body. No more electric-like shocks. No more nightmares and no more trembling. She still woke up to the buzzard wake-up service every morning to go to the bathroom, and she had some tinnitus in the daytime, which often was barely noticeable. She was getting better and all three of them saw the results in Megan's journal notes every week.

It was working.

Chapter Forty

Wednesday Night 9 p.m.

For Megan, having Rebekkah at the new place had its benefits and drawbacks. They hadn't spoken much in the last few years and yet they'd lived less than ten miles away from each other most of that time.

Rebekkah had made herself at home in the far bedroom. The twin home was elegant. Very nicely decorated and shaping up nicely. Ashley had the ability to get Megan moved in quickly.

"So, how's your therapy going, Megan?" The question was asked during a commercial break during *CSI*.

"It's fine."

"Are you feeling any better?"

"If you're still thinking I'm crazy, you can forget it."

"You're not crazy, dear. You've just had some bad things happen to you. When you're well, we'll be happier."

"Are you saying this has been hard on you? It's not like you're ever around to help."

"Well, I'm here now. I've never dealt with schizophrenia and…"

"I *don't* have schizophrenia. I'm not crazy. I have tinnitus and auditory hallucinations and that's it."

"But I thought…"

"You were wrong. This is all no big deal. The tinnitus is getting better. I'm getting better. Daniels says that in another six to twelve months

I won't hear the compressor anymore, whether the buzzard is real or not."

Rebekkah was smart enough to leave this area alone.

"Sounds like a real good man."

"He's funny and he's cute."

"Perfect credentials for a therapist."

"They work fine for me."

"OK."

"I think I'm going to write a book about all of this. How tinnitus can change your life. Make your life miserable. Even worse than being paralyzed…or anything. I'm sure a lot of people would buy it. I read that a lot of people have tinnitus."

"Well, sweetheart, then do that. You have the time and probably the money, if I know Ashley."

"God told me that I need to help people get better. They need hope. They need to know that their head can get quieter and it has nothing to do with their ears, at least not for most people. Look how much better I've gotten."

"That's true, you're a pretty normal person now."

Megan shot Rebekkah a glance. Her aunt saw that *CSI* was back on. As far as Megan was concerned she was never… not normal.

"Should we watch?" Rebekkah wanted to get past that blunder.

"Yes. Let's watch it together."

***

It had been nine days since Megan's last visit to see Daniels. Although he used it often, he'd so far been avoiding using regression hypnosis with Megan, until she was substantially improved. He wanted her to be able to trust the process… and him. Today was the day.

Megan confessed that she'd been having second thoughts about whether the buzzard was or wasn't sending radio messages any more. She was quite understandably confused and uncertain.

"What's it going to be like?" She was more than a little worried, even with Ashley sitting right beside her.

"It's going to be an experience that will help desensitize your emotions to your tinnitus. Something we've already had a lot of success with…and…something to offer you insight, from the inside of your mind, as to what the actual cause of the tinnitus is. When we're done with the process you'll be able to tell me the answers to your questions."

"Really."

"Yep. That's the deal."

"Should I try and relax?"

"Not necessary."

"But I thought you had to relax to have hypnosis."

Daniels smiled. "I remember when I had tinnitus. There was not a day that I could come close to relaxing. I know yours is a lot better now but I'd simply like you to be alert, if that's OK."

No sooner had he said "alert" than Megan relaxed. She was noticeably calmed.

"First, do I have permission to touch the back of your wrist or your shoulder while I'm working? There are times when it might be useful."

"Sure." A spark of enthusiasm emanated from Megan. The last time anyone did anything other than kiss her forehead was a decade ago. The wrist was as good as any place to begin!

"OK, great. Close your eyes and take a deep long breath in. Take your time. Gently exhale and do the same thing again. Notice your breathing….and again in…good…and out nice and slow…wonderful.

"Now, Megan, I want you to picture a box in your mind. Any kind of a box will do as long as you have it in your mind…good…now, in your mind put a check mark on the box and draw a circle around it. Perfect…and let that picture go dark.

"Megan, I want you to take me to a time recently when your tinnitus was really bothering you. When you're there, tell me everything you see, feel, and hear. Don't leave anything out."

"It hasn't been bad lately…oh…with Aunt Rebekkah, watching *CSI* last week. She got me all stressed out and stuff."

"Take me through the event as it happened, step by step, moment by moment…in the first person as you re-experience it again."

"OK, well, *CSI* was coming on and my aunt said to me, 'You know you're just about normal again.' I got kind of upset and during the commercial the compressor... tinnitus turned up pretty loud. I was nervous for the first time in a long time but I do what you always tell me to do and that's to immerse myself in whatever I'm doing. So I ignored her and watched *CSI*. It was a good show. Gil is obviously in love with this woman who runs a fetish house. I don't know the name of it...in Vegas...and he believes that she might be guilty of a murder but by the end of the show it turns out that he figures out that she's innocent and she isn't too happy about it."

"And the tinnitus?" Marc scribbled furiously on his notepad as Megan talked. He starred certain sentences, circled others. Ashley had no idea what hieroglyphics he was using or what coding system he had, but his fingers were flying as fast as she could talk.

"It was fine by the end of the show. Didn't bother me at all. Maybe a three...you know...it was there, but only annoying."

"OK, now Megan, I want you to take me to an earlier similar incident where your tinnitus was really bothering you."

"Anything?"

"Any time is fine."

"Well, when I found out that Mary was going to be in the psychiatric ward, the compressor got really loud. Just like the buzzard used to do when he wanted to punish me."

"And what happened specifically? Tell me everything that you notice and observe."

"Well, I was at Bill's and when I woke up there was a note by my bed stand saying that he and Mary had gone to Mayo that Mary wasn't feeling well and he'd be home in a few hours. He left me his cell phone number. When he got back that afternoon, he told me what happened and the compressor came on *really* loud. It scared me and may have shaken me like it did in the old days. I was really scared and upset. When he said she was in the psych ward I started crying. It wasn't long before I talked to Ashley and I think I yelled at her pretty loud. I was so angry. Nothing's wrong with Mary. Just because she hears the buzzard is no reason to put her in the psych ward."

She finally took a breath. Daniels didn't want her going down this path. He wanted to get her on the tinnitus trail, not the judgment-about-Ashley trail…and he wanted to track it to its origin…or whatever the unconscious mind of Megan said that origin might be. He had no idea what he would find. He worked another hour or so on this specific chain of events moving slowly backward toward the genesis. He continued to scribble away and had filled half of a legal pad of yellow paper. Ashley said nothing but watched, fascinated.

"OK, Megan, good job. Now, I want you to take me to an earlier similar incident and tell me everything you see, hear and sense."

"I'm lying in bed at 4190. It's just after midnight and I hear them upstairs having sex. The giant vibrator is on. It's shaking the ceiling and the walls. They're screaming. It sounds like she's going to have an orgasm but I'm shaking and the compressor is so loud and it sounds like someone is laughing at me. There's a 'knock knock knock' on the buzzard's door. It's the manager and they let him in. He and the buzzard say, 'Megan, Megan, Megan' at the same time. It's terrifying! They're laughing because I can't have sex. I'm helpless! They're rubbing it in my face. The vibrator goes on 'high' and shakes me out of the bed. I'm shaking from head to foot. I can't believe how scared I am. I wish Mary would come in the room. *'Mary!'* She isn't coming. I start to cry. I'm weeping. No tears will come out and I can't get up. They stop laughing but the compressor is now turned on high too. They're torturing me. I want them to stop. Please make them stop. *Please make them stop!*"

She was indeed shaking as she sat on the loveseat next to Ashley, completely unaware that Marc was turning pages and writing away at what looked to Ashley to be a verbatim transcrip of what Megan was saying. For what reason, Ashley wondered, had Daniels asked Megan to go through this event over and over again? He seemed to be stuck on it. There was no apparent reason. She wished he would just move on.

After almost three hours of processing, when Megan was in a bored state and could repeat the night's events with almost zero emotion, Marc smiled. The trauma had been processed and eliminated.

"OK, Megan, well done. I want you to take me to an earlier similar incident where you were scared because of sounds or people talking."

"I hear 'knock, knock, knock' and a woman's voice says 'Marnie, Marnie, Marnie.' I'm scared. My heart is pounding. My palms are sweaty. I feel helpless. I feel terrified. Mother walks in the door and I wake up from a dream."

Daniels looked up with a start. He was as alert and focused as Ashley had ever seen. He repositioned himself on the couch. He quietly turned the page and said, "Good now…go to the beginning of the event and tell me everything you see, feel and hear…add in all the extra details now."

"I hear, 'knock, knock, knock'. A window is open. A woman's voice says, 'Marnie, Marnie, Marnie.' I'm terrified. My heart is going to jump out of my chest. My palms are sweating. The poor woman is having a horrible nightmare. Someone is going to hurt her and she can't wake up. But Marnie's mother walks in the door. She's an evil looking woman but she doesn't hurt Marnie. Oh my God. It's Marnie…the movie…the Alfred Hitchcock movie. Oh my God. The first time I heard, 'Megan, Megan, Megan' it was really Marnie. Oh my God. The tapping of the window shade drawstring against the glass window. Marnie's mother. Her nightmare. Oh my God. The first time it was Marnie… and Sean Connery came to her rescue. Oh God, no one came to my rescue. Why couldn't there have been someone to come to my rescue? I couldn't wake up from the nightmare either. No one was there. No one to hold me."

And she wept, repeating, 'Marnie, Marnie, Marnie' over and over again. Minutes later she had settled down and Daniels continued to write furiously, drawing arrows to and from various sentences on his legal pad. He finally looked up. She was hunched over and her weeping began to subside.

"Megan, I want you to listen to my voice. We are here in 2011. We are here in 2011 and it's now the right time for you to know that you also are in 2011. Can you tell me what my name is?"

"Marc."

"That's right. Can you tell me who is sitting next to you on the loveseat?"

"Ashley."

"That's right. Can you tell me where you are?"

"In your house in the den."

"Very good. Megan, when you feel comfortable you can open up your eyes and know that you have done beautifully."

It was twenty or thirty seconds before Megan opened her eyes. When she did, Marc's were there to meet hers. His eyes, often sharp and questioning, were now soft and sympathetic. Kind.

"It was Marnie."

"I know, Megan."

"I mean, It was the movie that started all of this, wasn't it?"

"That's probably right."

"What does it all mean?"

"I think the best thing for you to do is simply know that is what really happened. You now know a lot more than you did before. The movie was something that became woven into the fabric of your being. But there's still more that we need to address next time."

"Can't we do more now?"

"Megan, we've been going for hours. I think we'll pick this up next week. I'd encourage you to not speak with anyone about your experience while your mind processes all of this. We just did surgery and we don't want anyone to be checking to see if the surgery was successful or not. We all know it was."

"OK, can Ashley and I talk about it?"

"I don't think so. I think you guys can go out to lunch at that Mexican place and I think you can flirt with your favorite waiter. There'll be plenty of time to talk next week."

"I feel light, like I weigh thirty pounds less. Is that normal?"

"Very much so. You had a big weight lifted from you. You'll notice the difference over the next few days."

"Thank you, Marc."

"You're welcome."

"Should I watch Marnie between now and next week?"

"It's going to be airing?"

"No, I have it on DVD."

He stared at her.

"Really? Bring it in next Tuesday. I'd like to go through it. It's been twenty years since I've seen it and frankly don't remember much of it…might help. But no, please don't watch it on your own."

They said their goodbyes and soon they were off. Daniels closed the door and rubbed the back of his neck. Clients never knew that the weight they felt removed was moved to Daniels's neck and shoulders. He was exhausted.

"A goddamn Hitchcock movie. So the sound… tinnitus… the voices heard while sleeping, Marnie's mom, Connery, the buzzard maybe, but what about the paranoia? Where the hell does that come from?"

He put the water glasses into the dishwasher and went to his bedroom. He looked at the pillow and buried his face in its softness.

***

Megan laid her head on the pillow, still thinking about how loud the compressor had been while in hypnosis and how quiet it was right now.

It's there, but I don't ever remember it being this quiet. I wonder if the hypnosis is working?

Megan's aunt came in the door and tucked Megan in.

"Thanks, Aunt Rebekkah."

"How ya feeling?"

"Pretty good. Better than in a long time."

"Therapy must have gone well today?"

"It really did. We did hypnosis. First time. It was fascinating."

"That's nice honey. Now, you're off to bed. Physical therapy tomorrow, right?"

"G'night, Rebekkah."

"Night, dear."

For the first time in a long time she laid her head on a pillow and quickly fell fast asleep.

***

She could hardly see her face. But the man must have been able to. She sat on the chair with her legs spread wide open. She wore a blue bikini bottom and a t-shirt that was made for someone half her size. Her nipples were magnets for the man. He walked toward her and she simply waited for him. There was no sense of urgency, nor of boredom. It was all as it should be. He had a small waist and broad shoulders. Tan. Light hair that had been bleached in the sun. He had tan lines beneath the swim trunks.

He came closer and she raised her hand squeezing what had just become firm. She used it as a handle to bring him closer. She didn't smile or frown. She sat up just a bit and teased him. He would have to earn the rest.

Her right hand pushed him away. She tugged at the bottom of her bikini and pulled it to the right. He knew what to do next.

He knelt in front of her, then entered her. She was ready. She pulled her t-shirt up to reveal her breasts, then reclined back on the chair and rested her arms on the chair. She watched him. He moved in and out. The angle was difficult to maintain because the seat of the chair was higher than he was and she was higher yet. But she would do nothing to adjust for that.

She tightened around him and came quickly, and just in time, as he was only moments behind her.

She looked straight into his blue eyes. He had broken a sweat. As he pulled out and away from her she grabbed him and pulled him close to her once again.

She touched his face, kissed him once more, urgently.

She mouthed the word "tomorrow." She let him go and he put on his clothes and walked out the bedroom door. The room was enormous. Most houses could fit in this room. Today everything took place on a chair. And he'd be back tomorrow.

"Megan, Megan, Megan…"

She woke up, her heart still racing from her dream. She wanted to go back to sleep but was never able to get back to a good dream when she wanted to. Why? You can get to all the bad dreams without trying. The good ones, never.

She'd heard the voices and realized that they were not "real." The compressor was there but quiet. She felt good, even with the sweat from her dream.

Chapter Forty One

Three Days Later

"What do dreams mean?"

"Hopes and fears." Daniels responded instantly, without hesitation. Then he qualified his instant response. "There's two parts to dreams. They play out your hopes and fears, and they also mimic the emotional content in the brain that is predominant in the course of the day. The story line often doesn't mean anything, but the emotions you feel during the dream show you what's running your system. Why? Been having interesting dreams?"

"Not really. Just wondering."

"OK. Well, today we need to solve the other half of the genesis puzzle."

"The what?" Ashley was curious.

"The genesis puzzle. Last week we found out that ..."

"That Marnie was important in starting the voices, the 'Megan, Megan, Megan.'" Megan knew he was going there. She had given it much thought in the past week.

"But there's other stuff we don't know that I think we will in a few hours."

"OK." Megan looked uncertain but she knew that she could trust Marc. Her tinnitus...the compressor sound, had been way down from a week ago. Maybe just at a level two or three on average using the 1-10 scale they had for tracking their progress.

"Do you want me to relax?"

"No, that's OK, Megan. Just like last time. I'll ask you to take me places and tell me what happens, and you go ahead and do it in the first person as much as you can. Experience it all. Feel it all."

"OK. I will try."

He grabbed his yellow pad and two pens. He looked at Ashley who had gotten out her Day Runner. Apparently she was going to take notes as well. Good for her, Marc thought.

"Megan, I want you to take a deep breath in…slowly now…and as you begin to exhale I want you to close your eyes. Excellent.

"Now Megan, you can get as comfortable as you want, move around if you like. Find a position that feels right. OK. Good.

"Now, Megan, I want you to take me to a time recently when you were really scared. Worried. Fearful. When you felt terrorized perhaps. Take me there and tell me everything you notice, observe and feel. Go there now and then begin."

There was a pause. Part of Megan didn't want to go there as instructed, but she was going to because she wanted to know what was deep within and she wanted to make Daniels happy. He had helped her so much.

"We're in a hotel room in Chicago and people are shooting at us."

Instead of writing his eyes came up from his paper and looked at her. She was evidently there again, and she was scared.

"The glass breaks and Mary says we have to leave now. We pack everything, really fast. I call down to the front desk and see what is going on. The man says there was a shooting between gang members and they've all run away. But I know he's covering up because this is the buzzard and his henchmen. He's trying to kill me. We have to leave. My heart's beating so fast. My hands are sweating. My head is throbbing. And the compressor is unbearably loud."

Daniels could see some of these symptoms recurring now. She was as "there" as she could be.

"The valet brings the car up. We haven't waited long. It's the red Mercedes. The convertible. Such a pretty car. We get inside the car and

Mary starts driving. She is racing toward the interstate. It's a few miles away but she's going fast.

"She sees a car chasing us. She starts to go faster and faster. The people in the buzzard's car begin shooting and hit our car twice. I duck and Mary keeps driving. They keep shooting and missing.

"We finally get to the interstate and my heart is racing. We want to lose the buzzard and get away back home but they get on the interstate too.

"A state trooper pulls us over. We tell him that we're being chased by the buzzard, that the buzzard was shooting at us, but he doesn't believe us. We were going fast. Really fast and he had his ticket book out. He was going to write a ticket.

"He told us to wait in the car. As he walked past the back of the car he saw two bullet holes. I don't know what he thought but it took a while before he came back. He told us that there were gang members seen shooting a red Mercedes on the North side. We told him it was the buzzard, then we realized that he was going to let us go, so we kept quiet.

"He takes the license number of our car and we tell him who we are and how to get a hold of us. I guess it matched the information on Mary's license.

"We drove and drove fast again until we got to Grand Avenue, I think, in Gurnee where we pulled off and found a place where we thought we'd be safe."

As the fear began to subside, Daniels wanted to get her back on the track that had so nicely been opened.

"Megan, I want you to take me to an earlier similar incident. Tell me everything you see, feel and hear."

"OK, well, I'm in a bathroom and I've got my head in a wastebasket and I'm screaming at the buzzard. I want him to know what he's doing to me. He's punishing me and I want the sound to be horrible for him too.

"I'm shaking from head to foot. I'm on the floor. This goes on for a long time and no one comes to help. No one. I'm there on the floor all by myself and no one comes, and they are torturing me."

"Megan, what do you hear? Voices or sounds?"

"I hear both. He's saying my name over and over again and the compressor is super loud. It's insanely loud. My God. It's horrible. Make it stop. *Make it stop!*"

"Good job, Megan. Now listen, I want you to take me to an earlier similar time when you felt just like that."

And she did for an hour and a half…when they stumbled upon another surprise.

"There's a man in the attic. He's a young man. I think it's the buzzard's son. He's looking through a peephole in a bathroom. There is a woman there getting out of the shower. She's scared because she hears noises. The buzzard gets on a phone and calls her and she answers it and he tells her exactly what she's doing and she gets terrified. She feels helpless. She goes to look at the door locks but in just a moment the buzzard bursts through the ceiling and kills her.

"Only her pet cat lived. And then Grissom comes and Catherine from the crime lab and they start to…oh…this is *CSI*. I'm watching this on TV. I thought this was happening to me. It's exactly like what happens to me. It's scary because this is what has been going on for so long. They hide above. They drill holes in the ceiling and the walls, drop the listening and video devices down and watch every move you make and then torture you."

"Megan, you're positive you are watching *CSI* here?"

"Yes. I'm sure."

"And the woman gets killed by the man hiding in the ceiling, the attic, the next floor up?"

"Yes, he does this to a lot of people; he has dozens of holes and wires. He's evil. God, he's scary. They need to kill him."

"*CSI*, right?"

"Yes. *CSI*."

"Go forward to the end of the show. How does it end?"

"It's kind of ambiguous. You get the idea that this is going to happen again, that the case isn't really over."

"And it scared you?"

"Yes, because it was just how I felt, being a fish in a fish bowl. People come to look, feed me and leave. It's not a good life."

"You thought the buzzard was on *CSI*?"

"Well, sort of, I guess. The guy upstairs was the same as the buzzard. I mean, he tortured that woman. It's what he did to me."

"Do you think he still tortures you?"

There was silence for what seemed like eternity.

"I don't think so."

"Do you know that the man in the attic with all the wires, the video and the audio. He's an actor, right? He went home that night, had a glass of wine and the next day went to another set and he was in another TV show. Right?"

"I think…I mean…he is cruel. He tortures me…but he can't because he's an actor in a TV show. He's…"

"He's guest-starring on *CSI*, right?"

"Yes. That's right."

"And this is make-believe, right?"

"But it's based on a true story."

"And you know that because…"

"All *CSI's* are based on a true story."

"OK. But this man, is he the buzzard?"

"No. He's not."

"But you remembered him as the buzzard. You were sure it was him. You told me word for word what was happening in the TV show and you thought that it was happening to you. But it wasn't."

"Well, I don't know if it was happening to me. I don't think it was. It was on TV. I think I got confused and I thought it was happening to me. I don't know. It's confusing now."

"Before you saw this show were you ever scared that people were chasing you?"

A long pause. Megan searched her memory. "I don't think so. I think this was when I thought people were chasing us. Of course, I thought there were people torturing me before this."

"Were there people torturing you in real life?"

Again… a long silence. "What did you say?"

"Were there people torturing you in real life?"

"I don't know. There might have been."

"When you and Ashley searched for holes and wires and surveillance equipment, what did you find?"

"Nothing."

"You found *nothing* at all three places you went to?"

"That's right."

"And where did you see this *CSI*?"

"I think we were in Las Vegas. We went there because the people were torturing me back home."

"And what do you think about the man in the ceiling now? Do you think he was torturing you?"

"No. Of course not. He's an actor on TV."

"So was anyone torturing you?"

"I think at first there was and then maybe they got bored and quit. Then maybe all of this was just one long bad memory that I was always thinking about."

"You can see how it was easy to think that something that you thought was really happening to you, actually was happening on TV, right?"

"Yes."

"The two things, TV and real life, seemed to blur together to be one event, right?"

"Yes. That's true."

"And do you think that could happen with other events in life, too?"

"I guess so. Sure."

"So would it surprise you if something else that was terrifying to you might have simply been something you saw on TV that really had your attention, that had you in suspense?"

"Yes, I think that's true."

"OK, Megan. What's my name?"

"Marc."

"And what was the name of the show you saw the person in the attic on?"

"*CSI*."

"What network is that on?"

"CBS."

"Where is the show filmed?"

"Los Angeles and Las Vegas, I guess."

"And where was that scene filmed?"

"In Los Angeles, I suppose."

"And when they were done filming for the day, could they have all watched TV together or done something fun, or were they all scared of each other?"

"I guess they probably went home until the next day and filmed some more."

"For the TV show?"

"Yes."

"OK. When you feel comfortable you can open your eyes and return to the present."

Megan opened her eyes. This time there were no tears. But there was a drifting feeling of paranoia… leaving. It felt good. Megan would never call it paranoia of course, but she did say, "I don't feel very scared anymore."

"Good."

"Ashley, isn't that something? I had something to do with this too."

"I think it's…" Ashley was about to get cut off firmly by Marc.

"I think it's too early to talk about this, and next week we'll look at what it all means, OK? Let's not talk about today's session with anyone. We'll catch up next week. Fair enough?"

"Yes, OK."

Megan wanted to talk about her experience but clearly, Marc didn't want to hear it. Megan looked at the clock. They had been there for over two hours. It seemed like minutes to her.

"Listen Megan, here's what I want you to do for the next week. I don't care whether the buzzard was doing this yesterday, a month ago or six months ago. I want you to live the next seven days as if it's all tinnitus. You hear *'Megan, Megan, Megan'* wake you up in the morning, simply say, 'I'm so glad I have a way to wake up so I get to the bathroom.'"

Megan smiled. "I guess that is true. If I didn't have the buzzard wake-up service, I'd be a lot of work for my aunt."

"You know what, Megan, that's a really good point. I never thought of that before. If the wake-up service didn't wake you up in the morning, we'd have a lot of problems. I'm not so sure we want to get rid of that part of this experience!" Marc smiled at Megan.

"And the rest of the day, any time you hear your tinnitus because you aren't wrapped up in something else, immediately think: This was once really annoying, and it's now just a minor distraction.

"You're getting better. You're very suggestible and I think that where self-suggestion is overvalued in most cases, in your case, I think it's good medicine."

"OK. I'll do that. Do you think this is going to go away?"

"Yes. For the most part it will be gone sooner than most cases I've seen."

As he closed the door he sighed with great relief. It had been an exhausting session, but rewarding. Most of the puzzle pieces were now together. Between a TV show, a movie, and tinnitus, mixed with a suggestible mind, dying for an explanation, and a schizophrenic housekeeper, it was a recipe for hell.

He found his favorite pillow and buried his face into it once again.

Chapter Forty Two

September 19

Day 3652

Six weeks had passed since the "*CSI* Session." They had had three sessions in that period. Megan was feeling better. The wake-up service didn't always wake her up in the morning and sometimes there was a price to pay for that. Other mornings, she was just fine, waking up as any other person would.

Both of those were good things.

She was starting to walk faster, stand straighter, look better. Her body was beginning to return to the shape that God had made for her. She had dressed rather elegantly for today. She didn't look like she did ten years ago, but she really did look quite good.

Everyone was in a good mood today.

She told Marc that on a recent trip to Vegas with her Aunt Rebekkah, of whom she had grown quite fond, and her Aunt Jane, whom she couldn't stand, she had been awoken by the Jane Wake-Up Service. "Megan, Megan, Megan" had been in Jane's voice. She had seen her in a hypnagogic dream. She had asked Marc about it. He remarked that her waking up seemed to be associated with only bad things and bad people. She smiled and had another "aha" experience.

Today's session brought something new for all of them. Ashley was brimming with excitement. Megan could hardly contain herself.

"What are you guys so happy about?"

Soon they were telling him.

"I want the world to know my story about how I got well from tinnitus."

"You're well?" He had to ask.

"My tinnitus is less than one in volume almost all the time, almost every day. I want you to write a book telling the world about what happened to me. It will give people hope."

"I'll do that in my spare time, Megan. Yes, I will. Megan, I want to give you something special."

He handed her a sealed envelope. It was a birthday card.

"Today isn't my birthday."

"Ten years ago today this all started. The accident. You've come a very long way and I rather think that it is your new birthday."

Daniels' repair work was done and with time, Megan would now be OK. He wouldn't have believed it. He hadn't wanted the job, but here she was looking good, speaking quite clearly, and she was happy. Not just happy to see him, but really happy.

***

Alberto was good-looking, and Megan kept looking at him. Megan had ordered a combo plate. They were celebrating her birthday and she was staring at the guy she'd been flirting with for over a year. Alberto was 5'10" and perhaps thirty-five years old. He was a good waiter and probably made twenty dollars an hour, including tips. Nice looking guy and there was no wedding ring on his finger. Megan had inspected that finger many times.

Ashley ordered and spoke with the woman who was refilling drinks. Megan was daydreaming. Alberto was standing in the pool. She had swum out to him. The water gave her much greater flexibility than walking did. In the water she couldn't hear well at all. She had taken her hearing aids out before getting in. She was wearing a two-piece bathing suit. Her legs looked bruised and scarred, and probably always would. The ball in her eyelid would probably be there forever. The metal in her head was never going to be removed. When she looked down at her body, she knew she wasn't twenty-seven anymore. She was thirty-seven, and she actually looked pretty good for thirty-seven. Many of the scars on her body had completely disappeared. She didn't just look OK, she looked *good*. Her legs and her eye were distracting, but aside from that she was comfortable with herself.

Alberto stood in the middle of the pool. Megan didn't take long to get to him. She was surprisingly strong in the water.

The water made her body weight easy for her to support.

She took her top off and Alberto grinned from ear to ear. And she could see that he was happy to see her.

She stood perhaps six feet in front of him. The water was up to her waist. She covered her breasts with her hands. Alberto frowned.

She put her hands over her head then behind her head. She had done this before, long, long ago.

The sun was warm. Alberto walked toward her and lifted her up. He brought her out to where the water was just four and a half feet deep.

She looked into his eyes and she felt something she hadn't felt in a decade. God, it felt good.

And then his body tensed and he groaned. He held her tight.

He returned her gaze.

***

"And Megan, would you like another margarita, or would you like an iced tea?"

She blinked. She heard silence. Complete silence. There was no buzzard. There was no compressor. There was no vibrator. She knew in that moment that she was whole again.

"Alberto?"

"Yes, Megan, what would you like?"

"Would you come to lunch with me next Saturday at my apartment in Edina? It's very nice and I'd like you to come, just the two of us."

"You mean a date? With you, Señorita? It's been so long since I've been on a date. Yes, I would like that very much, I would be honored. Eres muy bonita, Megan."

No tears came to her eyes. She wished they could. But she felt it inside. The joy of being beautiful to one person was the same as being beautiful to everyone.

It was her new birthday.

It was a very good day.

Dedication

I wish to dedicate this book to my dear friend Janet Snyder, whose daily life struggles inspire me to be a better, more compassionate person. Her traumatic journey ultimately led Dr. Kevin Hogan and me to write this book in hopes that her courageous story would be a source of inspiration for all who read it.
Cheryl Boldon

For
Mark, Jessica and Katie
Kevin Hogan

Shattered is dedicated to the millions of tinnitus sufferers in the world today, in hopes that its message will give them the courage to come forward and receive help so that tinnitus can be obliterated in our lifetime.
Jan Snyder

Acknowledgements

I am very grateful to my employees and to friends who humored me, and saw to it that my needs were met. Most of all, I am very grateful to my best friend, Cheryl Boldon, who patiently dragged me from doctor to doctor and hospital to hospital trying to get me a cure for an illness I wouldn't even admit I had.
Love,
Jan Snyder

I would like to express my deepest gratitude to my family members and friends who provided counsel, creativity, understanding, and support before, during, and after writing this book. To my dear husband Bruce and my daughters Lauren and Cory Anne who supported me throughout the entire ordeal and who understood and accepted the sacrifices that had to be made in order to bring this book to fruition. To my mother Janet Belsaas-Baldwin and my brother Randy Domstrand, I thank you for your creative contributions that made *Shattered* an even better book. To my brother Bill Domstrand and my sister Mandi Kliche, I thank you for reading the many manuscript versions and offering suggestions. To my dear friends Vicky Chancellor and Senada Zakariasen, I thank you for your counsel, which kept me sane during all the insanity.
Cheryl Boldon

Shattered was completed after years of work with the help of the best editorial and creative team I've ever worked with. Elle Phillips did a brilliant job with the cover and interior design. Rachel Hastings was ever so patient and methodical with rewrite after rewrite. Her story and character editing was superb. Jill Balin in New York first handled her author with great care and wisdom in addition to making the book what it is today. Jill corrected thousands of manuscript errors and caught all kinds of glitches that needed repair along the way. Truly an amazing job. All mistakes and errors of any kind in *Shattered* are those of the authors. A special thanks to Mark, Jessica and Katie, who have now survived #20. Living with an author "in progress" is no treat for anyone.
Kevin Hogan

Jan's Message of Hope for Those Who Suffer

Tinnitus is a disturbance which affects about ten percent of the world's population. We are way behind in achieving a cure. We can't even decide on how to pronounce it!

I was helped the most by Dr. Nicholas Rogers, my psychiatrist, who accurately diagnosed my hearing of voices and sounds as tinnitus; and by Dr. Kevin Hogan, who counseled me and guided me medically, with his excellent book, *Tinnitus: Turning the Volume Down.* In fact, his book is essential for tinnitus sufferers everywhere. At my American Tinnitus Association support group, one of the members referred to it as "The Bible"!

With best wishes,

Jan Snyder

Dear Reader:

Jan's story is far broader in scope than this work of fiction could ever encompass. It's true that after her accident she was in surgery for thirty-six hours, in a coma for over a month, and when she awoke she had no idea where she was. She would soon learn that she had lost her husband and her entire way of life. She couldn't communicate with anyone on the outside, and for quite some time, no one knew whether Jan was understanding what they would communicate with her.

Most people in that situation would have simply given up and died. Jan's very survival of the physical destruction to her body makes her amazing. She possesses a tenacity of spirit which allowed her to do ceaseless hours of therapy to learn how to walk, and to talk, and even to take a drink of water. To be looked at in a dark light by the world, to be seen as completely disabled, which she was, is something that you and I wouldn't want to have happen to anyone we love. But the more remarkable story is that she began to hear voices, experience full body tremors, and severe tinnitus, which are far more disabling than any physical issues that she (or probably you) would ever face. What really got Jan well in the end was the mission that God had given her to get this book into your hands, as well as the love of her Trustee, who wouldn't quit until she was well.

Kevin Hogan

About the Authors

Kevin Hogan
Author of twenty books including *The Psychology of Persuasion, The Science of Influence* and *The 168 Hour Week: Living Life Your Way 24/7.* www.kevinhogan.com

Janet Snyder
Janet Snyder was a successful drugstore entrepreneur and happily married woman of twenty-three years when she was hit by a drunk driver in 1988. She was in a coma for five weeks, hospitalized for seven months, and had three years of round-the-clock nursing care before rebuilding her life. She could not walk, talk, stand, feed, or dress herself. But despite the utterly desperate circumstances, Jan went from being an atheist to a believer. She saw how God helped her through every stage of her rehabilitation. If Janet can believe and trust God, thereby making her life better, anyone can! Presently, Janet lives independently in Plymouth, MN with her cats Amos and Andy. She still drives a Mercedes.

Cheryl Boldon
Cheryl Boldon has been a Trustee for the Janet Snyder Irrevocable Trust since 1990, managing all trust assets. She is also Chief Executive Officer for SouthWest Station, LLC and SouthWest Station Management, LLC. Cheryl was past President and CEO of Drugstore King, Inc. (DBA Snyder Drug and Butler Drug) from 1988 to 2001. She received her MBA in 1992, and was Governor Carlson's Appointee to the 1995 White House Conference on Small Business. She has been happily married for twenty-four years and resides in Minnetonka, MN. Her husband Bruce Boldon is a West Point graduate with a distinguished twenty-two-year military career and is currently Chief of

Operations for the U.S. Army Corps of Engineers. Cheryl is the proud mother of two beautiful daughters, Lauren Michele and Cory Anne. Lauren is working on her Ph.D. in nuclear science, researching pyrochemical reprocessing of spent nuclear fuel, and Cory Anne is working toward her Bachelor's Degree in Education.

READERS' QUESTIONS

1. How might Megan have felt about being trapped in a body which didn't work? What would be your worst nightmares about that? What would you think about all day long?
2. Is this novel a story of inspiration to you in any way? Or was it "just" a thriller?
3. What is the greatest struggle described in this book?
4. How did Megan feel when people stared at her everywhere she went? Is there a difference between being disabled and handicapped, and if so, what is it?
5. Loss features heavily in Megan's life after the accident. What were the most significant losses and how did she respond to those?
6. Few family and friends show up in Megan's life except at Christmas and to stage the intervention. What might keep you away from a relative or loved one in similar circumstances?
7. What might Ashley have been feeling when no matter what she did, she couldn't get help for Megan?
8. Did having money help or hurt Megan through this ordeal? Consider resources, therapy, Mary, etc.
9. Megan showed enormous determination in learning to walk and speak again. Do you suppose everyone would be able to persevere, or would it take a special kind of person? What do you think you would be like under those circumstances?
10. At any time did you as a reader believe the radioing was actually happening to Megan?
11. Checking herself into the hospital, Megan risked being committed permanently. What might she have been feeling when she voluntarily checked herself into the psych ward and what led her to

trust Ashley so deeply? How would you feel? Would you let anyone institutionalize you under any circumstances?

12. If you had a relative or friend suffering from tinnitus, what would you suggest they do? If they were suffering from schizophrenia what would you do? What's the difference between the two?
13. Why do you think Marc Daniels took Megan on as a patient, when he no longer saw other patients?
14. Daniels was certain Megan had both tinnitus and schizophrenia. Where did he draw the line between the two problems?
15. What was Daniels' realistic appraisal of Megan's chances of recovery? Why do you suppose that psychiatry and psychology have not been able to help more with schizophrenia?
16. Megan felt betrayed by Ashley's inability to believe everything that Megan knew to be true. To what extent is our reality purely governed by our beliefs, and how were Megan's beliefs changed to find a new reality?
17. How could you use the belief-change methodology Daniels employed with Megan, to change reality for yourself when in a disagreement with others?
18. What do you think it is about "talking cures" that make them work, when they do work?
19. When did Megan start feeling like a "normal" person again? What were the signs?
20. How did Megan's relationship with God impact everything that happened to her? Do you have a faith that would support you through something similar? Do you think that some faiths and belief systems might be more useful than others in dealing with a situation like Megan's?